To Stacy,
Read this book
now.
Then share it,

Bless you,
Dean
Lincoln
Minton

The Universal Essence

Dean Lincoln Minton

Inquiries should be addressed to:
Pulpwood Press
P.O. Box 35038
Panama City, FL 32412

Library of Congress Cataloging-In-Publication

Dean Lincoln Minton

The Universal Essence /Dean Lincoln Minton/ Fiction
-----2nd ed.
        p.   cm.
        ISBN: 978-1-888146-85-1

ACKNOWLEDGEMENTS

The birth of this book would not have been possible without help from Lynn Wallace, Michael Lister, and my brother, Eric.

Special thanks to those whose helpful commentary shaped parts of this book, including Lynn Barrett, Robert Perry, Dr. Charlton Prather, Hank and Grace Russell, Nancy Sanders, Beverly Shown, Mark Thurston, and Kenneth Wapnick.

Special thanks to those who provided technical knowledge and hands-on experiences, including Charles Courtemanche, David Dickle, Calvin Jones, John Shafer, and Willard Smith.

This book is dedicated to my wife, Mary,
for inspiring the quest.

Cast of characters in order of appearance:

Jacob: Blacksmith of the Free Town.

Count Edzard: Ruler of the East Mark, son of Derek.

Crayfish: A beggar in the Free Town.

Peter: A serf from a farming village.

Gabriel: The village fool, Peter's older brother.

Rosamund: A serf from Peter's farming village.

Lord Lothair: Marshal of Count Edzard's castle, nephew to Lord Arnulf, cousin to Father Ulrich.

Father Ulrich: Son of Lord Arnulf, recruited by Bishop Bernard.

Bishop Bernard: Ruler of the Free Town and its valley, situated in the heart of the East Mark and below Count Edzard's castle.

PART I

Catalysis
and
Calcination

CHAPTER 1
THE PROPHECY

"Why?" Jacob asked again. The answer was surely simple. It always was. If only simplicity was not the most difficult thing in the world.

Jacob was a master of the world, until this day.

He was above every mortal weakness, until this morning.

He was free from fear until it slithered back like a snake unseen in an overgrown garden. Fear bit him during his dawn communion.

"Why?" he asked and waited for the answer. He stood alone in his blacksmith shop. Charcoal hissed under the furnace. Hot embers popped in the forge. But no answer came. For years the answer came immediately, but not today. Still, he had faith. The counselor would answer soon.

Jacob picked up the warm, metal disc, the result of today's communion. The metal shone with a yellow luster like gold. But it wasn't gold. It was brass. Since becoming a master, he had helped lead, tin, copper, iron and all sorts of metals and things change back into gold. He did it every day. But not today. He let the metal disc fall to the ash-covered floor with a soft thud. Why had today's communion produced brass instead of gold?

He waited and stroked his white beard. Still no answer came.

Why wouldn't the counselor answer him?

Jacob longed to hear something or, at least, to sense something from that which is beyond any sense. But he sensed only fear coiling to strike again.

He scratched his white mane with growing impatience. Perhaps he should look for the answer himself. Perhaps one of his tools failed during the communion. He inspected the smelting furnace for cracks and it seemed whole. He checked the crucibles for impurities and found none. He greased the bellows, even though they were already well oiled. He restacked sheets of copper and ingots of iron as neatly as before. He shuffled containers of herbs and powders from one shelf to another. He rearranged hammers, chisels and rasps that hung from pegs on the wall near the forge and anvil. He reorganized knives, nails, drills, hooks, and scrapers that were already neatly displayed for his customers. He carried a pot of water from the well within his shop to the slack tub by the forge, and then another pot, and then another until water sloshed over the edge of the hollowed out stump and onto his boots. Only then did he pause and realize that his busyness was a cover for restlessness, an affliction he had not suffered for years.

The answer lay not in the world but in the mind. He took a few deep, calming breaths and lifted a book of ancient writings onto the tilted study table. He focused on its vellum pages, on its verses and diagrams, and turned his mind inward. Everything lies in the mind, every answer, too.

A distant commotion interrupted his study. It sounded like children shouting and weapons clattering. He knew all too well the sound of spears beating shields.

He swung open the shop's double doors and stepped into the street. Below his hilltop home, most of the valley and the town hid under an early morning fog, a common condition when cool fall air slid down the hills to mix with remnants of summer's humidity. The gray cathedral spire thrust out of the fog like a nail through a wool blanket. Beyond the spire to the west, on the opposite side of the fog, a hill in the shape of a wedge cut into the heart of the valley. The count's wooden tower and stockade perched upon the wedge's rocky point and seemed to lean over the valley.

The shouts of children and the rhythmic slapping of spears against shields grew louder. Jacob's neighbors stepped out of their wattle and daub houses and watched from beneath the eaves of their thatched roofs. From out of the fog below, a group of squealing children scampered up the hill toward Jacob's house, the last building on the town's eastern edge.

Behind the children, young Count Edzard and his warriors spurred their horses up the hill. Dew glistened on their chain mail tunics. They beat their spears against their shields in unison and guided their mounts with their knees. No foot soldiers followed, apparently because the count wanted to move quickly, urgently. Edzard jerked his head from side to side like a small, nervous dog. The oversized iron bowl tied to his oversized chain mail hood flopped each time he jerked. Jacob counted eleven grim warriors and one short priest before he and his neighbors bowed their heads to the passing warriors.

"I'll be back with Maynard's head," the count yapped above the clatter. "I'll be back with Maynard's head."

Fear bit Jacob again.

The small count led his warriors on a little used road eastward toward dark lines of trees and thunderstorms that blocked the rising sun.

Between the rhythmic clapping of weapons, Jacob heard metal clinking in his shop. Someone was handling his tools. The intruder must have come in the back door.

As the last warrior rode by, Jacob slipped back into his home and recognized a beggar lifting a hammer from a wall peg. He slid up behind the thief and asked, "Do you need anything, Crayfish?"

Crayfish jumped toward the open back door but bumped against the bellows. He staggered and dropped the sack he held with his teeth. The sack clanked on the floor and a knife as long as a finger rolled out. Crayfish curled the toes of his crippled left leg over the knife and hissed, "You scared me, dirty Jew."

Jacob swept the sack off the floor before the beggar could grab it with his one good hand.

"Give me de sack." The beggar's breath stank worse than his ragged tunic. "De sack ish mine." His arms, legs and face seemed made of damaged pewter, gray skin pocked with sores. Muddy, blond hair stood as rigid as twisted spikes of bronze. One clear, blue eye flashed like polished steel. The other eye squinted between two swollen spoons of flesh. The beggar's jagged, black halo stabbed the air with the ferocity of a thousand iron knives.

Jacob sensed the beggar wavering between fleeing and attacking. "Don't be afraid." Jacob placed the coarse hemp satchel on the worktable and pulled a couple of his hammers from it.

Crayfish waved his right arm, which ended abruptly at the wrist in a handless stump. "Didn' want no tools. I come to help you clean your home, help you do sorcery."

"It's alchemy, not sorcery. One is selfless, the other selfish."

The beggar wiped tears from the swollen eye. The puffy flesh around the eye glistened pink and purple. "Give me de sack."

Jacob pulled a round of bread and links of sausage from the bottom of the sack. Except for healing herbs, Jacob never kept food in his home. "You've been cleaning other homes, too. You waited for people to step outside when the warriors passed. Then you snuck in the back door. If they catch you stealing again, they'll cut off your other hand."

The beggar snatched his empty sack from Jacob. "What people do when dey catch you doin' magic? You pretend to be a blacksmid, but I know you do sorcery." He limped backwards, snorted and spit yellow mucus into the water well. "Nobody gots a well for demselves, inside dey home. Dat's Jew magic. Sorcery."

Jacob said, "Wait. Let's tend to your eye. Have a cup of birch beer."

Crayfish stopped. "Birch Beer?"

Jacob pointed at the wooden pitcher on the worktable. "Help yourself. What happened to your eye?"

Crayfish hesitated a long moment and squinted at the wooden pitcher. "Talon beat me."

Jacob carried two small, wooden boxes from a wall shelf to the worktable and retrieved a pot of hot water from the forge. He stirred powders from the boxes into the pot. "Your partner, Talon? Pour yourself a cup."

The beggar put his empty sack back on the worktable and poured the dark liquid into a wooden cup. He drained the cup with one swallow and poured another. "I hate Talon. He beat me. Lord Maynard said we could go east wid him and live like warriors in de wild lands. I didn' want to live under de bridge no more. But Talon wouldn' let me go. He beat me - said I slow everybody down - said I too crippled." He pointed at his left leg, bent backwards below the knee like a dog's hind leg. "I hope Lord Edzard catches Talon, kills him." He gulped the birch beer and poured a third cup. "Ooooh, dat makes my tongue cold. What you cookin'? Dat for me?"

"Flaxseed and fenugreek," Jacob said. The salve's fetid odor seemed pleasant compared to the beggar's stench. "Bring me a fresh elm leaf from that shelf."

Crayfish put the empty cup down and hobbled across the shop with the small knife still hidden under his curled toes. He paused over the brass disc on the floor. "What's dat?"

"That was a mistake. It's brass. Take it if you want. You can exchange it for bread and sausage."

Crayfish returned with the leaf and the brass disc. "I like dis mistake. Gots any more? Show me how to make it. I be de novice, you be de master." He filled his cup for the fourth time.

Jacob spooned the yellow paste from the pot onto the green leaf. "The shop doesn't need an apprentice."

"You gots no food. I help you. In a few weeks de market fair begins. I know ways to gets food from de fair. Talon ish gone so I need a new partner wid two good hands. I show you how to gets food and you show me how to make mistakes." Crayfish pushed the brass disc into his sack and flashed a discolored smile.

Jacob fanned the salve with his leather apron. "Why steal when you already have everything? Where were you when the Lombard caravan was robbed on the bridge?"

Crayfish lost his toe grip on the hidden knife. He waved his handless arm in Jacob's face and grabbed the knife again with his toes. "No. No. Not me. Lord Maynard robbed de foreigners. Den he ran away. Talon and runaway serfs go wid him. Some of de count's slaves, too. Everybody go but me. Hope dey all die."

"Now be still. Let's put this salve on your eye." Jacob smeared the paste on the beggar's bruised eyelid. "It's good you couldn't go. Poor Maynard won't get far."

"'Poor Maynard?' Why you say 'poor Maynard?' He murdered old Count Derek."

Jacob shook his head but stopped when the beggar's steel blue eye pierced him.

The beggar said, "Why you say 'poor Maynard?' You know someding nobody else knows? Ow!" He jerked his head back from Jacob's hand and dropped the empty cup. "Be careful."

"Sorry," Jacob said. His hands trembled. "Do you want another cup?"

"No. No more birch beer. I saw you go in de forest when old Count Derek went huntin' wolves. Count Derek was killed on dat hunt. What you doin' in de forest?"

"Hunting fenugreek, elm, and other healing herbs, with the bishop's permission. Now be still." Jacob tried again to spread the salve evenly over the beggar's swollen eye.

"Count Derek, his warriors, de women from de castle and you, all in de forest before he died. You saw de old count and Lord Maynard, didn' you? Ow!" Crayfish jerked his head away again. "What wrong wid you?"

Jacob tried to will his hands still. The writhing serpent within bit Jacob's heart.

The beggar's cold eye cut Jacob again. "You shake, you say 'poor Maynard', 'cause you know Maynard didn' kill Count Derek."

Jacob looked away and busied his hands, wiping the salve from his fingers on his tunic. "The affairs of the world are beneath me," he repeated to himself. "The affairs of the world are beneath me."

Crayfish swept the bread and sausage from the table into his sack and limped to the front door. "Maybe you killed de old count."

Jacob pointed at the beggar's feet and said, "Leave the knife."

Crayfish uncurled the toes of his crippled leg and dropped the small knife. "I tell everybody de Jew killed de old count."

"You should return that food to its rightful owners."

Crayfish hissed a long while before replying, "You tell nobody I steal dis food, and I tell nobody you killed Count Derek." He hobbled out of the blacksmith shop.

Jacob rubbed his writhing stomach and sat on a bench. He closed his eyes and took a few deep breaths. "Detach from the world," he whispered. "Cleave to the universal essence." After a few more deep breaths, fear released him but remained within, coiled and ready to strike again. "What's happening to me?"

"*Nothing*," a familiar voice whispered back.

Jacob jumped up. "Counselor. Where have you been?" he asked the invisible advisor. "Why didn't you tell me what happened this morning? Why didn't the ritual make gold? Why didn't you answer me?"

"*The answer is always given, but not always heard.*"

Jacob nodded. That was true. The counselor spoke to all people all the time. Was Jacob, like so many others, blocking the counselor's voice?

"*Yes.*"

What barrier had he erected? He knew of none.

"*Unless you are nothing, something will always be in your way. An apprentice will help you see the barrier.*"

An apprentice? Jacob shook his head. An apprenticeship in alchemy demanded too much from most people. The sacred art flipped the world upside down. Its transmutations churned the weak into madmen or sorcerers. A suitable apprentice would have to be solid as lead and noble as gold. Not one of the town's residents was strong enough and wise enough to learn its powers.

"*A simple stranger, a fool, will knock on your door and call you master.*"

A simple stranger? A fool? Jacob didn't want an apprentice, especially a foolish apprentice. He was happy living alone as the town's only blacksmith. Why would he need an apprentice?

"*You are in danger.*"

Jacob scratched his bushy white head. How could he be in danger? He was, after all, a master alchemist, connected with all creative powers, detached from all earthly concerns. Not even death could touch him. The only thing that could possibly hurt him was himself.

The prophecy came swiftly and silently. "*The fool will save you from yourself.*"

Fear bit Jacob again.

CHAPTER 2
BROKEN PROMISE

Peter stood at the edge of the forest under a spruce tree and bit his fingernails. He peered into the woodland where the last remaining blackness of night resisted dawn's light. He saw nothing and heard nothing but the patter of water droplets slipping off leaves in a misting rain.

"Battle not started yet." He shivered and spit out a sliver of fingernail. "The warriors need me. I gots to go to the battle."

"Go no no," his elder brother Gabriel said. "Battle ish prattle no tattle."

Peter looked over his shoulder at Gabriel. The older brother wore his usual stupid grin. Gabriel bent over and brushed rainwater off his short blond hair, revealing the large cross Peter had shaved on his crown. A spirit had possessed Gabriel since childhood and, although everyone believed Peter's elder brother was harmless, Father Ulrich ordered the fool should never be without the protection of the magic cross. Peter shaved the cross neatly onto his brother's head every few days to scare away bad spirits. Gabriel wiped his face with his soggy tunic and stood straight again, head and shoulders above Peter.

Behind Gabriel, the warrior's spears leaned against the tree trunk and their horses stood tied to buckthorn and holly bushes along the forest boundary. Beyond the horses, the creeping dawn revealed ripe fields of beans, rye, cabbage, and turnips, all drowning in standing water from a series of hard rains. As long as outlaws hid in the forest, the serfs dared not work in their fields, drain the water, and save their harvest. Farther away, in the midst of those fields and nearly obscured by the drizzle, lay Peter's hamlet and, slightly above those huts, the stockade. The rest of the serfs were hiding inside Lord Arnulf's house within the stockade.

"They all afraid," Peter said, "everyone but the warriors and me and you, and you too stupid to be afraid. Wish I made no promise to Rosamund."

"Rosamund," he whispered again and sighed. His chest ached at the sound of her name. He sought every opportunity to be near her, to see her smile, hear her voice, feel her touch.

Last month when Peter thought he and Rosamund were alone, he gave her a brooch he had carved from alderwood and she kissed him for the first time. He kissed her back and kissed her again and then again. She pressed herself against him and he sank within her softness, losing himself in caressing eddies. Their boundaries dissolved in rushing currents - skimming, brushing, gliding, caressing. His cousin, Karl, crashed upon them and knocked him away from her with a wooden rake.

Peter touched the scab on his forehead where Karl's rake had struck him a month before. "You showed Karl where we were." Peter spun around and stabbed a finger into Gabriel's broad chest. "You followed me like you always do, and Karl followed you, and he found us, and he attacked us, and I beat him away from Rosamund with no help from you, and then he ran off, and he told Gisela about us, and he lied, and he lied some more."

His elder brother nodded.

Peter shook his head. "Old Gisela says I too feeble for Rosamund. I gots to go to the battle. Then they won' laugh at me anymore. They won' make me cut weeds or collect dung. That's children's work. They will honor me." He gestured toward the forest. "When I help the warriors, they see I more than a serf. Maybe a warrior will teach me to use a sword. I could be like Edzard's grandfather." He gazed into the forest and recalled the story of the slave who had saved his lord in a battle, who was made a warrior and later a count. "Then I ride back to the hamlet. They will bow their heads to me. Yes. And I will leave again, leave them all behind, except Rosamund. I take Rosamund with me."

Gabriel nodded and said, "Go away away to play play the way to go away."

Peter jabbed Gabriel's chest again, "Yes. Away from you, and Karl, and old Gisela, and all the other stupid serfs."

Count Edzard's horse neighed and kicked Father Ulrich's horse, an unshod mare that had once bitten Peter.

Peter grumbled, "Stupid to stay with crazy horses. I gots to break my promise, and Rosamund gots to forgive me, and she gots to forgive God, 'cause Father Ulrich says God makes everything happen, and if I break a promise, ish 'cause God made it happen." He waved at Gabriel. "You stay. I gots to hurry."

"Go no no," Gabriel said. "To Rosamund to promise."

Peter turned toward the forest, ducked under a branch and sprang over a fern. Something scratched his bare feet and snagged his knee-length breeches. In the dim light he recognized the thorny fingers of a young hawthorn bush, a home for she-devils. The bush grimaced and reached for his other leg. He tore himself loose and scampered back under the spruce tree.

Peter focused on the hawthorn bush and saw no she-devil. "Rosamund goes in the forest by herself. She doesn' care about custom. She not afraid of she-devils, or monsters, or bogs or Magyars or Jews. She found Maynard and the outlaws in the forest. She told the count where they are. I gots to be brave like her." He grabbed a spear from the tree trunk and swung it at the bush, slicing off the uppermost leaves. The bush quivered but didn't fight back.

"Guard forces and fears horses and spears," Gabriel said.

Peter whacked the thorny bush a few more times. "The warriors don' need us both to watch their spears or their stupid animals. The warriors need me. Count Edzard said he didn' have enough warriors. Including Father Ulrich, there were, ... uh ..."

Gabriel pointed at the horses. "Twelve one count thirteen."

"Quiet," Peter barked. He counted all his fingers while keeping a tight grip on the spear. But the warriors numbered more than ten and he didn't know what numbers came after ten. "You don' count past three," he said to Gabriel. "You wouldn' be here if it weren' for me. I told the warriors how brave I am. They took you only because you followed me. You the biggest serf, but they don' know you a half-wit."

Gabriel nodded and said, "Half-wit all-wit all alike."

Beyond the battered hawthorn bush, the forest appeared more open, empty, and safe as dawn stretched gray fingers into the black recesses of the woodland. Monsters, she-devils, and spirits did not like the light of day. If Rosamund wasn't afraid to defy custom and walk through the forest alone, then neither would he be afraid.

"So close to the battle," Peter continued, "so close to that meadow where Rosamund saw the outlaws. Stupid not to go the rest of the way." He beat the hawthorn bush flat to the ground. The she-devil had either fled the bush or died with it. "Never gets another chance. Half my life ish gone. I more than 10 years old."

"Fourteen years old," Gabriel said. The foolish grin spread across his square jaw.

"Why bother talking to you?" Peter muttered. He returned the spear to its place beside the other spears upright against the tree trunk. "Stay here," he said to Gabriel. He ran and leapt over the dead bush.

"Go no no," the elder brother called after him.

Peter sprinted up a gentle slope in the misty light, veering wide around a few suspicious shrubs, weaving between towering evergreens and oaks with trunks as wide as a man was tall. A blanket of wet pine needles muffled his quick steps. In places the air stank from rotting stumps. In other places the fresh scent of pinesap cleared the senses.

The slope grew steeper the farther he ran. His wet tunic hung heavier from his shoulders. His legs tired and stumbled as he jumped over logs. When he saw the top of the hill, he slowed to catch his breath and to sweep clinging, blond hair out of his eyes. Rosamund said the outlaw camp lay in a forest meadow on the other side of the first hill.

Huge water drops fell randomly from the high forest canopy. Some drops spattered on his head, plastering hair down again over his eyes. No birds sang overhead. No animals rustled underfoot. Only his footsteps, his panting and the patter of water drops disturbed the silent forest.

A man's cry froze Peter in mid-step. Beyond his sight on the other side of the hilltop, the battle exploded with sudden fury. Clashes of iron on iron pierced the moist air. Shouts and screams rushed over the hill.

Peter threw himself behind a small tree. With each metallic clash he crouched lower against the tree. With each awful scream he pressed closer to its warty bark. Heavy footsteps pounded up the other side of the hill but stopped short of the crest with a shriek. He heard a thud and a frightened wail, which was cut short with another thud.

Peter fumbled along his hemp belt for his finger-long knife, worn thin and brittle from years of weeding. Serfs carried knives, but men of honor carried swords. The warriors had said the outlaws carried swords stolen from a merchant caravan. The outlaws would laugh at his little knife and slice him to pieces with their stolen swords.

Maybe he should go back to the horses and spears.

But Count Edzard's grandfather had saved his lord from armed Magyars with his bare hands. Slaves were not allowed to carry any sort of knife. But he, Peter, carried a knife.

He should stay and prove his honor. This was his best chance, probably his only chance.

He shook like a weed in a rain shower, pointed his little knife at the hilltop, and waited for the battle to spill over the crest.

CHAPTER 3
THE STOCKADE

"I wasn' looking for trouble - just mushrooms - found outlaws instead," Rosamund said. Hadn't she explained this ten times already?

Nearly every woman frowned at her. Some leaned against timbers that supported the roof and divided the alcoves along the walls. Others huddled under links of sausage and sacks of powdered dye hanging from crossbeams. Gisela and her helpers stirred pots over the central fireplace. The aroma of boiled flowers drifted with the smoke through Lord Arnulf's large one-room house. Rainwater dripped into muddy puddles on the floor of rammed dirt and straw. Children cried, sheep bleated, and chickens clucked in a din commonly heard in the village community building, not in their lord's house. Rosamund could hear Lord Arnulf's wife reciting prayers in a curtained alcove nearby.

Outside his house, Lord Arnulf and his male serfs guarded the stockade walls and the larger farm animals.

Rosamund stretched her stiff legs out from where she sat on the floor and leaned against the wall near the front door. "I found bits of wool, fine red wool. They were stuck to brambles and twigs. I followed the bits to their camp." She rolled her head back against the wall and a hand-sized flake crumbled off the wall onto her shoulder, exposing the house's skeleton of twisted reeds packed in mud.

Rosamund's grandmother, Bertha, brushed wall chips from Rosamund's shoulder and said, "Rosamund ish a brave girl. She found the outlaws. She warned us. We are safe in Lord Arnulf's house 'cause of her. Father Ulrich went to get help 'cause of her. Count Edzard knows where to find his father's murderer 'cause of her. She ish smart."

White haired Gisela hobbled on her walking stick from the fireplace. "Smart? She ish trouble. She ish headstrong. The girl thinks she knows everything. No one asked her to pick mushrooms. Do any of you trust her to know the difference between a stone mushroom and a deathcap?"

A few women shook their heads.

Gisela sat with a grunt across from Rosamund and glared. "No one goes alone into the forest. It ish against custom. Alone with wild animals, spirits, monsters, Jews. Not good. She needs a beating."

Most of the women nodded.

Rosamund's face grew hot.

A little boy asked his mother, "What ish Jews?"

His mother answered, "Slave traders that steal children and eat them."

Gisela pointed at Rosamund. "Lord Arnulf gots to choose her a husband. She ish old enough now. We gots to make sure he gives her to Karl. Karl can beat some sense into her." She knocked her stick against the bottom of one of Rosamund's bare feet. "God ish punishing us. We cannot drain the fields 'cause of the outlaws. The crops will rot. God ish punishing us 'cause you break the custom." She thumped Rosamund's foot again.

Bertha grabbed the end of Gisela's stick and shook it. "Leave her alone. She ish a brave girl. She warned us about the outlaws. If only someone had warned us when the godless Magyars hid in the forest. When I was a little girl ..."

Gisela yanked her stick from Bertha's grasp and rolled her eyes. "Oh, no. Not that story again." All the women turned away.

Grandma Bertha looked at a wide-eyed little boy. She spoke to the boy in a voice loud enough for all to hear, "When I was a little girl, Lord Arnulf's grandfather brought us to this valley. We came with his slaves and ploughmen. We came for a new life. We came to a new valley between the unholy Slavs in the east and the holy Empire in the west. But then from the south, from Gog and Magog, came the Magyars, and they rode out of the forest pulling two horses behind each one, and they carried lances with linen streaming from the tips, and they screamed 'hooy, hooy, hooy' like wild demons, and they had brown skin, and black eyes, and long braids of black hair, and their arrows were tipped with iron forged in hell, and their bows were made of devils' horns.

"They killed all the animals, and all the slaves, and all the ploughmen, and all the serfs working in the fields, and their horses trampled all the crops, and their axes felled all the fruit trees. I was a little girl, and my mother grabbed me, and carried me into the stockade, and Lord Arnulf's grandfather shut the stockade door, and his warrior sons killed every demon Magyar that climbed over the wall, and the wild Magyars set fire to the stockade, and we prayed to be saved from Satan's demons, and the stockade fire was slain by rain from the storm god Donner."

Rosamund flinched at the forbidden name of a god known only to the oldest serfs.

Gisela turned and squawked, "Shut up. Don' talk about the old gods."

Bertha continued, "If some brave person like Rosamund had warned us about the demons in the forest, then all the serfs and slaves and ploughmen could have hidden in the stockade and they would have lived. That was a terrible time, the end of the world."

The front door creaked open and misty, gray light seeped inside. Lord Arnulf limped through the door and wiped rainwater from his bald head. "Is it ready?" he asked.

Everyone bowed their heads. Rosamund lowered her head but watched through her blond strands as the old warrior wobbled to the central fireplace.

Gisela climbed up her walking stick until she stood as tall as her crooked back allowed. "Yes, sire. I boiled the flowers of Saint Johnswort to cheer our men."

Lord Arnulf grabbed a pot from the fire with a gloved hand and limped back toward the door.

"Excuse, sire," Gisela said, her head bowed. "Bertha ish telling the young ones about the old gods. Tell us, sire, about the new gods and the end of the world."

The old warrior stopped. His rusted chain mail tunic nearly blended into the sooty walls and curtains behind him. His watery eyes glanced about the crowd until they found Bertha. "Look at me, Bertha. The old world is gone. The old gods are gone. The bishop says another thousand years have begun, the time of which the apostles spoke. The true faith of the church will overpower Satan's warriors; Magyars, Saracens, Jews, Slavs, Norsemen. Yes. The end of the world. End of time for a thousand years. Don't speak of the old ways, Bertha." He opened the door and went out into the grey, wet dawn.

"What ish thousand years?" a little girl asked.

Her mother answered, "More than all our fingers and toes."

Bertha kept her head down and rubbed dirt from between her toes. Gisela sneered at Grandma Bertha and Rosamund before hobbling back to the fireplace to oversee the preparations of other medicines.

Rosamund watched Gisela from her seat by the door, noting how much comfrey root, birch bark, and rabbit fur Gisela diced, ground or cooked into salves, poultices, infusions, and decoctions. She wanted to learn Gisela's art but the village healer refused to teach her. Rosamund learned much by watching Gisela's helpers and by visiting the forest, noting how birds, squirrels, and rabbits chose nuts, berries, and grasses. Gisela's helpers coughed and gagged when a rabbit skin fell and burned in the fire.

Gisela scolded them, "Hurry. We gots to be ready for the wounded."

Rosamund hoped Peter would not be one of the wounded. He promised to stay away from the battle. She shook her head. If he hadn't bragged to the warriors, they wouldn't have taken him. If only he could be more practical.

She pulled from her cloak the brooch Peter carved for her in the shape of a wolf. He had presented it to her with stammering words, shining blue eyes, a tender touch. They kissed and melted into each other's arms, and for a while she floated free in the currents of life essence, released of that vague, yet constant yearning to be free of the village, of custom, of the whole world. Karl found them and raged as though jealous, beating poor Peter with a rake. He might have killed Peter had not Gabriel pulled Karl away and snapped his rake in half.

She studied the wolf brooch in a dim slice of dawn that slipped under the front door. The wolf's tail curved up to a point for hooking one side of her cloak and its front paw curved down for hooking the other side. Peter was clever with small carvings. With his weeding knife he carved many of the village spoons and ladles, decorating them with twisting vines, leaves, and animals. Even Lord Arnulf's wife asked him to carve her combs and hairpins. He was always ready to help anyone. She whispered a prayer for his safety. When would he realize he didn't need a sword to help people?

The incised ridges on her wooden brooch stood out in a sudden beam of sunlight that vanished in a moment. Rosamund watched the cracks in the doorjamb and waited. After a short time, tiny streaks of light cut through the filmy air and disappeared again.

"Grandma. Did you see that?"

Grandma Bertha smiled and nodded.

Rosamund jumped to her feet and reached for the door.

"Rosamund, stop," Gisela called. "What are you doing?"

"The rain ish gone," Rosamund said and opened the door. Sunlight and clean air poured through the doorway.

The sun sparkled off the stockade's wet timbers, which stood as high as the thatched roof on Lord Arnulf's house. Some of the upright logs swayed outward and others inward straining against hemp ropes that bound them together. Along the base of the wooden walls, large, flaking, holes grew from years of rot in the moist earth. In the space between the encircling stockade and Lord Arnulf's house, serfs, cows, and oxen basked in slanting sunlight.

Each serf clutched a knife, an ax, or a scythe. Only Lord Arnulf held the proper weapons for war, but neither he nor his weapons had seen a battle in many years. His rusted tunic showed tears where brittle ringlets had broken. The dull point of his sword pierced the frayed end of its discolored sheath. His spear functioned as an oversized walking stick, whose blunt end stabbed the ground each time the arthritic warrior struggled to stand or battled to walk.

He pointed at the sun shining through a patch of blue sky just above the stockade wall. "This is a good omen," he called to Rosamund.

She walked into the sunlight, followed by women and children, chicken, and sheep. Chattering and nervous laughter mixed with the clucking, bleating, and mooing of farm animals. A low cloud blocked the sun.

"Something ish moving," Karl shouted from his perch atop the stockade wall. He pointed toward the eastern forest.

The villagers grew quiet.

Karl's voice pitched higher. "Peoples coming from the forest."

Everyone rushed to the stockade gate, opened it, and peered at the dark forest boundary. They stood quiet and still except their hands, which clasped and twitched. Lord Arnulf limped forward until he stood, swaying, in front of his serfs at the top of the ramp that led into his rotting stockade. His wife plowed through the crowd to a place beside him. Rosamund stood on her toes and strained to see the distant figures.

Lord Arnulf asked, "Who is it, Karl? Outlaws?"

After a long moment, Karl shouted in near panic, "Don' know."

CHAPTER 4
BATTLE

Peter hugged the small tree with one arm and pointed his trembling knife with the other. Men stopped screaming. Iron stopped ringing. Only the sound of falling drops from rain-laden trees continued to patter. The battle beyond his sight ended quickly.

Cheering erupted from the other side of the hill. The wet forest dampened the voices. Peter couldn't tell who celebrated: warriors or outlaws. The shouts came closer.

Peter's knife shook so much it nearly fell out of his hand. He should run back to the fields, back to the stockade, back to Rosamund.

No. He had left the stockade with the warriors and if he returned without them, the villagers would never respect him. He would help the warriors regardless of how they fared in battle. They might need him now more than ever. "Act like a true warrior," he whispered. "Remember Edzard's grandfather."

Peter stepped out from the tree, his heart pounding.

Something large moved on the outer edge of his vision. His heart stopped. He jerked sideways, swinging the knife behind him in defense. A tall man caught Peter's hand and yanked the knife from it. The burst of terror changed to surprise when he saw the tall man was neither an outlaw nor a warrior, but Gabriel.

"You gots to stay with the horses," Peter shouted and snatched his knife back.

Gabriel spoke softly, "Horses tied to trees want to please no more sunder thunder paining raining -"

"Shut up," Peter screamed. He pushed Gabriel's chest with both fists. "You ruin everything. You gots no mind."

Gabriel remained in place, as though rooted to the ground like a tree. "Grind the lowest mind sting find the highest mind sing." He looked past Peter to the hilltop.

"Go away," Peter grunted as he pushed against his unmovable brother. Something heavy squished the ground behind Peter, and then again, closer. He choked and spun around. His bare feet slipped on the soggy ground and he flipped backwards, dropping his knife. His back hit flat and his head bounced off a hard root snaking along the ground. The leafy canopy above swirled until a shadow blocked his view. After a dazed moment he was able to focus on the shadow before his face. A pair of lifeless eyes looked back at him. Peter screamed and the unblinking face of death soundlessly screamed back, its open mouth drooled blood onto Peter's tunic. Peter scooted away on his elbows and vomited.

"You stinking sacks of ox dung." The head lifted away until Peter saw it clearly, impaled on the sword of the count's marshal, Lothair. "I told you to guard our horses and spears." Lothair spoke crisply, not slurred like the speech of serfs. Slashes crisscrossed his leather-covered shield. Blood splattered his tunic and hood. A small dent marred his bowl-shaped helmet. His angular head sat on a neck as thick as Peter's thigh. His short, black beard bristled and his thick eyebrows scowled. He stood as tall and broad as Gabriel.

"Horses tied to trees like to please," Gabriel said. "Weather fair not to scare not fair to scare -"

"Shut up, you worthless turdhead." Lothair shook his sword with its skewered head at Gabriel. "I should kill you here and now."

Peter jumped up and stepped between Lothair's sword and his brother. "No. Please, sire." He bowed his head and wiped his mouth. "Spare him. I left him w-w-with the horses. I w-w-wanted to help you and the count and the other w-w-warriors. My fault. My fault. He only gots half a w-w-wit."

"You're both halfwits," Lothair growled. He pushed the skewered head into Peter's chest, smearing more blood across his hemp tunic.

Peter gagged and backed into Gabriel. His knees shook and almost buckled.

Lothair pointed down the hill. "Check the horses. Make sure they're well tethered. Then tell your lord that we killed Maynard and his outlaws."

Peter swallowed the bile in his throat. "Thank you, sire." He picked up his knife and sprinted down the hill without looking back. His racing heart gave strength to his weak knees. He ran between trunks of ancient trees and snapped twigs from younger trees that stood in his way. His brother lumbered just behind. It seemed only a blink of the eye before they returned to the spruce tree and the warriors' spears.

At the base of the hill they pushed through underbrush, which marked the edge of the woods. When they broke out into the fields, sunlight burst through a break in the clouds and the trees cast long shadows over them. Only then did Peter's fear subside.

"We have victory," he whispered to himself. "And Lord Lothair sent me on a mission." Peter checked Lothair's horse first and double knotted its reins to a young oak. He pulled the knot especially tight to please Lord Lothair. He inspected the tied reins of the other horses while Gabriel stroked their noses. At the end of the line, the count's amber-colored stallion grazed on a clump of dill. Peter paused by the count's horse and looked across the fields to the distant hamlet. A low cloud scudded before the rising sun.

A few squat huts clustered around the bottom of the earthen ramp, which led to the stockade entrance. The stockade walls of swaying, rotting timbers circled the top of a low mound. A few people, mere specks at this distance, dotted the top of the wall and gathered at the stockade gate. Rosamund surely stood among them. He wished he could return to the village on a horse like a warrior.

"Stay here," Peter said to Gabriel.

His brother shook his head and walked toward him.

"No. This time you stay here. I gots to tell them about -"

Pain ripped Peter's upper arm. He gasped, jumped aside, and tore his sleeve free from a horse's clinched teeth. Blood trickled from a finger-long tear in his arm where the count's horse nicked him.

The animal stared at him with black eyes on either side of a white, star-like pattern on its forehead. Its lips curled as though to grin.

Gabriel touched Peter's shoulder.

"Stay," Peter jerked away from his brother and rubbed his aching arm. "Watch the animals from hell."

He turned and ran toward the stockade. He sped down a raised footpath between two fields of rye in standing water, past a small clump of woodland fenced in for pigs, and over a field of leafy, soggy cabbage. He would tell everyone about the victory. They would respect him. Rosamund would love him. His pinched arm hurt less the faster he ran.

After a few minutes, the sun returned and warmed the back of his wet tunic. He veered off the path and sloshed through a muddy field where he and other serfs had harvested lentils a few days before. His feet grew heavier with caked muck and his pace began to slow. When he got within hailing range, he stopped running and began walking. Above his heavy panting, he heard Karl shouting.

"Ish Peter."

Peter straightened his back and lifted his head. He had been to the battle. Karl had not.

"Ish the fool, too."

His brother jogged up beside him.

"Go back..." Peter gasped, "to horses ... I went ... to battle ... I gots to tell ..."

Gabriel laughed and trotted past him. Peter ran again to catch up.

"They running from the battle," Karl shouted to the crowd at the gate. "We lost."

Everyone tumbled back into the stockade, everyone but Rosamund. She stood unmoved until Gisela and her helpers dragged her inside and shut the gate.

Gabriel stopped near a field of mature turnips. Peter stepped in front of his brother, raised his knife into the air, and shouted, "We won." He panted a few moments before shouting again, this time louder, "We won. We won."

The stockade gate opened again and the serfs flooded down the ramp toward Peter and Gabriel. Rosamund ran with the surging crowd. She held her head high and sure, not stooped like the other serfs. Her long, blond hair fluttered away from her unblemished face. She waved and smiled, glowing in a flood of grayclad serfs.

The villagers splashed into the turnip field and gathered around the brothers. "Are we safe?" they shouted. "Are they gone? Are they coming?" The serfs milled about, jostled, and waved their arms with excited gestures. But every one was careful not to step on the leafy stalks.

"Wait," Peter shouted above the clamor. "Wait for Lord Arnulf."

More serfs gathered. Their questions scrambled louder over

each other. "Are we safe? Where are the warriors? Where are the outlaws?"

Peter tried to scowl like Lothair. "Lord Lothair the Angry told me to tell our lord."

Rosamund moved to the front of the noisy crowd. She wore his brooch. Peter reached for her.

"Peter." Lord Arnulf's voice stilled the serfs and they bowed their heads. Peter lowered his arms and his head. The lord of their valley hobbled forward, helped by his lady and his spear. He touched the blood stains on Peter's tunic and asked. "What blood is that?"

Peter shouted, "Outlaw blood, my lord."

The lady inspected Peter's bitten arm. "What happened?"

"A battle w-w-wound, my lady," Peter stammered.

"You were in the battle?" she asked. "How so? Where are the others?"

"They coming, my lady. Lord Maynard ish dead. So are the outlaws."

Lord Arnulf sighed. "What about Ulrich? Tell us about the battle."

Peter kept his head bowed according to custom. He put his knife under his belt and wished it were a warrior's sword. "Lord Lothair the Angry sent me. He gots outlaw head on his sword." Peter winched at the memory.

"My nephew is alive," Lord Arnulf said. "Good. What about Ulrich? Tell us what happened."

"The outlaws w-w-were over the hill, just like Rosamund said. The count led us into the forest and w-w-we attacked."

"What about my son?"

Peter had not seen the Father Ulrich since the warriors disappeared into the forest. "He w-w-was brave, too." His voice cracked.

"What's wrong?" Lord Arnulf's wife asked. "Is he hurt?"

In the corner of his downcast eye, Peter could see Rosamund's dress. Next to her stood Karl. Peter's face grew hot. "He killed many outlaws."

"Look at me, Peter," his lord said.

Peter raised his eyes but not his head. Worry creased the faces of his lord and lady.

"Tell me about the battle, about Ulrich," the old warrior said.

Peter chewed a fingernail a moment and began to lie.

CHAPTER 5
VICTORY

The sky cleared as Peter told his story. "The forest w-w-was thick like the stockade w-w-walls and it w-w-wouldn' let us pass, and Count Edzard told the spirits of the forest to open, and they did, and w-w-we passed through." Rosamund, Karl, and the other serfs raised their heads. "At the top of the hill w-w-we came to a monster bear, and the bear tried to stop us, and Father Ulrich told the bear to kneel before the count, and it did and w-w-we passed by."

Lord Arnulf's hairy, white eyebrows fused into a frown. "A bear?"

"Yes, my lord." Peter raised his voice a notch. "Your son, Father Ulrich, tamed the w-w-wild animal just like Saint Jerome from the bishop's magic book."

The serfs nodded. They had all seen those stacks of square cut sheepskins, scraped clean and bound together at one end. Father Ulrich called it a book. Monks had marked the skins with a caustic blend of oak gall and iron salts in water. Father Ulrich called the markings letters and pictures. Before returning the book to the bishop, he used it to teach the serfs that new saints of the church had replaced the old gods of memory. Rosamund asked to learn about the letters and Peter asked about the pictures, but Father Ulrich said serfs could not learn those things.

"Saint Jerome tamed a lion," Peter said, recalling a picture from one of the magic books. "Daniel tamed many lions, big, red cats w-w-with hairy -"

Lord Arnulf raised his hand. "Tell me about the battle."

"The monster bear let us pass," Peter continued. "and w-w-we crossed over the hill, and the rain stormed harder, and w-w-we couldn' see, and I told the spirits in the storm to stop, and they did, and w-w-we..."

The men murmured and the women giggled. Rosamund frowned.

"Ish true," Peter said.

"From tillage to pillage," Gabriel chimed. "The serf with earth between the toes between the ears nothing but fears of flying lying."

Peter's audience laughed in a hearty chorus. Karl kicked a clump of mud at Peter. Rosamund looked red-faced to the ground. Gabriel smiled blankly like a fool. Lord Arnulf turned away and waved a hand at Peter as though he were shooing away a fly.

Peter's face burned. He wanted to run away.

"The count," someone called above the laughter. "Count's coming."

The warriors rode toward the village in a single file on a footpath between the flooded fields. Their oval shields bounced on their left sides. Their right hands held their spears aloft. Impaled atop their spears were dark, round lumps. Peter choked at the memory of the head on Lothair's sword.

The serfs shouted all at once. "They coming back ... Are they all coming back? ... They gots more horses ... four more horses ... What's on their spears? ... Father Ulrich ish coming."

The little priest stood in his stirrups and waved from the back of the file. He turned his horse onto a parallel path and galloped forward, past the warriors. The whole village cheered.

Lord Arnulf counted the warriors. "Edzard, Ulrich, and eleven warriors. Good. Everyone is safe. We'll celebrate tonight."

His lady smiled and wiped tears off her cheeks. "I should fetch a goose, nay, two geese."

"Father," the little priest called as he galloped closer. "We killed them all. None of us are hurt." The serfs parted to let him into their midst. His frail arms reined the horse to a stop on the raised footpath. He leaned down to kiss his parents and gave the reins to his father.

Peter stepped back from the stamping, drooling mare and rubbed his horse-bitten arm.

Father Ulrich unsheathed his sword and wrestled the cap off the sword hilt. Sacred bone fragments rolled out of the hollowed hilt into his hand. Making a fist around them, he held his hand aloft and shouted, "The holy relics of Saint Ursula gave us victory." He lowered his fist to his mouth and kissed it. The crowd cheered again.

He returned the bone chips to his sword hilt, took the reins again, and dismounted. Even though he stood straight and his father stooped, the top of his tonsured head reached only to the middle of his father's chest. His sword sheath dragged the ground.

"Your mother is preparing a victory feast." Lord Arnulf waved his wife away. She kissed her son again before taking Gisela and her helpers back to the stockade.

The little priest pointed to the approaching warriors. "Those three pack horses and Maynard's stallion are loaded with goods stolen from the Lombard. Red English wool, six rolls, and bags of silver pennies, first rate Lombard swords, and a crossbow."

The old warrior's eyebrows lifted. "A crossbow? Never seen one of those."

Father Ulrich frowned. "Edzard killed Maynard while he slept. Then he hid until the fighting was over. They were all runaway serfs or slaves or beggars and none of them knew how to use their stolen swords. It was no battle, it was murder."

Peter and the other serfs scampered back when Count Edzard and his warriors thundered to a stop before Arnulf and his son. The horses snorted, kicked, and trampled turnip stalks.

Count Edzard yanked the oversized, iron helmet together with his chainmail hood back from his small, blond head and pole-thin neck. He thrust his lance upward. On its tip was skewered a fleshy head. "Maynard the Fat," he howled. The corners of his mouth foamed. "My father's murderer."

The peasants cheered and the warriors beat their spears against their shields. Each spear point held a severed head. The count swung his lance in circles, splattering Peter and others with dark ooze from Maynard's head. Peter's stomach convulsed.

Lord Lothair spurred his horse up to Arnulf and barked, "I challenged his men to a fair battle. But they tried to flee. The vermin could never have carved their own fiefdom in the east. The Slavs would have boiled them and eaten them like mutton, in their fine English wool, holding their fine Lombard swords and their silver pennies."

"Did you find any gold?" Lord Arnulf asked.

"No," Count Edzard growled. "We searched everywhere. No gold."

Peter wished they had found gold. He had never seen gold.

Lothair motioned in Peter's direction and held out his horse's shortened reins. "You there. Halfwit. You tied my horse too tight.

I had to cut him loose." He turned to the count. "He's one we'll take back to the castle."

Peter smiled and puffed his chest. He had impressed Lothair. Rosamund looked at Peter with wide eyes and open mouth. Gabriel put a hand on Peter's shoulder.

"What?" Lord Arnulf said.

Lothair pointed a skewered head at Gabriel. "Take the big serf, too,"

"What are you doing?" Lord Arnulf said. "Why do you want these serfs?"

The count tugged his over-sized, metallic tunic over his narrow shoulders. "The pig-headed masons are taking too long to build my house. I want to finish it faster. I've taken serfs from other vassals." A couple of warriors behind Edzard rolled their eyes. "I'll take two of yours."

Lord Arnulf said, "My lord, I already sent you a serf, Paul, a bright boy. He's been away almost forty days, the time of my vassalage duty. He must be returned, and I've got to keep these other two because it's harvest time."

"My liege," the count growled, "that bright serf won't be returning. He was too bright. The bishop lured him away from us. He ran off and Lothair killed him in the monastery."

Just behind Peter, Paul's wife shrieked and collapsed. Her young children reached out to her crumpled, sobbing form. Rosamund helped the young woman off the wet ground and locked her frowning eyes on Peter before leading Paul's wife and children back to the hamlet.

Lord Arnulf looked at his son. "Why didn't you tell me?"

Ulrich looked away and shook his head. "Well, with Derek's murder and Maynard's trial, it didn't seem ..." He shrugged and shuffled his feet.

Count Edzard watched the young widow stumble away. "According to custom, you, his lord, have first pick of this man's possessions."

Lord Arnulf shook his head. "Paul had nothing."

"You must select a new husband for that girl. She's young and healthy. It's custom for the lord to reserve the first night with the bride for himself. As your lord, I might take that right for myself, tonight."

Arnulf scowled. "Leave my serfs alone."

"Don't make me remind you again that I'm your lord." Count Edzard looked at Peter. "I'm taking the little serf and the big serf with me. After I give Ulrich his part of Maynard's booty, I'll give you Maynard's stud for the serfs. You have only one horse, an old mare. I've heard a stud in a wooden collar pulls a plow better than two oxen. I don't want any more bright boys. Lothair tells me these two boys are addle-headed."

Peter stepped closer to Count Edzard and bowed his head lower. "I am battle headed just like Lord Lothair said. Please, my Lord Arnulf, let me go. But keep Gabriel here. Let me go and I come back to you as a w-w-warrior."

"A warrior? Humph," the old warrior said. "Peter's a smart boy but he lacks common sense. His brother, Gabriel, has no sense at all. No. These boys can't be traded for an animal like slaves. They're serfs and they're bound to this land, my valley."

"YOUR valley?" The count smacked his fist against his horse's neck. The animal lurched sideways and Peter jumped out of its way. "This is MY valley in MY county, and you are MY vassal. Your family couldn't stand up to the Magyars and so your family put itself and this valley under my family's protection. For that, your family owes my family forty days of armed service each year. But you are too old to fight. And all your sons are dead, except for this sickly priest." Count Edzard dipped Maynard's head over Father Ulrich. "This year you exchanged your war service for a serf who ran away before your service ended. For this and next year's service I'll take these two serfs. I'll take them now and you can have them back in a year. If you don't agree, I will declare your vassalage in abeyance and you will be an outlaw."

Lord Arnulf blinked heavily and bowed his head.

Father Ulrich stepped forward and said, "We accept your generous offer, my lord. We'll take the stud plus a share of the merchant's goods for me and a share for my father."

"A share for the worthless old man?" the count snarled.

The little priest spoke firmly but evenly. "My father held the stockade safe for your return from battle, and my mother prepares a victory feast. My father will use his share of the booty to exchange

They stepped back to let Count Edzard and the warriors ride past. The count reined his horse in the center of the village and barked, "Where is Bertha?"

The old woman stuffed the bone cubes back into her pouch and limped forward with her head bowed.

Rosamund looked for Father Ulrich. The little priest watched from the back of the line of warriors. He preached against the old gods, called their works sorcery, and threatened to exile anyone still practicing the old rituals. Had he seen Bertha's magic bones?

The count looked down on Grandma Bertha. "I'm told you're the eldest villager. You've lived from the time of the old ways."

"Yes, sire. I lived here before your grandfather came," she said to his horse's hooves.

The count tilted his head back. His long nose, narrow face, and short limbs reminded Rosamund of a small dog. He dropped a length of fine, red wool onto Bertha's shoulders. "May I also be blessed with a life as long as yours." He spurred his horse forward.

Grandma Bertha held the wool cloth a moment before shouting, "Bless you, sire. Long live Count Edzard."

The villagers cheered. They gathered around Bertha and touched the wool.

Lord Lothair untied four lumpy sacks from his saddle and dropped them at Peter's feet. "Two sacks of heads for you and two for the other fool. Get in line behind the packhorses."

Dark blood stained the bottoms of the gray sacks. Peter heaved a sack onto his back with both hands. He held it with one hand and tried to lift the second sack with his free hand. His arm shook and his legs wobbled. Rosamund struggled to help him lift the second sack. Its weight surprised her. Gabriel took the second sack from them and picked up the remaining two sacks. When Father Ulrich rode past pulling Lord Maynard's pack horses, the elder brother swung all three sacks over his shoulder and ambled forward.

"Thank you, Gabriel," Rosamund said. She kissed Peter's cheek. "Please be careful."

"Don' w-w-worry," Peter grunted.

He and Gabriel walked after the packhorses on the narrow muddy path, winding between the huts. Rosamund walked a few paces behind. "I come back a true warrior," Peter said to everyone.

"A true warrior when I come back."

Most villagers shook their heads. Peter's aunt said to her son, Karl, "Good riddance." Children laughed and swaggered behind Peter. Rosamund shooed the children away as she followed him.

The warriors snaked past the long communal building, around the dunghill and then followed a raised footpath between two fields of wheat.

By the time they reached the forest boundary, black stains at the base of Peter's sack had spread to the back of his cloak.

She stopped at the edge of the woodland. "Be careful," she shouted. She tried to shout again but her words choked on a lump the size of her heart.

He waved before wobbling around a turn on the forest path.

She knelt in the field and let her tears flow. Grandma Bertha knelt beside her and hugged her shoulders. She rocked Rosamund and dabbed her cheeks with her new piece of fine, red wool.

"He gots zeal, the fire of desire. That will help him," Grandma Bertha said. "The magic bones say if he does good, he rules the world. He comes back here with more power than he can understand."

Rosamund asked, "But if he fails, what do the bones say?"

Grandma Bertha looked down. Her wrinkled forehead creased into a frown.

The parade stopped and grew quiet before a two-storied structure, the grandest house he had yet seen. Stout timbers crisscrossed the walls. The windows were covered not with shutters of wood, but with a lattice of thin, translucent fabric.

A tall lord walked out the front door of the grand house and stood in the twilight. He wore red linen, leather boots, and a blue cloak so large that several children could easily find warmth within it. A conical hat on his high forehead tilted as if hurriedly placed on his head. Several priests with tonsured haircuts, black robes, and sword sheaths hooked to their belts filed out of the house and stood beside him.

Peter moved closer to stand near Lothair as the town's people bowed their heads. Peter bowed his head but raised his eyes to watch. Neither Count Edzard nor his warriors bowed their heads before the tall lord and his priests.

"Greetings to God, Count Edzard," the tall lord said.

Count Edzard stood up in his stirrups and raised his spear with its impaled head. "Greetings to God, Bishop Bernard. Do you recognize Maynard the Fat? I killed him with my own hands, the murderer of my father."

The bishop rubbed his clean-shaven chin and said, "Was he the murderer?"

The count shook his spear. "Only a fool would think otherwise."

The bishop's reply cut through the twilight air. "Now that Maynard's dead, we'll never know for sure. I will inform my lord, King and Emperor Otto the Third."

The count tilted his head back and looked down his long thin nose at Bishop Bernard. "And I will inform my lord, Duke Heinrich the Good."

Lothair growled, "Heinrich the Good for nothing."

The bishop looked at Lothair and said, "Your duke supports the emperor. And the emperor's subjects," he motioned to the silent crowd behind Lothair, "hear your every word. "

Lothair shook his sword with its impaled head. "His subjects, your people, count for nothing. The old duke was a real warrior, unlike his son."

Edzard nodded. "Your emperor exiled our lord and sent his

son, Heinrich, to the God damned monks, who taught him to read and write, things that make a man weak."

"They taught him the power of forgiveness," the bishop said.

Edzard thrust Maynard's head toward the bishop. "That's no power. That's weakness."

Father Ulrich dismounted and stood between the count and the bishop. "My lord," he said to Count Edzard. "Our new duke does not support old grievances. He made peace with Emperor Otto. It's time we make peace."

Edzard shook like a small dog. "Your bishop doesn't want peace. He's a schemer like his emperor. He's trying to weaken me. Look at the wife he chose for me."

"She came from the emperor's court," the bishop said. "Your father saw it as a way to mend our troubles."

"My father was a fool. He married me to a servant's daughter."

Bishop Bernard spoke slowly as though speaking to a misbehaving child. "Lilli's mother was first lady-in-waiting and had great influence at the court before she died. She was a Greek noblewoman like the Empress herself, versed in many secret arts."

"And what was Lilli's father?" Edzard snapped. "Nobody knows."

The bishop winced and looked away.

Father Ulrich replied, "People say her father was from the emperor's family."

"Shut your muzzle," the count barked at the little priest. "You are my vassal and you serve me, not the bishop."

Father Ulrich bowed his head. "Forgive me, my lord. With your permission, I'll take leave of you now. My father needs me to help harvest the fields."

"Go back to your useless father," Count Edzard growled.

Without another word, the count turned his horse westward and the warriors followed. They rode out of the town's square and onto another street.

The residents seemed to lose their enthusiasm for the count's parade. They returned to their homes a few at a time as the procession wound through the streets. Parents pulled their children away. Doors to the houses along the way remained shut. The warriors twirled the severed heads and beat their shields with waning vigor until they, too, lost their zeal. Their sour lips spoke no words, their grim eyes looked only forward. When the warriors reached the opposite side of the free town, they were again alone.

The count led his warriors over a bridge broad enough for five men to walk abreast. A small river gurgled beneath the bridge. A gaunt figure crawled out from under the bridge pilings at its opposite end.

"So glad you gots Maynard and Talon. Bread for a beggar?" the waif lisped to each warrior crossing the bridge. One of the beggar's legs bent backward below the knee and one arm ended in a stump at the wrist.

The path divided in three ways just past the bridge. The left way followed the river south, lined with a few meager fields and huts like those in his village. The right path disappeared after a few paces over the edge of a large rock quarry. Peter followed the warriors and packhorses along the middle way, which skirted the edge of a quarry and then twisted up the barren south side of the bluff to the stockade above.

Peter strained to see into the quarry, barely visible in the dimming twilight. Someone grabbed his arm and he jumped with a start. It was the beggar.

Peter shook his arm free. "Gots nothing to give you."

The beggar said, "Wanted to see how strong you are. You won' last long."

CHAPTER 8
THE CASTLE

"Wake up."

A gruff voice and a kick in his ribs woke Peter. It took him a moment to remember he lay on a bed of straw in the castle stables, in a stall shared with his brother and six other serfs. His cloak and shoes were piled with the belongings of others in a corner. The back of his tunic crackled stiff from dried outlaw blood. He rubbed straw from his face. His arms ached.

Ledmer, a stocky serf, kicked Peter again and motioned toward dawn's faint light. "Gets up. Go."

In the courtyard, Lord Lothair stood with arms crossed and watched a couple of serfs pull three mares from the stables. Guy, a tall, lanky serf, handed Peter a bread crust with something like white mold inside. Peter sniffed it.

"Eat it," Guy said. "White bread. No body here eats brown bread. The warriors eat the heart of the bread. They give us and the dogs the crust."

Peter took a cautious bite. The bread tasted thin, not like bread but like something under bread. Under bread? He had heard that before. He remembered Lothair had said the count was under bread. Brown bread was heavy and coarse, but this under bread was light and noble.

He chewed the under bread and studied his surroundings. Since he and Gabriel arrived in the dark, this was his first real look at the castle courtyard.

The swaying walls of the timbered stockade indicated that it, like Lord Arnulf's stockade, was rotting at the base. But there the similarities ended. The count's fortification was far larger. Ladders led to walkways just under the top of the parapet. Against the walls leaned several wattle and daub shanties, some open and some enclosed, which he assumed contained storerooms, stables, kitchens, and barracks for the foot soldiers, servants, and their families. At the back of the courtyard rose a tower, many paces high and across, and made of thick timbers.

"The count and countess eat on the bottom floor," Guy said, pointing to the tower. "They sleep on the top floor. Count Edzard wants a stone tower."

In the center of the castle grounds, men in clean tunics and leather boots erected scaffolds around the beginning of a stone house, the count's new tower.

Guy told Peter as they walked past the scaffolds, "Those men are free masons, building him a tower with a cellar and three floors. He wants it taller than the bishop's house."

The warriors who had attacked Maynard mounted their horses. Lothair waved as they rode out the gate.

"They gots to go back to their valleys," Guy said. He pointed to a shanty as the serfs walked to the stockade gate. "Lord Lothair sleeps there. He ish landless, gots no valley. His father lost his valley in a quarrel with Derek the Ram. If Lothair ish a good marshal, Derek promised to take a valley from the wild Slavs and give it to him. Now Derek ish dead."

Peter followed the serfs leading the mares out the castle gate and down the bluff. Fog the color of lead covered everything in the valley except the cathedral spire, which pierced the leaden air with real solidity. At the first hairpin turn in the steep road, the serfs came upon an upright spear topped with an outlaw head. Peter gagged and kept his eyes down as he passed it and all the other impaled heads displayed at each sharp curve.

"The count gots to show off his victory," Guy said.

Peter wanted to wash his stiff tunic free of dried fluids from those heads as soon as possible.

The road descended steeply through layers of fog, until it flattened near the edge of the quarry. Narrow plots of rye and barley near the bluff seemed almost barren compared to the robust fields on the opposite side of the river. A ragged family mowed a sparse plot near the bridge.

"Slaves on this side of the river," Guy told Peter. "Some left and died with Maynard. Now their heads sit on the spears behind us. On the other side of the river, monks and free merchants. The valley belonged to Edzard's grandfather until the emperor took it away and gave it to the church. Derek wanted it back. Edzard wants it back, too. The bishop gots the best farmland and hunting" Guy pointed across the river. "Old Count Derek always went there to hunt. He died there."

The beggar crawled out from under the bridge on the count's side of the river and hissed as the serfs turned north onto a footpath. On the bishop's side of the river, a few women washed linens in a boulder field at the water's edge. Their children played in one of the river's mud flats between tracts of boulders. The houses behind them appeared as great shadows in the fog.

The footpath led the serfs to the bottom of the quarry where more masons cut blocks from the heart of the rocky spur.

Guy pointed at a long building on the chiseled ground. "The masons lodge there. They built the cathedral with stones from this quarry."

Peter, Gabriel, and the other serfs loaded blocks of stone on the mares and on pallets as long as a man. They teamed up in twos to carry the pallets. The man in the rear, in addition to holding one end of the pallet, pulled a loaded mare by the reins tied around his waist. They ascended the winding road, delivered blocks to masons in the courtyard, and then descended for another load. The sun burned away the fog and burned the serfs' already sun-darkened skin. The stench of the rotting heads along the castle road nauseated Peter. When it was his turn to lead a mare, he chose the one with the longest reins, hoping to distance himself from another horse bite.

Except for a brief rest to hear mass from a priest, the serfs carried blocks until darkness forced them to stop. The next day Peter awoke with stiff and painful muscles.

Peter's mugwort leaf crumbled away. "Ish there a mugwort bush close by?" he asked.

Ledmer laughed and asked, "Why? You tired?"

While Peter unloaded blocks, he watched the courtyard activities. Every morning Lothair taught the garrison of four foot soldiers the art of war. They improved their agility and accuracy against a manikin, clubbing a target shield on one of its arms while ducking its opposite arm as it spun around to strike its assailant. They trained their hands, eyes, and ears to act as one while practicing sword swings with long wooden batons as thick as Peter's wrists. They built their strength in a war game with a leather ball, which they stuffed with sand, vinegar, and an old chain mail tunic. They fought over the ball, kicking, hitting, and throwing it and each other from one side of the courtyard to the other. After the game, they opened the ball and removed the chain mail, now clean and shining.

Sometimes Count Edzard fought in the games. When he held the ball, the soldiers let him pass by faking falls. When a soldier held the ball, he always let the count catch him. But Lothair always played in earnest and, whenever Lothair joined the game, the count retired. A few times Countess Lilli watched the games, but she never smiled at a comic fall, never winced at a bloody clash, and never cheered her husband.

"The count does not plow her furrow," Ledmer said and snickered. "He prefers young widows."

"She ish of child-bearing age," Guy said. "But she ish a foreigner with strange ways."

She seemed to glide across the courtyard, and she carried her head high with the same assurance as Rosamund. Her brown eyes entranced Peter. Her dark skin glowed with a golden hue unlike the red-brown skin of sunburned serfs. In sunlight her black hair reflected the blue tint of the moon. She always wore an embroidered, full-length dress, sometimes red, sometimes blue, adorned with many bracelets, armlets, amulets, and necklaces that sparkled like stars.

"Yes, that ish gold," Guy answered Peter's question. "She always wears gold and silver. Mostly gold."

One day, as Peter unloaded stones in the courtyard, a loud thwack echoed through the stockade. A brawny mason ducked just before something popped against the stone wall behind his head. A splintered stick with a twisted iron tip struck the dirt at Peter's bare feet.

"Crossbow dart," Guy said. "Bounced all over the courtyard. Count Edzard don' know how to use it. Lothair won' touch it, not honorable he says. So they gave it to him." Guy pointed to a foot soldier, who aimed the crossbow at the manikin. Before he could fire it again, Edzard yanked the weapon from him.

The count strode to the brawny mason. "I saw you duck. You're quicker than a dart. You could learn the art of war and how to use this damned thing." He shook the crossbow in the air. "I need more warriors and I could make you a foot soldier in a year's time." He picked up a scaffolding stick and gave it to the mason.

"Show me how you would swing a sword."

The mason leaned the stick against the wall, bowed his head and said, "You honor me, sire. I am free to work when and where I please, unlike a foot soldier, a warrior, or even the highest lord. I'm happy to remain a free mason and to serve you."

The count snarled and marched away.

Peter picked up the scaffolding stick and imitated some of the swings he'd seen during sword drills. If he were as quick as the mason, then Count Edzard would ask Peter to learn the art of war. He practiced swordplay with the stick each time he descended to the quarry.

On the day of rest all the castle residents, except Lothair and the serfs, descended to the cathedral. Peter was finally allowed to wash his tunic and cloak free of outlaw blood in a water trough. He rejoined the other serfs, who sat against a wall facing the empty courtyard. Peter slouched against the wall and let the wet, cool tunic sooth his aching muscles.

"No, no, no," Ledmer whispered and waved his arms at Guy. "Maynard killed old Count Derek in the bishop's forest. Custom in the bishop's valley says trial ish with witnesses and oaths and oath helpers. Maynard wasn' hiding in the monastery. He was waiting for witnesses, for oaths."

Guy shrugged. "No matter where Maynard killed the old man. Maynard was the count's vassal, subject to customs of the count's land, not the bishop's. They share many customs, Konrad's customs, but not this custom. Here trial ish with red-hot irons."

Ledmer shook his head and pointed at the stockade gate. "If they let us go to High Mass in the cathedral, we could learn more about this. Edzard keeps us here with Lothair, afraid we hear what the monks say. They say Maynard didn' kill Derek the Ram."

"No," Guy said. "The count ish afraid we will breathe the air of free men."

Ledmer said, "No need to worry. We happy to be serfs."

"Not me," Peter said from his slouch. "I not going to stay a serf."

"What do you mean?" Ledmer whispered through clenched teeth. "Don' do something that keeps us here longer. I gots to go home, back to Lord Norbert's valley. Don' be stupid."

"I am not stupid," Peter said. He sat up, tilted his head back and looked down his nose like Count Edzard.

"The last boy from your village, Paul, he was stupid," Ledmer said. "He ran away to the monastery. The monks put a bell rope on him to protect him. But there not enough magic in that bell rope. Lothair went to the bishop's house for Maynard and killed Paul instead. He gave the bishop a copper penny for his life."

"That was not right," Guy said and the others nodded. "Konrad's custom says the serf's lord gots to come for the runaway. Lothair was not Paul's lord."

"Lothair the Angry does what he wants," Ledmer said. "What done twice becomes custom. If Lothair does it again, it becomes custom, Lothair's custom." He shook a thick finger at Peter. "If you run away, he pay a penny for your life, too."

Guy frowned at Peter. "Konrad's custom says if a serf stays a year and a day in the free town and his lord doesn' come for him, that makes the serf free. If you run away and Lothair kills you, he makes a new custom that anyone can find and kill a runaway, not just the serf's lord. Then none of us gots a chance to be free."

"Not going to run away. Not going to stay a serf," Peter said. "I am going to be a warrior." He sneered like Lothair.

The serfs broke into derisive laughter.

Ledmer sneered back. "You? A warrior? You going to be squashed in your first battle."

Peter pointed to the scab on his arm where the horse bit him. "Already been in battle. Gots wounded in battle with Maynard the Fat."

"You told us already," Ledmer said. "Your fool brother don' say ish true. You lying."

Gabriel grinned stupidly. Ledmer and the others frowned.

Peter walked to a stack of long, heavy batons used to practice swordplay, grabbed one and threw another at Ledmer. "Pick up the stick. I show you how I fought in battle."

Ledmer's sneer dropped from his face. Guy's frown opened into wide-eyed fear.

Peter said, "Come on, you stinking, thick dunghill. I gots to improve my skill. Wish Count Edzard was here to watch me."

The serfs scrambled to their feet and bowed their heads.

Even Peter's older brother stood servile before him. Peter was surprised and smiled at their submission until he heard an ice-cold command.

"Bring me that stick," Lothair barked.

Peter turned with a start. The tall warrior stood a few paces behind him

Ledmer delivered the baton and backed away.

Lothair swung the baton and growled, "Since the little serf says he's been in battle, it wouldn't be honorable to fight someone who hasn't. I'll be the champion for the loud serf." He marched at Peter. "If you want to improve yourself, little serf, then choose a true challenge. I am your challenge."

CHAPTER 9
THE DUEL

Peter gripped the long baton with both hands to stop its trembling.

The blackbearded giant swaggered toward him. Iron ringlets in his armor glinted in the afternoon sun. He stopped within striking distance, pulled the chain mail hood over his head and growled, "Attack me, like the warrior you want to be."

Peter hesitated before swinging his baton. Lord Lothair stepped back to let Peter's stick glide past and then stepped forward to push Peter in the ribs with the end of his baton. Peter tripped over his own bare feet and sprawled onto the castle yard.

Lothair looked down his crooked nose. "That's not the way of a warrior."

Peter's face flushed warm. He glanced at the other serfs. All but Gabriel watched with wide eyes and open mouths. His brother grinned like a fool.

Peter jumped up, bowed his head and said, "I can learn the w-w-way of a w-w-warrior, sire."

"Did you say you fought in a battle? Show me how you fought."

Peter raised his head and his stick. Lothair seemed unconcerned, leaning with one hand on his stick. Peter swung his imaginary sword with all his strength. Lothair lifted his baton, stepped forward, and deflected the blow without blinking. The impact rippled through Peter's hands and stiff muscles.

Peter lifted his weapon above his head and sliced downward. Lothair veered aside. Peter's stick thudded into the ground.

Peter slashed hard upward. The warrior stopped the assault dead with his own baton.

Peter retreated a step and cut the air again. Lothair pitched forward and knocked away Peter's baton.

Again and again Peter hacked at the warrior. Lothair batted away every blow as if he were swatting at a fly. With each contact, Lothair moved forward and Peter backward. Before long, Peter's hands hurt, his arms ached, his lungs gasped, and his attack slowed.

After a sluggish swing from Peter, Lord Lothair said, "Tell me, little serf, what makes you think a serf can become a warrior?"

Peter lowered his baton and panted, "The count... comes from a family ... of slaves."

Lord Lothair grinned and nodded.

Peter felt encouraged. "You said he ish... iknorant miskreant." He didn't know what the words meant but he wanted to show he could speak the crisp language of lords.

Lothair's grin dissolved. "What?"

"Ik-no-rant-mis-kre-ant. You said ... he ish like ... under bread."

"Underbred?" Lord Lothair glanced over his shoulder at the serfs standing on the other side of the courtyard. "I did not say that."

"You told your uncle ... at my village ... You said the count ish ... under bread."

"Quiet." Lothair glared through frowning eyebrows. "Ignorant turdhead. Dangerous turdhead. If Edzard hears you say that ... if he hears you say I said that ..." He stared at his baton.

Peter shuffled his feet, surprised at Lothair's sudden anger. The warrior must have misunderstood him. "You said the count ish ..."

"I said quiet, you stupid gnat. I'll lose everything if..." Lothair bared his jagged teeth like a dog. "You must never speak again." He lifted his baton over his shoulder.

Peter jumped back. The warrior swung lethally and missed completely. He swung again and Peter jumped out of the way again.

Gabriel's laughter echoed through the courtyard.

Lothair's face turned crimson. He lurched toward Peter and howled, "Stand ready to die."

Peter jerked his baton up to block the next assault. The fury of the strike propelled his own weapon back, bouncing it off his forehead. Lights gyrated around the courtyard and blocked his sight. He held his stick blindly before him.

He sensed Lothair's next attack and shifted his baton to deflect it. The whack of wood hitting wood pierced his ears. The blow knocked his baton back against his shoulder.

He staggered sideways, slipped on horse dung and fell. Lothair's baton whooshed above his head before his bottom thumped the ground.

Peter rolled aside to escape Lothair's downward thrust. It thudded into the dirt and raised a puff of dust.

He scrambled to his feet and jumped backwards. Lothair's stick cut through empty space he had just occupied.

The tall warrior howled again and followed his retreating target. A lightning upward blow snapped Peter's baton back against his nose.

Peter tasted warm blood on his lips. He felt more than saw Lothair's blurring swirl and instinctively countered another crushing assault. The crack echoed off the courtyard walls and shook his imaginary sword from his grasp. The baton flew over a water trough a few paces behind him and rattled off the stable wall. He backed up to the knee-high water trough and shook like a frightened puppy.

The warrior lifted his long baton with both arms above his head, prepared to execute a condemned prisoner.

Peter raised his arms and half turned away. He tripped over the water trough and fell backwards as Lothair delivered the final blow.

Peter heard a snap just before his head bounced off the hard packed ground of the courtyard. A couple of dazed moments later, he realized that he still lived, that Lothair had missed. Peter looked through a fog of whirling lights to see the warrior standing on the other side of the water trough, stick in hand.

Peter swung his legs off the trough and jumped to his feet. White pain shrieked through him. Agony squeezed a scream from his lungs. His legs buckled and he collapsed. The courtyard reeled with such violence he had to shut his eyes. His hands felt for the source of the pain and found, just below his knee-length breeches, his right leg bent backward. His watering eyes opened to examine the broken leg. The shin glowed red where the baton struck but the skin wasn't torn.

Lothair stepped over the trough and nudged Peter with the end of the baton. "You gave a good fight, little serf. If you had lived, perhaps, you could have learned to be a warrior." He raised his stick again, ready to end Peter's misery.

"Oh God, please," Peter whispered and held his breath.

Through tears of pain, he half saw a large hand reach up behind Lothair and grasp the end of the baton. Lothair spun around and found himself face to face with Peter's older brother.

"Stop attacking," Gabriel said. "Give to live live to give and forgive. Stop attacking."

Peter wiped his eyes and sat up with a grunt.

Lothair looked at Gabriel with a confused squint. After a moment he shook his lethal baton free from Gabriel's grasp. "Go away, fool."

The big serf remained, standing as tall and broad as the dark warrior. Lothair pushed him but Gabriel stayed rooted to the ground like an old oak. Lothair pushed harder a second time and nearly fell backwards.

The warrior thrust his baton at Gabriel's chest. The elder brother yanked it out of Lothair's hands. With a quick flick, he tossed Lothair's stick toward the stockade gate.

Before the baton could hit the ground, Lothair jumped over Peter, snatched up Peter's lost wooden weapon. He lunged at Gabriel, swinging and grunting.

Gabriel stopped the baton's motion in midflight with one hand and jerked it from Lothair's grip. In one swift move, he grasped the thick baton on each end and broke it over his knee. After the snap of heavy wood echoed through the courtyard, he dropped the splintered halves to the ground. "Stop attacking," he repeated.

Lothair's bearded jaw dropped open, his eyes widened, his face flushed dark. He shook his fist at Gabriel and at the other serfs watching from across the courtyard. "I'll kill you all," he howled and whipped his long, double-edged sword from its sheath.

"Lothair. Stop." The count's high-pitched bark shot through the courtyard.

Lothair stood still, sword trembling. Gabriel bowed his head. Peter looked over the water trough to see the count in his sagging chainmail armor walking toward them from the stockade's gateway. The countess followed, sparkling with many gold and silver necklaces over a vermilion dress. Behind her came the foot soldiers, the servants, their wives and children, and the horses, all returning from High Mass at the cathedral.

Lothair pointed his sword at Gabriel. "He attacked me."

Count Edzard stopped at the water trough. "I saw what happened from the time you broke the boy's leg. The big serf never laid a hand on you. 'Stop attacking,' he told you. What audacity. And he defended himself well, better than any warrior I have. He broke your battle baton as if it were a twig. What strength. You should teach him to attack with the same skill."

Lothair lowered his sword and frowned at the count. "What?"

The count pointed at Peter. "You're not to hurt him or any of the other serfs. How can I give you a fief of land? You'd kill all your serfs in a fit of anger. You're not fit to rule your own valley."

"You promised to give me a valley." Lothair's voice shook.

The count turned to Peter. "You're no good to me as a cripple. Go back to your village. Tell Arnulf there's no need to replace you. This big serf is worth three men. Tell him his vassalage duty is fulfilled for the next three years because the big serf is staying with me. I need more warriors to protect me. Since that old man can't fulfill his war duty, I'll make his serf a warrior. Lothair will teach him the art of war."

Lothair shook his head. "But he's a serf. He's weak headed."

"Good," the count barked. "That's better than a head strong warrior." He pushed his lower lip forward and frowned at Lothair.

Lothair bowed his head and shifted his weight. "What about my valley?"

The count turned away and marched toward the tower.

Peter couldn't believe what he'd heard. Count Edzard didn't really want his fool brother to become a warrior, did he?

As the foot soldiers and servants dispersed, Lothair stepped toward Peter and held the sword's blade over Peter's head. "I can't believe what I heard. Did I lose my valley because of you?"

Gabriel leaned toward Lothair and whispered, "Worse if he knew what you curse." His words tripped like a song. "Sing his name his fame you gain."

"Shut up," Lothair snarled. He frowned at the sky for a few distracted moments before bending over Peter. "Swear by the holy bones of Saint George in my sword hilt that you will never tell -"

"Lothair." The voice sounded like Rosamund's.

Both Peter and Lothair straightened with a jerk. Lothair turned toward the voice.

"Come help with the Sabbath meal." The voice came from the tower's door, from the countess. Until now, Peter had never heard her speak. Her voice snared him like a dog on a leash. "Come here." Her command was resolute, yet seductive, demanding obedience while weakening the will. She stood in the tower's threshold. Her eyes held Peter and Lothair with a steady shine more alluring than all her gold and silver necklaces. "Put your sword away and come here now."

Lothair sheathed his sword and shuffled away without a word, as though dragged by the same leash that held Peter.

Gabriel took Peter under his arms and stood him up. Between waves of pain, Peter heard his brother babbling, "... you go I stay you grow what may..."

He caught a glimpse of his reflection in the water trough. Blood from his nose smeared across his face and a red knot glowed on his forehead. He looked again at his grotesquely bent leg. He could tell the villagers he crippled his leg in another battle. But they would eventually learn the truth. They would hear how he was expelled from the castle and they would laugh at him again. His aunt wouldn't want him back. A cripple would be a burden to whichever villager gave him shelter. Nobody would want him, not even Rosamund.

Gabriel continued gibbering, "... you grow I stay -"

"Get away from me," Peter shouted. He pushed Gabriel off and leaned on the stable wall. "You staying? Not going to follow me now? You always did before, like a pest."

"Stay to play you go but know could be good."

Peter took a step and pain rippled the stockade walls as though they were sheets of cloth. He struggled with one agonizing hop after another along the billowing walls toward the stockade gate. Tears rolled down his cheeks. He bit his lip and didn't look back.

Gabriel brought him his cloak and shoes.

"Go away," Peter cried. "Don' want them. Don' need them." He tore Rosamund's flask from his belt and threw it at Gabriel.

"Don' want to go home. Want to die. Gots to die."

At the gateway, Peter picked up the baton that had crippled him and used it for a crutch. He lurched out of the pitching stockade and down the barren hill in the late afternoon sun.

The steep road made his hopping descent treacherous. Sometimes he tripped and fell, screaming in pain, anger, and defeat. He retched until he was empty and then he retched some more. The afternoon hours dragged as he stumbled around each hairpin curve. Vultures, which had picked the last flesh from the skulls on the spears, circled above.

He cursed his luck and his elder brother. "The count ish going to make my fool brother a warrior. I told everyone the count would make ME a warrior."

Between shots of searing white pain, he thought of Rosamund. "She won' have me now. I just a cripple, a burden."

The break swelled into a pink ball below his knee. The hem of his breeches rubbed the ball with every hop. "Don' go back home. Hurt too bad. Want to die."

He reached the bottom of the bluff after sunset. The deepening gloom of twilight made the road nearly invisible in his blurring sight. At nightfall he came to the bridge.

Something deep within him voiced itself, "*Stop. Rest under the bridge.*"

He crawled under the bridge, settled against a piling, and stared with numb exhaustion toward the sounds of the river.

"You run away from de count?" a voice said from the blackness under the bridge, "My home ish your home. Anyding I gets for you? Anyding you want?"

Peter wanted death.

CHAPTER 10
UNDER THE BRIDGE

Each morning, fog hid Peter and the bridge behind dense layers of milky murals. Traffic on the bridge ceased when the fog was heavy, as though people believed mist to be solid.

For days, he sat with Lothair's baton at his side and leaned against a bridge piling without speaking, moving, eating, or drinking. A fist-sized ball, bright red and tender to the touch, ballooned over his broken shin. Each day his leg throbbed less. The memory of his disgrace stung less. He waited for death, for painless oblivion.

But the beggar's constant chatter made waiting difficult. "What wrong? You lost your fire, your zeal? You a little man. You gots to eat someding. You die if you don' eat." Sometimes the beggar prattled while lying in a nest of dirty blankets. Sometimes he jabbered while limping in circles around Peter. His left leg bent backward below the knee like Peter's, but the beggar's leg had hardened into that unnatural angle. "You can be my new partner. I lost my old partner. He went wid Maynard. Wanted to be a warrior. Now his head sits on a spear."

The beggar prodded Peter with growing persistence. "Why don' you gets dat leg fixed? Why don' you eat?" Each day he put a crust of bread in Peter's hand. Peter let it roll out.

One morning the beggar poked the Peter's broken shin. Peter screamed at a pain that drove his numbness away. His muscles and nerves, now alert with pain, tensed further under the cold intensity of the beggar's eyes.

"Good," the beggar said. "Now I know you still alive." He put his face close to Peter's and his steel blue eyes held Peter with furious tenacity. "You gots to live, gots to help me. I give you zeal again. I catch you a fish. Ever see a man fish wid his foot? Oh, but you a serf. Serfs never eat fish. Lords eat meat. Merchants and monks, too. Serfs eat porridge and turnips, only what grows in dirt. Hah, serfs only eat dirt. Well, I eat like a lord. I eat fish. Watch me catch a fish."

The beggar's eyes released Peter and he hobbled down the riverbank, his limp exaggerated all the more as his bare feet stepped

on worn boulders of different sizes. He slipped and fell into a wide
expanse of mud that lay beside the boulder field under the bridge.
The mud almost swallowed him, but he pulled himself free and
cursed. He lifted the torn hem of his breeches, waded two paces
into the water and sat on a large rock in the river. The gray mud
covering the beggar blended with the gray rock so that the beggar
and the stone appeared as one. He extended his good leg into clear
water up to his knee and his foot rested on the sandy bottom of the
slow moving river.

"Gods damn. Dat's cold. But not too cold. Summer almost
gone. River gets too cold for fishin' in winter. You watchin' me?
Watch me fish."

The beggar coughed and spit upriver. He watched his spittle
float toward him. "First time my leg broke, I didn' have a woman
to fix it. Went to de monks to fix it. Dey dragged me to every Gods
damn prayer mass. Dey put a bell rope around my neck. Custom says
nobody can hurt you, take you away, if de monks put a bell rope on
you cause you belong to dem. Dey tried to cut off my tongue 'cause
I curse too much. Look at my tongue." He waggled his squared
tongue at Peter and turned back to watch his spittle. "Gods damn
monks. I went to de Jew blacksmid. He fixed my tongue."

Yellow phlegm floated past his knee. He coughed and spit
upriver again.

"But my leg gots broke again in de same place. Custom says no
good to fix someding broke twice. Went back to de Jew blacksmid
to get my arm fixed. Gods damn free men cut off my hand for
stealing. Dat's why I live on de count's side of de bridge. If dey
see me doin' someding, I run back here and dey won' hurt me here.
You gots two good hands. I need dat. You watchin' me?"

His spittle wiggled past his leg. He coughed and spit again.

"Gots to fix your leg. You gots no woman to fix it? Stay
away from de Gods damn monks. I take you to de blacksmid, de
Christkiller. He killed old Count Derek, too. But everybody blames
Lord Maynard."

The beggar spit up-river again. "People made de Jew live
out of town. But de town grows and now de Jew lives on de edge
of town. He gots a water well inside his house. Ish on top of a hill
but de well fills to de top. People say dat ish bad magic. Some

want him to leave town or die. But when people gets sick, dey go to him 'cause ..."

The beggar stopped. His eyes pierced the river water with iron intent. A shadow moved beneath the mucus bobbing at his knee. With a swift kick, the beggar splashed a shower of water over Peter.

The shock of cold water stung Peter. A fish as big as his foot flopped in his lap. He jumped up to rid himself of the struggling animal. A flash of pain from his leg threw him back against the piling. He crumpled into a heap and struggled to catch his breath.

By the time he was able to sit up again, the beggar had waded out of the river and held the writhing fish down with the foot of his crippled leg. The beggar bent over to study the fish. A beetle crawled through the beggar's blond hair, as though foraging in a stable's dirty straw.

"Today we eat fish like de count and de bishop." The beggar focused on Peter again. "You gots to eat, gots to stay alive, gots to help me 'cause you gots two hands. I can help you 'cause I know how to beg and steal. We can be partners."

Later that day the beggar pushed a cube of sun-dried fish into Peter's mouth and held Peter's jaw shut between his hand and his stump. Peter was too weak to resist. The flesh crumbled to slivers in Peter's mouth and he swallowed it, the first food he'd eaten in days, the first meat he'd eaten ever.

The next day, Peter ate a stale piece of white bread the beggar brought him. Under bread never tasted so good. The day after that, he ate a small link of sausage. It made his mouth oily and his stomach unsettled.

The days blurred and Peter wasn't sure how long he had stayed under the bridge. The red ball over his broken shin grew brighter every day. When the beggar forced him to stand and walk, Peter shuffled a few steps with the support of Lothair's baton.

Sometimes, before drinking from a glassy eddy on the river's edge, Peter peered at his reflection. Mud crusted the fuzz growing on his chin and pink sores spread over his graying skin.

On sunny afternoons the wives of merchants washed clothes in boulder fields scattered between the mud flats on the opposite side of the river. The beggar slipped into the free town whenever they scrubbed. The women gestured toward Peter and called him "Crayfish."

"Dey believe you are me. Dat's good." The beggar's blunted words stumbled off his wounded tongue. "We look alike so we can fool people. Dat's good." He gave Peter a rock hard crust of bread. "Harvest time ish over. Tomorrow de market fair begins. Lasts all week. Many new people coming. New peddlers. New dings to steal. Maybe you find someding for dat woman you like. What her name?"

"Rosamund," Peter mumbled. Crayfish never stopped pressing him about his village, the castle, Lothair, and Gabriel.

"You don' gots to be a warrior for her to like you."

"I am a cripple," Peter said, "A beggar. A crippled beggar." He pulled a muddy blanket closer and shivered in the warm autumn air.

"You whine too much, like a little wolf puppy." The beggar playfully rubbed Peter's head as he would a dog. "Good to be a crippled beggar."

"I am the lowest of the low," Peter groaned. His body warmed in an unhealthy flash and he discarded the blanket.

The beggar danced around Peter. "You don' work in de fields. Dat makes you better dan Rosamund. You don' work in de castle. Dat makes you better dan Gabriel. You do what you want and you take what you want. You gots no lord. No good to be a warrior. I know, 'cause I was a warrior."

Peter frowned at the beggar. "But you a cripple."

Crayfish locked his eyes onto Peter's with fierce audacity. The cold courage of the beggar's stare pierced him like a sword and sliced his disbelief to ribbons.

"You were a warrior?" Peter asked.

The beggar flashed a smile of broken, discolored teeth. "Yes. A great warrior. Went wid old Count Derek to lands where de women are dark. Derek loved dark women. I stole wid my sword. Got wounded in battle. Now I steal wid my head. I better dan a warrior. We can steal Rosamund away to de free town. You and her be free, like me."

A caravan of people and animals rumbled over the bridge. More traffic had crossed the bridge on this day than in the whole time Peter had lived under it. He shivered from another cold wave rolling through his body and wrapped himself in the blanket again.

The beggar waited until the rumble passed. "We gots to have food for de winter. A peddler from de sea came today wid big fish, split down de middle, salted and dried. I love dem chewy dainties. I saw cheese and honey, furs and linens. We steal enough to live like lords."

Peter shook his head. He baked inside the blanket again and he threw it off.

Crayfish stooped and fixed his cold eyes on Peter again. "You gots two good hands, little wolf. You gots to do dis for me, your friend, de wounded warrior. Maynard took all de beggars but me. I de only one left. People know me but dey don' know you. You can steal more dan I can. Den I take you to de Jew, gets your leg fixed. Den we gets Rosamund. Maybe we gets her before we fix your leg."

Peter looked down at his crippled leg and mumbled, "Don' want to be a thief."

Crayfish flicked a finger against the red ball on Peter's shin. Searing bolts of pain shot through Peter. He choked back a scream, tucked his knees under his chin, and shielded his leg with both hands. Beyond the throbbing in his ears, Peter heard the beggar hissing.

"You are my partner. I fed you. Kept you alive. You owe me your Gods damn life. You steal for me and we be rich and we gets Rosamund and we gets on her. I want to gets on her."

"Honor," Peter whispered. "I want honor, too."

Another merchant caravan rumbled overhead. Peter sat up and checked his leg. The sooner he stole what the beggar wanted, the sooner he would get his leg fixed. He would ask Rosamund to come to the bridge, to be free with him in this new life. His skin turned icy again in the warm air. He wrapped himself in the blanket once more.

Crayfish had saved his life. This new life was better than death. Or was it?

CHAPTER 11
THE MARKET FAIR

The next day the beggar pushed Peter out from under the bridge. Peter hobbled with the baton next to his throbbing right leg. He sizzled with fever one moment and shivered with cold the next. A warm sun slowly burned the fog away.

Crayfish jabbered without stopping as they entered the free town. "See dat man. He gots linens on two unshod mares. But he no richer dan dis man, wid linens on one mare wid iron shoes. Know why, little wolf? Peddlers pay de count to use his roads when dey come to de bishop's valley. Two copper pennies for a shod horse. One penny for an unshod horse. Look at dat herder. He gots all dat cheese on his back 'cause nobody pay for goods brought on foot. Only merchants and nobles use coins."

The streets became more crowded as foreign merchants streamed out of the houses. Some ladened merchants stopped in the doorways to thank the host families for their hospitality. Some spoke with slurred speech like serfs, others with clipped diction like noblemen, and a few others with strange accents.

"People so excited," Crayfish whispered. "So many dings to see. Nobody watch behind. Ish de best time to steal."

Peter staggered with the flowing river of people until the crowded street burst into the central market square. The crowd spread over a field covered with people, animals, blankets, tables, and tents. The beggar led Peter through displays of brown, yellow, and green linens coarse and fine, and around rolls of white and gray wool thick and dyed. Peter gawked at blocks of different colored cheeses, slabs of meat smoked black, dried herbs and roots in baskets, wild mushrooms ranging from spicy, orange fingerlings to white caps from stone mushrooms, furs of bears, foxes and wolves, cured hides of cattle, sheep and pigs, metal hooks, hammers and sickles, spades, pots and pans, clucking hens, bleating lambs and squealing piglets. The tangy scents of spices and dung mingled in the dusty air.

Wicker cages held small animals. Makeshift pens contained larger beasts. Most foods and skins lay on low tables or carts, their sellers waving to bring in buyers and swat away flies. Peddlers spread metal wares over blankets on the ground, with buyers stepping around them, occasionally stooping and picking up a piece. Men in travel-worn clothes unrolled swatches of linen and wool from the backs of pack animals and cut them with shears to the desired length for ladies in elegant dresses. Well dressed men and women, robed monks and ragged peasants bartered and bargained in a noisy riot of color. The cathedral's tower soared over one side of the confusion; over the other side the count's stockade loomed on its high, rocky bluff.

Crayfish gestured as they limped down the fairway between shepherds, herders, and peddlers. "Dat yellow-haired shepherd ish a Slav. Dey gots round faces and high cheeks. De monks go east and make de Slavs go to prayer mass. See dat man wid black hair. He gots a round face too but he half Magyar."

Crayfish stopped at a display of iron tools. "For a cow, you gets four iron tools. For a sheep, you gets a pot. For a pot, you gets a handful of nails. For your little knife, maybe two nails."

Peter checked for his knife under his belt. It was gone.

The beggar chuckled and handed the knife back to Peter. "Don' worry, little wolf. Don' want your knife." He wrapped the toes of his crippled foot around the rim of a pot.

A big, bearded merchant waved a hairy hand at the beggar. "Go away, Crayfish. Let go of the pot, you thief."

Crayfish released the pot from his toe grip. "No, Hugo. You a dief. You want too much for de Jew's iron." He shouted at the crowd. "Don' buy from Hugo. You pay too much."

Hugo stepped toward Peter and Crayfish. "I'll break your other leg." The beggar skipped away.

Peter hobbled quickly to catch up with Crayfish. "I saw Hugo before. He came to my village, to see Lord Arnulf, to trade iron tools."

"Never been to de fair, little wolf?" the beggar asked.

Peter knew of the annual event from old Bertha and others who accompanied Lord Arnulf on his yearly journey to the count's castle. Arnulf and other warriors met at the same time each year to honor the count and to trade in the market fair for items that were either difficult or impossible to make in their own valleys. Not even Bertha's colorful descriptions prepared Peter for the noisy, bright confusion. Peter forgot his leg pain in the cascade of exciting new sights, sounds, and smells.

Crayfish pointed toward the end of the market square. "Dere ish our Gods damn Bishop."

Peter looked up, awed again by the tall stone basilica, a majestic backdrop for the market fair.

"Not dere." The beggar thumped Peter's head with his stump. "In de big house. Second floor. Hangin' out de window."

Leaning from the open bay window of his palace, the bishop raised a red, gloved hand and boomed a blessing into the town square. Many turned toward the bishop and much of the noise subsided. The low, pointed hat, sitting squarely on the bishop's head, made him look taller. He extended a pastoral staff, whose metallic decorations glinted so brightly that it surely reflected the light of heaven. The angel white fabric of his sleeve fluttered in a breeze as he swept the staff over the crowd.

"Looks like a goose wavin' his wings over a flock of Gods damn sheep," the beggar said and hobbled off.

Peter nearly tripped over his crutch and felt again a piercing pain from his leg.

"Bernard traveled and saw many fairs wid his cousin, de emperor," Crayfish said. "When de old bishop died, de emperor made Bernard de new bishop. He started a fair here. Every year de fair gets bigger and bigger. De bishop lifts de usury laws for de fair 'cause tradin' leads to usury and gamblin' and whorin'. De more sin people do, de more shame dey feel, de more dey give at mass. Dank God, I gots no shame."

They limped past a group of men, huddled together, engrossed by something at the center of their circle. Peter stopped when they moaned and cursed in unison. Most of them extracted a brown coin from a small leather pouch hanging on their belt and threw it into the group's center.

"Dice." Crayfish pushed Peter away. "De holy disciples played dice to find someone to replace Judas. You gets a choice of games, little wolf, after we pluck a few purses. Dey are hangin' from belts like ripe plums."

At the central fountain the crowd became thicker. Not only was the pool's water in great demand, but it also seemed to be the place where merchants exchanged news. A few wore long robes with many pockets. Each pocket contained a scroll or several sticks. Some merchants sat on the low walls of the pool and marked scraped sheepskins with sharpened goose quills dipped in black liquid, and others added notches to their sticks with knives.

The beggar spat and pushed Peter through the crowd. "Dey count what people owe. On de last day, dey put a bank on two barrels. People call dem bankers. Dey change coins, pennies for deniers, shillings for ducats and florins."

A few merchants gathered around a dark skinned man with a long beard as he counted beads strung between the sides of a shallow wooden box.

"A Jew from de land of Saracens," Crayfish said. "Gots a magic box dat counts numbers."

A monk bumped into the beggar and said, "Crayfish, you smell so bad, Satan himself would throw you out of hell."

The beggar said, "He drow me out, but he keep you." He spat on the monk's feet and scampered into a part of the fair where the crowds were smaller.

Peter limped after him. In this, the west end of the market fair, buyers and sellers dressed in brighter colors and softer linens. They bartered at blanket-covered tables within large tents. Some tents were barrel shaped, others were square cubes and a few were simply a sheet suspended on four poles. The sellers kept their horses and oxen tethered behind their tables.

Shining swords lay arrayed on one table, each with a hollowed hilt to store magic bones from dead saints, bones used to empower the warrior with strength from heaven, and to swear oaths before a witness in heaven. Across the way, a cloth merchant displayed rolls of vivid red and dark blue wool, along with pieces of finely embroidered linens. Another merchant presented baskets of dyes including long red madder roots, blue woad leaves, black dyeberries and dried yellow flowers of dyers weed. Under another tent sat pots of salt and honey. On the next table a merchant with dark eyes, skin and hair like that of Countess Lilli arranged pouches of seeds and powders between baskets of roots and nuts, all unknown to Peter.

Crayfish pointed at a basket of black seeds. "I traded a few peppercorns for a hen. Ate chicken eggs until de Gods damn count rode over my hen. Den I ate chicken meat." He pulled Peter closer. "Peppercorns easy to steal. I busy de Greek peddler, make him look away. You take a handful. We be rich."

Peter wiped fevered sweat from his brow and glanced around. All the merchants and their patrons were surely watching him. He looked at the beggar to protest.

The beggar pierced him with ice blue eyes. "You owe me your life, little wolf. You gots two good hands. Do dis for me, your friend, de wounded warrior."

Peter shivered. Sweat soaked his muddy tunic. He could almost hear his leg throbbing.

The beggar cast his cold eyes around the fair. "We find someding easier, 'cause ish your first time, 'cause you scared."

He pushed Peter forward with his stump and pointed with his hand. "Candles. You need a handful of peppercorns for just one candle. Gods damn monks burn dem just to tell time from one damned prayer mass to de next."

The beggar studied a barrel tent at the end of the fair. Inside the tent, a high pile of fish, split lengthways into halves, lay stacked on a blanketed table. The fish measured as long as an arm, far larger than any fish the beggar had kicked out of the river. Their smoke-colored meat sparkled with salt crystals.

Beside the table stood a plump monk in a clean black robe. He brushed his fingers through his freshly tonsured haircut and spoke with an equally plump young man in an ankle-length, fur-lined cloak over a leather tunic. The young merchant listened and stroked his thin red beard and long red hair.

The strange language of the monk flowed gracefully. The merchant responded haltingly, his well-fed hands flew with gestures to fill the gaps between his words. As he stumbled through the language, his ruddy complexion flushed to match his hair. The words sounded like those Father Ulrich recited during prayer mass.

"Latin," Crayfish whispered. "De Norseman don' speak our tongue. Don' speak much Latin, too. He gots big stockfish. One stockfish lasts all winter."

"Salutis et virtutis," the monk said and walked away with a stockfish under each arm. The merchant waved with one hand and with the other dropped two shiny, white coins into a pouch tied to his belt. He scanned the crowd for new buyers and caressed a tiny box dangling from a strap around his thick neck.

"See de relic around his neck? He gots magic bones in dere. Only de rich buy magic bones of a saint. Look how he keeps his back to de fish. See how de blanket on de table goes all de way to de ground. You can hide under de table, behind de blanket and nobody sees you. He gots two horses and four oxen tied to de table. Rich, young, and stupid. Felix et beatus."

"You speak Latin?" Peter asked.

"I teach you Latin after you steal for me. Go behind de tent and between de oxen. No one can see you. I busy de Norseman and you crawl under de table. Wait 'til someone buys a stockfish. After he takes de coin, de fat foreigner waves and smiles, blessed by his saint, so happy wid himself. Dat's when you grab a stockfish and run out between de oxen. If dere's trouble, I busy him again." He pushed Peter away.

Peter shivered and limped on his stick to the end of the market square. He hesitated, but the beggar's cold glare pushed him on. He circled around the outer limit of the square until he stood behind the merchant's animals.

With quiet grunts, he climbed down his crutch to his left knee and crawled between the oxen, keeping his right knee suspended but dragging his stick and his foot on the ground. His leg's dull throb catapulted to a sharp stab with each movement. When he reached the backside of the table, the angry red knot on his leg touched the ground. A shot of blinding pain stiffened his already tense muscles. He gritted his teeth, blinked away stars, and continued crawling. Sweat fell like rain from his brow.

"Pretty fish." The beggar's hiss pierced the murmur of the fair as Peter sat down under the table and behind the blanket that hid him. "How much, fat man?"

"Go avay, thief," the Norseman shouted.

Peter's heart stopped. The foreigner spoke the local language. This was bad.

"Fish. Goot fish," the Norseman bellowed.

The foreigner could yell thief and call for help in the local language and Peter couldn't run and they would catch him and they would cut off his hand for stealing and -

"Who wants to eat such ugly things," a young man said, unseen on the blanket's other side. Peter had heard that voice before, from a time that seemed so long ago. "These are caked with too much salt. Salt ish too valuable to waste." It was Peter's cousin, Karl. "As my wife, you will not waste like this, will you?"

A female answered, "I don' waste anything." It was Rosamund's voice.

Peter sat up with a start and bumped his head on the table above. "Rosamund? Karl's wife?" he whispered. "No, never."

With one hand, he lifted the blanket that draped down the front of the table and reached out with the other hand, ready to spring out and take her away from Karl. The heavy Norseman walked by and Peter felt the full weight of the foreigner on his fingertips. He jerked his fingers out from under the leather boot and the table above him thumped.

Someone lifted the blanket and kicked gravel under the table. A rock bounced off Peter's inflamed shin. The shock of pain knocked him onto his back.

"Goot fish. Goot fish," the Norseman shouted outside.

Peter held his leg and choked back tears. He wanted to hold Rosamund in his arms and then stand against Karl and then ...

And then what? What could he have done? He would have staggered before Rosamund, a cripple expelled from the castle in disgrace and unable to defend himself against Karl.

Maybe Rosamund would speak of him. Maybe she would say she preferred him, Peter, over Karl, because he's brave and high-minded. He rocked himself quietly and listened.

CHAPTER 12
MOURNING PETER

Rosamund stepped back as the fish merchant barreled between his table and the two serfs in a show of aggressive protection. He slipped and slammed his hand against the table to steady himself. The redfaced, redhaired merchant frowned at the ground where he had slipped. He lifted the blanket and kicked the offending pebbles under the table. He looked up and bellowed over her head, "Goot fish. Goot fish."

"Let's go," she mumbled to Karl. "We make him nervous."

"Look at his oxen," Karl said. "Smaller than ours. Their coats and manes are thicker."

Karl loved animals. He knew the appetites, personalities, sleeping and mating habits of every village animal. For advice on their welfare, Lord Arnulf always asked Karl.

"Fish. Goot fish," the foreigner called.

Lord Arnulf had exercised his duty and arranged for her to marry Karl, but only if Peter agreed. Despite Gisela's protest, the old warrior decided on this compromise to balance the wishes of the village women and that of Rosamund. On this annual visit to honor Count Edzard, Lord Arnulf brought Rosamund and Karl to talk with Peter. Karl said he would persuade Peter, with his fists if necessary, to let her marry him. She expected Peter would ask their lord to delay any arrangement for her marriage until he returned to the village.

"Fish. Goot fish," the merchant shouted.

Rosamund shook her head. If Peter hadn't been so loud and witless, Lothair wouldn't have killed him.

Karl took her arm. "Still thinking about Peter, aren't you?"

Grief broke through her again, as it had last night when she learned what happened. "He was stupid," she sputtered. "I hate him ... Only a fool ... would fight a warrior ... And then they ... they sent him away ... to die ... to die, alone."

"Stop crying," Karl said. He looked away and fidgeted. "He may not be dead. Maybe he's begging, like that cripple."

She wiped her eyes and followed Karl's gesture to a gray figure standing still in the colorful swirl of the market fair. One of his legs twisted backward below the knee. One arm ended abruptly at the wrist. He leaned over the table of a dark-skinned merchant and said, "Give me just one peppercorn." His stump dropped onto the table, tipping a pouch over. A few black seeds rolled out and one seed dropped off the edge of the table.

The merchant jumped around the side of the table and shouted, "Go away, thief." He pushed the cripple away and put the seeds back in the pouch.

The cripple limped a few paces, stopped in the shadow of a tent next to the fish merchant and picked what appeared to be a black seed from between the toes of his crippled foot. He caught her watching him. His blue eyes reminded her of Peter until he scowled at her with black hatred.

"Fish. Goot Fish," the fish merchant bellowed.

"No," she said to Karl. "He would never sink so low. A thieving beggar? No. He had high dreams, noble dreams. But then he fought Lothair. How stupid. He was such an ... idiot." She began to sob again.

Karl said, "You gots to be my wife now."

"Yes," she said and covered her face with her hands.

"Stop crying," Karl said. "Stop crying. You gots to obey me. Stop crying."

"Karl," Lord Arnulf called.

Karl and Rosamund bowed their heads. She stifled her sobs.

Their lord hobbled up to the fish merchant's tent. "Go to the dye merchant over there, Karl. I've traded some iron for some powdered dyes. My wife will love them. They're already sacked up. Three sacks. Just bring them along. Here Rosamund, take this bag of salt. We'll stop by the bishop's house and say good-bye to Ulrich before we leave."

Rosamund looked up to receive the hemp sack from her lord. Towering behind his old, bald head was Lord Lothair. The fish merchant stepped forward, smiled and spoke a few halting words in a language Rosamund recognized from Father Ulrich's ceremonies.

"Latin is for monks and merchants," Lothair snarled. "I will have none of it."

The big foreigner bowed his head and whispered, "Goot fish. Very goot fish."

Lothair pointed at Rosamund, "I know this serf. Look at me, girl."

Rosamund wiped tears from her cheeks, but she did not look at Lothair.

Lothair growled, "She's the one who found Maynard in the forest."

Lord Arnulf frowned. "She's grieving Peter, the one you beat to death."

"Ah, yes. The little serf with the little mind. He was no good alive."

"His brother thinks he's alive," Arnulf said.

"Well, Uncle, do you believe the ramblings of that big fool?"

"No. A bog may have swallowed him or his body might be in a bear's lair."

Rosamund shook her head to free her mind of those dreadful images.

"If the little serf isn't dead ..." Lothair pointed at the gray cripple. "See that beggar over there? He was a serf once. Konrad's custom lets a runaway serf become a free man after a year and a day in the free town. If I had been his lord, I would have found him and killed him. If our little serf isn't dead, he will be when I find him."

Lothair turned to the merchant. "I want six fish." He pulled a few white coins from a pouch tied to his sword belt and tossed them on the table. "It's for the count. Understand? The count." He pointed at the stockade which seemed to lean over the free town. "He always sends me out to fetch things. I'm nothing but a lap dog to the inferior coward."

"You're not a lap dog," Lord Arnulf said. "You're the count's marshal. You enforce the customs, train warriors, manage the count's household. That's an honorable fief."

"It is no honor. It is servitude," Lothair barked. "His family's vulgarity shows itself in his every God damned whim. But if you made me your heir, Uncle, I could get away from his dishonor, his conceit, and your valley would be safe with me. I need a fief of land."

Rosamund glanced around the market. Several merchants stopped what they were doing to listen. The fish merchant weighed Lothair's coins on a set of scales.

"Hasn't Edzard promised you a valley?" Lord Arnulf asked in a low voice.

Lothair's black beard seemed to bristle. "He'll break his promise just like his father did. Listen to me, Uncle Arnulf. If you give Ulrich your valley, he'll give it to the bishop and Edzard will want it back. Edzard wouldn't challenge little Ulrich to a fair battle. No, instead he'll murder my little cousin while he sleeps, just like he killed Maynard, because our count has no honor."

The red headed foreigner stepped between them, his arms full of fish, and whispered, "For this silver, five fishes."

Lothair slammed his fist on the merchant's table shaking the fish and the blanket. "I said SIX fish. I could raise your toll fees, you turd eating insect. You merchants are infecting the whole world. I would enjoy exterminating every one of you pests."

The merchant's eyes widened in his round face. His ruddy complexion reddened all the more. With a trembling hand, the foreigner picked up another fish.

Lothair grabbed all six fish from the merchant's arms and picked up a seventh fish from the table. "This extra fish is for your insolence to me, Lothair the Angry, a warrior from an honorable family of warrior chieftains." He looked sideways at Lord Arnulf. "Have a safe journey back to our valley."

The tall warrior swaggered away with his arms full of fish. He plowed into the market crowd as if it were nonexistent, blindly bumping common folk out of the way with his noble elbows. With each collision, the dried fish jumped in his arms and his swagger turned into a stagger as he juggled the fish.

From Lothair's loud and witless talk, Rosamund saw something akin to Peter. If Peter had become a warrior like he wanted, would he have lost his gentleness? Would he have become like his hero, his model warrior, Lothair the Angry Bully? She would never know now that Peter was dead.

CHAPTER 13
THE LION'S DEN

Peter chewed his bleeding fingernails under the fish merchant's table. He scarcely noticed waves of fevers and chills washing over him. Fine dust, kicked from the ground by the foreigner's tethered animals, drifted in the still air before Peter's nearly unseeing eyes. The stench from growing piles of animal dung nearby barely pierced his sense of smell. He hardly heard the fish merchant's hawkings, his frequent customers, their protracted haggling, the shuffling of stockfish and all other market sounds filtering through the blanket that covered the table and hid him.

His mind spun in a different world, drowning in a whirlpool of Rosamund's words. "She said I would never be a thieving beggar," he whispered to himself again and again. "But I am a thieving beggar."

He repeated her insults and spiraled farther down. "Said I am stupid, a fool, idiot. She hates me."

He plunged ever deeper into the dark hole of her betrayal. "Said she gots to be Karl's wife. Wish I were dead. Should have died under the beggar's bridge."

"Ssss."

A low hiss penetrated Peter's gloom.

"Ssss."

The gray beggar was crouching between two oxen tied to the back of the merchant's table. He waved his arms in jerky motions. "Steal a fish. Don' sits under table all day. Steal a fish."

Peter stared past the beggar and the oxen in the shadows. From the angle of the shadows, he slowly realized the morning had turned into late afternoon.

Crayfish scowled. "You waits too long. Steal a fish."

Peter no longer saw the beggar's piercing eyes as signs of courage, but as tools of deceit. "He was no warrior," Peter whispered. "Just a runaway serf."

Peter groped for his walking stick and crawled out from under the table toward the beggar. He stood the baton on one end and climbed up hand over hand, grunting in loud gasps until he stood on one foot between the oxen.

"You crazy?" the beggar hissed. "Everyone see you." He fled, reeling away on his own crippled leg.

Peter leaned on the long baton for a few moments within a dizzy darkness, wobbling from side to side, not caring if he were discovered, not caring about anything.

"Thief," the fish merchant cried from across the table.

The darkness cleared and Peter hopped out between the oxen, groaning each time the hem of his breeches flicked the swollen ball below his knee. He managed a few hops before felled by a sharp blow to the back of his head.

"Thief," the Norseman shouted in his ear.

Several merchants rushed to Peter and held him down. He closed his eyes while hands groped through his tunic and breeches. His leg throbbed, his body burned and he was thankful for the switch from mental anguish to physical pain. "Please kill me," he whispered.

The groping stopped. "He's got nothing," someone said.

"No thief?" the fish merchant asked.

"He's sick," another said. "Bad sick. Half dead. Stay away from him."

Peter heard feet shuffle away and felt a light kick to his ribs.

"Go avay," the Norseman said.

He opened his eyes. The Norseman and other merchants were walking away, rubbing their hands on their clothes as if they had touched something filthy.

Peter climbed up his walking stick and hobbled off, determined to find death. He wanted to die alone, away from Rosamund, Lothair, and the beggar, away from the free town, the castle, his village. He left the market fair and searched the town, seeking with singular purpose that road, which would lead him out of the bishop's valley and to the end of his life.

Parents pulled playful children from his way. Traders turned their pack animals from his path. Residents and visitors returning from the fair stared at him, a few offered help. He ignored them all. The shadows had lengthened, the day would soon end and so would his misery.

While he hopped through the streets, clouds swept over the

setting sun and brought an early twilight. Fewer and fewer families and merchants shared the road with him. They retired to their houses and lit resin-soaked bundles of reeds, which cast fitful shadows on the walls. After a time doors and windows thudded shut against the approaching night.

He stumbled onto the road on which he had entered the free town. It would take him up a hill, out of town and into the forest where he could finally die. He began his ascent, sweating in the cold air.

Halfway up the hill, he heard again that familiar hissing. "Whats you doin', little wolf? Goin' to gets Rosamund?"

Peter didn't stop or look back. "You lied to me. Said you were a warrior."

Crayfish tugged the back of Peter's tunic. "You never lie, little wolf?"

Peter kept his aim on the hill's blurring summit. Earth and heaven merged into a single, fevered twilight.

"Where de little wolf goin'? To de Jew?"

Peter didn't answer. Talk was meaningless. Life was meaningless.

"No, no, no. You gots to stay wid me. I need your hands. When de Jew fixes your leg, he won' lets you walk 'til after de fair. First we gots to steal. Den we fix your leg."

Peter kept hobbling up the hill, leaning heavily on his stick. With each step forward, the pain from his crippled leg stabbed deeper.

Crayfish staggered around in front of him and blocked his way. "Look at me. I need your hands. You owe me your life."

The beggar seemed only a shadow, dark and without substance. Peter bumped into Crayfish and limped around him.

"You owe me your Gods damn life. I kepts you alive."

Peter continued forward. Without warning, his walking stick flew out of his hands and he pitched forward.

"You owe me," the beggar shouted and kicked at Peter's head, back, arms, and legs.

Peter heard other people shouting and saw shadows swirl around him. A shadow pulled Crayfish back, but the beggar broke free and kicked Peter's crippled leg.

Peter heard a snap and saw blinding, white agony. His lungs expelled a hoarse wail. Stars whirled in the middle of the shadow world. His hands searched for his crippled leg and found it dangling, limp and lifeless, below the knee. Distant voices floated around him.

"Stop."

"Go away."

"Leave the boy alone."

"De leg broke twice." The beggar's hissing seemed far away. "Now little wolf always be a cripple. Nobody can fix it. Not even de Jew."

A plump, balding head hovered in the midst of swirling stars. "Let me help you," it said.

"No," Peter gasped, searching blindly for his walking stick. "Leave me alone."

Another face with dark, curly hair floated into view. "Our neighbor is a bone setter, a healer. He can help you."

"Go away," Peter screamed. "Want to die." He found his stick and swung it in wide circles around him. The disembodied heads fled.

He tried to stand, but collapsed in a writhing spasm. He struggled to his knees, fell forward and retched. With concentrated determination and his stick grasped firmly in one hand, he crawled forward on his hands and knees. Each movement that dragged his lifeless leg with him sent shocks through his fevered frame. Each breath began with a sharp inhalation and ended with a grunt. Tears streamed off the end of his nose.

The ruts in the road slithered like snakes. The houses on either side swayed, their walls inhaled and exhaled in undulating waves. Forms shifted and exchanged places with their own shadows. The rippling sky-ground shimmered between black and blue.

Voices circled Peter as he crawled upward. Sometimes he understood a word or two.

"... help ..."

"... healer ..."

He stood on his knees and swung his stick at the discarnate speakers. The spirits retreated and hovered in the distance. He continued crawling and felt the hill's incline leveling. The forest was not far away, home to spirits, wild animals, and death.

"Take me," Peter whispered to the spirits. "I'm ready."

He set his walking stick upright and climbed up its shaft hand over hand. Airy shadows from the world of spirits replaced the world of solids. He hopped once and the twilight world danced in his agony. His mind struggled to free itself from his body and its misery. He gritted his teeth and hopped again. The shadows jiggled again and waves of pain searched for his nearly detached mind.

A spirit in the shape of a snake gleamed before him. It coiled and swallowed its own tail. Its golden glow beckoned him and he reached for it. The soft world of shifting shapes rushed upon him. He felt its unexpected hardness knock against him as he fell into its rigid arms and lay still, ready to die. "Take me," he whispered to the shadows of death. "Please?"

At the creaking sound of an opening door, light exploded onto the shadow world. A figure moved through the door and crouched like a wild animal. Its mane glowed red around a shadowy head. Peter knew the animal from pictures in a magic book Father Ulrich had borrowed from the bishop.

"Dear God, a red lion," Peter whispered.

A spirit deep inside his floating mind said, *This is your master.*

Peter whispered, "Master, take me."

The lion swept down upon him and carried him into its den.

CHAPTER 14
JACOB'S OFFER

A gray light trickled into Peter's darkness. The light grew stronger and turned to gold. He opened his eyes. The light shone with such intense purity he had to shut his eyes again. A wet, musty odor thickened the air. Gisela must be boiling roots for another of her remedies.

He moved his hands over the soft, finely spun linen beneath him. He seemed to lie on a flattened sack as long as he was tall. Faint rustles from his movements indicated the sack was stuffed with straw. Under the stuffed linen his hands felt the hardness of a wood platform. The tiny ripples of wood grain were smooth, not splintered like the rough-hewn structures in his village. Below the low platform, his fingers touched the floor. The hard packed ground contained no slivers of straw, as was usual, but was covered with dust so fine it made his finger tips slippery.

He turned away from the light and blinked his eyes open again. Not more than two hand's length from his nose, the shadow of his head fell upon a wide timber joining two mud-covered walls in a corner of a room. Other timbers divided the walls into panels roughly one pace wide, similar to the construction of Lord Arnulf's house and the courtyard buildings of the count's castle. Sunlight shone in a bright square on him and his corner. From the sun's warmth and angle, he guessed the time to be late afternoon.

Why wasn't he up and working at … at what? Where was he?

Peter sat upright and swung his legs over the platform. A bolt of pain threw him against the wall. The sunlight dimmed.

"Don't move." The voice came from the light. "The leg needs rest to heal itself."

A pain throbbed in his leg. He remembered it was broken. What else had he forgotten?

A shadow placed a small sack on his leg and picked up a similar sack from the ground. The shadow moved into the light and said, "Let the poultice dry in the sun and absorb the bad humors."

"Who ish there?" Peter asked.

"My name is Jacob." His words were crisp, spoken like a nobleman.

Peter examined his broken leg, held straight between two splints. The inner stick reached from his groin to his instep, the outer stick from his hip to his heel. Linen strips tied the splints securely to each other. His trouser leg was rolled up to mid-thigh. A small moist sack, shining bright in the sunlight, lay over the break below the knee.

"You did this?" Peter pointed at the splints.

"Yes." The deep voice came from just below the light. "When you came here yesterday, your body was nearly dead."

Peter held his hand up to shield his eyes and squinted into the light. The bright sun stared back through an open window. Dark silhouettes of the cathedral spire and the count's stockade appeared beneath the sun. Faint sounds of the market fair drifted through the window. He looked into the shadows on either side of the brilliant beam and gripped the linen sack on which he sat. "Where ... what ..."

"This is my shop, my home. You're sitting on a mattress. That's a bed of straw packed in a sack. Loose straw is a fire hazard. You're as safe as you want to be, Peter."

Peter squinted to where Jacob probably sat under the windowsill. "How you know my name?"

"You were delirious last night and you said a lot. You said you wanted to better yourself and your world. You talked about Crayfish, Lothair, Gabriel, and Rosamund."

Confused memories slowly ordered themselves. He remembered how Lothair beat him, how Gabriel displaced him, how Crayfish bullied him, how Rosamund betrayed him. He remembered a shadow world and a lion – a red lion – just before dying. But he didn't die. He shut his eyes and moaned, "Oh God. I wanted to die. I still want to die."

"It's no accident you came here, Peter. You can still get what you want and more. You'll be stronger and more powerful than you ever dreamed. You can do it by learning alchemy."

Peter blinked at the light. "What ish all - to - me?"

"Al - che - my. Alchemy is the sacred art of transmutation."

"Trains my day shine?"

"It's a way of changing yourself and your world from the base to the noble, from the weak to the strong. You can be an alchemist."

Peter could distinguish the top of Jacob's head against the bottom of the windowsill. His bushy hair glowed in the sunlight like the mane of the lion Peter saw in the shadow world. "I can be a ... a ... all to mist?"

"Alchemist. Yes." The shadowy head beneath the window nodded. "But it's not easy to learn, and learning isn't enough. You must experience alchemy. Transmutation occurs when experience reaches from the sacred core of your spirit, strikes through your mind, and takes hold of your physical world."

Peter leaned forward. "What?"

"You work with things, with matter, and as you do this you restore yourself to your original nobility. The alchemical meditation changes how you see the world. You help the world restore itself to its original purity, like base lead changing into noble gold."

"Gold?" Peter rubbed his eyes. The sun yellowed as it moved lower but it still blinded him.

"Gold is not the purpose of alchemy. The true alchemist is interested only in helping everything return to nothing."

Peter didn't understand. "How do I ... uh ... How long ...?"

"We'll start tomorrow with simple things. When you're well, we'll take on more difficult tasks. If you're clever, you might finish the apprenticeship in three years."

Peter sighed. "Could have been a warrior in one year."

"An alchemist is mightier than a warrior."

"Humph," Peter grunted and held his hand up to shield his eyes. To his left, he could make out a large table. About fifteen paces away a smaller, higher table sat in a corner of the house. Next to the small table, light seeped through the cracks of a shuttered window. "So, after three years, I be a ... a ... all - can - mist."

"No," Jacob said. "After you've passed the test at the end of your apprenticeship, you'll become a journeyman. Then you'll travel for another seven years and learn from other masters. After that, you'll do a masterwork, and if you succeed, you'll become an alchemist. But if you fail at any point, if you use the powers you recovered for anything other than noble purposes, you'll slip backwards. You'll slip into an abyss blacker than the one you felt yesterday and you'll drag the rest of the world with you."

Light outlined a large set of double doors in the north wall on Peter's right. He squinted harder to see a cone as tall as a man and nearly as wide as a tree rising from the floor in the middle of Jacob's house. Was it a fireplace, an oven? Beyond it, close to the opposite corner, light showed around the edges of a small, closed door in the southern wall. "Why me?" he asked.

"It wasn't my choice." Jacob's tone dropped lower. "The counselor wants you."

"Who?"

"The one who guides us home," Jacob said. "Novices of alchemy are usually more mature, more stable. But the counselor said to offer you the apprenticeship because you would save me from myself."

Peter shut his eyes. "Strange. Not sure I want ... whatever it ish."

"Peter, do you want a world where you're strong instead of weak?"

Peter looked up and shielded his eyes again. "Yes."

"Do you want a world you rule instead of a world that rules you?"

"Yes." Peter detected a block about two paces wide near the cone. A second fireplace?

"Do you want a world where you have no enemies?"

"Yes. Of course." Peter strained to see roots, stalks, and twigs hanging from the lower rim of the thatched roof. Shelves on the upper walls were filled with containers. Below the shelves, many black objects hung on the walls. Were they tools? Why so many?

"Do you want a world in which the power you've hidden is revealed and dispels all your deceptions?"

"What?"

"Never mind, Peter. You don't understand this now, but you will. It's only necessary that you're willing to search and to change. You will see your responsibility in everything, not only the things you do, but also the things others do."

Peter sat up higher, gritting his teeth against sharp spasms from his leg. The bottom edge of the sunbeam had moved up past his leg as the sun sank lower. The poultice on his shin appeared nearly dry. He pointed at the sack. "What?"

"Comfrey root," Jacob said from beneath the window. "We'll have to apply it every day."

Peter reached over slowly, grunting with each stab of pain, and lifted the poultice. Beneath it a pink circle had replaced the red ball.

Jacob said, "The infection was lanced, drained of poisons, and cleaned with an onion. That tea next to you broke your fever."

Peter picked up a wood cup from the ground and sipped its bitter contents. "Yech."

"It's cold, isn't it?" Jacob stood, silhouetted against the window. "You need a hot cup. It's a tea of willow bark, bitterwort root, and black mullein flowers."

Peter spit on the floor. "Black mullein." He spit again. "Used by witches."

"And by saints." Jacob carried a steaming cup to Peter and blocked the blinding sunlight.

With the sunlight blocked, Peter could clearly see Jacob's white hair and beard, his gray leather apron and heavy boots. "You the blacksmith," he gasped. His breath stopped.

"You can learn smithing too." The Jew put a full cup on the floor next to Peter and picked up the empty one.

Now Peter could see that the large block was a forge and the cone was a furnace. A square anvil sat on a stump between the forge and the furnace, and behind that Peter could just make out a low stone wall, probably the accursed well Crayfish had mentioned. The beggar said that the Jew had killed the old count. Peter's heart beat faster.

"Alchemy and smithing go well together," the Jew continued. "With alchemy you'll have no needs, but smithing will allow you to move through the world without arousing fear."

"No. Not with a Jew." Peter struggled to stand, but the pain from his leg slapped him down.

"Don't move," the Jew said.

The Jew stepped away and the low sun blinded Peter again. He couldn't see the Jew, but he could feel his penetrating eyes, as if the Jew was looking through him, seeing his thoughts and feelings.

Finally the Jew said, "You're worried about my Jewishness. You'll learn alchemy as a Christian would, using the church's methods and symbols. That's a promise. My master was a cleric of your faith."

"Father Ulrich says Jews gots no church, no faith." Peter studied the back and front doors for an escape from the slave trader, the child eater, the sorcerer, the murderer.

"The Jewish faith gave birth to the Christian faith," the Jew said. "You'll learn the language of your church, Latin."

At the foot of the mattress Peter saw his walking stick. Perhaps he could beat the Jew with it and run away. "Latin ish for monks and merchants. I will have none of it."

"The first book you'll read will be the Bible."

"A Jew can not touch the magic Bible book."

"Your Bible was written by Jews, for Jews -"

"Liar."

"Jesus was a Jew who -"

"LIAR," Peter shouted. He lunged for his baton but crumpled in agony before he could reach it.

The Jew walked to the window and stood in the sunlight. The sun had moved lower in the sky, changing from yellow to orange with the coming sunset.

Peter heard voices outside the blacksmith's shop. He could yell for help.

"Peter, if you choose not to be my novice," the Jew said quietly, "then you are choosing physical death."

Peter glared at him, hoping his frown might keep him away. "I choose death. I am going to the forest to die like I wanted." The voices outside grew louder. Maybe the town's people knew the Jew had taken him. They were probably coming to rescue him.

"Lothair will kill you first," the Jew said.

"Good." Peter said. "Let him. I want to kneel before him. I want to submit -"

The shop's double doors swung out and light from the street flowed into the shop, revealing every dark corner. His rescue had come. A gaunt figure hobbled through the entrance and danced in front of Peter.

"Dis is where he hides," the beggar shouted and pointed a

handless stump at Peter. "Now de runaway serf dies."

The light from the doorway dimmed, swallowed by the dark warrior standing on the threshold.

"Lothair," Peter whispered and shrank into the corner.

The Jew bowed his head.

CHAPTER 15
CLEVER WORDS

"Lord Lothair," Peter whispered. "Please, no."

The blackbearded warrior marched into the shop and blocked the sunbeam streaking from the window. Light glinted off iron ringlets of the warrior's chain mail tunic and hood. Next to the Jew in his charcoal-stained apron, Lothair looked every bit a martial menace.

Peter pressed his back against a wall panel and wished the wall would let him break through. The reeds within the mudpacked mural creaked but did not yield.

The beggar hobbled back to the shop's entrance and grimaced at Peter. "Dere is de runaway serf, just like I told you. Kill de serf and pay me."

Behind the beggar, several men, women, and children from the free town crowded around the doorway and leaned forward, their eyes wide and their mouths ajar.

Peter struggled to stand, hoping to run out the open door. Pain from his leg slammed him back onto the mattress, chopping his breath into short, quick gasps.

"Don't move, Peter," the blacksmith said with head bowed.

Lothair frowned at the splints on Peter's legs and the poultice fallen on the floor. "What's the little serf doing here?"

The Jew spoke to Lothair's boots. "He has been asked to be my apprentice, sire."

Lothair's lips pushed up, bristling the short hairs on his chin. He snarled with exaggerated disgust, "The runaway serf has become an apprentice to the Jew blacksmith."

Crayfish hissed, "Kill de Jew. No. Cut off his hand for stealing de serf."

"Blacksmith." Lothair's bark thundered through the shop. "Hold out your hand."

The Jew raised his right arm, hand open and palm up.

Lothair plucked a dull, brown coin out of a leather pouch tied to his sword belt and dropped it into the Jew's open hand. "According to Konrad's custom, I must pay the master for the death of his apprentice. Here's a copper penny."

The Jew closed his hand around the coin and lowered his arm. The cracks between the fingers of the Jew's right fist glowed in the sunbeam.

On the Jew's left, more people from the street craned their necks around the door jamb and looked at Peter. A low murmur of disapproval circulated through the crowd.

Crayfish hobbled to Lothair. "What about me, sire? I told you where he ish. Give me a penny, too."

Lothair reached again for his belt and unsheathed his long sword.

Peter gave a short shriek and pushed his back harder against the wall. His arms shook.

The beggar retreated to the shop's door, beyond the range of a swinging sword blade. "Gets my penny later," he said.

The old Jew did not move, but remained behind and to the right of Lothair. The light on the Jew's fist grew brighter.

Lothair grasped the sword hilt with both hands, stepped up to Peter and lifted the blade above his right shoulder.

"Oh God," Peter whispered. His body stiffened. The wall behind him groaned.

A flash of light froze on the sword's polish. Every sound stopped and waited in expectancy. After a long moment that seemed unnaturally suspended in time, Lothair's grunt disturbed the quiet and he swung the sharpened metal.

Peter watched the blur of iron slicing through the air toward him with unblinking, fascinated horror. Terror petrified his every muscle. The iron blur flew forward and Lothair's fingers sprang open. A resounding thud vibrated through his rigid body as the sword's tip embedded itself into a thick wall timber above and left of his head. The sword protruded from the wall at a right angle, its hilt wobbled from side to side. Peter exhaled with a gasp.

Lothair stared wide eyed at his empty hands. "What the devil? How did it ...?" The dark warrior's eyes narrowed into a frown and his lips pursed into a tight, thin line. He pulled back his metallic hood, and ruffled his thick, dark hair into a shag of random patterns.

"Why does Lord Lothair wish to kill a lowly serf?" the Jew

asked, his head still bowed. The light on his right fist radiated brighter.

Lothair grasped the sword hilt with one hand and pulled. The blade refused to slide free. He wiped his palms on his armor and grasped the sword with both hands. He grunted and jerked, but couldn't free his sword from the stubborn timber.

"Is Lord Lothair afraid of what the little serf knows?" the Jew asked quietly.

Lothair's face reddened. He whirled and marched to the old man. "Look at me, Jew."

The blacksmith raised his head, his white beard and hair contrasted sharply with the warrior's black shag. Lothair bent down and thrust his face close to the Jew's.

"What does the dirty Jew know about that?" Lothair snarled, nose to nose with the Jew.

"Peter said much last night while fever boiled his brain. But he repeated only what everyone else knows." Without looking away, the Jew waved his left hand toward the doorway.

Lothair turned his head and stared at the crowd in the street. All but the small children quickly bowed their heads.

The Jew spoke so softly, Peter could barely hear him over his own thumping heart. "Peter may have heard you secretly insult your lord," Lothair jerked his head back towards the old Jew, "but you, Lord Lothair, do not keep your loathing of Count Edzard a secret."

"Shut up," Lothair growled. "I could kill both you insects."

"You'd have to kill the whole town. Your secret is common knowledge. Yesterday, at the market fair, while speaking with your uncle, didn't you refer to your lord's family as being vulgar and to your lord as having no honor?"

"My uncle would not betray me," Lothair growled lower. "He feels the same way I do."

"Just because you come from a family of esteemed chieftains, doesn't mean you're always surrounded by likeminded warriors. The common people you ignore so well have eyes to see and ears to hear. Many of the people at my door heard you at the market fair. They saw your transparent sentiments. You can't kill them all."

Lothair looked back to the doorway. The men, women, and

children had shuffled closer. In response to his glare, the spectators lowered their heads again.

The Jew's fist glowed so brightly that Peter could see finger bones through the skin. The light seemed not to come from the setting sun but from the copper penny within the Jew's fist. The blacksmith pressed his hand into a fold of his apron, as though to hide it from the crowd and Lothair. The Jew continued quietly, "The only person who will betray you, Lord Lothair, is yourself. You must keep your resentment of the young count to yourself. If you don't, you could face exile or worse. That would be unfortunate, because Peter needs you."

Lothair turned from the crowd to Peter. "Ah, yes. The little serf." He strode toward Peter and grabbed the sword hilt with both hands. "I'm going to kill the runaway serf."

Peter pushed against the wall with renewed vigor. "Please, Lord Lothair. I w-w-won't tell anyone about anything. I don't know w-w-what you said that w-w-was bad."

Lothair put his boot against the timber, just above the embedded sword. "Shut up. You are runaway serf vermin. Running from serving your lord. Infecting others with notions of freedom from duty. That's reason enough to kill you."

The blacksmith bowed his head and raised his voice. "Does Lord Lothair want to be known as the slayer of defenseless serfs?"

The warrior pulled the sword with his hands and pushed the timber with his foot until his face turned crimson. The sword remained fast. "What sorcery is this?" he muttered. He pulled and pushed again, grunting loudly.

"Custom dictates that a runaway serf be taken by his lord," the blacksmith said, loud enough to be heard over Lothair's straining.

The redfaced warrior released his immobile weapon. "My uncle is his lord. I'll be lord of his serfs someday." He looked at Peter. "If you hadn't run away, you'd be submitting to me."

The blacksmith said, "You gave the copper penny to me, not your uncle. Who is Peter's lord? Custom requires the master be paid after his servant is murdered, not before."

Lothair marched again toward the blacksmith and howled,

"What the devil does it matter who his lord is or when his dung-filled master is paid? Damn the custom. I'll make a new custom."

"As the count's marshal, you may," the blacksmith said and shrugged. His right hand lifted over the fold in his apron and only a faint yellow glimmer showed between the fingers. "When the marshal does something twice, it becomes the custom. You killed one of your uncle's serfs after giving the bishop a copper penny. If you kill this second serf, you'll make a new custom."

"A good custom," Lothair snarled.

"A serfkilling custom," the old man continued, "that will forever bear your name. The previous marshal, Lord Konrad, is remembered for his customs. This new custom will bear your name. You'll be remembered as a serf slayer among serfs. Wouldn't you rather be remembered as a warrior hero among warriors?"

Lothair shifted his weight from one leg to the other and placed his fists on his hips. "I am already that."

"Then you would dishonor your good name and your family's name by killing another serf and making a new custom in your name. What honor is there in killing helpless serfs or sleeping warriors?"

Lothair frowned at the floor. "Do not equate me with Edzard."

For a long time, the two men stood silent and still. Each passing moment lingered longer and longer, allowing Peter's thoughts to clear and his fears to settle. His breathing slowed, his heart grew quieter, and his muscles relaxed little by little as each silent, calming moment passed.

Peter looked through the window. The red sun seemed to balance without the slightest movement on the hilly horizon. A tree swayed in the breeze with unnatural leisure. A butterfly flew past, its wings fluttered sluggishly as if the air had thickened into syrup. The normally rapid chirping of crickets drifted through the window in singular, lazy notes, one slowly following the other, punctuating the quiet with delayed staccato. Lothair, the Jew, the beggar, and the crowd in the street stood still and all expressions of hatred or concern melted away in the arrested moment.

A loud thud beside the mattress startled Peter. He looked for the source with a stiff jerk. The sword had come loose from the timber and fallen, hilt first, to the hardpacked floor. The lethal blade pointed upward, hesitating for a long, lazy moment before falling, first slowly, then quickly, toward him.

Peter's heart jumped. He pushed himself against the wall, away from the falling sword. He gulped as the sharpened blade struck his chest broadside. Its tip lay atop his racing heart.

Lothair picked up the sword by the hilt but kept the sword's tip pointed at Peter's heart.

Peter pressed against the wall. "Please, Lord Lothair," he whispered. "Gots to think w-w-what w-w-would happen to your good name?"

"Shut up," Lothair barked. "The Jew is clever enough and needs no help from you. I do not want to be remembered for killing serfs. But there's more than clever words here. There's sorcery, too ... an unholy alliance ..." His eyes looked past Peter in distracted thought.

After a moment, Lothair lifted the sword tip from Peter's chest and pointed it heavenward. Light shimmered off the unsteady blade and betrayed his trembling hands. For the first time, Peter saw fear in Lothair's eyes. The tall warrior kissed the hilt of his sword. "May Saint George protect me. I swear by his holy bones I'll find an honorable way to be rid of you and your unholy master." He slid his sword into its sheath.

With his head still bowed, Jacob walked up to the warrior and held out his right hand. "Here's your penny, sire."

Without looking at Jacob or the coin, Lothair accepted it.

The beggar ran to Lothair and tapped his metal tunic. "No, sire. Kill de serf. Give me de penny."

Lothair walked past Crayfish to the shop's door as if he'd heard nothing. The crowd backed away.

"He owes me," the beggar shouted and waved his arms. "Kill de serf and pay me."

Lothair spun around in a metallic whirl and hurled the penny. The coin thumped the beggar squarely on his forehead. Crayfish staggered and fell backwards onto the shop's floor.

"Stay away, Crayfish," Lothair barked, his eyes wild like a frightened dog. "For all I know, you too have made a pact with the devil." He turned and walked quickly down the hill.

The town's people mumbled to each other and slowly dispersed.

The dazed beggar rubbed a red knot on his gray forehead and then searched the floor on his knees with frantic enthusiasm before pouncing on his prize. "Yes!"

Between the forefinger and the thumb on his one hand, the smiling beggar held the penny up in the glow of sunset. The coin reflected not the dull glint of copper, but a bright, yellow sheen. "What metal dis?" He hobbled toward the blacksmith, but held the coin just out of the old man's reach.

The blacksmith answered, "Looks like gold."

The beggar's gray skin seemed to lighten. "Lord Lodair ish very generous."

Jacob pointed at Peter. "It would seem the boy no longer owes you anything."

The beggar closed his hand around the gold penny. His gray skin darkened. "Dis penny comes from Lodair, not de little wolf. He still owes me." He danced out of the shop. "Wid a gold penny I gets a winter cloak, ... and boots, ... and a hen, ... and a stockfish, ... maybe two stockfish..." His words grew fainter as he descended the hill.

Jacob pointed out the doorway. "You can go now," he said to Peter. "Or would you rather be an apprentice of alchemy?"

Peter stopped pushing against the wall and slumped onto the mattress. After a long sigh, he closed his eyes and answered, "Yes."

PART II

Distillation
and
Sublimation

CHAPTER 16
THE FIRST LESSON

"How do I turn a copper penny into gold?" Peter asked.

Jacob lit a candle with a hot charcoal, and shut the doors and windows against the twilight. "An alchemist must learn cleanliness," he said and gently lifted Peter onto a stool. The splints held Peter's broken leg straight out from the stool. "Breathe slowly, in through your nose and out through your mouth. Clean your mind by concentrating on each breath. A quiet mind gives life to the body." He helped Peter out of his muddy clothes and poured a cup of water over Peter's head.

The shock of cold water sent shivers through Peter. He let Jacob scrub away encrusted river mud from his hair and torso. He focused on filling his lungs with the wax-scented air. Spasms of teeth-gritting pain interrupted his measured breathing. But each slow breath calmed him and warmed him against the chilly water. A soothing glow flowed through him and eased the pain.

After cleaning and drying Peter, Jacob carried him back to the mattress and laid a blanket over him.

Peter shut his eyes and drifted away, far from pain, far from fear.

Clanging metal woke him. It took him a moment to remember where he was and what had happened. The slant of the sun's rays told him the hour was noon. Even though a whole night and half a day had passed, it seemed he'd slept only a moment. He pushed off the blanket and sat up with a grunt, careful to move his broken leg as little as possible. He pulled his clean, dry tunic from a peg in the wall next to him and slipped it over his head.

The blacksmith was putting tools into a hemp sack. "There's no food in the shop, but a few tools can be exchanged for a good store of food in the market fair. Go back to sleep."

The distant din of the market fair wafted through the open window on the west and the open double doors on the north. Peter craned his neck to look out the double doors. Lothair or Crayfish might be lurking outside. "No. Don' go. You gots food up there." He pointed at dried plants tacked upside down on ceiling beams, and at shelves packed with containers and pouches.

"Those are for healing, not eating," Jacob said. "You need a new poultice, don't you?" He set the clinking sack of tools aside and pumped the bellows to the forge. The cone-shaped furnace and the forge shared a pair of bellows, which could be swiveled from one to the other.

Peter leaned forward. "Show me ... all to ... all kept ..., please."

"Alchemy." Jacob stirred a pot on the forge. "Alchemy is everywhere. Look around you."

Nearly everything in the shop seemed related to stories Peter had heard about smithing; tools hanging from the walls, an anvil on a stump, the forge, and the bellows. Through the half-open southern door, he saw a cherry tree and a garden of onions, chamomile flowers, tall catnip plants, and spindly caraway stalks. He saw nothing magical.

The blacksmith strained the pot's liquid through a piece of linen and folded it into a small pouch. "Everything you see teaches us how to uncover inner nobility." He pointed at the bellows. "Controlled breathing of the bellows feeds the fire and enhances the healing power of comfrey root. Your controlled breathing enhances your inner processes, your healing."

Peter nodded. "Slow breathing gots me warmer, leg hurts less."

Jacob replaced the dried poultice on Peter's leg with the wet, warm one. "Now, let the mattress teach you to lie down and rest. You'll have food soon."

"Don' go. Not hungry. You gots to show me something else, please. Something to stop Lothair ... and Crayfish, too."

Jacob's eyes softened and Peter felt that tingling sense again, as if Jacob was looking through him. The alchemist said, "Lothair and Crayfish are not waiting outside. It will be some time before Lothair finds the courage to attack you again. You need to rest. You're still weak."

"Not tired. Please. Show me what all-kept-me does."

"Al-che-my," Jacob said. "Alchemists do what everyone else does, except we see it differently, and that makes all the difference in the world."

"I gots to have al-che-my to protect myself."

"Nothing protects you," Jacob said. "When you understand this, you know you are invulnerable." In a shallow, clay-covered basket he gathered hot charcoal from the forge and fresh charcoal from a dusty bin. From the worktable he lifted a small square anvil about one-fourth the size of the larger one on the stump. He placed the basket and the small anvil on the floor next to Peter along with two chainmail tunics, a platter of open-ended iron ringlets, wire, and tools.

"This is a lesson in alchemy," Jacob said. "Maynard the Fat's hauberk was torn into two halves so that Count Edzard might have two hauberks which fit him. You will make each hauberk whole.

"Put a single ringlet against a hot charcoal. Blow a long and steady breath with this tube on the charcoal." He exhaled slowly through a river reed. "Breathe until the open ends of the ring turn red. Then scarf them like this." With a pair of pincers, he flattened and bent the ends in opposite directions. "Put it back against the charcoal. Blow slowly until the ends turn orange."

Peter memorized every move.

"Punch a hole in each end but don't split the iron's fiber." The blacksmith laid the ring over a tiny pit on the anvil and punched a hole in the flattened ends with a needle and hammer. "You'll need to sharpen the needle again after a few rings." He pointed to a file. "Mend the tear in a hauberk with the ring. Rivet the ends together." He slid the open ends through rings on either side of the tunic's tear, pinched the ring shut, inserted a wire through the punched holes, snipped the wire close to the ring, and flared the wire tips with a tap of the hammer.

"Look at the interlinked rings," the blacksmith said. "A central ring holds four neighboring rings in place. These four rings are the four elements: earth, water, air, and fire. The fifth ring, the 'quinta essentia,' unifies all elements. Remember this each time you close a ring. Breath slowly in your nose and out your mouth, and each time you exhale say 'Benedicamus Domino.'"

"Baynaydeekahmoosdohmeenoh," Peter repeated. "Are these magic words? Will they keep Lothair and Crayfish away?"

The alchemist picked up the clinking sack of tools. "With proper breathing, chanting, these words carry Latin monks to a new understanding. When you learn Latin, you'll learn what the words mean." He waved and stepped outside.

Peter pulled a hauberk over his lap. If anyone attacked him while Jacob was away, he would cover himself with the chain mail armor and call for help.

He prepared each ring for its place in the armor, connected it to the center of the four interlinked rings, and unified the four elements. With each exhalation, he chanted "benedicamusdominoo oooooooh." With each repetitive movement, his attention narrowed on pinching and hammering. His mind lightened, his leg hurt less, fear melted away, and the soothing glow from the night before returned.

Sometimes children stared at him from the shop's entrance. At other times well-dressed merchants and foreigners walked in and asked for the Jew blacksmith.

After a while, Peter's arms grew heavy and his chants became whispers. He slumped against the wall to rest and shut his eyes for just a moment. He dreamt of chain mail armor turning into gold.

When he opened his eyes, he saw through the opposite window an indigo sky nibbling at the amber glow of an aging sunset. He sat up and a jolt of pain reminded him of his broken leg.

"Careful," the blacksmith said and closed the window.

Peter sniffed the air and his stomach growled. "Bread?"

"Baking in the furnace," the blacksmith said. He placed a new poultice on Peter's leg and gave him a tiny brown cube. "Eat this. It will quiet your hunger until the bread is ready."

Peter popped the cube into his mouth and gagged on the over-powering sting of salt. "Aaaach. What ish?"

"Stockfish. The longer you chew it, the less salty it becomes." Jacob carried a flickering candle to the small, tilted table and opened a book. Stacked on a chest at the foot of the table lay other books, similar to the bishop's magic book. "Eat it slowly just as you learned to breathe this morning. Bless it because, in so doing, you bless yourself."

"Ish this al-che-my?" Peter asked.

"Eat in silence, like the monks do," Jacob said. "Concentrate on eating and blessing."

Peter chewed the dried fish. The tough little cube softened and swelled, broke into pieces, multiplied and filled his mouth. After a long time, he swallowed the last sliver from the cube and asked, "Can you give me ... the power to ... change things?"

The alchemist looked up from his study table. "No one can give you a power you don't already have and you already have all the power there is."

"Then ... how do I make things change?" Peter asked.

"Things change by themselves."

"But you make things change. The copper penny turned to gold. I saw you do it. Did you make Lothair's sword slip out of his hands? I want to turn his sword into lead. I want to make him kneel before me. I gots to hurt him 'cause -"

"A true alchemist is never selfish and never does harm. An alchemist helps things change with permission."

"Permission? Who gives you permission?"

"The things that change."

Peter frowned. "Can you show me how to do it?"

The alchemist closed his book and stood up. "As a novice, you'll learn my way for change, but you must improve on my way and make your own way."

"Your way ish the right way," Peter said. "I saw it. I believe it."

The alchemist opened the furnace door with a large pair of tongs. He removed a crucible and shook it until a round loaf of bread fell onto the worktable. He cut it in half and scooped out the steaming heart. The sweet smell of baked grains filled the shop. "What we believe is true today, we may not believe tomorrow. You're wrong to think my way is right, but you'll receive my best instruction and my frank admiration." He laughed and shoveled hot charcoal from under the furnace onto the forge. He placed two pots on the forge. Into one pot he dropped a handful of mixed herbs and into the second, rolled oats. "You will learn, oh, let's say, six powers."

"Good," Peter said, his mouth watering. "I learn them after I eat."

Jacob sat on a stool between Peter and the forge. "You'll learn them next year."

"Next year?"

"First you need a well built furnace," the alchemist pointed at the conical furnace, "within which the soft dough of your latent powers may be baked until they are raised and firm. A furnace requires four qualities: clean walls to reflect heat inward, a door to allow openness, a crucible to shape an ideal, and a fire to burn with zeal. How will you build your furnace?" He pointed westward, in the direction of the count's castle. "Come down from your barren hilltop. Come down to your fertile valley." His hand swung to point at Peter. "Come to the quarry of the prima materia and build your furnace from the philosopher's stone."

In the glow of charcoal behind Jacob, his hair and beard blazed like a fiery mane, a vaguely familiar image to Peter. But Jacob's words confused him. He listened for a time to the hissing charcoal and his own rumbling stomach before commenting, "I came down from the castle and ... I saw the quarry in the valley."

Jacob's shadowy face nodded and said, "Universal essence."

Peter repeated what he thought Jacob said. "You - invert - all - sense."

Jacob chuckled and said, "Good description. Listen to the words again. U-ni-ver-sal es-sence."

"U - nee - ver - sahl - es - sens," Peter repeated slowly. "What ish?"

The alchemist walked behind the forge and pumped the bellows. "Universal essence can neither be explained nor ignored. We either know it or desire to remember it. We've erected three barriers on the road to the quarry of that knowledge. These barriers are created by our own deceptions and, though they appear solid, they are but clouds." He laid straw and wood on the charcoal. The kindling flared and smoke obscured him.

He swept his hand through the smoke, breaking it into swirls. "The first barrier is fear of our world because we imagine it is hostile."

He broke the stream of smoke with his hand again. "The second barrier is aggression. Whether in deed or thought, whether for vengeance or protection, we act with aggression because of our fear."

His hand again swept through the smoke. "The last barrier is shame because of our aggression and fear. These barriers seem terrible, but they have no substance. You can pass through them as if they were made of smoke."

Jacob leapt onto the edge of the forge and jumped through the thin smoke. He seemed to fly several paces before landing with a light thud before Peter's mattress.

Peter sat back, startled at the old man's youthful agility.

"Beyond these barriers," the alchemist said, pointing at Peter's chest, "is the quarry of your loving, unassailable, and undefilable essence."

"Under - fiber - essence," Peter repeated.

The alchemist walked away. "After you have built your furnace with your quarry stones, you will hear and see better." He returned with a cup of tea, a wooden spoon, and porridge in the hollowed out bread, "This tea will help you rest. Eat the frumentry and bread slowly, in quiet, with reverence."

Peter poked his finger in the porridge to test its heat, blew on it a moment to cool it, and slurped. He'd not eaten warm porridge and brown bread since leaving his village. He gobbled the porridge and washed it down with Jacob's tea, which smelled like primrose flowers and hops. When the porridge was gone, he stuffed his mouth with pieces of bread. Before he could finish the last few bites, a sudden drowsiness washed over him. He stretched out on the mattress and mumbled, "Left you some bread." Through half shut eyes, Peter saw Jacob take the bread and empty cup from his mattress.

"Thank you, Peter, but an alchemist does not eat."

"Are you going to bed without eating?"

"An alchemist does not sleep either," Jacob said.

Peter's eyes opened wide. "What do you mean?"

"An alchemist eats and drinks nothing, and doesn't sleep," Jacob said. "Sometimes alchemists dine with others so as not to arouse fear, and eating is often a pleasant experience. But alchemists have no needs and are never tired, hungry, or sick. We are sustained by nothing." He dropped the leftover bread into a container and replaced the lid. "Go to sleep now."

Peter couldn't sleep. For most of the night he watched candlelight jitter nervously on the ceiling while Jacob studied a magic book. He had accepted Jacob's ability to turn copper into gold because he had seen it with his own eyes. But nobody lived without food and sleep. Everybody in the world, even animals, had to eat and sleep. If Jacob didn't, then he wasn't of the world.

And if he wasn't of the world, what was he?

CHAPTER 17
REFLECTIONS

Peter did not sleep that night, jumping every time the Jew turned a page in his book. The next morning he ate his fill of leftover bread. But the bread seemed no less. It even seemed to have grown. What kind of magic made bread grow?

The Jew ladled water from the well that Crayfish called bad magic. A spring in a house and at the top of a hill seemed unnatural. Was the Jew an enemy of nature, a sorcerer?

Through the shop's open front doors drifted cool air and the hubbub of merchants leaving grand homes for another day at the market fair. Perhaps he could find refuge in another shop, become an apprentice to a less menacing merchant.

A sudden cry startled Peter. A plump, balding merchant led a whimpering boy by his ear into the blacksmith shop. The merchant stomped his leather boot and shouted, "Tell Jacob what you want."

The barefoot boy appeared two or three years younger than Peter. He bowed his head of short, dark curls and murmured, "Please, Master Jacob, please make three scrapers."

The merchant stomped again. "Tell him why."

"Three of my master's scrapers ... were lost."

The merchant slapped the back of the boy's head. "You lost them gambling at the market fair." The redfaced merchant slapped him again and the boy fell to his knees.

The Jew held back the merchant's hand and said, "Thomas, please stop."

Thomas shook his hand free. "Custom says we must beat novices for their own good. The master must be respected. Tell Jacob what you'll give him for the scrapers."

"My dinner ... every other night for six months."

"Once a week for six months is enough," the Jew said. "Give it to my novice, Peter." He turned to Peter and said, "Master Thomas is a furrier who lives across the street. Lucus is his apprentice."

Peter nodded to both of them and they returned the nod saying, "Greetings to God."

"You're too generous," Thomas said to the Jew, "but I'll

accept that."

Lucus kissed Thomas' hand. "Thank you, master."

Thomas yanked Lucus off the floor. "We're late getting to the fair." He pushed Lucus out the front doors.

Peter handed the Jew the leftover bread and picked up the unfinished chain mail tunics. He began to work each ringlet, but he didn't concentrate on breathing, or chanting, or the elements, or the universal essence. Instead he concentrated on the Jew's every move.

The Jew added a mound of fresh charcoal to the forge. He pumped the pair of bellows with a lever and placed a thick iron rod in the dome of white-hot charcoal. As one bellow blew, the other drew breath, working in tandem to insure a steady stream of air.

The tiny creaking of the lever, the muffled tapping of valves within the bellows, and the low rushing of air into the forge provided a steady rhythm for the distant humming commerce in the market square. Wary raps from Peter's hammer drummed against the rhythm. Sparks of burning charcoal flew up from the forge, glowed with life, died quickly, and settled as gray dust to the ground near Peter's broken leg.

After a few long moments, the Jew said, "As an alchemist, the first quality you'll need is reflection. As we learn about the images we have of ourselves, we can replace them with nobler images. Life reflects what we think. Our life and our world changes when we change our minds." He brought the iron rod to the anvil and hammered its bright red tip.

Peter's nerves jumped with each metallic clang.

The Jew hammered the tip into a flat, broad crescent and put the rod back into the dome of charcoal, heating it a hand's length above the flattened end. He pumped the bellows and watched the iron. "Charcoal is heaped into a mound to reflect heat back into the center just like the clean, interior walls of the furnace. The hotter the iron, the softer it becomes and the easier it is to shape. So we shape our stubborn lives. Why do you want to be a warrior?"

Peter said, "Warriors are strong and good and free."

"Did you hear that from legends or see that yourself?"

"I been with warriors," Peter said. "I been in battle. I fought beside Count Edzard."

The Jew looked at Peter with a penetrating gaze. "When honestly reflecting on yourself, you learn to be honest, and you stop believing your own lies."

Peter glared back.

The Jew set the handle of a chisel into a hole on the worktable so that its sharp edge pointed upward. He carried the rod to the table and set the bright, red section on the upright chisel. With a blow of the hammer, the chisel nearly cut the rod in two. The Jew slipped on a glove, grasped the scraper and, with a quick twist, freed it from the iron rod. He bounced the cloven point of the scraper's handle on the anvil until the handle's point was round.

The Jew said, "Enough with honesty. Let's reflect on it later." He threw the rough scraper into the slack tub next to the anvil. The water crackled on contact with the hot iron. He put the tip of the rod back into the fire and pumped the bellows.

Peter continued working on the chainmail ringlets.

After a time, the Jew spoke again. "When reflecting on yourself, you grow more tolerant of others because you see others as reflections of what you are or had been. Would a great knight be tolerant?"

"Tall-or-ant?"

"Tolerant. It means to honor those who look, act, or think differently from you."

Peter answered reluctantly. "A knight would honor good people."

"What if all people are good?"

Peter remembered stories of saintly warriors told by Father Ulrich. "He would honor people who stand against wrong, give food to the needy, shelter to the sick."

The Jew said, "Would he honor a blacksmith, a Jew, who gave you food and shelter, who stood against Lothair?"

Peter focused on riveting ringlets into Edzard's armor and mumbled, "No." The charcoal on the forge hissed.

The Jew put the glowing end of the iron on the anvil. "No?" He struck the hammer against the rod. "Custom allows a less tolerant master, like Thomas, to beat you for such disrespect." He struck again and again.

Peter whispered to himself, "A sorcerer don' need to beat his apprentice. A sorcerer would strike him dead with a curse."

The hammering stopped. Peter kept his head down but looked up through his eyebrows. The Jew held the hammer suspended and gazed at Peter with unfocused eyes. Had the Jew heard what he'd said? Peter tensed.

The shop was quiet. The distant hum of the fair seemed to retreat in fear. Not even the charcoal dared to hiss.

After a long while, the Jew's voice cut the silence. "A fructibus eorum cogniscetis eos."

The curse froze Peter's muscles. He squawked, dropped the ringlets, and fell like a rigid pole against the wall. He clutched his straining chest and his heartbeat roared in his ears.

The Jew laughed and put the iron back into the mound of charcoal. "Those are no evil words but a quote from your Holy Scriptures. It means, 'By their fruits you will know them.' Since you've been here, your cup has overflowed with good fruits from a good tree, has it not? Reflect on this for awhile."

Peter looked at the poultice and splints on his throbbing broken leg. Until now the Jew had protected him, sheltered him, fed him. He leaned again over the plate of ringlets and tried to breathe calmly, think clearly. Maybe Jacob wasn't a bad man, but he was still a Jew.

"Good," the Jew said. "Now that you've reflected on yourself and on me, let's look at how you see the world. What do you think of Jews?" He placed the hot iron over the upright chisel and dealt it a blow.

Peter hesitated, but resolved to answer truthfully. "Jews steal Christian children to sell for slaves, or for ... murder." His voice trailed off and he instantly regretted his answer.

The Jew blunted the scraper's cloven end on the anvil. "Before coming here, had you ever known or seen a Jew?"

"No. Just heard people talk. Probably not ... true."

The Jew threw the scraper toward the slack tub. Cool water snapped against hot metal slipping below its surface. He put the rod in the fire for the last of three scrapers. "Some lies contain a seed of truth. This lie is partly true."

"True?" Peter stiffened. "Did you, do you ..." He choked on his words.

The Jew squeezed the bellows a few times and stared into the fire. "At one time, yes," he finally answered. "Hebrews are in all lands: Latin, Greek, and Moslem. So it's easy to travel, to find comfort and aid, to trade exotic goods. Slaves were my goods, especially blond haired, blue eyed, fair skinned Slavs, pagans from northern lands who brought high prices in southern lands. The Latin Church disapproves of the slave trade to Muslims, saying that souls purchased by infidels and heretics would be lost from heaven. In truth the churchmen fear the Slavs would join the swelling ranks of Muslims besieging Christian lands. At first the churchmen bought Slavs from me and urged their princes to buy them too, at low prices, of course. Then they sent missionaries and warriors to the Slavs to make them Christian. With the empire expanding, more and more of my slaves were Christian.

"Sometimes poor Christian parents sold their unwanted children to slave traders. When they couldn't sell their children, they left the little ones in the forests to die. They blamed the Jews for the disappearances of their children, inventing stories of child theft and ritualized murder." He brought the glowing iron to the anvil and struck it again and again.

Peter held his breath until the violent hammer lay silent and the Jew returned the iron to the fire. The shadow of a cloud drifted over the shop and the air filled with dread.

The Jew removed the hot iron and set it upon the chisel. "We never stole or murdered children, but we were blamed for crimes committed by lying, murdering Christians." He struck the scraper once, twisted it free, blunted its handle on the anvil and threw it into the slack tub. The water popped with anger. He looked directly at Peter. "It was easy to hate you Christians."

Peter picked up the little hammer and pretended to scarf a ringlet. He kept a wary eye on the Jew, ready to swing the hammer in defense, and hoped someone would come through the open shop doors to save him.

"Aren't you glad," the Jew said, "that my hatred is long gone?" He laughed and pointed at Peter's hammer. "No need to defend yourself, Peter. My love for Christians is as great as my love for Jews."

The cloud moved off and the air lost its heaviness.

A tall merchant walked into the shop. "Greetings to God, Master blacksmith. I need a few sturdy hooks."

The blacksmith pointed at an array of hooks hanging from pegs on a wall, "Greetings to God, sir. If those hooks aren't what you want, more can be fashioned to your liking."

He winked at Peter. "We'll continue our discussion later."

CHAPTER 18
IMMORTALITY

Peter enjoyed Lucus' first visit. The novice furrier brought him dinner and relief from the Jew's lessons.

"Have you heard the old count died with his hauberk up and his breeches down?" Lucus asked.

Peter slurped boiled cabbage seasoned with rye seeds and nodded. "Why don' anybody suspect Lothair," Peter said with his mouth full. "He was mad at old Count Derek."

"Lothair is always angry," Lucus said. "Everyone but the bishop knows Maynard killed Derek. Edzard found Maynard's ring next to his dead father."

"But that doesn't mean Maynard killed him. Lothair could have put that ring there."

"Maynard was the last person to see Count Derek. They say the hunt went badly that day and everybody was scattered all over the forest. Lothair tried to round up everyone. He sent Maynard to find the old count. Maynard came back all mad and shaking, wouldn't tell anyone what happened." Lucus leaned forward. "He killed the old count because ... well ... because Count Derek used him like a woman."

Peter frowned. "What do you mean?"

"Count Derek liked dark skinned women, used to boast about the dark women he raped in southern lands. Maynard had dark skin."

Peter stopped eating. "But Maynard was a man."

"That didn't matter to Derek the Ram."

Peter's stomach knotted. He gave the last bite of cabbage to Lucus. "Why didn' Lord Maynard go to his own valley and stay away from the old count?"

Lucus licked the wood platter clean before answering, "Maynard had no valley. He was landless, a bastard nephew of the duke and, he was half Magyar, or half Saracen, or half Greek or half devil. Nobody knew what his father was. The duke sent him here, to the eastern fringe of the western empire. Maynard came here as a child. Derek used him like a woman."

The knot in Peter's stomach tightened and he grimaced. "What ish the custom for a man loving a man?"

Lucus whispered, "Banishment. Exile. But custom is wrong. Love is love, regardless. But Derek didn't love anyone. He used people. He was the count and he didn't care about custom. So it was fitting that Derek died with his hauberk up and his breeches down."

Peter motioned at the Jew. "Why don' he tells me about these things?"

"Master Jacob doesn't talk about people. He only talks about ideas. He's a good man." Lucus picked up his platter and bowed his head to the blacksmith before leaving.

"It is good to make friends," the blacksmith said to Peter. "Alchemists are not hermits. But don't talk about alchemy until you know what it is. Otherwise, you'll get yourself in trouble."

After a week the fair closed, foreign merchants left the free town, and orders for new tools slowed. Most residents of the free town came to the shop not for tools but for treatments for ailments that local remedies had not cured. The blacksmith gave them roots, herbs and advice, "Afflictions grow from seeds of faulty reasoning. Sever the roots and they'll wither away." While he prepared teas and potions, the locals talked of trade and weather, the death of the old count and Maynard, the intrigues of the bishop and the new count. Peter paid special attention to rumors that Lothair had not set foot again in the free town. The blacksmith never offered an opinion or a tidbit of gossip and, after the residents left, he would advise Peter, "Avoid the tangled undergrowth of worldly affairs."

When they were alone, the Jew prodded him with questions, forcing him to examine thoughts and feelings about himself, others, and the world. Concentrated reflections lessened Peter's hunger and fatigue. Slow breathing and chanting honed his concentration.

Latin exercises were welcomed breaks from reflection. He memorized the alphabet and, after six weeks of practice, he could read and speak simple sentences scratched on the shop's dirt floor. Rosamund would have been proud of him.

On the day of winter's first snow, Peter finished linking the last ring of universal essence in Edzard's chain mail tunics. "When do I finish all this reflecting? I want to move on."

Jacob covered a pot of leeks in broth and placed it on hot

coals in the forge. "Reflection is a process that's never finished. But since you want to move on, you can start walking. You've sat on that mattress long enough."

"Walk?" Peter shook his head. "No. Not yet."

The blacksmith sat on a stool next to Peter and asked, "What have your reflections taught you about your body?"

"When hungry or sick, I can control it with my thoughts. My mind makes me strong."

"Your mind can't make you strong. It may seem to help your imperfect body, but your mind is also imperfect. It can't control anything by itself. Your mind is either flowing with creation or fighting against it, but your mind never controls creation. It's only a tool, like your body."

"Then why do you make me do these mind exercises?"

"To sharpen your tool. To learn its use. Just as the furnace walls are used to reflect heat inward, so is your mind used to reflect thoughts inward, to cook yourself in your thoughts. Trouble, which seems to attack from outside, actually has its source inside. Do Jews still scare you?"

"No. Not like before."

"Jews haven't changed but you have. The Jews of your fears existed only in your mind. Do you still distrust me?"

Peter looked away. "Not as much. My thinking has changed."

"Good. An honest answer. Do you still lie to hide your perceived shortcomings?"

Peter's face burned with embarrassment. He shook his head.

"You're learning to use your mind instead of letting it use you." The blacksmith held out his hand to Peter. "Let's walk together."

After a moment of hesitation, Peter picked up Lothair's baton at the foot of the mattress, grasped Jacob's hand, and grunted to his feet. He balanced all his weight on his good leg, which wobbled from six weeks of disuse. He took a deep breath and chanted, "Benedicamus Dominoooooooo – uh oh." He toppled onto Jacob.

The blacksmith held him up and said, "Open the door of your furnace and let the universal essence use your tools. Every step you take, however small, brings the rest of the world with you, because the world is your body, not this little sack of flesh with puny arms and legs."

Peter gripped Jacob's hand tighter and dragged the splints half a pace forward. The tightly bound splints protruded below the foot of his broken leg. The pressure from standing shifted to the tight knots of cloth around his thigh and to the tops of the splints pushing into his hip and groin, thus keeping his weight off the wounded leg. He planted the baton parallel to the splints, hopped his good leg forward and groaned. His good leg ached. He tottered like a baby learning to walk.

The blacksmith said, "You may feel trapped within layers of skin, blood, and bone, hostage to their needs, appetites, and afflictions. But when you see the body is just a tool, it helps you realize that you are not the tool, that you are, in reality, the invulnerable craftsman. When the work is done, you put aside the tool because the tool is not the work, it's not you, it's not real. Take another step."

Peter dragged his splints forward, planted his stick and hopped with a grunt. "Not real? My body ish real. My leg ish really broken. If not, why you put splints on it?"

"Because your mind believes your leg is broken. With a sharpened mental tool, you can cut through shifting layers of cloudy thoughts and feelings, which hide your true nobility. When you find your quarry, the unreal mind that holds deceptions dear disappears. Take another step."

Peter grunted forward again. "Are you saying my mind ish unreal, too? But that leaves nothing."

"Everything came out of nothing, so we must look for the nothing in everything. There is nothing more real than no thing. Reality is the only illusion."

"That makes no sense," Peter said. "My REAL mind says that if I don' sit down REAL soon, I am going to REALLY hurt my REAL body."

The blacksmith laughed and helped Peter turn around. With another hop, he was one step closer to his mattress.

"If nothing ish real, what the world for?" Peter asked.

"Healing, perhaps. What is your leg made of?"

Peter answered, "Skin, then blood, and then broken bones."

"Which of the four elements is your leg made of?"

Peter answered, "Blood ish water. Bone ish earth. Skin ish ... uh ... both water and earth."

"Take another step. Good. Now tell me what unifies the elements?"

"The universal essence."

The blacksmith nodded. "The content within the form. The power within every thing. Think of a hauberk. The rings of the four elements are all made of the same material: iron. If the rings are not connected, what do we have?"

"A pile of rings."

"Exactly. The prima materia in shapeless piles. We give it form, but we mustn't mistake form for content. We can shape iron into a hauberk, a scraper, a hook, or any number of forms with the help of our tools, only if we remember the content: iron. The universal essence is the content for everything. We shape its forms with our tools but never its content. One more step."

After the last hop, Peter's good leg buckled and the blacksmith helped him down to the mattress. Peter leaned back against the wall, clutching his walking baton, and whispered, "That ish too strange. I don' understand all this stuff. Why you want me to be your apprentice?"

The alchemist brought the soup pot to the worktable. "The counselor told me," he said and removed the pot's lid.

The smell of sweet leeks in broth wafted into Peter's corner and his stomach rumbled. He licked his lips and asked, "Has he been back since I became your apprentice?"

Jacob scooped out the heart from a half round of bread. "The counselor is here now." He ladled soup into the hollowed round and dropped shavings from a cheese block into the broth.

Peter glanced around the empty shop before asking, "What do you mean?"

"Spirit," Jacob answered.

Peter sat up. "You talk to spirits?"

The blacksmith brought Peter the steaming soup in the bread bowl. "There's only one spirit, just another form, another tool in the universal essence. It's everywhere, a friend, father, mother. It scared me, too, the first time it came."

"What happened?" Peter asked and sipped the soup.

"It told me to play dead. You'll hear the story later."

"Gots to hear it now, please."

Jacob returned to the worktable. "No. You must eat in quiet."

Peter put the soup down. "Then I eat later."

Jacob nodded. He leaned against the table and stared at a burning candle. After a few moments he said, "Before the freetown, before the empire spread this far east, this was a small village. A few Jewish families lived here, along with Slavic farmers and herders, and a couple of Latin missionary monks. At that time, your hamlet to the east was greater, a pioneer settlement of a Christian chieftain with many serfs and slaves and ploughmen."

"Were you all alchemists, I mean, you and the other Jews?" Peter asked.

Jacob's eyes seemed to stare at distant images. "No. We were slave merchants. We built the bridge across the river. This valley was between the Slavs in the east and north and our slave markets in the west and south. We felt safe here. When one of us was away, we looked after each other's families. We celebrated holy days and weddings together. My son married and had children. My daughter was about to marry. On the day of her wedding, the Magyars rode into the valley. My son, wife, and my grandchildren were killed. My daughter was carried into slavery."

"What about you?" Peter asked.

"Wounded, terribly." Jacob spoke softly. "During the slaughter, a voice spoke directly to me, counseling me to pretend death."

"That spirit saved you?"

"Yes. The Magyars assumed they had killed me. Everything was destroyed, except for me. Grief overwhelmed me. Hatred consumed me. Desire for revenge and fear for my daughter nourished my pursuit, my bleeding pursuit of the Magyars. I followed their trail to Lechfeld, some distance to the west. There news came that they lost a battle with the emperor. Only seven Magyars survived and the emperor cut off their ears and sent them back to their tribes, the On Ugar, with a warning never to raid again. But hatred pushed me after those last seven, to the south and east, until my wounds finally felled me a few days later. Christian churchmen found me near death and healed me in their monastery. They taught me alchemy."

"Ever find your daughter?"

"No."

"Know what happened to her?"

"No."

Peter sat in silence for a few moments and recalled Bertha's stories about Magyars. Something was wrong with Jacob's story.

"In my village," Peter said, "there ish a very old woman. She ish much older than you. When the Magyars attacked, she was a very small child. But you were a grown man, a grandfather."

The Jew turned to Peter with unfocused eyes. His gaze crawled through Peter's skin and scratched at his heart. "You don't believe my story," the Jew said.

Fear slithered back into Peter's mind. He picked up the baton. The thick wooden stick trembled in his tight grip. "Been a long time since the Magyars attacked. You gots to be much, much older ... or even ... dead."

"And that would be true if it were not for alchemy."

For a long while, the Jew's response churned through Peter's mind until a shocking idea burst through his fear. "Do ... do you mean you ... you don' gets old?" Peter's heart raced. "Ish that the meaning ... ish that the goal of alchemy?"

"That's the goal of life, to live forever and enjoy each moment." The alchemist pointed at the bread bowl next to Peter. "The meaning of life is to eat your soup before it gets cold."

Peter was no longer hungry.

CHAPTER 19
THE OPEN DOOR

White steam from Lucus' platter spiraled through still, winter air inside the blacksmith shop. Peter swallowed another mouthful of lentils before continuing his story. "So then Lord Helmut rebelled against Count Derek and the old count killed him and gave his valley to Lord Norbert and gave Lothair, who was Helmut's son, to the monks and the monks couldn' tame him 'cause he was a headstrong child and they gave him back to Count Derek."

Lucus nodded. "Yes. Well, so what?"

Peter glanced at the blacksmith who sawed a piece of wood on the worktable. "But don' you see?" he whispered. "Lothair hated Derek the Ram for killing his father and taking away his valley, and the old count kept Lothair loyal with a promise of land until Lothair saw it was a lie and he killed the old count."

Lucus shook his head. "You're saying that because Lothair broke your leg. Everybody knows Maynard killed the old count. The old count was hot with lust because Master Jacob was giving him vervain tea."

Peter gave Lucus the last bite of lentils and said, "Jacob gives many people vervain. It improves the fluids."

Lucus gulped the lentils without chewing them. "Vervain protects you from witches and attracts the favors of young women. It makes an old man lustful again. Master Jacob gave Count Derek many potions of vervain just before he died."

Peter remembered one of Gisela's secrets that Rosamund had once whispered to him. "In my village, when Lord Arnulf felt old and weak, the village healer buried a carline thistle root during the new moon and poured blood from a ram over it. Then she dug it out during the full moon."

Lucus rolled his eyes. "Typical serf remedy." He moved to stand and pointed at Peter's new footwear. "Leather. Very nice. Big enough to fit over your splints. You walking now?"

Peter grabbed his friend's cloak and pulled him closer. "Gots to know one more thing. How does someone live forever?"

"What?' Lucus said.

Peter asked, "You know someone who lives forever?"

Lucus smiled. "Last summer, Master Thomas and I were trading far to the south. We met someone the locals called a wizard. They said he never got hungry or sick or tired. I guess if you never got sick and tired, you'd live forever. He was a strange goat, never did anything without first asking a spirit he called 'the counselor.' But everyone respected him, especially the local warriors." He nodded to Peter, stood and bowed his head to Jacob before leaving the shop with his empty dinner plate.

Jacob shut the doors behind Lucus and laid a few cleavers and knives on a hemp cloth next to Peter. "These tools have to be sharpened." He brought Peter a bucket of water and a whetstone.

Peter dipped the whetstone in the water. "When does the counselor speak to you?"

Jacob measured a piece of wood. "All the time. The counselor is speaking to you now."

Peter stopped stroking the whetstone against a knife, cocked his head and listened. A charcoal popped in the forge and the wind whistled outside. "I don' hear anything," he said.

Jacob began sawing the wood. "You're too busy to listen. Sometimes the counselor breaks through your clutter in times of stress. But when you open your door, the counselor comes every day and all day as a voice or a vision or, more often than not, a feeling. Sometimes all you have to do is ask a question to get an answer."

"Then I ask how I gets respect from the warriors, from Lothair?" Peter said to the ceiling.

"You'll need to reflect on -"

"I reflected for weeks. I gots to try a question, please."

Jacob put down the saw and nodded. "Start with a sharpened mind."

Peter leaned back, closed his eyes and breathed slowly. "Benedicamus Dominooooooooooommm," he whispered, the last syllable humming in his mouth as his lips closed around it. After a few chants, the humming heightened his senses and concentrated his mind. He whispered, "How do I gets Lothair to -"

"*You gots the power now.*" A confident voice thrust itself upon him before he could finish his question. On its heels flew a shrill voice, "*For your sins, you will be hated.*" More voices rushed from dark recesses of his mind, each sounded like his own voice in different moods. *"You greater than Lothair" "You gots to be honored and worshiped and adored and -" "How dare you ask such a question." "I command you gets revenge on Lothair." "Follow the example Gabriel follows."*

Gabriel? Peter opened his eyes and shook his head. "Too many voices."

Jacob chuckled and said, "Bewildering, isn't it?"

Peter resumed sharpening the knife. "They just thoughts."

"True, but which thought belongs to the counselor? Spirit never flatters, interrupts, or commands. It is selfless. Don't get attached to the counselor because it's not real either, just another tool like your mind and body. You'll learn to discern the selfless voice from the selfish ones. But if you follow the selfish voices, you'll learn form without content and you'll deform your world like a sorcerer or a fool."

"A fool like Gabriel," Peter said. He tossed the finished knife onto an oily cloth.

"Your brother is no fool," the blacksmith said.

Peter frowned, selected a second knife, and brushed its blade. "When Count Edzard finds out what an idiot he ish, he kick Gabriel out of the castle just like he did me. My fool brother -"

The blacksmith interrupted, "Perhaps you should begin developing the second quality of your furnace." He pulled the furnace door out by a handle in its center. "How do we use this door?"

Peter said, "If I gets too hot from the heat of reflection, then I gets out the door."

Jacob laughed and said, "You're the heat inside and you're also the door outside. When you heart is open, you're open to boundless power." He slid the stone door back into the furnace. "But three barriers obscure your power."

"Fear, aggression, and shame," Peter said, proud that he remembered one of Jacob's lessons.

Jacob scraped splinters off a piece of wood. "You open your door by dissolving your self, becoming selfless."

Peter paused striking the knife. "How can I not be me? Nothing ish left."

"Exactly," Jacob said. "How can you not be you? You start by not judging anyone or anything, by accepting them as worthy of honor. Then you can serve them with detachment, without any effort, without any selfish interest in the outcome of your service. You can start today by … by accepting Gabriel as worthy of honor."

Peter threw the second knife against the first. "Gabriel ish not worthy of any honor."

The blacksmith scraped another piece of wood. "Well then, you can start by not judging Lothair, by not gossiping about him with Lucus."

Peter picked up a cleaver. "I don' gossip. I gets news." He brushed the cleaver hard.

"You can be more selfless by reducing the number of times you say 'I' when speaking."

Peter pushed the whetstone as hard as he could. "And you can reduce the number of times you say 'you' when speaking." Harsh scraping and brushing devoured all other sounds until he threw the sharpened cleaver to clang against the finished knives. He felt the penetrating gaze of the Jew and he glared back.

"Sorry, Peter. These are only suggestions. If you, or rather, if we reflect on it, we'll find many selfless ways to open the door, to discern what's true." The Jew fit the finished pieces of wood into a short-legged study table. "Sharpen those tools again, please."

"Why?"

The Jew brought the short table to Peter's mattress, picked up a sharpened knife, and pointed to a nick in its gleaming edge. "You dulled them again when you threw them against each other in anger. We must take care of our tools."

Peter growled, "Why don' you sharpen them with magic? You an alchemist."

"That would take away your freedom and power to act, and your responsibility for your actions." The Jew smiled and placed the magic Bible on Peter's new shortened table.

Raucous confusion outside interrupted their argument. Peter gladly pushed aside the tools, hobbled to the double doors, opened them, and peered out.

At the base of the hill, a group of children laughed and ran around a warrior who led three limping horses up the frozen road. The warrior walked backwards, pulling the horses' reins with one hand and stroking their noses with the other. His bowl shaped helmet and chainmail tunic glinted in the cold light. He was taller than any of the men watching from the roadside. He was as tall as ...

"Lothair," Peter whispered. He banged the double doors shut and cried, "Oh God. Lothair ish coming."

CHAPTER 20
THE COUNSELOR

"Gots to hide." Peter twisted his head from side to side, looking about the shop. "Nowhere to hide." He jumped when the Jew touched his shoulder.

"Wait," the Jew said.

Looking past him to the garden door, Peter cried, "Go out the back." He hobbled quickly, tangled his good leg in Lothair's baton and fell, arms flailing. His head bounced off the hard floor and his baton clattered against his splints.

The blacksmith bent down to check Peter's leg. "Don't move," said Jacob.

The front doors swung open and the tall warrior entered, a black silhouette against the bleak sunlight outside. Three dark horses stood behind him. Their icy breath spurted from their nostrils.

Peter squawked and his heart galloped.

The tall warrior took off his round iron helmet and pulled his chainmail hood back from his head. The light behind his darkened face shone through his tasseled hair like the halos Peter had seen in drawings of saints in the magic Bible. The children in the street hooted with scorn.

Jacob strode to the door and the children fled. He looked at Peter and said, "Those children fear Jews as much as you did." He turned to the warrior. "Greetings to God, Gabriel."

"Gabriel?" Peter squeaked.

Jacob laughed and said, "Did you think Lothair would let children taunt him?"

The warrior turned his face to the light coming from the entrance and Peter recognized his brother's foolish grin. Gabriel's hair had grown long over the cross shaved on his head.

Gabriel gave the reins to the blacksmith, walked to Peter, pulled him off the floor and hugged him. "Greetings to God, little brother," he bellowed.

Peter gagged from his brother's stench. "In a warrior hauberk?"

"His hauberk is not a pretty one," Jacob said. "Rusted and brittle. Holes in some places. And the aketon," the blacksmith pointed at the thick undershirt visible through a tear in the ringlets, "the aketon is caked with mud or manure or both. Lothair doesn't want you to forget you were once a serf."

Gabriel held his nose and said, "Sweet as spring planted fields."

The blacksmith roared with laughter.

Peter almost shouted his question. "You a warrior?"

Gabriel nodded. "No warrior just voyager they want to put soldier afoot no sword no stick will not permit to smite in spite what they think think me not."

"He never makes any sense," Peter said to Jacob.

"He said the young count wants to make him a foot soldier," the blacksmith said. "But he refuses to carry a weapon."

Gabriel turned and stroked the white star pattern on a horse's nose, the same horse that bit Peter the day of the battle with Maynard. "Frozen mud makes the stud wore and sore."

Jacob picked up the horse's leg and studied the hoof. "Poor creatures. Edzard neglects them every year until the frozen ground wears the hooves down." He motioned to Peter. "Come, have a look."

Peter backed away. "Don' like horses."

"Shoeing is part of smithing, but you can learn it later."

"Lothair won' come for hauberks," Gabriel said. "Sent me to come for whole works."

Jacob said to Peter, "Why don't you show Gabriel the hauberks you finished for the count," He tied the horses' reins to the circular doorknocker, dabbed a salve on their sore hooves, and shaped them with a knife and file. Then he formed the iron shoes on the forge and anvil.

Peter sat on his mattress and draped the chainmail armor over his lap. Gabriel folded himself onto a stool nearby. Peter explained how to make chainmail armor, how each ring was heated, scarfed, reheated, punched, pinched, and riveted.

Gabriel grinned and said nothing.

Peter explained how the central ring, the ring of universal essence, unified the surrounding rings of the four elements, how all the rings were made of the same essence and how this essence could be formed to make different things.

Gabriel grinned and said nothing.

Peter shook his head and bit his nails. It was useless explaining anything to a fool, especially a fool in stinking, rusting chain mail armor, armor that Peter should be wearing. He had almost gained the honor of wearing a hauberk, but Gabriel took his dream from him. Why couldn't Count Edzard see what a fool Gabriel was?

With the shop's doors open, the interior turned cold enough for the brothers to see their breath. Finally the blacksmith nailed the last horseshoe and said, "We'll load the hauberks onto the horses and you, Gabriel, can take them to the count."

"No," Gabriel said to the blacksmith. "You go the armor to bestow the count wants to see what makes Lothair flee he be no glee."

"Agreed," the blacksmith said. "When we give the count his new hauberks, let's ask him why you can't get a cleaner aketon and hauberk." He beckoned to Peter, "Give us the hauberks."

With a furious grunt, Peter swept the metal tunics from his mattress and threw them to the floor with such force that clouds of ash swirled into the air. "This fool gots the hauberk that was meant for ME. Life ish not fair." His shouts hung in an icy cloud.

Gabriel's eyes arched with concern. "What ish fair be seen by some obscene by some a dream fear blocks the plots of the living no harm when armed with forgiving."

Peter's eyes teared. "Shut up. You don' make sense."

The blacksmith picked up the crumpled hauberks. "He said life's fairness depends on how you look at it. Fear blocks life, but forgiveness removes fear, restores life."

Peter waved his arms. "He ish an IDIOT. How can you understand an idiot?" He limped up to Gabriel and thrust a finger in his face. "You are a FOOL. You were always a fool and you always be a fool. You never be a warrior. You took away MY chance for greatness."

"Greatness to all answer the call within," Gabriel said. "Without assert the hurt in vain no gain so stop and ordain let reign your greatness."

"He said greatness is within us all," the blacksmith said, "but aggression is a barrier to greatness. Stop attacking and let your nobility rule."

Stop attacking? The translation rang in Peter like the snap of a battle baton breaking over Gabriel's knee and echoing off the castle walls. His elder brother had spoken those words when he disarmed Lothair in the castle. His brother had saved him from death and all Peter could do in their first meeting since that time was to spit venom at his brother. Peter staggered back, collapsed on his mattress and let his tears fall. "I just a cripple ... attacking my fool brother. How can I ... How can I be great at anything?"

Gabriel sat beside Peter and put a hand on his shoulder. "Guilt shows the light ish bright within you know the pure endure within dig deep and quarry and don' you worry of barriers to warriors of infinite good."

Jacob spoke softly, "He said your shame proves that you know you're not expressing your noble essence. Go through your barriers to your quarry of unending good."

Peter wiped away his tears. "Barriers? You mean fear, aggression, and shame?"

Jacob nodded. "You just showed all three; fear of life's unfairness, aggression against your brother, and shame at your behavior."

It took a moment for Peter to understand. He nodded and mumbled, "Sorry."

"Nothing happened," Gabriel said and stood up. "Dig deep and quarry, and don' you worry. Spirit ish there. Do not despair."

Peter asked, "Does Gabriel know about the quarry ... and the spirit, too?"

Jacob took the horses' reins and said, "Some of us always hear the counselor."

Gabriel bowed his head to Peter. After he and Jacob led the horses outside, they shut the front doors.

Cold, white light from the winter sun streaked in thin rays through cracks around the back door and window, slicing into pieces the smoky air and the red glow from dying charcoal in the forge. Peter shivered alone in silent half-darkness and buried his head in his hands, ashamed of his behavior. "Oh God," he said. "Why do I gots to learn about these barriers?"

A small voice answered, *"You must see they are unreal, like a fog that clouds your source."*

Peter glanced around the shop for the person speaking but saw no one. He sat still and listened, but heard nothing.

"What ish my source?" he whispered. "God, universal essence, my quarry, or what?"

The voice was soft but clear. *"Yes."*

After a few stunned moments, he decided to test the voice. His next question was unspoken, asked only in silent thought. If God is so great, why wouldn't He get rid of the barriers for everyone?

The voice was everywhere, but distinct. *"That would take away your freedom and power."*

For a moment, Peter believed the counselor had spoken. In the next, he doubted it. He wavered between fear and elation.

CHAPTER 21
CHURNING BUTTER

Rosamund slipped through the double doors of the hamlet's communal building and scanned its smoky interior for Gisela and Karl. Nearly every villager labored inside, in the animal stalls, work alcoves, storage bins, or around the central fireplace. She spotted Gisela's gray hair and stooped shoulders in the pickling alcove halfway down the building's sixty-pace length. Karl brushed Lord Arnulf's horse in another stall at the far end of the building.

She pulled her winter cloak closer and touched the wolf brooch Peter had carved for her. Poor Peter. Beaten to death for dreaming too loudly. She, too, could be beaten to death for simply being herself.

She bowed her head to let her fine blond hair drape over her cheeks and hide the bruise under her left eye. Pungent smells of animals, cured skins and pickled cabbage churned her stomach. She stepped toward Gisela and stifled the rising nausea by concentrating on her newly repaired pigskin boots. Her mumbled greetings formed frosty clouds as she passed the chatter of children collecting frozen dung in the sheep corral, the grind of iron against a circular whetstone in the tool stall, the rasp of a saw in the carpentry booth, and the rustle of reeds from basket weavers around the central fire. She stopped at the pickling alcove, where Gisela directed her helpers to stir salt into a vat of steaming water.

Gisela shook a dried turnip in Rosamund's face. "Karl told us you would be late."

All activity stopped. The building grew quiet.

Rosamund tossed her hair back, no longer hiding her black eye. She should have known Karl would brag about it this morning. "I wasn' going out until I stitched the holes in my boots."

Gisela shook her head. "No excuse. Not even Karl can beat any sense into you." She pointed the turnip to the back of the building. "Take Frieda's place."

Rosamund felt the sting of critical eyes and disapproving whispers as she walked past other villagers to where Frieda and Grandma Bertha churned milk in two hollowed out logs. Rosamund held her head high and looked directly at Karl in the horse's stall.

He scowled back at her.

Frieda stood up and left her churning log without a word. Bertha greeted Rosamund with a toothless smile before doubling over her own churn in a coughing fit. Her coughs froze into tumbling billows. She wore the red wool from Count Edzard tied around her gray head. Rosamund hugged her grandmother, sat on the vacant stool, put her knees on either side of the churn, grasped the plunger with both hands, and began stirring the cream through a hole in the lid.

Pushing and pulling, she matched her frosty breathing to the thumping of the plunger. She inhaled deeply through her nose and exhaled through her mouth. After a time of rhythmic breath and movement, her mind eased and warmth spread all the way to her fingers and toes.

A sudden attack of nausea stopped her rhythm. She held her hand against her mouth and swallowed until the sickness left her.

"All the women know." Grandma Bertha's words drifted by as a white wisp.

"What?" Rosamund asked, knowing already what Bertha meant.

Bertha's lips trembled with cold. "You pregnant. Does Karl know?"

Rosamund shook her head. "So hard to talk to him."

Bertha touched Rosamund's stomach with a shaking hand. "Men too stupid to see it. Soon it be obvious. Don' gets Karl angry again. He can hurt your unborn. Might kill it. Be careful."

Rosamund squeezed Bertha's hand. "Thank you. You too old to be in the cold." She opened Bertha's churn and looked inside. "These not even half full. I scoop out yours into mine. Go sit by the fire where you belong. Makes no sense for both of us to do this."

"Custom tells us how much goes into a churn," Bertha said.

"We gots to do what right," Rosamund said, "not what custom."

"But when the cream hardens -" Bertha turned away in another coughing fit.

"I can do it," Rosamund said. "I am younger and stronger. Go over to the fire."

Bertha shook her head. "You gots a lovely, open heart. But

Gisela -" A coughing spell knocked her off the stool.

Rosamund helped her stand and led her to the fire. "Don' worry about me. Churning makes me warm." She fastened her own cloak around Bertha's neck with Peter's wolf brooch.

Rosamund returned to the churns and ladled one into the other.

Gisela stomped up to Rosamund's churn and thumped it with her walking stick. "What you doing?"

The communal house grew quiet again. All work stopped.

Rosamund scraped the last bit of cream from Bertha's churn into her churn and faced Gisela. "Grandma Bertha ish too old and sick for this work."

Gisela pointed a bony finger at Rosamund. "Gots too much in your churn. Don' do that."

"I work harder. Besides, I came late, so you can say I make up lost work."

"That don' matter. You cannot break custom."

Rosamund looked past Gisela and addressed the others. "Custom without heart ish no good. We gots to stop, think inside how we see custom, how we see each other and everything."

Gisela put her hands on her hips. "Let Father Ulrich do the preaching."

Rosamund sat and stirred the churn, pushing and pulling the plunger. "Gots to open our hearts."

The cream began thickening and the plunger began sticking. Doubling the cream seemed to require tripling the effort to churn it. Clouds of her frozen breath grew larger and came quicker as she panted from the strain.

Gisela tapped her foot on the ground. No one else in the building resumed work. Everyone watched the two women. Stirring the churn became more and more difficult but Rosamund refused to quit.

"Stupid girl," Gisela hissed and motioned to Karl. "Shut her up."

He marched forward, swinging his long arms, clinching his fists.

"Rosamund," he barked. "Shut up. Do what Gisela says or I blacken your other eye."

Gisela stepped aside.

"Don' touch her," Bertha called from the fire. "She ish with child."

Karl stopped a pace short of the churn.

Rosamund bowed her head and tensed, but didn't stop churning. She grunted against the stubborn plunger. "Gots to ... be like ... the saints -"

Something told her to duck her head. *"Hurry,"* it said. She hesitated and in the next moment, Karl's fist thumped her temple, knocking her onto the hard frozen ground.

Somewhere behind swirling lights, Karl growled, "Just shut up. Who you trying to be? Saint Rosamund?"

Darkness swallowed the lights.

CHAPTER 22
THE CRUCIBLE

Peter placed a cup of hot birch bark beer on the worktable before Father Ulrich and bowed his head.

The little priest spoke to Jacob sitting across the table, "We were shorthanded at harvest time. Praise God we finished before the first frost. I heard Peter broke his leg twice. That means he'll be crippled forever. I won't ask for his return since he can never work again. He would be a burden to us. But the villagers will be glad to hear he's alive."

"How ish Rosamund?" Peter asked.

"She and Karl are healthy. She's with child," Father Ulrich said.

Peter's head drooped lower. "Pregnant?"

"Yes. What message do you want me to take to the villagers?"

"Nothing," Peter mumbled. "Don' tell them anything." He hobbled back to his mattress, pulled his winter cloak tighter against the cold and chewed his fingernails.

Father Ulrich sipped his steaming cup. "I'll be spending less time in my father's valley because Edzard is threatening Bishop Bernard even more. When Edzard returned with Maynard's head on his spear, he didn't lament his father's death. No, instead he complained that his father and Bishop Bernard arranged his marriage to Lady Lilli. Strange behavior for a grieving son, don't you think?"

"Judge not, and you will not be judged," Jacob answered.

Father Ulrich continued, "While Maynard waited for his inquisition to begin, he confessed to Bishop Bernard many evil things, but not murder. He was adamant that someone else killed the old count. Derek was killed from behind, something only a coward would do. The monks think Edzard purposely dropped Maynard's ring by his murdered father and -"

Jacob interrupted, "Jesus didn't concern himself with worldly affairs."

Father Ulrich frowned. "How can a Jew know anything about Jesus?" He untied a leather sack from his sword belt and tossed it onto the table. It landed with muffled clinking. "Here are five pounds of silver. Fashion the silver into the shape of a cross. Make hollow places about half the length of a finger in each arm and cover those spaces with silver filigree. Bishop Bernard needs a reliquary. At this year's market fair he obtained four holy splinters from the cross on which our Lord God was crucified. On Christmas day, we'll display the holy splinters in the reliquary." He stood to go. "I didn't believe the rumors that you were wealthy until today." The little priest pointed at Jacob's study table to which was tied a candleholder for several candles. "Who can afford to burn nine candles at once?"

Jacob said, "A new candle is lit each day during Hanukkah, the Hebrew festival of -"

"Don't infect Peter with your false beliefs," Father Ulrich interrupted. "I expect to see him at mass when he's well enough. You're welcome, too. The true faith has spread to other nonbelievers: Norsemen, Slavs, Magyars. The end times have come and the true faith will rule the world for the next thousand years." He moved to the door. "Wouldn't you rather rule than be ruled?"

The blacksmith bowed his head and said, "We will make a reliquary fit for a ruler."

After Father Ulrich left, Jacob brought Peter a gray, stoneware crucible. "This is a good time to learn the furnace's third quality."

Peter spit out a fingernail. "Tired of cooking myself."

Jacob laughed. "Then while you're still hot, you can pour yourself from the crucible into the mold of your ideal. As a Christian, what is your ideal, your goal, your dream?"

"A true warrior," Peter grumbled. "That ish what I told everyone at the village. I can never go back."

"Who knows the way to become a true warrior? Who would you mold yourself after?"

"The count. No. Lord Arnulf, or his son, Father Ulrich, or the bishop or ... the saints?"

Jacob placed the magic Bible on Peter's short-legged study table at the foot of the mattress. "When a disciple asked who knows the way, what was the answer?" He flipped a few pages and pointed to a verse.

Peter read it and said, "Jesus Christ? How can He be my ideal? He was the Son of God."

"We're all children of God. We're all part of the universal essence."

"I am not Jesus Christ. I could not even copy Him."

"The ideal is not to be copied, but to be lived."

Peter shook his head. "How can you know anything about Jesus Christ?"

The blacksmith flipped another page and pointed.

Peter read the Latin aloud, "Jesus replied, ... 'Where I am going, ... thou cannot follow now, ... but ... thou will follow later." The blacksmith pointed to another page and Peter read, "... anyone who has faith in me ... will do what I have done. He will do ... even greater things.'"

Jacob walked across the shop and tossed Peter a ball of wax from a shelf. "This is your mind."

Peter caught the milky white ball that was twice the size of his fist. "Beeswax?"

"Yes. Soft and malleable." Jacob dropped the clinking pouch of silver onto Peter's mattress. "You will make the holy reliquary."

"But I never made one before. Never even seen one."

Jacob sat at his study table. "Good. Your work will be unrestricted by convention. Use your fingers and a knife to form the wax into a cross. Carve holes in each arm to hold the holy splinters. Open the door of your creativity to selfless service."

For the rest of the day, Peter worked the beeswax over a platter of hot charcoal; kneading, pushing, pulling, slicing, cutting, carving, and sweating from exertion. He finished the basic cross form with a rectangular opening in each arm as nightfall came early – too early, Peter thought.

"Yes," Jacob said. "At this time of year, we only have eight hours of daylight. Use the evening to plan how the reliquary will look. Impress your spirit with pictures in the Bible."

Peter flipped through pages of the Bible by candlelight. He studied the pictures in the margins and frontis pages. He marveled at twisting vines rhythmically crossing the pages, animals familiar and exotic leaping through leafy mazes, saints and prophets with sharply folded robes and golden halos gesturing under heavenly canopies.

The next morning, with his small but familiar knife, he carved those flat images into the wax. Leafy vines climbed and intertwined, foxes chased rabbits up and down and across, and in the middle of the cross, the head of Christ reigned within a halo of concentric circles. He forgot to eat and nightfall rushed unexpectedly upon him again.

The following day, he carved details; the serrated edges of leaves, the furry flanks of animals and the noble face of his ideal. Every time he thought he was finished, he'd find a new flaw and worked longer to complete a forgotten twist of a vine, to balance a group of leaves by adding or subtracting a single leaf, to groom the fur of the animals into more realistic patterns. That night he showed his work to Jacob.

"Very good," Jacob said. "Very detailed. Now bring a pot of clay, a bag of fine sand, and a bowl of water."

Peter assembled the ingredients and mixed them according to Jacob's instructions.

"First you impressed your spirit with your ideal," Jacob said as Peter stirred the soupy clay. "Then you formed your mind with the impressions of your spirit. Now your body will follow the impressions of your mind." The blacksmith tested the loam with his finger. "It's ready."

Peter placed the wax model face up on the floor and poured the mixture over it. "How can my body follow my ideal? Christ ish not here for me to follow."

Jacob answered, "Just as the clay conforms to the shape of the beeswax, so will you conform to the shape of your thought. Before you do anything, ask yourself, 'What would my ideal do?' and then do according to the answer." Jacob returned to his study table. "This layer must dry completely before you pour another coat. In this cold weather, that might take all night."

The next morning, Peter mixed and poured another layer of clay onto his model. While he studied from his shortened table, he frequently reached out from under his winter cloak to test the mold's dryness. The loam remained wet as midday approached.

"Why don' we fire up the forge, heat up the shop, make the

clay dry faster?" Peter asked.

"Would Christ be impatient?" the blacksmith asked from his own study table.

Peter grumbled, "Want it dry before Christmas. What you know about Christ anyway?"

"As much as any churchman."

"You don' know as much as the bishop."

The blacksmith smiled and nodded.

"No," Peter said. "He ish a great churchman … a warrior … a nobleman."

The Jew got up from his table and walked to the charcoal bin. "That's right. Bishop Bernard is a nobleman, a cousin to Emperor Otto. As long as the emperor controls this valley and other strategic dioceses around the empire, he stays informed of any rebellions his unruly dukes may be planning. Edzard's father plotted with Duke Heinrich's father to overthrow their emperor. Even though Heinrich the Good is not like his quarrelsome father, Bishop Bernard still needs to watch Edzard." He emptied a basket of charcoal onto the forge. "Temporal power, not spiritual power, is the bishop's primary role."

Peter said, "He ish a learned churchman."

The Jew pumped the bellows. Fingers of fire stretched above the charcoal. "True. And he seems more learned each time we meet."

"That ish how you learned the Bible, from the bishop."

The blacksmith retrieved another basket of charcoal. "Two thirds of your Bible are the Torah, the Prophets and the Writings, all of them Hebrew Scriptures. The last third, the Christian third, was taught to me in the monastery while healing from Magyar wounds."

He emptied the basket under the furnace and fed it breath from the bellows. "When you stay in a monastery, you must follow their rules. At sunrise we rose for the service of Prime. Those who couldn't work, the infirm such as me, were required to study the teachings of the Christ. Three hours later we celebrated mass at Terce and then we studied again. At noon came the service of Sext and after that, lunch. Speaking was forbidden while eating, and we listened to a brother read our studies from the refectory pulpit.

Then came a short service, Nones, and more study. Vespers was at twilight. We ate supper silently and studied again. After the service of Compline, we meditated on our studies in the Great Silence and went to bed. We slept in our habits and stockings to be ready to rise at midnight, and chant our studies for the service of Nocturnes. Before dawn we performed the service of Matins and Lauds."

The glow from both fires tinted Jacob's hair and beard red. The shop grew so warm Peter had to remove his winter cloak.

Jacob continued, "The Christian ideal was foremost in every study and service. Every hour of every day we added layer upon layer of learning." He tested the clay mold and motioned to Peter. "You're ready for another layer."

CHAPTER 23
THE THIEF

For two more days, Peter applied layers until the clay mold could support the weight of liquid silver.

After warming the mold in the furnace, he poured the melted wax out of the mold. Jacob checked the clay for cracks and residual wax before placing it on the floor by the furnace's fire. Peter added more fuel to the furnace and pumped the bellows.

Jacob dropped the bishop's silver coins into a gray stoneware crucible and laid a piece of charcoal on top of the coins. "This is a burnt offering to remove the impurities," he explained, "or, as a Christian would say, to resurrect the purity." He coated the underside of the gray crucible with charcoal dust, placed it into the furnace's white-hot interior with a set of tongs and closed the furnace door.

Peter pumped the bellows and timed his breathing with their movements. "Benedicamus Dominooooooooh," he chanted softly. After a time the familiar warm glow spread from his heart to his fingers and toes.

Jacob opened the door, removed the crucible, and placed it on the floor. The crucible's surface radiated intense heat. It was no longer gray, but mottled with deep black and golden orange craters and ridges, which moved as though alive in rivulets of superheated air.

Jacob swept away slag floating on the surface of the melt with an iron rod. "We'll return the slag to the bishop. Father Ulrich will weigh it and the reliquary to make sure we're returning all the silver. We'll each lose a hand if he thinks we've stolen any silver."

With the slag removed, the melt shone brilliantly. Heat from the melt prevented Peter from standing directly over the glowing crucible. He squinted obliquely into the seemingly clear liquid, past swirls of bright light into the bottomless depths. He forgot to chant and almost forgot to breathe.

Jacob picked up the crucible with a set of tongs and tipped it over Peter's earthen mold. The shop seemed to brighten as the shining liquid brimmed to the top of the mold. Jacob left a few drops of silver in the crucible. "We'll use the drops later to make the filigree."

They left the mold by the dying fire to cool slowly overnight. Peter scarcely slept that night and rose before dawn. He wanted to free his reliquary from its mold before breakfast, before anything else.

Under Jacob's guidance, Peter chipped away the clay mold. Jacob said, "Your ideal modeled first the subtle inspiration of the spirit, then the soft wax of the mental, and finally the hard clay of the physical. After everything's gone, what's left?"

Peter chipped off the last piece of clay. "Shining nobility," he said. He climbed up his baton, opened the back door and held his creation in the cold morning light.

The silver crucifix gleamed from its smooth surfaces and sparkled from its sharp edges, creases and points. It reflected a light far whiter and purer than that of the original metal. Peter studied the details on its surface, turning it first one way and then another to see how the light caught nuances of the vegetation, the animals, and the radiant Christ.

Jacob stood beside him and said, "It's beautiful."

Peter couldn't speak. He could only nod.

On the opposite side of the shop, the entrance doors creaked open and a cold draft blew past Peter. Someone in heavy boots and a hooded cloak slipped inside. The figure shut the front doors and bent over in an uncontrollable coughing fit.

"Remember to ask yourself what your ideal would do," Jacob said to Peter. He shut the back door and called to the visitor, "Greetings to God. Can we help you?"

The figure limped in a grotesque dance toward the fire in the forge. "Don' need no help from de Jew."

Peter's grip on the baton tightened. "What you doing here?" he gasped.

"Come to visit you, little wolf." Crayfish wheezed from within his hood and doubled over in a hacking fit so fierce Peter thought he would turn inside out. When he finally stopped coughing he said, "You owe me. Come back to me or I bring Lord Lodair back to you."

Jacob dropped a handful of white powder into a pot of water on the forge and said, "Crayfish hasn't come for you, Peter, but for charity."

"Don' need no charity." The beggar bent over again, coughing fitfully.

Jacob pointed at a shelf and said to Peter, "Bring him some horehound syrup."

Peter hesitated a moment. Remembering the crucible, he mumbled to himself, "What would my ideal do?" He gently laid the reliquary on the worktable and hobbled on his baton to bring Crayfish a small jug of cough syrup. After delivering the jug, he retreated a few steps, repulsed by the beggar's rotting stench.

"Take only a sip," Jacob said.

Crayfish pulled back his hood caked with frozen river mud, and guzzled the syrup. The beggar's matted blond hair and beard reminded Peter of a reflection he had once seen of himself in a calm pool by the river's edge. He had, at one time, looked like the beggar and probably smelled as bad. "*You were like him,*" a small voice whispered. "*You are him. Be compassionate.*"

Peter asked, "You need anything?"

"No. I gots more dan you. Keep a hen under de bridge. Gots many stockfishes. Sleep wid two wool blankets. See my cloak and boots. All I need ish two good hands."

"You spent the gold penny wisely," Jacob said, stirring the pot.

Peter said, "I heard that when you started buying things at the market fair, all the merchants checked their gold to make sure none was stolen."

"Dat penny was mine. Not stolen." The beggar scowled at Peter.

Peter tried to scowl back with disdain but the beggar's cold, blue eyes pierced his sense of safety. He turned away and silently asked himself; what would my ideal think? If it were not for his good luck, he'd still be a beggar. He was, in reality, no better than Crayfish. He shouldn't let the beggar's gray skin and red sores infect his judgement.

Peter said. "You deserve as much good fortune as anyone else."

Jacob removed the pot from the fire, pointed at a corner of the shop and said to Peter, "Get a horseradish root out of the sand. Make a poultice from it."

The beggar pointed at the pot. "What in dat?"

Jacob fanned the steaming pot and answered, "Water and imperial masterwort."

"What you -" A long coughing spell cut the beggar short. When he was able to catch his breath again, he took a few long swigs of horehound syrup.

Peter crushed the root on the worktable and leaned back, away from its stinging aroma. He glanced with watering eyes at the reliquary lying on the table and reminded himself to act according to his ideal. He wrapped the crushed root in linen and gave the poultice to Jacob. "I hope this help you," he said and touched Crayfish on the shoulder.

Crayfish swung his stump and knocked Peter's hand off his shoulder. "Don' need no help. 'Cept I need your two good hands." His eyes once again cut through Peter. "Come back to me. De Jew killed Count Derek. He kill you, too."

The blacksmith dipped the poultice into the warm broth, squeezed the excess water from it and carried it to the beggar.

"Dat stinks." Crayfish tried to push it away but was interrupted by another coughing fit.

"This will help you breathe better," Jacob said. He tied the warm poultice around the hacking beggar's neck, tucked it under his tunic and slipped the ceramic bottle from his hand.

The beggar grasped for the half empty jug. "No. Give me dat."

Jacob handed the bottle to Peter. "Give him a full one to take home."

"Give me a full one 'cause you owe me, little wolf. I saved your life."

"You tried to take it, too," Peter said and instantly felt ashamed at his retort. He brought Crayfish a full jug and said, "God bless you."

The beggar dropped the bottle into a bag tied to his belt and limped to the worktable. "You de best healer, better dan God damned monks. I give you dat gold penny back." He reached into his bag and, with a quick jerk, flipped the coin over his shoulder.

The penny flew past Peter and thudded onto the floor, sending a puff of fine dust into the air. Peter stepped toward the penny and saw that it wasn't gold, but dull, and it wasn't flat, but round. It looked like a - "Pebble?" he whispered.

He looked back at Crayfish, who was hobbling for the shop's doors. Peter saw a glint of silver in the beggar's hand. A glance at the worktable confirmed that the reliquary was missing. "STOP," Peter shouted and hopped on his splints toward the fleeing beggar.

Crayfish pushed a door open with his stump. The reliquary flashed in the daylight.

Peter lunged in a desperate dive, swinging the baton with all his strength in a longreaching arc. The tip of his thick stick hit something solid. He heard a yelp and a clunk at the same time.

Peter crashed to the hardpacked floor with a grunt and a clatter of wood splints. He turned his head to follow a thumping sound. The silver cross was bouncing end over end across the floor until it stopped at Jacob's feet.

The front doors slammed shut. Peter heard a muffled cry outside the shop. "You owe me, little wolf."

Peter struggled off the floor and screamed, "Stay away from me and my master, or I cut off your other hand. I hope Jesus Christ sends you to hell."

He limped to where Jacob stood studying the cross and grabbed it from his hands. Peter shook so much he could hardly see the reliquary, but when he was able to steady his hands, he saw the painstakingly sculpted face of Christ had been flattened.

Jacob said, "That happened when you hit it with your crutch."

"What we gots to do now?" Peter's voice choked.

"Melt it down and make another." Jacob put his hand on Peter's shoulder. "A good thing has come from this."

Peter looked up with teary eyes. "What?"

"This is the first time that you called me master."

CHAPTER 24
THE ZEALOT

Peter laid tools and house wares in neat rows on the worktable before Hugo. The iron peddler looked more like a bear than a man, with his short black hair, low sloping forehead, a beard that covered his cheeks right up to the dark rings under his dark eyes, a long nose above a thin mouth in a protruding jaw.

Hugo shook a fist at Peter. "Give us a fire, you stupid worm, or I'll break your other leg."

Peter jumped to the forge and pumped the bellows as fast as he could. Although the days were growing longer, winter still held the free town in its icy fingers.

The iron peddler pointed across the table at Jacob. "These prices are robbery."

"These prices are fair," the blacksmith said and turned to Peter. "You need more fuel, not more air."

Peter tore his eyes from the threatening iron peddler and looked at the charcoal. Air hissed through a few dying embers. He shoveled away the spent fuel and brought as much dried straw and wood to the forge as he could carry. With one pump of the bellows, yellow tongues of fire licked the bottom of the fuel. He dumped a second armload of kindling onto the forge and turned around to watch Hugo. As he had worked, Hugo's voice rose louder and angrier each time he asked the price of an item.

"That's enough." The iron peddler cut the air with his paw and looked down his snout at the blacksmith. "I'll bring to this town Christian blacksmiths, zealots like me. You'll starve to death."

"Bring them," Jacob said. "We'll join together in a guild, like the masons. We'll set fair prices, raise standards, and protect ourselves from unscrupulous peddlers."

Hugo stood up. He was a head above and twice as broad as most men. "What do you mean by unscru ... unscrop ... Damn Jew?" He marched around the table toward the blacksmith. "What do you mean?"

Jacob stood. "It's best you sit down."

The big man shoved the blacksmith with one hand. Jacob stood unmoved while the peddler stumbled back, as if he had pushed himself off a wall. Peter raised his baton and moved to help his master.

Jacob bowed his head and said, "Thank you, Peter, but you should tend the fire."

Peter returned to pump the bellows with one hand, but held his baton ready in the other.

Hugo glowered for a moment before rushing forward, pushing Jacob with both hands. Jacob remained solid and the hulking man pushed himself off the alchemist, tripped, and fell onto his wide rump. Fine clouds of disturbed ash swirled around Hugo.

"Peter," Jacob said. "The fire doesn't need any more air."

Peter turned to see the fire leaping high and bright, sending smoke and sparks toward exposed river reeds of the ceiling. He had loaded too much fuel, pumped too much air, and paid too little attention.

Heat from the fire intensified. The crackling flames reached higher. Twisting ripples of superheated air made beams and reeds in the thatched roof appear to flicker. At the base of the fire, the bright interior seemed alive with yellow charcoal writhing under wings of flames. Some sticks on the edge of the forge had not yet caught fire. If this unburned kindling ignited, the flames could grow still larger, could reach the ceiling and set it afire. He had to remove those sticks.

The heat was too intense to get within arm's length. He swung his baton at the fire's base, aiming for the unburned sticks. He knocked most of the unburned sticks and some of the burning ones from the forge to the floor. The fire on the forge lowered for a moment, but now flaming kindling stippled the floor.

Jacob appeared next to him with two pots and threw water onto the forge. A hissing cloud of steam surrounded Peter and Jacob. The steaming cloud around Jacob's head appeared to writhe. Objects on the wall behind Jacob flickered and rippled as though Jacob wore a hood and cloak of superheated air. Peter blinked and focused on Jacob's invisible cloak.

The creaking of the front doors drew Peter's attention. Lucus entered the shop with a platter of food.

Hugo picked up a cleaver from the worktable. "Filthy Jew," he grunted and hurled the iron tool.

Peter ducked. The cleaver whirled toward Jacob's head, curved outward where Peter had seen the invisible hood, and continued forward to crash into a wall.

Hugo pushed Lucus aside and slammed the doors behind him.

Jacob walked through the steam and smoke to help Lucus pick up the platter and strands of pickled cabbage off the floor.

Lucus coughed. "What happened?"

Jacob said, "A fire got out of control."

Lucus pointed at the scorched ceiling. "That was close. Your tribute could have been tripled."

"Tribute?" Peter's voice squeaked and his hands trembled.

"The free town belongs to the bishop and every resident gives a yearly tribute to the bishop," Lucus said. "If a house burns down by accident or on purpose, the resident's tribute is tripled until he builds a new house."

Peter said to Lucus, "You see Hugo throw a cleaver at us?" He turned to Jacob. "It curved around your head. There was something like hot air, something invisible around your head. I saw it."

"What?" Lucus said. "There was steam, smoke. That's all. You'd better sit down, Peter. You're shaking like a frightened puppy. I'm sorry about your dinner. It's all ruined." He carried his platter of dirty cabbage out the door.

Peter limped closer to Jacob. "You gots an invisible shield. I saw it."

"You saw a halo," Jacob said.

"You gots a halo?"

The alchemist began returning the tools from the worktable to the walls. "Everything has a halo. Do you want to see your halo?"

"Yes. Of course. How?"

"Hold out your hand against a dark background. Spread your fingers, relax and look between without focusing on anything."

Peter took a few deep breaths and concentrated on calming his hands. After a moment, he detected airy distortions close around his fingers. While he marveled at the shimmering layers surrounding his hand, the distortions turned milky white. "I see my halo. Ish white."

"Colors change according to thoughts and feelings."

"I can see something invisible," Peter said. "That ish great. Am I an alchemist, almost?"

Jacob replaced the last tool. "Everyone is an alchemist. Most don't know it."

Peter sat on a stool, his crippled leg held straight before him in unbending splints. "How long before I know it?"

"That's up to you," Jacob said. "You burn with desire to finish your apprenticeship." He pointed to the ashes under the furnace. "What is the fourth quality of the furnace?"

"Fire."

"The fire that nourishes desire and stirs you into action. Without the fire of zeal, the furnace walls do not reflect, the door serves no purpose, and precious metals within the crucible cannot form the ideal."

Peter looked at the blackened ceiling. "If I gots too much zeal, I burn my house down."

Jacob laughed and said, "Zealots have been known to burn down their own houses." He brought a small pot of well water and a turnip to the table. "Let's make your dinner."

Peter said, "Hugo said he ish a zealot. Zealots are bad people."

Jacob sliced the wrinkled turnip into small pieces. "We're all part of God. How can any part of God be bad?"

"Hah," Peter snorted. "How can Hugo be a part of God? Or Lothair? How can I be a part? God ish in the sky somewhere." He picked up a discarded piece of discolored turnip. "People are rotten." He threw the piece onto the forge, where it shriveled into a black sliver.

Jacob dropped the sliced turnip in the pot and placed it on the forge. "There is no rotten fruit in the Garden of Eden. Don't regret any rotten thing you think you've done. Regret cripples zeal and makes you look backward. Forgiveness releases regret and lets you move forward. You will understand that when you pass the test to finish your apprenticeship."

"What ish the test?" Peter asked.

"Forgiveness. The test is to forgive."

Peter waited for Jacob to finish answering his question. Jacob stirred the pot and said nothing more. After a few moments Peter asked, "Ish that all? Just to forgive? I thought my test gots be, maybe, some great work of magic."

"Only forgiveness heals the perception that you and others are rotten. Forgiveness is happiness. Offer the happiness you would want for yourself to everyone, no exceptions."

"That easy. I can forgive everyone right now."

The blacksmith focused on Peter. "Then do it."

"Well then, I forgive everyone. I forgive my brother Gabriel for becoming the warrior I was supposed to be. I forgive Rosamund for calling me stupid and marrying Karl. And I guess I forgive the beggar for being so vile."

The blacksmith doubled over with laughter.

Peter's face felt hot. "I did it, right?"

"You said it," the blacksmith said, stopping to catch his breath. "But you didn't do it." He chuckled a few moments more before speaking again. "What about Lothair?"

Peter slumped on the stool, looked at his broken leg and mumbled, "I forgive him, too."

"Do it. Don't say it."

"What do you mean?"

"Go to Lothair. Submit yourself to him."

Peter sat upright. "But he kill me."

"That would be to his disadvantage. Besides, he can't really hurt you because you're not your body."

"But I like my body. I want to keep my body. As long as I stay here in your shop, I safe from him."

The blacksmith said, "Your final test will be to go out to Lothair, to forgive him, and to kneel before him in selfless service. If you fail the test, if you misuse the powers of alchemy, you'll fall back into despair and you'll pull the rest of the world with you."

"If I can pull the world backwards," Peter said, "then I gots to be more powerful than the whole world."

"You are," the blacksmith said. "The world is a thing, just like your body or your mind or your spirit. All things push and pull each other. You can push and pull all things, all of creation."

"And the universal essence, too?" Peter asked.

"No. The universal essence is no thing. When you submit to

Lothair, you're releasing all things and submitting to no thing."

Peter struggled to his feet and hobbled to his mattress. "Cannot do it. Won' do it. I want Lothair to submit to me. I want him to respect me, to fear me."

The front doors creaked open and Lucus entered with his platter. "Master Thomas washed the cabbage and boiled it." He gave it to Peter. "I added a little honey."

"How nice," the blacksmith said. "Let's add the turnips to it and make a feast for Peter."

Peter's dinner tasted neither sour like pickled cabbage nor bland like dried turnips. It was sweet and plentiful. But Peter wanted no more than a few bites. He had lost his appetite.

CHAPTER 25
GOLD

Jacob roused Peter from a deep sleep in the middle of the night. "Your fire is out," Jacob whispered. "We must rekindle your zeal."

Jacob arranged items on the worktable by the light of a single candle while Peter pumped air to the furnace. They chanted in unison "Benedicamus Dominoooommmmm," humming the last syllable until their lungs emptied.

Between chants, Peter yawned and listened to the rhythmic tapping of valves in the bellows, the low rush of air through the nozzles, and the steady drum of rain on the roof. Outside the shuttered windows and closed doors, distant thunder rumbled closer. He struggled to stay awake. His ears blended their chants with the sounds of the bellows and the storm, and his mind grew ever lighter until it seemed ready to detach, to float above.

Jacob placed three crucibles inside the furnace, closed its stone door, knelt before it, and bent his head as if in prayer. The air above him twisted like hot eddies from a fire. His flickering mantle grew and stretched upward. Objects on the wall behind his head appeared to dance. With sturdy shelves and iron tools wavering in the air, the shop appeared less solid, less real. Jacob stopped chanting and looked up with glassy eyes to the ceiling.

Peter followed his gaze to the ribbons of heat leaping and twisting from the vent at the top of the furnace, soaring upward through the shop's smoke hole and into the sky. His mind wanted to fly with the invisible rivulets to the heavens above but his hand on the bellows' lever anchored him to the earth below.

Jacob raised his palms above his head and called out in Latin, "One is the all."

Lightning illuminated the cracks around the shop's closed doors and windows.

Jacob stood up, lifting his arms higher. "And by it, the all, and in it, the all."

Thunder boomed overhead.

Jacob seemed to rise still higher. The floor beneath his feet shimmered and Peter couldn't tell if Jacob stood on his toes or floated above the ground. "And if it does not contain the all, it is not." He lowered his arms and bowed his head. "Thy will be done, as above, as below." His shoulders began to rock and the rocking motion spread until his whole body shook.

When Jacob collapsed to his knees, Peter became afraid for his master. Fear snapped the wavering world back into focus and made it solid once more. He released the bellows and hobbled forward. "Master, what wrong?"

Jacob jumped to his feet, hugged Peter's shoulders and laughed. "Everything," he said at last. "Everything is right." He dressed in a heavy leather apron and gloves, picked up a set of tongs, and opened the furnace door.

Peter stepped back as streams of intense heat leapt free from the furnace's white heart.

Jacob removed three glowing crucibles and placed them on the floor. A shimmering halo of hot air surrounded each container. He swept an iron rod over the top of the melt in the first crucible. Slag clung to the rod in black clumps and a shining orange liquid appeared beneath the slag. "Copper," Jacob answered Peter's unspoken question. "From the mountains of the Greeks."

Jacob moved to the second crucible and swept its surface clean of slag. "Tin," he said as Peter studied the bright white liquid. "From the mines of the Kelts."

The third and largest crucible was empty. Jacob poured first liquid tin and then liquid copper into the empty container. Orange and white bands seemed to spiral past the bottom of the crucible, through the veil of solid earth and into a realm of unworldly light.

Jacob pulled a handful of white powder from a leather pouch and said, "This is the earth of zinc." When he dropped the powder into the spiraling melt, it hissed, crackled, and steamed. Peter backed away from the acrid steam and Jacob threw more handfuls of powder into the noisy brew.

Jacob retrieved a ladle of flaky ash from beneath the furnace and stirred it into the melt. Dark swirls formed and clung to the iron ladle, coating it like smooth, black syrup. "Lead," Jacob said and removed the ladle after sweeping up the last dark swirl.

He poured the crucible's contents into a shallow depression

on the floor.

Thunder crashed overhead.

Peter hobbled closer for a better look at the yellow puddle. Jacob filled a pot from the well and tipped it over the liquid metal. When the cold water hit the hot melt, a flash like a bolt of lightning blinded Peter. An explosion roared. Everything in the shop rattled. Peter covered his eyes and staggered back until he stumbled against the worktable.

"We thank Thee," Jacob said in Latin.

Peter rubbed his eyes for a long while before he could again distinguish anything in the shop. The explosion had not overturned any tables, collapsed any shelves, or tossed any tools from the walls. The candle on the worktable still burned. But the doors and windows had been thrown wide open. A cool, damp breeze flowed through the shop. The rain had stopped and thunder rumbled away in the distance.

Jacob was kneeling by the well and dipping a large metal platter in the cold water. The platter shone yellow like the beggar's gold penny.

Peter limped closer. "Could that be ... ish that ... gold?"

Jacob handed the disc to Peter. With his baton tucked under his arm, Peter held the gleaming saucer with both hands. It was warm, heavy, and maybe ten times the size of his hand. Its clean yellow sheen reflected the flickering candlelight.

"It ish ... so much," Peter whispered.

The alchemist wiped tears from his eyes. "More than the bishop or the count and Lothair have hidden away,"

"Lothair gots gold?" Peter gave the gold disc back to the alchemist. "We gots to hide it."

"We must return it," the alchemist said. With a flip of his wrist, he threw the platter over his shoulder. It flashed as it tumbled through the air, upward, to the peak of a high arc, and then downward until it splashed into the well.

"Master," Peter cried and lurched to the well's low wall. Half an arm's length below, his wavering silhouette appeared on a surface of disturbed water like a broken dream. He probed the well with his stick but couldn't feel the bottom. "Can we gets it out?"

"Why? Your zeal is rekindled. You don't need it anymore."

Peter sat on the well wall and shook his head. A golden gleam near the depression on the floor caught his eye. He pounced on it and cupped in his hand a warm droplet of gold the size of a small pebble. He scoured the floor for other orphaned droplets but found no more. "Don' throw this one away. Can I keep it?"

The alchemist chuckled and nodded.

Peter said, "I want it because I want more things."

"The more you want, the less you have. The less you want, the more you have."

"But we can make more gold and have all there ish."

"We already have all there is. What good is gold when we already have it all?"

"Why don' you make gold all the time? Why you gots to be a blacksmith? Why do I gots to learn smithing?"

"The value of any trade is not what we get for it, but what we become by it. No one becomes an alchemist without excelling at some type of work. Besides, if you were wealthy and without a trade, wouldn't people accuse you of sorcery?"

Peter nodded. He didn't want to be accused of sorcery. "Master Jacob, I want to finish my apprenticeship. I certain you know what ish right. Sorry I doubted you. I was stupid."

"Doubts are uncomfortable, but never stupid. Don't be so certain. If you are certain, you are closed-minded and arrogant. If you are uncertain, you are open-minded and humble. This world is forever changing and uncertain. Nothing and only nothing is forever certain. You must find your own way back to that eternal certainty. Learn from my way, but don't accept it as right. Don't accept everything you hear me say or see me do."

Peter frowned. "I know you made gold. I saw it. Can you teach me?"

"You already know how, but you've forgotten. Forgiveness will help you remember. Help me close the windows and doors, and then you can go back to sleep."

Peter didn't want to go back to sleep.

CHAPTER 26
THE SPOON

Another wave of cramping clawed Rosamund's belly. She curled into a ball on her pile of straw, grit her teeth, and gasped between groans. After a few long moments, the pain eased and she sighed.

Karl grabbed the puppy's head again and laughed. The dog flipped over several times and pushed its paws against Karl's hands. It barked, jumped into his lap, and chewed one of his thick fingers.

"Ouch," Karl yelped and shook his hand free. He stood and opened the hut's door. "No more. Now gets out of here."

The dog stopped barking and cowered.

Damp, cold air settled over Rosamund like a wet blanket. Karl nudged the puppy with his boot. "Hurry. Getting cold in here." The dog bolted outside and Karl shut the door. "People should be like animals." He sat with his back to her and stirred the charcoal of the earthen fireplace in the center of the hut.

Another cramp twisted Rosamund's insides. Her hand moved over the small bulge at her stomach. She was in her sixth month, wasn't she? Too early for childbirth. Since yesterday, the cramps had grown more intense, each one lasting longer and coming more frequently. And more worrisome, the baby within her belly had stopped moving.

The pain ebbed and she wiped tears from her sight. She rolled over and faced the wall. Scratches on the mud-packed wall caught her eye and, when she rubbed off the soot, she discovered the pattern of a wolf.

"Peter," she whispered. Rosamund had found many of his etchings: pigs, geese, oxen, trees and people. He told her that scratching pictures into the smoky walls of this hut was his only solace during long winters with his cousins, an aunt, his brother, and any livestock they brought inside to keep the human inhabitants warm. Only Karl and Karl's mother remained, and Rosamund now slept where Peter had once slept.

After Christmas, Father Ulrich returned from the free town with news that Peter was alive. Why hadn't Peter sent her a message with Father Ulrich? She frowned and turned away from the wolf etching.

Another cramp squeezed the air from her. "Karl," she gasped. "Getting ... worse."

"You gets over it," Karl growled. He kept his back to her and poked the fire.

The grip on her stomach grew tighter. "No, Karl. Gets your ... mother ... please."

"You always sick. Don' know why mother made me stay with you today."

"Ish different. Not ... bad stomach. Ish -" A jolt of pain stopped her breath. She doubled over again. After a long, groaning while, the cramp released her and she could breathe again.

Karl stirred the fire. "Mother be home soon. Be quiet."

Her baby fell lower in her belly. Was the baby coming? But it wasn't the right time. Too early. She squeezed her buttocks together and gasped, "No."

Karl spun around and glared. "What?"

Rosamund spoke through gritting teeth, "Gets your mother."

"I told you to be quiet," Karl snarled.

"Gets your mother."

Karl stood and looked down on her. "A woman gots to obey her man. You act like a man."

She whispered, "Something wrong and -"

"Right," he barked. "Something ish wrong. You wrong. Everyone says so. Everyone laughs at me 'cause you don' obey me. Custom says you gots to be silent and listen to me, your man. Father Ulrich says God ish the head of man and man ish the head of woman. That stack of sheep skins told him so."

"You mean the Bible," she said.

"Shut up," he howled, his face red.

Rosamund struggled to sit up. A small red spot stained her dress below her belly. The wool padding between her legs, which absorbed the trickle of blood yesterday, could not contain it now. "Bleeding -"

"Shut up." He shook his fist. "I told you to shut up."

A sudden cramp struck and she ground her teeth. The baby

slipped lower again. She pressed her legs together, determined to stop it. The pain cascaded into agony that seemed to drown her. "Gets your mother," she gasped.

Above the flood of agony she heard Karl howling, "Shut up. Shut up."

Her body contracted, pushing the unborn child down. She wasn't ready. The baby wasn't ready. Another contraction crashed over her. She reached between her legs and pushed against the wool padding. Hot liquid soaked the straw beneath. Her water had broken. What could she do now?

"*Let go.*" The quiet voice broke through the torrents.

She could force her will to stop the birth, couldn't she?

"*It will kill you.*"

She let go of her determination to stop the baby. "Gets your mother," she screamed.

A flood of spasms crashed over her. She floundered on a wave of wet straw. Pain sucked her into its black whirlpool. She shut her eyes and screamed for help. A vague sense that Karl was kicking her surfaced in her screaming nightmare.

A woman's voice washed past. "Karl. Stop it."

Another voice swam by. "Don' you see what wrong?"

"Gets out of here," said another. "This ish women work."

Many hands rolled Rosamund over onto her back and lifted her legs. Voices floated over her while wave after wave of contractions swept her under.

"Push," someone said.

"Push," said another.

Rosamund obeyed the voices until a final terrible spasm released her. Warm darkness silenced the pain and the voices. She drifted on a bed of soft nothingness.

A cool hand on her forehead awoke her. She saw Karl's mother.

Karl was howling outside the hut. "God damn woman. How could she do this to me?"

"He ish a bad boy sometimes," his mother said, her eyes red and her weathered cheeks wet with tears. "I hope he can forgive you."

Rosamund looked through the smoke hole in the ceiling, to

the blue sky. "I always forgive him," she said. "If I didn', I never be free."

A small cramp squeezed her insides. Rosamund moved her hand to its source, her stomach. Her belly was flat. The pain passed quickly and something slipped out between her legs. She sat up with a start. At her feet, Grandma Bertha swept a bloody lump and red straw into a sack.

"What that?" Rosamund asked.

"The afterbirth," Karl's mother said. "Lay down. Ish over now." She began sobbing.

Rosamund smiled and looked around the hut. "Where ish my baby?" she asked.

Bertha wobbled to her feet and wiped her eyes with her red wool shawl. Rosamund saw Bertha's mouth moving and heard her speaking but couldn't understand what she said.

Rosamund remembered her child was three months early. "Where ish my baby?" she asked, her voice rising.

Grandma Bertha looked away and Karl's mother covered her face.

Rosamund's back stiffened. "Where ish my baby? Where?"

The door opened and cold light flooded the hut. Bertha carried the bloody sack outside while Gisela and a few other women entered. They shut the door and everyone but Gisela avoided Rosamund's eyes.

"Does she know yet?" Gisela asked.

No one answered.

"I want to see my baby." Rosamund's voice trembled.

"That was the devil's child," Gisela said. She dropped her walking stick and slapped a long-handled wood spoon into her open palm. "The head was no bigger than my thumbnail."

The women encircled Rosamund.

Her mother-in-law pushed her back onto the straw and held her shoulders down. Other women pulled Rosamund's legs apart.

Gisela waved the spoon over Rosamund and said, "For the good of all, we gots to scrape you clean of the devil's seed."

CHAPTER 27
HAMMERING POWER

Jacob pumped the bellows and the forge roared hot again. He hammered a red-hot rod to a point with four blows on the anvil and said, "It's time to remove the splints."

Peter looked up from the open Bible on his study table. A shaft of warm afternoon sunlight reached for his mattress. Gentle spring breezes brought the scent of valerian flowers through the open doors, and helped cool him as he sat wearing only his breeches. He replied in Latin, "Have thou seen I can read a whole chapter without asking what the words mean?"

Jacob did not answer in Latin. "Don't change the subject." He laid the rod on a thick cleaver standing upright from its handle hole in the worktable. With a hammer he struck the rod about half a finger above the point. He slid the nearly severed point into a hole in the center of the nail header, an iron disc tied to a wooden handle. He twisted the point free and returned the rest of the rod to the forge, setting it beside two other thin rods.

"It's time to free your leg," Jacob said. Four blows from the hammer against the top of the severed point shaped the nail's rosehead. With a tap on the table and a flick of the wrist, the new nail flew out of the nail header and into the slack tub, snapping as it hit the cool water to join other nails beneath the surface.

"That is the fortieth nail thou have made since noon," Peter continued in Latin. "See how well I count?"

"You can't avoid it any longer." The blacksmith knelt before Peter and removed the short study table to one side. "It's time to take off the splints." He rolled up the trousers on Peter's crippled leg.

Peter grumbled in his native speech, "Leg broken twice ish always crippled. That what custom says."

The blacksmith untied the knots holding the slats in place. "Custom doesn't say you can't walk on it. The beggar broke his leg twice in the same place. He not only walks, he runs."

Peter grimaced as the blacksmith peeled the boards from his white, wrinkled skin. He pointed a shaking finger at his bony leg and its scales of dead skin. "Look at that. Don' want to walk."

"Why?"

Peter pouted.

Jacob said, "Is it your way of purging your shame?"

"No," Peter snapped. His eyes welled with tears and he whispered, "I am a cripple. I could have been a great warrior."

"You're already great. Now is the time for you to use the first power of alchemy, hammering power."

Peter wiped his eyes. "How do I gets hammering power?"

Jacob answered, "By acting with faith."

"Faith? Don' I gots to learn the steps of a magic spell?"

"First step; reflect deeply to find the truth of your being in your quarry. Second step; open your door so that your truth fills your world. Third step; melt truth in your crucible and pour it into your mold. Fourth step; act on your truth with zeal. Faith is to the world what hammering is to the blacksmith. If a smith doesn't hammer, he doesn't make anything useful. Use the power of a hammer and walk, knowing you are healed now and forever." Jacob held out a hand.

Peter shook his head. "I do it later."

"When compared to forever, later is meaningless. There is only now and forever."

Peter looked away. "I want to study."

The blacksmith flipped a few pages of the Bible on Peter's study table and pointed. "What can you do when you have no more than a seed of faith?"

Peter glanced at the page. "Move a whole mountain? No."

"Some of us have to break the mountain with our hammer and move it one stone at a time. Let's walk one step at a time." The blacksmith held out his hand again.

After a moment's hesitation, Peter grasped the baton in one hand and the blacksmith's hand with the other. With a grunt, he allowed himself to be pulled up. He balanced on his good leg and held his shriveled leg stiffly out before him.

"Bend your leg a little," the blacksmith said, putting his free hand under Peter's arm.

Peter bent his leg and a terrific pain shot through him. Every muscle contracted.

The blacksmith's voice echoed off a wall of pain. "Each day you'll have to bend it a little more until it's back to normal. Have faith."

Peter shook his head. "It hurts. I gots to have ... confidence."

"Confidence is not faith. Confidence comes from accepting your deceptions as true. Now, take a step."

"My pain ish no deception," Peter muttered and planted his baton a half pace forward. With his bad leg extended in the air, he hopped once with his good leg. The jerking hop bent the knee of his crippled leg. Pain rushed through him again. "Argggh. Damn Jew." He lowered his head and cringed. "Sorry, master."

"You're forgiven," Jacob said. "This time don't hop."

Peter stared at the floor. "I am so sorry, master."

"Don't worry. Nothing happened. Find what's beyond your deceptions. Hammer the knowledge of what you find into forward motion. Put your foot flat on the floor in front of you."

"Sorry," Peter said and lowered his crippled leg without bending his knee.

"What's your true nature?" Jacob asked.

"I am a person with nobility inside," Peter said.

"No. You're nobility with a fortress outside, like a bird with a rock tied to its feet. Hammer that belief into action. Put your weight on the healing leg and move the other leg forward."

Peter sucked in a deep breath, put his baton and his bad leg forward. He quickly slid his good leg up next to the bad one. Instead of the pain, he felt a dull ache.

"Good," Jacob said. "Take another step in faith."

With the foot of his crippled leg resting on the floor, Peter moved forward another step, careful not to bend the knee. Sweat dripped from his brow. "Can I go back now?"

Jacob helped him return to the mattress in three slow steps. Peter sat with a grunt. Jacob brought Peter a sack of three hammers and a bowl of syrupy grease. "We must oil our tools or they will rust."

Peter sighed and dipped his fingers in the bowl. A thick drop of oil drooled onto his trousers as his fingers greased the iron surface.

Jacob added more charcoal to the forge and pumped the bellows. Damp charcoal popped and hissed. "Fear, aggression, and shame are holding you back. You know deep inside they are not real. No thing is real. Act on that faith, hammer it into something useful." A piece of charcoal snapped, shooting a spark into the air and falling as ash to the floor.

Peter oiled another hammer. Another drop of oil fell to join a pool on his lap. "Yes, yes, I remember: my body and my mind are not real. Not even that spooky voice, the counselor, ish real. But it all feels real. How does hammering power change any of that?"

"Just as a hammer shapes iron, belief shapes the world. Once you believe you can walk, then you can walk. Faith tells me you can run, too."

Peter oiled the third hammer and put it aside. "I gots to see proof."

The blacksmith looked at Peter with penetrating eyes and said, "Be careful. You need only ask and you will receive."

Peter squirmed under the blacksmith's probing gaze and put his hands on the floor to shift his weight. A solid coating of floor ash stuck to the grease on his palms and fingers. He held up his hands for the blacksmith to see. "Right now, I ask for soap and water. Will I receive that?"

Jacob smiled and walked out the back door. Peter heard him chipping soap from the block they had boiled in the garden the day before. Maybe he should step outside, walk forward with courage like … He tried to think of a brave person who did things others were afraid to do. Rosamund came to his mind. At the thought of her pregnant with Karl's child, he winced.

A piece of charcoal exploded in the forge, sending a large ember into the air. It hissed in an arc up and then down, streaking with flaming brightness onto Peter's oil stained trousers.

Peter knocked the ember from his lap with a quick backhand. The hot cinder flew back toward the forge and landed on the ashen floor. But a glowing piece stuck to the back of his hand.

"Ow," he cried and shook his hand vigorously until the burning fleck flew away. He put the burned knuckle in his mouth and sucked it.

The smell of burning oil filled his nostrils. He looked for the flames, his knuckle still in his mouth, and found his lap afire with blue flames.

He scrambled to his feet and reached for the knot in the rope that held his pants. But the knot was burning, too. He slapped at the flames. One of his hands caught fire.

"Aiiee!" He waved his burning palm through the air with rapid strokes. The flames on his hand fluttered out, extinguished by the quick movement.

The fire in his lap licked at his exposed stomach.

MOVE, panic screamed in his head. MOVEMENT PUTS OUT THE FIRE.

Peter took a step toward the center of the shop. The forge with its own fire confronted him. The furnace, table, and well seemed too close.

MOVE, screamed his panic.

He bolted out the open front doors. To his left people in the street, their mouths open, eyes staring, blocked his flight. He turned right and ran with stiff legs up the empty road toward the forest.

FIRE IS HOT. FOREST IS COOL. MOVE.

He swerved right again, off the road, and sped through a field of wheat seedlings, a short cut to the forest.

"Peter." Jacob's voice penetrated his panic. "Over here. There's water."

WATER. Peter cut sharply to the right, in the direction of Jacob's voice.

Jacob waved from the garden and pointed at the shop's back entrance. "Jump in the well. Hurry."

Peter ran past his master, through the back door, and jumped. He flew half the length of the shop before splashing feet first into the well. The shock of cold water tightened every muscle.

For a moment he sank into liquid darkness. With a few rigid kicks he swam to the surface.

His master extended a hand from above. "Not only can you run, but you can swim, too." He pulled Peter out of the well.

Peter gasped for breath and shivered with cold fright. "I burned," he panted.

Jacob examined the blackened hole in Peter's breeches. "No. Only the grease burned. But we'll have to get you new trousers."

Peter held out a trembling hand. "I burned my hand."

"A few blisters here and there. The ash covering your palms protected your skin."

Peter checked his hand, stomach, groin, and legs. He squeezed the pouch tied to his charred belt and felt his gold pebble still within. He saw the discarded splints on the floor and remembered his broken leg. An aching pain returned to his stiff knee.

"You're lucky for someone asking for trouble," Jacob said.

Peter waved his arms. "I didn' ask for this."

"You wanted proof of my faith."

Peter's voice rose higher. "Did you do this?"

"No," Jacob said. "You did this. You asked for it."

Peter wobbled to his mattress, sat down with a groan, and leaned against the wall. Water from his breeches soaked into the straw stuffed mattress. He stared at his shriveled leg, which ached more with each passing moment, and said, "I ran. I jumped. I swam."

Jacob laughed and said, "On the surface, you don't think you can walk. On a deeper level, you believe you can run but don't want to. On the deepest level, you know you can fly. And then you acted on that knowledge." He tossed Peter his serf's tunic. "This will cover the hole in your pants. Let's go into town and find you some new trousers. Or would you rather run?"

"What if we meet Lothair?" Peter took a deep breath and added, "I need my stick."

"Do you think that little stick will protect you?" Jacob said. "Real protection comes from the second power of alchemy. That's your next lesson."

CHAPTER 28
CLEAVING POWER

Peter ran for the nearest cover, a holly bush next to the road, and vaulted over it with his baton. He crouched and watched through the bush's prickly leaves.

Count Edzard, Lothair, and several mounted warriors rounded a bend in the forest road. The count's chain mail tunic, the same Peter had repaired from Maynard's old armor, fit Edzard well. A newly waxed shield hung by a strap from his left shoulder and glistened whenever he rode through a shaft of late afternoon sunlight. He carried an iron-tipped lance in one hand. His sword sheath dangled from a belt decorated with shiny studs. Behind him came Lothair, his armor dull, his shield scarred.

Jacob pushed his two-wheeled pushcart to the side of the road and bowed his head.

The count reined his horse to a halt before Jacob and the procession stopped. His horse tossed its star-marked head and stamped with impatience. "What is the Jew doing in the forest?"

Jacob said, "We're mining iron and making charcoal with the bishop's permission."

"We? Is the little serf with you?"

"He's in the bushes, sire," Jacob said.

"Ah, I see." The count stroked the blond fuzz growing from his chin and turned to Lothair. "He's as afraid of us as we are of him."

Lothair's face turned crimson against the green foliage.

The little count spurred his horse forward. Lothair followed, giving Jacob as wide a berth as the road allowed. The rest of the mounted warriors, nine in all, passed with the same caution.

Four foot soldiers trotted behind them. One of them carried the crossbow strapped to his back. Two others carried a small round shield and an ax. The last foot soldier carried no weapons and led a heavily loaded mare. Peter recognized the tall man's foolish grin within his chain mail hood.

Gabriel released the mare and embraced Jacob. He ran around the holly bush to Peter.

"Go away," Peter whispered. "I gots to hide."

Gabriel laughed out loud and hugged his crouching brother. He bounded back to the waiting mare and trotted off to catch up with the warriors.

Peter limped back to his master. His muscles ached from their work at building a woodpile. That morning, at first light, he and Jacob had entered the forest, scraped a ten pace wide circle free of grasses and roots from a saddle between two hillocks in a forest meadow next to the road. Then they cut six young tree trunks into poles about the length of a man, anchored the poles in a tight circle in the middle of the cleared ground, chopped pine trees into pieces half the length of a man, carried the logs to the saddle, leaned the logs upright against the six central poles, added a second layer of logs on top of the first, and covered the wood pile with a blanket of dried pine needles.

After Gabriel's mare disappeared in a cloud of dust, Jacob pointed to the top of one of the hillocks. "Throw dirt on the wood pile from that hill." He turned and climbed the opposite hillock.

Sticky pinesap glued Peter's hands to the shovel and to his baton. At the top of the hill, beneath short grasses, he found soft, dry dirt, with no stones or roots to impede his digging. "They going to a battle?" he asked.

"The warriors? Yes. To their annual raid," Jacob said. "Edzard will capture weaker counts and hold them for ransom. He calls his vassals every summer for forty days of armed service. He leaves one foot soldier to watch his tower. His father, Count Derek, could extort a year's provisions in twenty days. His grandfather, the first count, didn't need to steal at all. For Edzard, peace means poverty."

"You make battle sound like robbery," Peter said, shoveling and breathing hard. Sweat dripped from his brow. "You ever seen a real battle?"

Even though Jacob had cut three times as many trees as Peter and shoveled dirt at twice Peter's rate, he seemed hardly affected. "A real battle? Yes. Too often," Jacob said. "The Greeks move large armies over good roads with supply wagons. Arab commanders flank and outflank each other on open plains with masses of riders on giant stallions." His words skipped to the rhythm of his shoveling. "The Magyar tribes travel light on small horses with bright streamers fluttering from their spears, overtaking their fleeing foes and killing them with small bows and iron tipped arrows as though they were hunting forest animals. In our part of the world, warriors fight private wars with private armies. They capture and ransom each other, steal livestock, murder peasants, burn villages, plunder merchants."

Peter said, "If that true, the free town ish not safe."

"It isn't," Jacob said. "If Edzard could take the free town, he'd collect the tribute the bishop now receives, and if he burned the free town while taking it, he'd collect triple the tribute until the merchants rebuilt the town. No free man would be allowed to leave the valley until they did so. As of now, all the count can get are tolls that merchants give for using his roads to and from the free town. And then Edzard must give two thirds of his tolls to Duke Heinrich. As long as the Emperor is strong, the free town is safe. If the bishop's lord and protector weakens, Edzard would be the first to fall upon us."

They threw dirt onto the mound for a long time in silence until Peter stopped to catch his breath and wipe sweat from his brow. "You make warriors ... sound like outlaws. Warriors fight that ... good may conquer evil."

Jacob said, "When everything is one and the same, who is the conqueror? Who is the conquered? Who is good? Who is evil?"

Jacob descended the hillock and motioned Peter to come down. Jacob seemed not one bit winded. Not one drop of sweat glistened on his brow. He instructed Peter to pack the dirt evenly on the mound with the back of a shovel while he dug a few small draw holes into its base at regular intervals, filled them with kindling and lit them with flint and iron.

After packing the mound, Peter lay in the meadow among white and yellow chamomile flowers. Every bone hurt and his throat was dry. He stared at the sky with numb exhaustion. The clouds grew rosy with the approaching sunset. At this time of year, daylight lasted sixteen hours.

He called to Jacob, "We gots to hurry ... to gets back before dark."

Jacob lit the kindling in the last draw hole. "We're not leaving a smoldering fire. We must stay here for several days."

Peter sat up. "Several days?"

Jacob pointed at Peter's half eaten bread on a blanket. "You have food, blankets, there's water, berries, and mushrooms in the forest."

Peter stood up. "And wild animals and monsters and spirits."

The blacksmith walked around the mound and placed rocks in front of the draw holes. "If the fire goes out in the mound, the wood won't char and we'll have to start over. If the fire bursts out of the mound, the wood will burn to ashes and the wind could carry the fire into the forest. We have to stay and tend the fire."

Peter backed up to the mound and scanned the meadow boundary. The strong, resinous scent of the forest thickened in the dimming light. The air grew heavy, harder to breathe. Rustles in the undergrowth betrayed the creeping advances of invisible spirits. Tree roots could become fingers of sleeping monsters, who awoke hungry at moonrise. Nightfall would turn nature into something supernatural.

Beyond the meadow's boundary, one of the bushes moved. The bush seemed to be seated against a tree, like a ...

"Bear," Peter gasped. He pulled his knife out and gripped his baton tighter. "Master," he shouted. "A bear."

The bear swiveled its great head to look at Peter and Jacob.

Peter put the knife in his teeth, picked up a rock the size of his fist, and hurled it. The rock struck the bear's belly.

The animal grunted, dropped onto all four paws, and ambled toward Peter.

Peter threw another stone. It sailed harmlessly over the bear's head. By now the bear had crossed half the meadow. "Run, master," he cried and his knife fell from his teeth. He stooped to pick it up, but the bear was too close. He jumped back, leaving the knife on the ground, and thrust the baton at the animal. The end of the stick poked the bear squarely on its snout.

It stopped and rubbed its snout.

Peter scooted sideways around the mound.

"Wait," Jacob said softly.

The bear followed Peter around the mound.

"Run, master." Peter swung the baton, hitting the side of the bear's head.

The animal stopped again and shook its head.

"Stop." Jacob's tone remained calm.

Peter's heart raced. His second swing skipped off the top of the bear's skull.

The beast snarled and bared its teeth.

Peter jabbed the stick in its face.

It reared up on its hind legs and swung its claws.

Peter deflected the animal's claws with his stick. He stumbled on the base of the mound and fell against it. "Help me," he screamed.

"Please stop," Jacob boomed.

The bear stalled. It stood still, upright on its hind legs.

Peter's every muscle froze. It seemed even his heart stopped beating.

Jacob stepped through the stillness and stood between Peter and the bear. With his back to the animal, he said firmly to Peter, "The bear has been with us all day." He turned to the animal and touched its head. "Did my apprentice knock you on your head?"

Peter said through clinched teeth, "You talking to a bear?"

"You can talk to him, too," Jacob said. He held up his hand and spread his fingers. "Thank you for your company. Go in peace."

The bear lowered itself to all four paws, turned, and lumbered back into the forest.

"You talk to animals?" Peter asked with shrill disbelief.

"When you cleave to the universal essence, you feel united with everything, including animals. Cleaving is the second power of alchemy. It's like being in love."

Peter punched the air with his stick. "I been in love before, but I couldn' talk to animals." He noticed for the first time that the mound on which he leaned was very hot. He pushed himself off and rubbed his seat. "I couldn' even talk to Rosamund without stuttering."

"Real love is not cleaving to one special person, but to all. We're all the same content in different forms. What was the lesson of the hauberk?"

Peter ran his trembling fingers through his hair and struggled to remember. "The right arm of a hauberk thinks ish different from the left arm, but they connected, all one piece of armor, made of the same thing; the universal essence."

Jacob pointed at Peter's chest. "You're not limited to this little body. You're connected to the trees, the animals, the sky. The world is your real body. Cleaving power is your armor. No animal, no person can hurt you. Cleaving power makes you invulnerable, not because it protects you from evil, but because it dissolves evil and good, both."

Peter retrieved his knife and scanned the meadow boundary again. "Evil ish out there. A true warrior loves to hate it." He examined deep scratches on his baton from the bear's claws.

Jacob walked around the charcoal mound, stopping at places to press a hand against its blanket of dirt. "A true warrior forgives and loves what was once feared and hated."

Peter limped behind Jacob. "But you hated Christians once."

"My hatred was strong," Jacob said, "until Christian monks took me into their home, healed my body, mind and heart, taught me alchemy. Then they sent me back to the Magyars."

"To the Magyars? Why? To fight them? To gets your daughter back?"

"No. They sent me to the Magyars to be a Christian missionary."

"What? How could that be? You a Jew."

"Jew, Christian, Moslem, an alchemist is all. Teaching a despised religion to a hated race was my test of forgiveness, of love and submission. That finished my apprenticeship. You must also learn to love Lothair."

Peter shook his head. "You want me to love Lothair? Hah. What would I gets in return? Pain and probably death. I gots to love someone who loves me back."

"Don't get caught in emotional undergrowth. Look for greater meaning." Jacob laid his hand flat against the mound. "Put your hand here and check the temperature."

Thunder rolled through the forest as Peter pressed a hand to the mound. Heat radiated through the dirt so intensely that Peter had to remove his hand quickly.

"It's too hot," Jacob said and kicked a stone to cover the draw hole below. "Beneath the surface of the mound, the core is changing.

Which of the four elements make up wood?"

Peter touched the sticky pinesap between his fingers. "Water and earth."

"And air, too," Jacob said. "Each element has two of four qualities: cold, hot, wet, and dry. Forms change when the qualities act on each other." He pointed at the smoke escaping through the vent at the top of the mound. "Right now, the dryness of fire is acting on the wetness of water in the wood. The smoke is white with steam. Later the smoke will turn yellow and heavy when the heat of fire acts on the coldness of earth within the wood. And in the end, when the smoke turns blue and wispy, what's left?"

"After water and earth burn away, only air ish left."

Jacob nodded. "The wood becomes charcoal, light as air, the perfect fuel for our furnace. If we lived only within this earthen cover, we would know only the emotion of burning wood, its pain and fear. But being outside, being detached from it, we can recognize a greater purpose to charring wood in this way. Detach from all, but connect to the all." He checked the temperature at another part of the mound. "Too cool." He stooped and opened a draw hole.

"First you tell me to connect with everything," Peter said, "and then you tell me to detach from everything." Another rumble of thunder, closer this time, moved through the forest. Peter smelled rain in the air. "If everything ish the same essence, why don' you talk to the storm like you talked to the bear? Tell it to rain on Lothair and not on us."

Jacob walked to the pushcart. "Remember what the good Jew Matthew wrote: 'God lets the sun rise on the evil and the good and lets the rain fall on the just and the unjust.' Why? Because we're all equal in His eyes. Cleave to the recognition of our unity, but cleave from the emotion of our separateness." He picked up a deep basket and pick ax from the pushcart. "It's an hour before nightfall, enough time to fill the basket with iron. One of us must tend the mound. The other must dig for iron. There's an outcropping of iron in that direction." He pointed to where the bear had disappeared in the underbrush. "Which would you rather do?"

Over the next several days Peter tended the mound alone and listened to the distant taps of Jacob's pick ax. When a section became too hot, he closed the nearest draw hole and opened it again when it became too cool. He stayed awake most of the night, watching the meadow boundary, and took short, fitful naps during the day. Every afternoon, rainstorms swept through the bishop's forest and, although Peter saw lightning and heard thunder, he never felt a single drop of rain. Every night he sought answers about the power of cleaving from the man who seemed to rule the weather and wild animals.

CHAPTER 29
THE BISHOP

Jacob and Peter each held a handle while pulling the cart. The pushcart bumped along easily because the black logs were charred to the core and light as air.

Jacob said, "The bishop wants to speak with you."

Peter released his handle and froze in midstep. "With me? Why?" He gripped his walking stick tighter and hurried forward to resume pulling the cart. His hands and clothes were black with charcoal dust. He assumed his face and hair were also black.

Jacob smiled. Only a few black smudges marked his face and clothes. "Don't worry. Bishop Bernard is only looking after his flock."

The bishop's wheat fields flanked both sides of the road leading out of the forest. A few Slavs, all of them slaves of the monastery, and a few novice monks pulled discolored seedlings from the furrows. Beyond the fields and at the end of the road, the cathedral spire reached for the late morning sky.

"The fields look unhealthy," Jacob said. "Weeks of drought and now too much rain."

"When he wants to see me?" Peter asked.

"As soon as possible," Jacob said. "The first three carts of charcoal belong to the bishop. It's our tribute for harvesting iron and charcoal from his forest."

When they arrived at the back of the monastery, a tall, noble priest, the son of Lord Norbert, directed them to a windowless, musty storeroom.

"Thank you, Father Kristoph," Jacob said. "Would you tell our lord Bishop Bernard that my apprentice is here to see him?"

Father Kristoph sneered, "I'll tell him the Jew and his boy are here."

Peter and Jacob stacked charred logs in the storeroom. When they unloaded the last armload of charcoal, Bishop Bernard walked into the room followed by Father Ulrich.

"Greetings to God, Jacob," the bishop said. Light from the open door reflected off his clean white, red, and gold garments.

Jacob bowed his head and replied, "Greetings to God, my lord bishop."

Peter mumbled greetings and bowed his head. He shifted his walking stick from hand to hand and rubbed black dust from his palms onto his tunic.

The bishop said, "We've had too much rain. Blight is ravishing our fields. Pray to God to save us from famine, Jacob." He stepped in front of Peter. "Look at me, Peter,"

Peter pried his eyes from the bishop's studded sandals strapped over scarlet stockings to look into his lean and angular face. The bishop smiled faintly, his lips straight and narrow. Eyes the color of a robin's eggs nestled beneath brown, bushy eyebrows on either side of a chiseled nose.

Behind him stood Father Ulrich, dressed in the black robe of a priest with his sword hanging from his belt. Even though he wore the belt high on his chest, the tip of the sword sheath dragged the ground.

The bishop said, "Jacob says you made the reliquary for the holy splinters of the holy cross."

Peter stiffened, unable to speak or even to nod.

"It was a beautiful piece of work," Bishop Bernard resumed. "I want another silver piece, an image of God enthroned, to put on my pastoral staff. I want you to make it. When you finish digging holes and cutting trees in my forest, come to the cathedral for more silver. Why haven't you been coming to mass?"

Peter focused on the embroidered crosses on the bishop's chest. A border of gold thread confined the crosses to a narrow band that rose up to the bishop's collar. Peter coughed and forced his lips to move. "My leg, sire ... crippled."

Jacob said with his head bowed, "If Peter is well enough to make charcoal in our lord bishop's forest, he's well enough to attend mass."

"Good," the bishop said. "Don't worry about Lothair the Angry. He hasn't been to mass since he killed that last runaway serf. I should have hidden that bright, young man in one of my chests. Lothair would not have found him. He came from your village, didn't he?"

Peter nodded.

"I've heard you're bright, too. Have you been learning Judaism?"

"Learning to smith and ... to read the Bible and -"

"Reading Latin?" The bishop's episcopal ring flashed as he placed his fingertips on his lips. Lines of thought creased his high forehead. "Someday you'll be reading more than the Holy Book. Do you know that a new millennium is upon us?"

"Millennium ish Latin," Peter said. "It means a thousand."

The bishop smiled and nodded. "Yes, very good. For true believers, it means a time when heaven rules on earth, when the true faith dominates the world. Although each race may search for heaven with their own beliefs, some beliefs are truer than others. If you, Peter, were to renounce your belief in the true faith for Judaism, you would be guilty of apostasy."

"I - paused - to - see," Peter repeated.

"Apostasy," the bishop said slowly, "is the greatest of all sins. God hates this sin above all others and requires you forfeit your possessions and your life."

"Oh no, my lord bishop. I believe the true faith. I not done this great sin."

Jacob said with bowed head, "Are some sins greater than others?"

"Of course," the bishop said. "Many are small but some are dangerous."

Jacob said, "It sounds like there are many, many sins,"

"They are unlimited, as if every aspect of us is at war with God. And God hates it and demands retribution."

"Then the fear of God seems reasonable," Jacob said. "But don't you, my lord bishop, teach that God is love? Why then would He hate us and hurt us for our mistakes?"

"Raise your head and look at me, Jacob." The bishop smiled. "God is nothing but divine love. We're hurt by demons, agents of Satan who tempt us and punish us."

"Agents of Satan tempt us and punish us," Jacob repeated. "If I tempt Peter to renounce the true faith, that makes me an agent of Satan."

Bishop Bernard frowned. "Well ... yes."

Jacob resumed, "And if you punish Peter for apostasy, that

makes you an agent of Satan."

Father Ulrich snarled, "Filthy Jew." He put a hand on his sword hilt and stepped toward Peter and Jacob.

Peter's legs buckled. He dropped to his knees, bowed his head, and jumped with a start when the bishop roared with laughter.

The bishop recovered his breath and said, "Stand up, Peter. Don't be afraid. I can always count on your master to turn the world upside down. Are you learning his wise irreverence?"

The blacksmith helped Peter to his feet and said, "Peter has been learning how to cleave to divine love."

The bishop looked at Peter and said, "Come to mass and you'll learn there's no substitute for divine love."

"Then why do you look for a substitute, my lord bishop?" the blacksmith asked.

The bishop walked to a storage box, brushed off its lid and sat down. "I see that my Jewish friend wants to make another point. With what am I trying to replace divine love?"

"Why are you recruiting the sons of the count's vassals?"

The bishop pointed at Father Ulrich. "A noble calling is best served by noble men."

"Since they have sworn allegiance to both the count and the church, who becomes their lord when they inherit their fiefs?"

The little priest looked away and shifted his weight.

The bishop smiled slightly. "You are a smart Hebrew. You know 'The Peace of God,' the church edict." He looked at Peter. "This edict limits Edzard and all warriors to forty days of warfare each year. It requires them to spare all priests, churches, and livestock." He looked back at Jacob. "Edzard is stretching those limits. His intentions against the church force me to defend it. If I don't take from him, he'll take from me. That's the way of the world."

"Is that the way of God?" Jacob asked.

The bishop stood and frowned. "How is this related to a substitute for divine love?"

"Why do you make yourself stronger and the count weaker?"

"Safety. Security. Control."

"That's your substitute for divine love. There is no safer

place than love's embrace if you detach yourself from the way of the world."

The bishop looked at Peter and asked, "Has Jacob talked to you about detachment yet?"

Peter nodded.

"Yes," the bishop said. "It's one of Jacob's favorite topics." He turned to Jacob. "But take care that your detachment is tempered with compassion for the world and its ways, otherwise it becomes aloofness." He nudged a pile of charcoal with his sandal. "My safety, and that of the free town, is less secure since I learned Count Derek's murderer is still alive."

"That's the first third of the charcoal we owe you," Jacob said. He motioned to Peter and pointed at the door. "With your permission, we'd better get back to the forest and -"

The bishop interrupted, "There was a witness to the old count's murder. Or are you too detached to care?" He looked to Peter. "But perhaps your novice would like to know."

Jacob shook his head but Peter nodded.

"Good," the bishop said. "Then I'll tell you, Peter, the truth about the murder."

CHAPTER 30
THE WITNESS

"Since the murder happened on my land," the bishop said, "I convened the trial and invoked the custom of the free town to call for witnesses both noble and not. None stepped forward. It became a futile exercise anyway because Edzard declared that Lord Maynard the Fat was not subject to my customs."

Peter nodded. He already knew some differences between the customs of the bishop's valley and those of the count's lands.

"After Maynard fled and died," the bishop continued. "I heard the confession of a witness who had seen the murder. I can't divulge anything disclosed during the sacrament of penance, except that Maynard was not the murderer."

Peter caught his breath. Here was confirmation of something he had suspected. "Lothair?" he whispered.

The bishop frowned.

"My lord Bishop Bernard," Jacob said, bowing his head. "We really must go."

The bishop waved a hand. "I've said too much. Go and bring me the rest of my charcoal."

Peter limped behind Jacob out of the storeroom into the hot midday sun. "What you think of that?" Peter said and shaded his eyes from the light.

"It's not important," Jacob said.

"He said the murderer ish still alive," Peter said. "I knew it."

Jacob pointed over his shoulder at the storeroom. Bishop Bernard and Father Ulrich stood in the door. "Don't talk of this anymore," he said.

Peter lifted one of the handles and, together with Jacob, pulled the cart away from the monastery and back on the road to the forest. Peter wanted to hurry but Jacob kept the empty, clattering cart bumping along at a careful pace.

When they passed the last of the monastery's novices and slaves in the blighted wheat fields, Peter asked again, "What you think about the bishop's witness? He said Maynard didn' kill the old count."

Jacob stared ahead at the forest. "Slow down. Don't pull so fast."

"The murderer ish still alive."

Jacob didn't look at Peter. "When Edzard hears that his father's murderer is still alive, he'll imagine enemies where there are none. He'll make false accusations and lose friends. He'll become weaker and Bernard stronger. Let's not become a part of Bernard's scheme."

"Scheme? The bishop wouldn' lie, would he?"

"He isn't lying."

"Did the bishop tell you already? No, wait. He wanted to make sure you heard it. But you acted like you didn' want to hear it, as if you already knew. You know it already?" Peter thought he saw Jacob nod, or it may have only been the rocking motion of the cart as they pulled it over a hole in the road. "How you know it? The witness told you, too?"

"It's better not to speak of this," Jacob said.

"Please, I gots to know what you know."

Jacob shook his head. "It would only distract you from your lessons."

"Then make it a lesson in alchemy."

Jacob looked into the clear mid-day sky for a few moments. "You're more than my apprentice, Peter. You're also my friend. What you're about to hear, you must never repeat." He wiped sweat from his forehead, leaving a large smear of charcoal on his face. "Let's make this a lesson in detachment, in disinterested love."

"How can love be disinterested?" Peter asked.

"You can love the world, its people, its things, its drama, without taking an interest in the outcomes. When we support a certain outcome without understanding the greater meaning, we're only acting in self-interest."

Peter nodded. "Yes. Good. I understand. Now let me hear what you know about the murder."

Jacob turned to him. "Are you sure you understand? How will you act when you hear the truth about Derek's murder?"

"I will act ... disinterested, detached."

Jacob looked forward to the forest and wiped sweat from his brow again. "There is only one witness to the murder and that witness has never kneeled in Bernard's confessional."

"Who?"

"Me."

Peter fell into dumbstruck silence. The rattle of the empty cart bouncing along the narrow road provided an uneven tympany for his confused thoughts.

"You were in the forest that day?" Peter asked finally.

Jacob's eyes seemed glazed. "Yes, harvesting herbs and roots with the bishop's permission."

"Are you sure you the only witness?"

"Yes."

"And you didn' confess to the bishop?"

"No. Jews are not allowed any of the sacraments."

"Then there was only you and the murderer, and if you didn' talk to the bishop, that means the murderer ish talking to the bishop. Ish he admitting his crime to the bishop?"

"No."

"How do you know that?"

"Bernard would be devastated if he knew who the real murderer is. Besides, rumors from the monastery place the blame on someone other than the real murderer."

Peter stopped in the road. "That means another innocent man will be accused."

"Keep pulling. We have more charcoal to haul."

"Who cares about charcoal? An evil man let an innocent man be accused and he ish going to do it again. We gots to stop him."

Jacob stared ahead. "You're not acting disinterested. We'll talk about it no more until you rise above it and see its greater meaning."

"What ish the greater meaning?" Peter asked.

Jacob bit his lip before finally answering, "Hard to tell."

"That tells me nothing. Who ish the real murderer? What are we going to do about it?"

"Nothing. Detach yourself from your interest in this. Nothing happened because everything is nothing."

Peter jabbed his stick in the air. "We gots to do something."

"Yes. You can refuse to join Bernard's scheme, refuse to spread his rumors. And when you hear one, tell everyone that it is only a rumor and not based on truth. Remember to cleave yourself from the world."

"Why didn' you tell the bishop what you knew? Didn' you feel terrible when Maynard was accused and killed?"

Jacob's forward stare hardened. "An alchemist should not get entangled in emotional undergrowth."

"But we gots to care. We gots to challenge the evil that -"

"Evil?" Jacob turned a frowning face toward Peter. "Nonsense. We must stay detached and rise above the nonsense." He looked away, and the furrows deepened on his brow.

It was the first time Peter had seen Jacob frown. They pulled the cart without speaking past the outermost wheat field. When they reentered the forest, Peter pressed again, "We gots to care."

Jacob stopped the cart abruptly and spoke through clenched teeth. "Don't speak of this again to me or to anyone else. Go to the back of the cart and push."

Peter bowed his head and took his place behind the cart. He had never seen his master angry. Jacob's unique serenity had been shattered. Why?

CHAPTER 31
THE RABBIT'S TOOTH

Rosamund dropped mint leaves into a boiling pot of dandelion roots, centaury, and thousandleaf. She took a deep breath of steam, filled herself with the herbs' powers and blew the healing breath in Karl's direction. The aromatic vapors pushed the stench of sweat and blood to the corners of their sweltering hut.

Over the past three days, bad humors in Karl's blood had weakened him. This morning, no one could wake him.

His mother held her wrist against his forehead. "He ish burning up again," she whispered and pulled away his blanket. Red and purple veins in his right arm streaked from the rabbit bite on his hand all the way up to his shoulder. Small knife cuts, some scabbed, others oozing, dotted his discolored veins.

Rosamund left the pot on the fire and knelt by Karl. She couldn't find a pulse at his clammy wrist. Only when she pressed her fingers deep into his neck could she feel a faint but rapid beat. "Poor Karl. I gots to put wormwood oil in his tea."

"Wormwood ish only for the stomach," his mother said.

"It also makes the heart beat stronger."

"No. If you use too much, ish poisonous. No one trusts you since you brewed elder trees."

Rosamund touched her belly. After the miscarriage, after the vigorous scraping of Gisela's spoon, she cried for days and bled for weeks. Her stomach became bloated, her urine bloody, and she was too weak to work in the fields until something, a small voice, told her to cook the young shoots of the accursed witch's tree, the elder tree.

She returned to the pot and blew more steam at Karl. "Those elder shoots healed me."

Karl's mother said, "Who told you to do that? A spirit, a demon?"

"No. I followed custom for weeks and ate nettle leaves and washed in teas of bistort root and oak bark and I didn' gets well until I tried something new."

"Karl ish sick because of you." The older woman wiped her eyes.

Rosamund said, "He tried to kill a rabbit and it bit him. The baby rabbits were friendly and Karl likes animals and I thought we could feed them together and maybe he like me again."

His mother glared at her. "Karl should beat you for wasting food on wild animals. Mold ish killing our fields. Food will be scarce this winter."

The door creaked open and Gisela hobbled in, her walking stick in one hand and a knife in the other. She shut the door and said to Rosamund, "Give me the pot."

Rosamund said, "It cooking dandelion -"

"Too late for that. Wash it out and bring it back to me."

"Don' bleed him again," Rosamund said.

"We gots to drain bad blood out." Gisela searched Karl's right arm for new place to cut.

"It makes him weaker and -"

Karl's mother slapped Rosamund. "Shut up. Do what she says." She slapped her again.

When Rosamund carried the small steaming pot outside, the villagers clustered at the door grew silent. Some of the women, Gisela's helpers, followed a few paces behind Rosamund as she walked between a couple of huts, around the communal building and past the dung hill to a shallow stream that trickled beside the village and the stockade.

Grandma Bertha beat a wet tunic with a stick on a stone by the stream. Wet garments hung on a nearby tree. Bertha's red wool shawl stood out amongst the gray fabrics of the serfs. "Bleeding him again?" she lisped.

Rosamund sighed and poured her herbal brew on the ground.

Bertha stared down the women watching from the side of the communal building and said, "Gisela knows more healing than anyone."

Rosamund rinsed the pot in the stream. "Wish I could help."

Bertha hugged her. "The best you can do ish to see him wake up in your thoughts."

Rosamund nodded. "Then the vision becomes real."

Rosamund returned to the hut with her head down, not because she couldn't look at her neighbors' accusing frowns, but because she worried about her husband. She didn't love Karl, but she didn't want him to suffer either. She shut the door of the hut behind her to keep his illness confined inside.

Karl's mother and Gisela crouched on either side of him. Gisela laid a rabbit's tooth on Karl's bitten hand and said, "Come out, black humor, come back to your home. Come out of the blood and into the bone. Come out of the bone and into the flesh. Come out of the flesh and into the skin. Come out of the skin and into the tooth, back to your home."

She put Rosamund's pot under his right elbow and cut a dark vein. Yesterday and the day before, his blood flowed quickly and filled the pot several times. But today it dripped slowly. His blood spread over the bottom of the pot and his pale skin faded.

Rosamund sat in a corner and imagined Karl awake and speaking.

Karl's mother shouted, "His eyes are open. Oh, thank you, Gisela. He coming back." She kissed his forehead. "My baby coming back. Karl, ish me, your mother."

"Mother," he whispered. Only his eyes and mouth moved.

"Yes, darling," she said. "The person that brought you back from death ish here, Gisela."

"Gisela," he whispered.

Rosamund knelt by him. Her heart opened.

He looked past her with glazed eyes.

His mother said, "Your wife ish here, too. The witch."

"Witch," he whispered and shut his eyes.

Rosamund blinked back tears.

His mother said, "Karl, darling. Wake up. Please, darling."

Karl's skin turned bluish white like the moon.

His mother pushed Rosamund away and said to Gisela, "Bleed him again, please. Do the tooth spell again."

Gisela again ordered the black humor to return to the rabbit's tooth. She cut his arm in a new place and his blood oozed again. By evening it had not filled half the small pot. Regardless of how often or how deep she cut him, she couldn't get enough blood out of him.

Rosamund sat on the opposite side of the hut and imagined

strands of love connecting her to Karl, to his mother, to Gisela, and to the rest of the village. She envisioned white streams erasing darkness. Her vision glowed brighter when she saw herself leaving the narrow confines of her village. Perhaps she could find a way to leave, just as Peter had the year before.

Karl never woke again. Two days later, he was buried.

CHAPTER 32
WELDING POWER

Jacob said, "Envision it and it will take shape. Make your thought into a thing."

Peter carved a ball of beeswax into his vision of God - a square jawed, broad shouldered warrior-alchemist on a studded throne. A few days later, after he chipped away the clay mold, he could see what shape his vision had taken. He delivered the silver ornament himself to Father Ulrich, who admired it and weighed it.

When Bishop Bernard affixed the shining ornament to his staff, the monks and merchants praised Peter's workmanship. Thereafter, Peter attended most morning masses and every Sunday mass.

Every visit to the cathedral's cavernous heart inspired him with awe. After his eyes adjusted to dim light streaking from narrow windows, he examined the walls, painted in earth tones with scenes of saints and sinners, and he studied the capitals of columns carved into creatures and thickets. From his place at the back of the cathedral, he stood on his toes to look over the heads of merchants and novices, beyond the count, the countess, their foot soldiers and servants, past the bishop, his canons and monks. Beyond the assembled humanity, on the high altar in the chancel, his silver reliquary shone like a star. When Bishop Bernard lead a procession through the forest of free men under the mountain of stone, his silver staff ornament sparkled with every step, like heaven on earth.

At each mass, merchants shuffled about the cathedral and conducted business. They talked about trade, weather, blighted fields, and Count Edzard's motives for murder.

"Edzard is the only person who benefited from his father's death," Lucus said.

Peter said, "Last year, you said Maynard killed the old count."

Lucus said, "Count Derek died face down with his sword sticking out of his back like a cross on an altar. He wouldn't have given his sword to anyone except his own son."

Peter shrugged. "Only a rumor. Don' gots to talk about it."

Master Thomas said, "Do you know the stocky serf, one of those building Edzard's stone tower?"

"Ledmer? Yes," Peter said. "From Norbert's valley."

"Edzard kept him an extra year and wanted to keep him two more," Thomas said. "The serf got angry and insulted Edzard. Lothair buried him in a hole below the stone tower."

Peter said, "I hope ish just another rumor."

Thomas nodded. "Lothair has started coming back into the town on the count's errands. I'll ask him and let you know."

Lucus said, "Did you hear the latest story about Gabriel?"

Peter always went to mass with Master Thomas and Lucus. They protected him from Crayfish, who begged at the cathedral entrance and took every opportunity to kick Peter.

With the arrival of autumn and the annual market fair, Jacob and Peter bartered away most of their tools and utensils to visiting merchants and nobles. Everyone complained that dried and salted foodstuffs were trading for twice their normal value because of a poor harvest. Peter avoided the market fair for fear of meeting Lothair.

One evening after the market fair had closed for the day, Thomas and Lucus brought Peter a bladder of wine and a pot of honeyroasted nuts from their trading trip to the south. They celebrated that Peter, after residing a year and a day in the free town, had become, according to custom, a free man.

The market fair ended, the days grew colder, and commerce decreased. One frozen morning, Jacob returned from a meeting with the bishop and placed a scroll on Peter's mattress. "This is on loan from Bishop Bernard, the Emerald Table of Hermes. According to legend, Hermes was the son of Adam and the father of Alchemy. Study it and tell me what it means."

Peter unrolled the scroll and read the short Latin passage. "Don' understand any of this," he said and read aloud in Latin. "What is below is like what is above, and what is above is like what is below, to accomplish the marvels of the one."

Jacob nodded. "What we do outside ourselves is what we are doing inside, and what happens inside happens outside, too. Thoughts make things and things make thoughts. When we recover our inner nobility, our golden state, we can help the rest of the world recover its noble golden state." He piled charcoal on the forge and pumped the bellows.

Peter read another passage, "Thou shalt separate the earth from the fire, the subtle from the gross, prudently and with judgment."

"Perhaps that refers to the golden body," Jacob said.

"Ascend with the greatest wisdom from earth to heaven, and then descend again to earth, and unite together the powers of the superiors and inferiors."

"That may be the golden mind," Jacob said.

"So shalt thou obtain the glory of all the world and ignorance shall flee from thee."

"That might describe the golden spirit," Jacob said.

"This has more fortitude than fortitude itself, because it surrounds every subtle thing and fills every solid thing."

"Could that be the universal essence?" Jacob said. "What do you think?"

Peter closed the scroll. "I don' gots to study. You can tell me what to think."

Jacob said, "Study without thinking is useless, but thinking without study is dangerous. Learn from everything, not just from me. Form your own opinions. If you limit your knowledge, you limit your creativity. When you're aware that you create all the time, then you can create with purpose." He took the scroll and brought Peter a wide book. "This is a collection of works from famous alchemists like Democritus the Greek, Kleopatra the Copt, and Mary the Jewess."

While Jacob heated the end of one thick iron bar and the middle of another thick bar in the forge, Peter turned the parchments. Peter paused at pictograms sprinkled through the text and at illustrations of containers with names like kerotakis, cucurbit, alembic, and pelican. On one page he found a familiar picture; a snake, half dark and half light, curled in a circle and eating its own tail. "Ish our door knocker."

"Yes. Ouroboros is the symbol of balance and continuation. Everything is circular. The beginning and the end are the same."

Peter read aloud the Latin words beneath the drawing of the snake, "Creation rejoices in creation, creation consumes creation,

creation brings forth creation."

Jacob hammered the glowing end of one of the thick bars into a wedge and put it back in the fire. "It's time you learn the third power of alchemy, welding power." He hammered a shallow recess in the center of the second bar and motioned to the first bar. "Take that iron and help me weld these two bars into a cart axle."

Peter slipped on work gloves and removed the first bar with the end wedge. Dark scales splotched the bar's red-hot point.

Jacob pointed to the sandbox on the worktable. "Turn it in the flux."

Peter rolled the hot end in cleaned river sand. Granules of sand melted into a milky glaze around the iron. He returned the bar to the fire and pumped the bellows.

Jacob sprinkled sand over the hot scales in the flattened middle of the second bar and placed it back onto the forge. "A good flux removes impurities from the iron's surface. It melts into the iron's crevasses to insure a good weld between two bars. Vision insures the weld between thoughts and things. Our thoughts, fears and desires are forms within the universal essence just as solid things are. With vision, thoughts become things."

Peter mumbled, "My thoughts don' become things. I wanted Rosamund to love me and she don'. I wanted to become a warrior but then Gabriel …" He shook his head.

Jacob said, "Everyone complains about their life, but no one complains about how they think about their life. Our adventures are parables of our thoughts." He removed the second bar to the anvil. The hot yellowish-white middle hissed. A glassy liquid had replaced the dark scales. "Bring the other bar and hold it against this middle."

With a small sledgehammer, Jacob pounded both hot irons into a T shape and scrapped the intersection with an iron brush. He and Peter and returned the T bar to the fire. "You may yet become a warrior," Jacob said, "but not in the form you expect." They brought the T bar back to the anvil. Jacob hammered and brushed it again.

The laughter of children outside the shop's entrance interrupted their discussion. Gabriel opened the doors and entered the shop. Except for a yellow cap with short floppy horns, he looked the same, wearing the same rusted armor and the same foolish grin. Behind him, three horses snorted frosty clouds in the doorway and a group of children giggled in the street.

The children fled when Jacob walked up to take the horses' reins. "Greetings to God, Gabriel. Good to see you again."

Peter cringed when Gabriel hugged him. But the elder brother no longer smelled like a stable. The aketon beneath his armor seemed clean, almost snow white.

Jacob said, "I heard you saved Count Edzard in his last raid. Rumor says Edzard stayed in camp as usual and sent his warriors off to pillage. But while they were away, his own camp was attacked."

"Defenders knew that he be coming and set a trap for him becoming," Gabriel said in a lilting voice. "Edzard sent men to look ahead was took instead."

Jacob said, "They say you unhorsed the warriors without using any weapons. They say you disarmed ten warriors."

Gabriel shook his head and held up five fingers. He and Jacob burst into laughter.

"They say," Peter projected his voice over their laughter, "they say you put those warriors back on their horses and sent them away before Count Edzard could demand a ransom. He was furious."

Gabriel pointed to his yellow hat. "He knows not what to make of me but he knows what not to make of me."

"What on his head?" Peter asked.

"A fool's cap," Jacob said.

Gabriel nodded. "Stories to tell and weave a spell to fight fatigue within his home, my strength ish seen to stand between and fight intrigue within his home, first floor of stone can now enthrone the count, the countess and me, so we stay and play the Keltic zither, because fear ish near and makes him wither."

Peter shook his head. "He ish not making sense again."

Jacob translated, "He said the first floor of Edzard's stone tower is finished. He lives in the tower with the count and countess. He's there to entertain Edzard and to protect him. Rumors that his father's murderer is still alive have frightened Edzard."

Peter pointed at his brother. "Has he moved from the stables to the stone house?"

Jacob and Gabriel nodded together.

Peter looked away and frowned. He couldn't believe his brother's good fortune.

After a moment's silence, Jacob called to Peter, "Come over here. It's past time you learned to shoe horses." He placed a stool and a sack by the cold doorway. Upon the stool he set a cup of salve, a handful of nails, a hammer, a file and a pair of clippers. He turned the animals around to face outside and tied their reins to the circular doorknocker, Ouroboros.

Peter limped to the horses, more to get away from his fool brother than to learn something new. He had seen Jacob shoe many horses and none of the animals had bitten or kicked the blacksmith. Nevertheless, Peter moved with caution to a horse's flank and held his baton between himself and the beasts.

One after another, Jacob lifted each hoof and held it between his thighs. "This shoe is good and needs only a new nail here and here. After you nail them, turn down the points and file them smooth. This next shoe is loose and the hoof worn. Remove the shoe and trim the inside of the hoof here, file the outside here, and then file the bottom until it's level. Put the hoof shavings in the sack. Now this shoe's been thrown and the hoof's sore. Numb it with the salve and then measure it for a new shoe. It won't take me long to make new shoes." He walked to a corner of the shop and retrieved a suitable iron bar for horseshoes.

Peter leaned his baton against the wall, turned his back to the horse's head, and held a hoof between his legs. He looked over his shoulder and saw the horse looking back at him through clouds of frozen breath. "Don' think I can do this," he said.

Jacob dumped fresh charcoal on the forge. "Use welding power. Create a vision that you will shoe the horses and then follow that thought with your hands and tools."

Peter took a deep breath and whispered a chant. He envisioned tooling the first hoof to perfection, not for his sake, but for the animal's well being. He began filing, trimming, and measuring. He envisioned a flawless shoeing for the second hoof and set to work with zeal. Jacob handed him a warm horseshoe and he nailed it onto the third hoof. His vision grew sharper with each completed horseshoe.

On finishing the first horse, he began working on the second without a moment's hesitation. He trimmed, filed, measured and shoed each hoof exactly as he envisioned.

He moved to the third horse, picked up a hoof and glanced confidently over his shoulder.

The horse's head turned toward him and Peter recognized the white star on the horse's forehead, the same horse that had bitten him at his village over a year ago. Its lips curled like a sneer and revealed its large teeth.

Peter concentrated on the hoof and tried to set his thoughts to shoeing, but memories intruded on his vision. He remembered how the horse had turned on him without warning. He thought about the sting of its teeth on his arm, the blood and the ache that followed. He trimmed, filed, nailed, and looked over his shoulder. He pinched his thumb twice and drove three crooked nails. Just as he finished hammering the last nail on the last shoe and was ready to flee, he felt his upper arm clamped between equine teeth. "Ow!" Peter jumped back.

The horse kicked and its new iron shoe struck Peter's hammer with a loud clang. The tool flew out of his hand and across the shop. The horse kicked again. Peter ducked and the hoof clipped the top of his head.

He scampered away and cried, "I could see that coming."

Jacob inspected Peter's bleeding head. "It's just a scratch. Why did you see that coming?"

"That animal bit me a year ago. I was afraid he do it again."

Jacob rubbed a salve on Peter's arm. "Your fear gave you a nasty bite."

"I didn' bite myself. That crazy horse bit me. It kicked me. It could have killed me."

Gabriel stroked the white star on the horse's head. "Good horse horse good if could would please give ease."

Peter limped to his mattress, to the book of famous alchemists. He flipped the pages of the book and rubbed his sore arm. "None of the famous alchemists ever had to shoe a horse." He turned away from Jacob and envisioned a visit by a famous alchemist who would show him a painless way to alchemy.

Three months later, his vision became solid.

CHAPTER 33
THE FAMOUS ALCHEMIST

Father Ulrich opened the door to the bishop's house and led Jacob and Peter inside. Peter stopped and leaned on his baton a moment to adjust his eyes to the darkness. One room filled the first floor, which was longer than and twice as wide as Lord Arnulf's house. Thick beams rose from the earthen floor to a high ceiling. Thin, oiled linen that stretched over narrow window openings kept out some cold but let in little light. The waxy bite of pine-scented candles thickened the still air. In the center of the room burned a fire, nearly enclosed with stone and tile.

Bishop Bernard leaned on a high backed chair on one side of the fire. His leaner face betrayed that not even he had escaped the winter's famine. "Greetings to God, Master Jacob. I'm glad Ulrich convinced you to come. You brought your novice. He can stay and watch."

Next to the bishop, in the room's only other chair, sat Countess Lilli in a long dark dress. A small dog lay on her slippers, obediently warming her toes with its body. Her gold and silver amulets, armlets, and bracelets flashed in the firelight. When she turned to watch the three arrivals approach, her eyes sparkled with curiosity and seemed to probe Peter as someone would probe murky waters with a stick.

Four canons in priestly robes, all sons of noble vassals to Count Edzard, conversed behind the bishop and the countess. Frosty clouds formed when they spoke in the winter air. Their sword belts were pulled tight over their thin stomachs.

Across from them waited the four town eldermen, merchants elected by local free men to petition the bishop for matters of the town's welfare. Master Thomas stood amongst them. His cloak sagged over his smaller frame. He wore stockings and sandals since he and Lucus had boiled their boots for soup.

After an exchange of greetings, Father Ulrich joined the churchmen. Jacob joined the merchants and Peter stood behind the town eldermen. Peter's mind sparked with excitement while his stomach groaned. He had eaten nothing but thin herbal soup since the town's store of grain was depleted after Easter.

With the exception of the countess, no one else from the castle attended. What if Lothair would arrive? Peter looked around the room and saw a couple of chests as long as a man. He could hide in one of those chests.

The bishop sat down on the chair and said with a loud voice, "Let's begin."

Boots thudded down the stairway from the second floor. A tall, slender man descended in a blue robe that flowed like the finest linen. The stranger held his head high and cast his eyes upon his audience with cool dispassion. His gray beard, domed forehead, and sharp nose conveyed wise nobility.

"Greetings to God, all you esteemed free men." His deep voice commanded respect. "I am Master Augustus. I was a student of Olympiodorus and the teacher of Geber and Rhases."

Peter's skin tingled at the mention of famous alchemists he knew from Jacob's books. He ignored custom and moved forward to stand beside Jacob.

Master Augustus gave Peter a faint smile. "I was a counselor to Pope Sylvester and to the late, great Emperor, Otto the Third."

The famous alchemist walked behind the fire and leaned forward. The fire's light cast unearthly shadows up his face. He raised his arms and his voice. "The end time is upon us. The first thousand years ended in chaos." He looked at the bishop. "What did a council of bishops declare about the end time? Tell us, Bernard, about chaos."

The bishop cleared his throat. "Well, the council said we are in the midst of the falling away, the coming of the Antichrist, the coming of chaos."

Augustus crossed his arms. "The horsemen of the apocalypse are riding throughout the world. Our King and Emperor Otto died childless. Who will be elected the new king? Will he be a friend to the church, someone the Pope can crown holy emperor? And if a good and strong king is elected, can he stop the chaos? No. Men of noble birth are disrupting trade," he pointed at the merchants, "robbing churches," he pointed at the churchmen, "and stealing from each other." He raised his hands. "We need to protect ourselves. We need more weapons."

He put his hands on his hips. "Heaven sent us the worst

famine and the coldest winter ever, didn't it?" He nodded his head vigorously.

Peter nodded his head together with Augustus.

Master Augustus continued nodding. "The summers are either too dry or too wet. The weather is changing. We need extra food for coming famines, don't we?"

The merchants and churchmen nodded with him.

"What will save you from the destruction of the new millennium?" He walked to the front of the fire and whispered, "Gold." A large yellow coin appeared between his thumb and forefinger. "An unlimited source of gold will get you a storehouse of food, an array of weapons, a chest of warm clothes. Gold will keep you safe as God counts each year to the end of time."

"Does the Eternal count the years?" Jacob asked.

Augustus frowned. "You are the Jew, aren't you?" He turned his back on Jacob and spoke to the churchmen. "How else would God know it was time to unleash chaos if He didn't count a thousand years?"

Jacob smiled. "Since Moslems are not yet half way through their first thousand years and Jews are between their fifth and sixth millennia, then we must assume God's chaos is intended solely for Christians."

The churchmen muttered and the merchants shuffled away from Peter and Jacob.

Augustus thrust his chin forward. "God does not concern himself with unbelievers. He cares only for the true faith, and its thousand years of service."

"What does a thousand, or nine thousand years matter?" the blacksmith said. "When compared to eternity, any time is nothing, less than a blink of -"

Augustus stamped his boot. "The only time that matters is the end time. It was written in the Holy Scriptures. It was made in God's mind." He turned to the bishop, lowered his voice and spread his arms. "Its chaos is everywhere."

The blacksmith said, "If we think chaos is everywhere, then it will be."

Augustus answered through clinched teeth. "Chaos is not created by our feeble thoughts. Chaos is a divine sign of the end time. A Jew cannot understand that."

Peter's face burned with embarrassment. He edged a step away from the blacksmith and glanced about. Everyone scowled except the countess whose painted lips smiled.

The blacksmith said, "The end time is only a form in the minds of fearful people who want their questions about life answered in their own lifetimes."

"Blacksmith," Bishop Bernard called. "The end time is not just a mental form. If God lived here amongst His people, He would not care to hear that His divine patterns exist only in our minds, in our imaginations."

The blacksmith bowed his head. "My lord bishop, if God lived here, His truth would disturb His people so much, they would burn His house down and run Him out of town."

The merchants' jaws dropped open. The canons' eyes widened. The bishop broke the stunned silence by chuckling.

Augustus stepped up to the blacksmith. "Abel, the son of Adam and Eve, was a gentlemen and the ancestor of all gentlemen. But you," he pointed a shaking finger in the blacksmith's face, "are a descendant of Cain, the peasant and ancestor of all peasants. Your words betray your blood line. But what could one expect from the race of people that killed our lord Jesus?"

"What was the blood line of Jesus?" the blacksmith asked.

Augustus stepped back. "Jesus was a gentleman, of course, on his mother's side."

The bishop's chuckling gushed into laughter and he doubled over in his chair. The bemused expression of the countess remained unchanged. The merchants and the churchmen stirred and murmured. Augustus scowled with barely contained rage.

The bishop regained his composure and said, "No more talk. Show us how we get an unlimited source of gold to protect us from the chaos of the new millennium."

Augustus waved to a bench, which displayed a set of scales and weights, a pair of tongs, a tall cup brimming with a liquid, three crucibles and a set of small, hand-sized bellows. He gave his gold coin to Thomas. "Weigh this and put it in a crucible of your choice. Don't touch any of the crucibles or you'll disturb their pure essence." He produced a red pebble and presented it to the bishop.

"Tell us, Bernard, what this is made of."

The bishop scratched the pebble with his fingernail. "It's a red powder encased in wax."

Augustus took the pebble from the bishop and held it high. "This is the philosopher's stone. When this is projected into a crucible with a seed of gold, the gold will grow. At this hour, in the sign of Taurus with the moon in Leo and Libra in ascendance, the heavens are in the right position to project the king of the red lion."

After weighing the gold, Thomas dropped it into a stoneware crucible. The coin thudded softly on the bottom. Augustus deposited the philosopher's stone into the same crucible with a graceful sweep of his arm. He lifted the crucible with a set of tongs and placed it in the fire's heart.

"Come here, Jew peasant," Augustus called to Jacob. "Enclose the fire and feed it the breath of life."

Jacob enclosed the open side of the fireplace with stones and placed tiles on the top. Then he pumped air with the hand-sized bellows through a space at the base of the fire.

While Jacob worked, Augustus explained, "Everything is made of the prima materia, the basic reality behind all forms. The prima materia is divided into four elements; fire, air, water, and earth. Everything contains these elements. The elements each have four qualities in varying degrees; dry, wet, hot, and cold. A thing can be changed into another thing by the quality they possess in common. We've all seen wondrous transformations, haven't we? Where does dew come from? Air has wet and hot qualities. Water has wet and cold qualities. Through their common quality, wetness, air transforms to water and becomes dew."

His listeners nodded their heads. Peter nodded vigorously and wondered why Jacob couldn't explain alchemy as simply as this.

Augustus ordered the blacksmith to stand away. He removed some tiles and stones with a set of tongs, retrieved the glowing crucible and poured its yellow contents onto the earthen floor before the bishop and the countess. As his audience crowded closer, he picked up the cup of liquid from the bench and tilted it over the glowing small puddle.

Peter looked away, expecting the exploding light he had seen in Jacob's shop. The sparkling gold necklaces around Countess Lilli's neck caught his eye. She was watching him, not Augustus. Their eyes met and Peter froze. Her dark eyes shimmered and held him fast. Her steady gaze seemed to reach into him and grope about his mind.

The cup's liquid crackled when it fell upon the golden puddle, but no light blinded the witnesses, no thunder shook the windows open.

The countess turned her eyes away and freed Peter from their grasp. He looked back at the palm sized disk, almost hidden beneath a fog of hissing steam.

Master Augustus crossed his arms. "Through the qualities they hold in common, gold is multiplied by the mediation of the philosopher's stone. See what it weighs now."

The merchants and canons huddled around the scales on the bench as Father Ulrich weighed the disk. Peter strained to look over their shoulders. An excited hubbub burst out.

"My lord bishop," Father Ulrich stammered. "The gold weighs twice what it did before."

Augustus raised his voice above the commotion. "Do you want to see another demonstration?" One hand pointed at the unused crucibles and the other produced a second red pebble.

"Yes," nearly everyone shouted at once.

Master Thomas held out several pieces of gold and shouted, "Use my gold."

Others shouted, "No. Use mine."

Master Augustus raised his hands. "The stars won't be properly aligned again until tomorrow. Anyone who wants their gold multiplied should leave it in my care tonight."

Peter opened his pouch, pulled out his gold pebble and stepped forward.

Augustus turned away with a sudden whirl, arms flailing, and grabbed Jacob.

The blacksmith had picked up an unused crucible from the bench. As Augustus grabbed Jacob's arm, the blacksmith tossed the crucible onto the lap of the startled bishop.

Jacob said, "These crucibles appear different from my own, sire."

Augustus plucked the crucible from Bishop Bernard's lap. "They're special. Not like something a rude peasant would use. I am a serious alchemist."

Jacob looked at the bishop and said, "A serious alchemist never takes himself seriously."

"Let me see that crucible," the bishop said.

Augustus stood still, both hands clutching his crucible. His mouth opened but uttered nothing.

The bishop held out his hand. "Give me the crucible."

After a long, quiet moment, Augustus handed the container to the bishop. His mouth twitched. "It's quite plain. There's nothing special about it."

Jacob said. "It appears to have a special base."

The bishop reached into the crucible. Peter heard the bishop's fingernails scratch inside.

"Wait," Augustus squeaked. "The special essence will be disturbed."

The bishop turned the stoneware so that firelight could shine inside. "There's a layer of wax and charcoal dust. Beneath that, a layer of gold."

Thomas picked up the third crucible and tested it. "This one has a false bottom, too."

Peter returned his gold pebble to his pouch.

Bishop Bernard said, "What's the custom for punishing a thief?"

"We cut off the offending hand," Father Ulrich answered.

Thomas said, "He used both his hands to trick us."

The merchants and clerics closed in a circle around the foreigner.

Augustus dropped to his knees and bowed his domed head. "Please, my lord bishop. I haven't stolen anything."

The bishop stood and let the crucible thud to the floor. "You're lucky your ruse didn't get that far. You may leave my valley with both your hands, but without your crucibles. Go now."

Augustus ducked spittle from his audience and walked with quick, light steps to the exit. He opened the door and the soft folds of his costly robe fluttered as he flew out of sight.

The merchants and canons lingered, examining the tools of

the hoax, talking and laughing about the experience. The countess quietly studied the stranger's gold. During the entire spectacle, her dog had flinched but had not moved from her feet, as though it was held in place by an invisible hand.

Bishop Bernard walked Jacob and Peter to the door. "Thank you for your insight, Jacob. Augustus captured my imagination. I thought he would enrich me."

"But he did, sire, just not with gold," Jacob said.

The bishop nodded. "If you get any more books of alchemy, bring them to my scriptorium for copying."

As Jacob and Peter walked home over the frozen streets, Peter asked, "Does everyone know you an alchemist?"

"It's no secret," Jacob said. "But most people don't know what alchemy is."

"Why don' you want me to tell people about alchemy?"

"What would you tell them?"

"Well, I would tell them a real alchemist can turn a copper penny into a gold coin."

Jacob laughed and said, "That's why you'd best not tell anyone about alchemy. When you learn alchemy's true nature, you can speak of it."

"I gots to learn faster. Why don' you teach me faster?"

Before Jacob spoke, Peter heard the answer deep inside, *"That would be dangerous."*

CHAPTER 34
ANVIL POWER

Peter leaned farther over the bluff to see the distant riders in the valley below. "Six warriors and ... one, two, three foot soldiers."

"Be careful you don't fall," Jacob said.

Peter looked down the sheer rock wall to the thick forest. The tops of evergreens beneath him swayed in a breeze and their piney scent drifted up the cliff. The distant riders traveled on the forest road through a meadow near the narrow southern end of the bishop's valley.

Peter squinted and wiped sweat from his eyes. "Someone walking next to the first rider. Gots a yellow hat. Gabriel."

"Count Edzard is keeping your brother close to his side," Jacob said. "He's taking only those warriors he trusts. Bernard's plan to weaken Edzard is working well."

"I wonder if -"

Jacob said. "Lothair is not on this summer's raid because Edzard feels betrayed by Lothair. Edzard sent his marshall to work secretly with other electors against the will of the bishops, against election of his duke, Heinrich, as the new king. But, as we know, Lothair cannot keep a secret and he failed."

Peter stepped back from the edge. "He smart to stay away from Lothair. Count Derek didn' and he gots killed."

Jacob stood still, facing the trees behind the cliff. He held a basket of herbs in one hand and raised the other hand, palm out, fingers spread. A doe walked slowly out of a thicket. It deposited a prized stone mushroom it held in its mouth into Jacob's basket. "Thank you," Jacob said.

Peter held out his hand. "Let me try that."

The deer took a step backwards and bounded into a thicket.

Peter sighed and said, "Dumb animal." He picked up his own basket of juniper berries, willow bark, primrose rootstocks, yellow gentian leaves, flowers, and other herbs.

Jacob stripped a few pieces of bark from a birch tree and added them to his basket. "What were we saying about the fourth power of alchemy?"

Peter limped with his baton to the same tree and picked a few more pieces of bark. "The power of an anvil ish like will power. I can push my will into the ground like a root. I can be unmovable, like you were when Hugo tried to push you around. I can change weather. I can slow time. I can command animals." He batted a fly away from his ear.

Jacob walked along the path that skirted the edge of the bluff, and studied the ground and undergrowth for healing herbs. "You cannot do anything alone. Creation bows to you only when you join your will to the universal essence. Anvil power comes not from willfulness, but from willingness, acceptance, submission. An anvil is like the universal essence – unchanging, unmoving. Hot iron bends on the anvil but it cannot bend the anvil."

Peter said, "What if I want to force my will?"

"Then the result will be deformed. Everything is joined. If you pull the right sleeve of a hauberk, the left sleeve follows. If you force the right sleeve one way and the left sleeve another way, then you'll tear the hauberk."

"How do I know which way to pull?"

Jacob stopped. "Be still, listen. Here's an example. Tell me which way the wind blows."

The still summer air pressed on Peter. He wiped sweat from his face. "Ish no wind."

"What is the nature of wind?" Jacob asked. "Listen, look, and feel."

Peter heard a low rush of air moving through the forest. Treetops on the far side of the valley beyond the meadow swayed. Soon the treetops on the meadow's near side began waving. The rippling movement drew closer, swept through the valley by an invisible power. The rushing grew louder and, when the wind flew up the bluff, it surrounded him with the gentle roar of rustling leaves and branches. The gust fluttered his tunic and his fine, blond hair. It cooled his skin and refreshed his mind. The branches around him swayed and then became still as the breeze moved on. The roar of the wind dwindled until, finally, the forest was quiet again. Below them, on the far side of the valley, another wave swept toward them.

"That is how you know universal will," Jacob said. "First, be still, reflect on its nature. Second, listen, look, feel for its presence in your open heart. Third, shape your will around it. Fourth, act on it."

Jacob picked a leaf off the ground. "Blow a leaf onto the wind."

Peter bent down and searched for a leaf as light and dry as the one his master held. When he found the right one, he stood and blew it toward the open air over the precipice. The wind from the valley blew up the bluff and the leaf sailed back into Peter's face. He staggered back and swiped the leaf away, breaking it into pieces. A fragment of the leaf lodged in his eye.

"That's what happens when your will blows against universal will," Jacob said. He blew his leaf in the opposite direction.

Peter rubbed one eye and watched with the other as Jacob's leaf flew on the wind through the trees and out of sight. Soon the air was still again.

Jacob continued up the path along the cliff, searching for herbs. Peter followed.

On the edge of the cliff, Peter spied a large domed mushroom. "Look, master. A stone mushroom." He bent to pluck it.

"Don't touch it," Jacob called. "Does it have a ring around its stem?"

Peter rubbed his eye again and stooped to the ground. "Yes."

"It's a death cap mushroom. If you touch it and then touch your mouth, your body will die in days, maybe hours."

"Yes, yes. I know. Why are we picking herbs? Ish work for women." Peter lifted his baton and swung his good leg back to kick the poisonous mushroom over the edge.

"Stop," Jacob shouted.

Peter shattered the mushroom into pieces with a swift, high kick. His crippled leg slipped on a mossy stone and he fell on his back against the sloping edge of the cliff. He slid forward on loose gravel, his walking stick slicing the empty space. The herb basket, his hand still grasping its handle, remained behind him on level ground, scraping toward the edge as he slipped over.

Peter's heart stopped. He spun around and scrambled, but too late. He slid over the slope and into the brink.

He felt a tug on the basket handle and he stopped falling. A cloud of bark, flowers, and leaves fluttered past him.

Jacob lay prone above him on the sloping edge. One arm extended down the rock face and grasped a side of Peter's basket.

Jacob's other arm held an oak seedling at the top of the ledge.

Peter swung against the cliff. "Master, use your power. Use your will."

"Can't do it alone," Jacob grunted. "Find a foothold."

Several rocky outcrops jutted out the cliff wall below him and to the sides. Within kicking distance, a small, scraggly spruce grew from a crack in the cliff.

"Hurry," Jacob said. "The seedling is breaking."

Peter kicked his legs up to reach the scrub and heard the sickening sound of ripping reeds. Both the handle he gripped and the basket side that Jacob held were tearing loose.

"Quick, give me your stick," Jacob shouted.

Peter swung his baton up as the basket broke apart. Jacob released the basket and reached for the stick, but it remained beyond his grasp as Peter fell. Peter stopped breathing.

While the air rushed past Peter, he saw above him Jacob slide over the edge with the uprooted seedling in one hand. His master tumbled after him into the empty space. Horror mixed with terror.

His feet hit an outcrop and flipped him backward with a slow somersault into the void.

We're going to die, Peter thought. A flash of calm acceptance released him from terror. Forgive me, master. If it's divine will, let it be. Was this the will of the universal essence?

"*No.*" He heard a familiar voice in the midst of air rushing past his ears. "*Extend your will into the stick. Let it join with you. Be as rigid as your baton.*"

He released the basket handle, grasped the stick with both hands, and held it stiffly over his head, as though he was an extension of the stick. His muscles hardened like the wood grain of the baton.

Halfway through the somersault, as Peter's feet pointed skyward, the end of the stick hit another outcrop. A loud crack echoed off the rock wall. The jarring impact vibrated up the stick through Peter's body. He balanced on the end of the baton, wobbling for a moment before toppling over. The stick vaulted him away from the cliff and into the top of a fir tree.

The first few twigs brushed him softly as he fell. The branches became thicker, snapping as he slid through them. Farther down, the larger ones ripped his clothes. He tumbled ever more slowly through each limb and lost his grip on the baton. The lowest boughs bounced him between them before letting him thud to the ground. He landed on a cushion of pine needles.

The landing knocked air from his lungs. He rolled on the bed of pine needles and fought to breathe. Lights twirled before him until a black ring closed in and snuffed them out.

After what seemed only an instant, cool wetness brought light to the darkness. His head throbbed. Nausea rose, ebbed, and rose again. He blinked his eyes open.

Jacob sat beside him, a wet cloth in his hand, his white eyebrows knit with concern. "How do you feel?"

"Headache," Peter groaned.

"Willow bark tea is brewing now. You've got bruises and scrapes, a knot on your head, and your tunic and breeches are torn to shreds. Other than that, you're fine."

Peter sat up. Every muscle ached. He checked his belt for his gold pebble. He still had it. He looked up at the tree above him. A row of broken branches reached to the sky. His walking stick balanced on a mangled bough.

"I wish I had my stick." He held up his hand and spread his fingers.

A breeze moved through the forest. The trees swayed, showering Peter with broken twigs. His baton thudded to the soft forest floor beside him. One end of his stick was split.

He focused on Jacob. His master wasn't scratched or bruised. His clothes weren't torn. "You fell, too," Peter said. "What happened to you?"

Jacob pointed at the bluff. "A shrub caught me."

Peter followed Jacob's finger to that small, lonely, scraggly spruce near the top of the cliff. A large bird, an eagle perhaps, alighted on its crooked branch. The rock face on all sides of the tree was sheer.

Peter said, "No way to gets down from there, unless you could fly."

Jacob smiled.

CHAPTER 35
THE HEBREW

"This is Peter, my apprentice," said Jacob in Latin.

Peter limped into the dark blacksmith shop from the bright street.

"This is Yitzak Azrielides," continued Jacob and waved a hand to a figure dressed in black. "He is a journeyman of alchemy from the city Tulaytulah in the Caliphate of Cordoba, the land of the Moors. He has come to learn from us as we shall learn from him."

Yitzak stepped forward and bowed. Light from the street reflected off his balding forehead, making his long, dark hair and beard appear even darker. A large nose dominated a narrow face the color of tree bark. The journeyman's black breeches, tunic, and mantle gathered in soft folds of fine linen. A bulky pouch hung from a leather strap over his shoulder. He spoke to Peter in a strange guttural language.

"Thou must speak Latin," interrupted Jacob. "Peter does not understand Hebrew."

Yitzak raised his eyebrows. "La'az? Forgive me, Peter Yahkovides. From thy name I should have known thou art a Gentile." He spoke Latin with guttural vowels.

"I am a Christian. I have just come from Mass."

"Thou art young. Art thou married?"

Peter shook his head.

Yitzak turned to Jacob. "Master Yahkov, tradition tells us to teach only mature apprentices, or at least, married ones. Without the stability of marriage and experience, the secrets of the sacred art can make one unstable."

Jacob nodded. "True. But sometimes we must work outside the limits of tradition."

Yitzak pulled from his pouch a polished ram's horn twice as long as his thin hand. "My master Azriel instructed me to present thee, Master Yahkov, this Shofar." He laid it gently on the table.

Peter reached out to touch it.

Yitzak wagged a finger at Peter. "The Shofar is only for the rabbi."

Jacob said, "Master Azriel taught me how to blow it." He lifted the horn to his lips and blew a cheerful bellow.

Yitzak waved both hands and called out above Jacob's trumpeting, "It is to be blown only for the days of renewal and atonement. That is tradition." The journeyman shook his head as Jacob returned the horn to the table. "Thou do many things that are not tradition, not mizvot. Thou wear two kinds of thread. Thy garden is planted with two kinds of seed. Thou do not -"

Jacob interrupted, "Dear Yitzak, when thou dine at our table, thou shalt be happy we planted more than one kind of seed."

Yitzak's face grew darker.

Jacob put an arm around Yitzak. His white hair contrasted with the journeyman's black hair. "Thou art correct to follow the mizvot, for that is thy way."

Peter asked, "What is mizvot?"

"Commandments from the Bible, from what thou call the Old Testament," said Jacob. "There are over six hundred commandments."

Yitzak said, "Strict adherence to mizvot brings one closer to Adonai, blessed be His name. For the good of the world, everyone must follow the laws."

Awkward silence followed, disturbed only by the staccato of hammers in the town center.

Finally Jacob said, "Yitzak shall be staying with us during the market fair."

Peter nodded. He saw many foreign peddlers in the cathedral. They were filling the market square with their animals, carts, tents, and tables. Tomorrow would be the first day of the weeklong fair.

"Yitzak needs to find a place to conduct his business," said Jacob. "Go with him, Peter, and help him get ready."

Yitzak led Peter through the back door to a pair of packhorses grazing in the mowed field. Peter kept away from the animals, wary of another bite, and suggested the journeyman lead them while he showed the way.

The noonday sun warmed the autumn air and burned away most of the morning fog. Above the disappearing mist, the cathedral's spire and the count's stockade overlooked the valley. The new second story of Edzard's stone tower peeked over the stockade walls on the rocky bluff.

They descended the hill and Yitzak said, "The fog was so thick, it was easy to lose the way."

"How did thou find Master Jacob?" asked Peter.

"Master Azriel told me to look for the door knocker in the shape of Nechustan."

"Ouroboros, the circular serpent?" asked Peter.

"The same," said Yitzak.

"What sort of merchant art thou?"

"I am not a merchant. I am a physician and a surgeon."

"I have heard of that. Physicians attend only the noble."

"Physicians are scholars who work with their minds. Surgeons are common people who work with their hands. I normally care for the noble as a physician. But I also help commoners as a surgeon for tikkun olam, that is, for repairing the world."

At the bottom of the hill they turned a corner and the hammering sounds from the town center grew louder. Peter asked, "How did thou learn thy trade?"

Yitzak pulled a leather belt from a sack bound to the lead horse's back. Attached to the belt were loops and sheathes, each holding a tool. He draped the belt over his shoulder and pointed to a small crystal vial in a loop. "From a brewmaster I learned how to taste sugar in a person's urine." He pointed to a short, thin knife in a sheath. "From a master stonecutter I learned to remove gall stones. A quick plunge into the belly," he stabbed downward, "dig out the demon stone with a quick flip," he twisted upward, "and stop the bleeding with a salve of frankincense, aloe, egg whites, and rabbit fur."

Peter shuddered.

Yitzak continued in Latin. "From a master barber I learned trepanning." He pointed to a metal tube with saw teeth at one end. "Poisonous humors burst from my patients after I cut a hole in their skulls." He pulled a long, thin knife from its sheath and pointed it at Peter's crippled leg. "Injury attracts blood. Blood stagnates and decays. It must be drained. I can make thy injury well again."

Peter discretely hobbled a pace away. "I thank thou, Yitzak, but I prefer to limp."

Without warning, a clawing grasp took hold of Peter's

shoulder from behind and lifted him by his tunic. The linen tightened around his neck and strangled his breathing. For a confused anxious moment, he dangled in the air.

Lothair hissed in Peter's ear. "The little serf has learned the language of pigs." He heaved Peter across the road.

Peter landed on his hands and knees. He spun around and crouched, ready to jump away in an instant.

The autumn sun gleamed dully from Lothair's chain mail. He stepped up to Yitzak and growled, "You look like the devil himself."

The journeyman did not bow his head, but countered Lothair's frown with fearless eyes. "Vaht does the knight vahnt?" Yitzak asked in the native tongue.

"The count vahnts a toll," Lothair mocked the journeyman's accent. "He sent me, his accursed servant, to collect it. Every thieving merchant who enters the God damned bishop's valley must travel on the count's roads. You have two shod horses. Therefore, you owe four copper pennies."

"I vahnt to read this law," Yitzak said.

The tall warrior leaned down, almost touching Yitzak's large nose with his closely cropped black beard. "It's custom. There's nothing for you to read. We have no use for reading and writing."

Yitzak produced a few coins from the pouch hanging on the shoulder strap.

Lothair studied the coins before putting them in his own pouch. He scowled at Peter and said, "Does the Jew beat you enough?" He clinched his fists and took a step toward Peter.

Peter leapt back, slammed against a wall, and fell. For a dazed moment he leaned on the building.

The journeyman ran forward and held up a hand to block Lothair's advance.

The warrior marched into Yitzak's arm and stopped abruptly, as if he had crashed into a sturdy limb of an old oak. He staggered back and his black eyebrows rose in wonder. He hesitated a few moments, fidgeting with his sword belt and tapping his foot.

Yitzak said, "Does the count vahnt you to collect tolls from other foreigners?"

Lothair growled at Peter, "You're always protected by

sorcerers." He marched away.

Yitzak helped Peter up and they continued down the street.

Peter asked in Latin, "Did thou use the power of the anvil, of will?"

"Will is a tool of the magician," said Yitzak.

"Art thou a magician?"

"Everyone is a magician."

"You could have pushed Lothair or knocked him down."

"If will is used to disadvantage another, the magician shall also suffer a disadvantage."

They rounded a corner to enter the market square and the busy confusion of preparations for the fair. Foreign traders shouted in strange tongues as they directed their animals, anchored tents, and hammered tables. Whiffs of exotic spices and animal dung mixed in the dusty air. Peter led Yitzak through the frenzied activity to a town elderman, who pointed the surgeon to an area reserved for dealers of more expensive, finer wares. Yitzak received the end spot, across from the redhaired Norseman and his table of stockfish.

Peter scanned the crowd for Lothair while Yitzak laid a blanket on the ground, erected a lean-to tent, and hammered a stool together. When finished, he washed his hands with a liquid whose aroma stung Peter's eyes. "The hands of a physician must always be clean, the nails manicured," said Yitzak. Under the stool, he placed an open shallow box with beads strung from one side to the other.

Peter examined the box. "I saw something like that two years ago. How does it work?"

"The abacus is for counting," said the journeyman. "Each number holds a spiritual truth for alchemists."

"When shalt thou become a master alchemist?" asked Peter.

"At the end of my journey, I must do a great work."

"Did thou have a test to finish thine apprenticeship?" asked Peter.

"Yes, of course. I had to forgive an enemy. I was filled with the wonder of Malkut."

"Malkut?"

"Has Master Yahkov not taught thee the Sefirot?"

Peter shook his head.

Yitzak glanced at the other merchants. "Do they speak Latin?"

Peter said, "All of the merchants and many of the monks know Latin."

Yitzak motioned Peter to sit on the blanket and began whispering, "In Genesis, the Creator, blessed be His name, formed the universe with ten utterances. These are the ten Sefirot, the divine principles."

With the hammer handle, he scratched on the ground ten circles arranged in a rough diamond and pointed at the top circle. "The first Sefirah is Keter, the crown. Then comes wisdom, then understanding." He indicated each successive circle. "Then love, then strength, beauty, victory, glory, foundation, and finally Malkut, the kingdom. The Creator, blessed be his name, spoke in Hebrew, and divine meaning fills the letters of the Hebrew alphabet." He drew twenty-two lines between the circles and wrote a symbol by each line. "They weave the Sefirot into a ladder of mystical ascension."

Peter pointed at the bottom circle. "Thou art here, the kingdom."

Yitzak shook his head. "No. Well, yes. I felt it once. Malkut."

Peter indicated the top circle. "Then Master Jacob is here, Keter, the crown."

"No," said Yitzak. "The Sefirot are not stages of growth. They are divine principles, emanations. They are like divine water springs, they either wash thee clean or drown thee."

"How do thou use the Sefirot in alchemy?" asked Peter.

Yitzak looked up at the afternoon sky. His distant eyes gazed into heaven. "First concentrate on each Sefirah. Call out its divine name. Beg for the blessings of the archangel and the lower order of angels ruling that principle. See light everywhere. Search to know the beyond, which lies within. Annihilate your mind and absorb the wonder of the Sefirah. Revelation comes like an old friend thou have not seen in ages. The soul delights with trembling."

Peter ran his fingers along his belt to the pouch that held his gold pebble. "How do thou use the Sefirot to make gold?"

"Forgive thine enemy and submit to divine will. This ritual is called the stone of the philosopher. In the exalted moment, the voice of the alchemist lowers and vibrates the divine names of the

Sefirot. The sounds inspire baser matter to transmute into gold. I did it once." Yitzak looked down and sighed. "Only once."

"How do thou use the Sefirot with the furnace, the mixing of metals, the -"

Yitzak interrupted, "Is that the way of Master Yahkov? He must be one of those who assigns a metal to each Sefirah. But alchemy is a work of spirit, not metals. There is no need to toy with outer things when the goal is inner experience." He shrugged. "But dust may play with dust if it pleases dust. I have a small scroll, 'The Sefer Yetzirah.' I shall ask Master Yahkov to translate it into Latin for thee. Then thou shalt learn the traditions of the Sefirot."

An uncomfortable tingling crawled along Peter's back. He turned and saw Lothair glowering at them from the shadow of a nearby building within earshot. Yitzak and Peter stood quickly and led the horses away, leaving the blanket and stool to reserve the place for tomorrow's fair. Lothair followed them through the busy square.

"Does the knight understand Latin?" whispered Yitzak.

"No." Peter looked over his shoulder. "Well, maybe."

Lothair followed them out of the town center and through the streets to the road that led up to Jacob's house. Before Peter entered the blacksmith shop at the top of the hill, he looked back again. The tall warrior stood at the base of the hill, his legs apart and his arms crossed.

"Lothair attacked me," Peter told Jacob.

Jacob shook his head. Hollowed out rounds of rye bread filled with barley soup awaited Yitzak and Peter on the worktable. Jacob sat with them and talked to Yitzak in Latin about alchemy. Peter ate his soup and followed the discussions as best he could.

"To understand the powers, one must master the Sefirot," said Yitzak.

"Symbols are never mastered," said Jacob. "As we change, their meanings change."

Peter conducted business with visiting merchants while Yitzak and Jacob's discussion continued unabated.

Yitzak waved his hands. "The Emerald Table was found in Hebron by Sarah, wife of Ahbram, father of all Hebrews. It belongs to the Hebrews. Why say thou Adam found it?"

Jacob shrugged. "Because Adam is everyone and, thus, it belongs to everyone."

At twilight, Peter shut the doors and windows against the cool evening air. Yitzak and Jacob did not stop talking.

"Will draws power from creation to extend creation," said Jacob.

"But when the magician draws power to dominate creation," said Yitzak, "the magician must always defend what was won and defeat is certain."

Peter lit a candle for the two men and sat at the table. He understood little of what they said. As the night grew longer and the candle burned lower, he propped his head up with one hand, later with both hands. The hard stool and table became uncomfortable.

He went to his mattress and shut his eyes to rest just a moment. As he drifted into sleep, he heard Yitzak's warning. "Enoch did not die, for the Creator, blessed be His name, had taken Enoch to heaven and his skin turned to fire and he grew fiery wings and his body became full of eyes and he expanded to fill the universe and he received divine wisdom and all the archangels bowed to him. A heretic ascended and saw him and Enoch scorned him and the heretic returned to earth and declared there were two Gods. Enoch received sixty lashes for scorning the heretic. Beware that thou suffer not the same fate."

Peter dreamed that he had grown fiery wings and lived in a room atop the count's stone tower. A gentle nudge brought him out of his dream. He blinked his eyes in bright sunlight and shut them again.

"Wake up, Peter." Jacob's voice brought him back. "You have a visitor."

From the angle of sunlight streaking through the southern window, Peter judged that he had overslept. "Visitor?" he mumbled. He climbed hand over hand up his walking stick and rubbed his eyes.

In the shop doorway, silhouetted against the bright street, stood a woman. Her blond hair shone around her face.

Peter's heart stopped. "Rosamund?"

CHAPTER 36
THE MINSTREL

Rosamund's heart skipped as she ran to Peter and wrapped her arms around him. "Lord Arnulf brought me to the market fair. We only here two days. I ... I so glad to see you."

Peter held a long, thick stick with one hand and returned her hug with the other arm. "Rosamund, I ... I ..."

Rosamund stepped back, holding his hand in hers. It felt larger, stronger than she remembered. She caressed his fingers and said, "You stopped biting your nails."

Sinewy muscles sculpted his arms and a broad chest filled his tunic. His blond hair was clean and trimmed above a face grown fuller, a jaw more square and stubbled with a thin day-old beard. He stood taller than she did.

"You grown up," she said.

"You, too," Peter said. His blue eyes stared at his wolf brooch pinned at her chest. Or was he staring at her breasts?

She giggled and turned away. He pulled his hand away from hers. Looking back, she saw that he too was embarrassed, gazing redfaced at the ground. It reminded her of his original appeal, his gentleness and sense of honor. She yearned again for that summer, two years ago, when his attentions showered her. Together they had shared hopes and dreams.

"Blacksmith," a warrior called and strode through the shop's double doors. "This blade needs sharpening." He laid a sword on the worktable.

"Greetings to God, sire. Yes, it will be sharpened right away," Jacob said. "Peter, your help isn't needed now. Go see how our friend, Yitzak, is doing. Take Rosamund with you."

Peter shook his head. "But Lothair attacked me yesterday."

Anger flickered in Rosamund's heart. "If he does it again, I stop him. I defend you," she said.

Peter's face turned red again. "I can defend myself," he said and marched out the door.

She followed him into the crisp sunlight, and noticed Peter favored one leg over the other. He stepped with the stick close to his right leg.

"Does your leg hurt?"

Peter mumbled. "No. W-w-well, yes. Gotten used to it."

Discordant sounds of market activity drifted up the hill from the town center. Many people in the street greeted Peter with a cheerful "Greetings to God." But a few glared and a big, bear-like merchant muttered, "Jew's boy."

"What he says?" she asked.

Peter walked with his eyes down. "Jacob ish a Jew."

Rosamund put her fingers in Peter's hair and entwined his soft strands. "He helped you. He ish a good man. I heard what Lothair did to you. When you didn' come home, I thought you died. I was happy when Father Ulrich said you alive. And now you a free man, no longer a serf. Why didn' you send us a message?"

Peter moved away from her fingers, leaving her hand to stroke the air. "You married Karl."

"Everyone thought you died, and Lord Arnulf married me to Karl, and later we heard you alive. You didn' send any word."

The din of the fair grew louder as they descended. Peter returned the greetings of the town's residents but said nothing more to Rosamund. He kept his eyes down, never looking at her.

At the base of the hill she said, "You could have sent me a message."

"You had Karl's child," he blurted without raising his head.

Rosamund looked down. "The child died before birth. It was deformed. I cried and cried." The old grief welled up again. The tracks of people and animals in the road blurred through brimming tears. "And then Karl died. I sad about it and glad, too, so ashamed to be glad he gone."

Peter took her hand. "Sorry," he said in a voice as gentle as his hand. "I didn' know."

She wiped her eyes. "Everyone but Grandma Bertha think I a witch. They say a demon made my baby. Gisela wanted to kill the evil seed so ... she hurt me inside ... so I don' have ... more children."

Peter squeezed her hand. "W-w-what happened?"

She shook her head. "I don' want to talk about it. I trying to forgive."

He squeezed her hand again. "I forgiving my enemies, too."

Rosamund smiled and resisted the urge to embrace him. "Everyone made it through the famine last winter. We had a good harvest this year. Wish I could leave the village like you. You seen so many new things and you learning smithing."

He pointed his stick at the castle and told her how he made two chain mail tunics for Count Edzard. He pointed at the cathedral spire and told her how the bishop praised him for his silver reliquary and staff ornament. He stepped closer and lowered his voice. "I learning the sacred art of alchemy."

"What ish alchemy?" she asked.

They rounded a corner and entered the colorful chaos of the market fair. "I going to be stronger than any w-w-warrior," Peter said, barely audible over the riotous noise.

They walked through a swirl of color, smells, and sounds. Rosamund had seen it once before with Karl. But now it seemed brighter. They encountered beautifully dressed women and men, warriors in chain mail tunics, monks and novices with tonsured haircuts and clean robes. Peter stopped occasionally to introduce her to his neighbors. She swung Peter's hand as he led her forward.

He made her promise not to tell anyone about alchemy before speaking softly and intently about his apprenticeship. She strained to hear him above merchants hawking "metal wares," "Flemish linen," and "sheep from Bohemia." He led her past baskets of clucking hens and explained how he had become like a furnace, with walls for reflection, a door for openness, a crucible for shaping, and a fire for acting with zeal. She agreed that everyone needed these qualities. At the pots and pans he told her about hammering power. She knew one must have faith, must know what's true before one acts, and she told him about her efforts to help the villagers reform old customs. As they passed the furs of wild animals, he spoke of cleaving. She spoke of the connection she felt to everything, like the baby rabbits she befriended in the forest. While pulling her from rolls of linen, he instructed her on the power of welding. It seemed obvious to her that all things and actions begin with a thought and she recounted how she envisioned that she would leave the hamlet after Karl's death and then, a year later, Lord Arnulf asked her to go with him to the market fair. When she paused to look at strange, dried mushrooms and fruits, he explained how universal will was like an anvil. She explained that if she had not given in to the will of life, her miscarriage could have killed her.

What Peter described as the secrets of alchemy, seemed to her to be just plain, common sense, the obvious workings of life.

When they reached the end of the square, Peter stopped before a dark-skinned foreigner dressed in fine, black linen. They greeted each other in the same melodic language Father Ulrich spoke at religious services in her hamlet.

"Latin?" she asked. "You speak Latin? Can you teach me Latin?"

Peter beamed and answered in Latin.

She repeated his last words, "Poolchrah-teebee-fahceeays. What does that mean?"

"It means I want to teach you Latin," Peter said.

A merchant behind them shouted, "Fish. Goot Fish."

Peter's smile faded and he released her hand.

The dark man bowed from the waist and said, "Forgive me. I should speak the local language. My name is Yitzak Azrielides."

She bowed her head. "My name ish Rosamund. Peter and I come from the same vil -"

"Fish. Goot Fish." The booming call cut off Rosamund's words.

Peter pointed across the way and asked her with an icy edge. "Remember coming here w-w-with Karl?"

Rosamund glanced at a fish monger's table. "No." She took his hand again. "Forget about Karl. We can enjoy the fair, you and I."

Yitzak tapped Peter's shoulder and said, "This morning I vent to the stables because people told me a man vahs singing and telling stories there. He is an alchemist. He has visdom. Master Yahkov said your next lesson is visdom."

"W-w-wisdom," Peter whispered. "Gots to be the fifth power of alchemy. Thank you, Yitzak." He led her away. "Gots to see the w-w-wise man."

As they wove between the buyers and sellers in the square, Peter explained that the stables housed the free town's animals and an occasional traveler for a fee. But during the market fair, the animals were removed to accommodate the fair's many visitors.

He steered her into a low, long building midway down the market square. The stables smelled of sweat and dung, much like the village communal building. Specks of dust swirled and sparkled in shafts of sunlight from holes in the roof. People packed the chest-high stalls and faced inward, listening to an argument in the center of the building. The crowd burst into laughter and catcalls while Peter and Rosamund squeezed to a place within sight of the speakers.

"Gabriel?" Peter hissed.

She laughed, instantly recognizing the big, blond foot soldier in the yellow cap, standing head and shoulders above most of the crowd. A tall, broad shouldered priest stood and gestured in front of Gabriel.

Peter took her arm. "How can Yitzak think that Gabriel ish a w-w-wise man?" He tugged her back toward the exit.

Rosamund rooted herself to the ground. "Wait, Peter, please. He tells a story of Count Edzard's battle with Maynard the Fat. I listened from outside the great stone house last night. Your brother sings well and tells a good story."

The tall priest spoke loud for everyone to hear. "Church doctrine tells me how to think. I have all the wisdom I need in its dogma."

"The more wisdom you find," Gabriel said, "the more foolish you find yourself."

The tall priest said, "I learned the tenets of theology and I know that I know. You are a fool. You know nothing."

Gabriel nodded. "Knowing nothing ish knowing all. When you know that you know, you don' know, don' you know, Father Kristoph?"

"I know the answer to this world." Father Kristoph's voice was stern. "Do you?"

Gabriel answered, "Nothing. No answer. Never was an answer. Won' be an answer. That ish the answer."

Giggles and snickers drifted through the spectators until the tall priest turned away. "This smacks of heresy," he shouted and pushed his way to the stables' doors. Fitful murmuring replaced the crowd's mirth. Father Kristoph shouted "Heresy" once more before leaving the building. An uneasy silence settled over everyone.

Gabriel began skipping in a circle. The crowd shuffled back, giving him a small area in which to dance. His voice soared over the throng in a melodic song.

**The
answer
we discover,
we only recover
in the nothing we are.
We are the warmth of the sun shining.
We are the cold of the star twinkling.
We are the roar of the wind blowing.
We are the power of the oak growing.
We are the speed of the deer running.
We are the heart of the bear fighting.
We are the strength of the ox pulling.
We are the scent of the rose blooming.
We are the thrill of the lover kissing.
We are the mirth of the baby smiling.
We are the thought of all.
Grace, beauty, and glee
in the nothing
are
we**

After a moment of silence, the crowd answered with scattered applause.

Peter shook his head. "Pure nonsense."

"A beautiful riddle," Rosamund said.

Foot stamping and chanting replaced the applause. "Battle. Battle. Battle." Rosamund chanted and stamped her feet with the rest. She, too, wanted to hear his song again.

Gabriel raised his hands to quiet the crowd. He picked up a shallow wooden box with gut strings drawn tight across its length.

Rosamund squeezed Peter's hand. "That ish a Keltic zither," she said, proud of her new knowledge.

The crowd edged closer when Gabriel plucked a twangy melody and began singing:

**"A count from the East Mark sent me to embark
on this story of his glory,**

to sing his name, extend his fame
of his battle with Maynard the Fat, the Gory.”

Rosamund whispered, “Ish the song I heard last night.”

“Count Edzard looked long for the fiend
who had schemed
to attack and murder his father.
And though Maynard ish dead,
the count still dreads
that conspirators are fed
still
at the table of their lord and master.”

Gabriel plucked a darker melody.

Rosamund nudged Peter. “Have you heard the murderer ish still alive?”

Peter frowned and nodded.

“The count searched for their leader,
Maynard the strong,
Maynard the bold.
Maynard could hold six men in his hand
and twelve in the other.
Edzard came to a forest in his search for Maynard,
a forest so black and then
the forest closed its door and the count said no more
and told the woods to open.
Edzard marched through the woods, up a hill to a crest,
to a bear so fierce and grim.
The bear roared stop and the count said not
and made it kneel before him.
Edzard clashed with a storm whose waters were borne
to flood him and to kill him.
The storm screamed die and the count said fly
and told the sun to glisten.”

Without a word, Peter shook his hand from hers and pushed his way toward the exit. Rosamund hesitated in confusion before following as best she could. Just before the stables’ door, she caught up with him.

“Wait, Peter,” she said. “It just started.”

Peter spun around. “Lies,” he snarled. “W-w-why ish he

honored for telling lies?"

Lothair's growl came from the doorway. "Lies about a man afraid of his own God damned shadow."

Peter jumped back and raised his walking stick.

Lothair drank from a cup and swayed away from the doorjamb. "Why doesn't your fool brother sing about me, the real hero that day?"

"Leave Peter alone," she said, her voice trembling with anger and fear.

The tall warrior pointed at her with his cup, sloshing out some of the frothy brew. "Cavorting with serf girls, are you? You know your place is with stinking serfs. You and your fool brother."

Peter bowed his head and limped quickly past Lothair out the door. Rosamund felt Lothair's glazed eyes follow her as she sprinted through the doorway and into the market fair. More people crowded the square now, making it difficult for her to catch Peter, who seemed to run between the displays of copper pans, cheese barrels, fabric rolls, and pig pens. She overtook him at the far side of the square.

"Peter, wait." She touched his stooped shoulder but he continued forward. "Lothair ish so mean. Your brother ish no fool."

Peter stopped so abruptly that Rosamund ran into his back. "So my brother ish no fool but I am," he growled.

"What?" she said to his back. "I didn' say that."

He turned and snarled at her. "Yes you did. Two years ago. Here, in the market fair. You told Karl I w-w-was a fool."

"No. I didn'."

"Yes, you did. You said it over there." Peter pointed his stick at one end of the fair. "I w-w-was hiding under the stockfish table. You said I w-w-was a STUPID fool."

She looked in the direction of his trembling stick. He pointed to a large redheaded merchant and a table piled high with dried fish. "Fish. Goot Fish," the merchant bellowed into the crowd. A memory of that day with Karl two years ago cut through her confusion.

"Please, Peter. I don' remember what I said, and I thought you had died, and I was angry with you then. Try to see it in a different light. You had a foolish notion that you could be something other than a serf and it nearly killed you."

"I am something other than a serf," he barked. "I a free man and I don' care to be in the company of a lowly serf." He turned and marched away.

Her heart squeezed with shock. She tried to call after him but a gasp was all she could manage. After a few stunned moments, she followed him again. Her voice returned and she called to him, pleaded with him. He continued forward without glancing over his shoulder, limping with stubborn determination out of the market square and through the town streets. She stopped at the base of the hill and watched him limp up to the blacksmith shop on the edge of town.

Rosamund hurried back down the streets of the free town, through the market fair which interested her no more, over the bridge where a gray cripple called to her, up the steep road of the bluff on which half a dozen serfs carried stone blocks from the quarry, back to the castle stables where she and Lord Arnulf were lodged, back to her bed of straw where she buried her face and let her sadness burst out. She cried the rest of the day and into the night, sobbing herself to sleep.

CHAPTER 37
STEEL POWER

The bishop's silver jingled in a pouch on Peter's belt with every step he took across the frozen ground of the market square. The bishop had weighed a number of silver coins and commissioned him to cast rings with images of biblical figures. The bishop asked that the ring with the image of Saint Elizabeth be smaller than a man's finger. "Why he wants me to make a ring for a woman? Ish there a woman that he -?"

Jacob interrupted, "Don't entangle yourself in Bishop Bernard's affairs." He slung over his shoulder a sack of four sheep shears from the bishop. "What about you and your woman? You have a problem."

"There ish no problem with Rosamund. She ish not my woman." Peter limped through his words, which floated as icy clouds in the still winter air.

"Tell me again the steps in using the power of steel."

"First step: reflect on the problem from the highest vantage point."

"Then you can see that Rosamund can't hurt you," Jacob said.

Peter's face burned in the cold air. "But she did. She told Karl I was a stupid fool. I heard it. I certain of it."

"Certainty is rigid, brittle, and ultimately weak," Jacob said as they left the market square and entered a street. "When you know you know, you really don't know. Wisdom is knowing how little you know."

Peter thumped his baton against the ground. "I know what happened."

"Do you see her as flawed, imperfect, because you thought she hurt you?"

"Yes."

"Do you see yourself as flawed?"

"Sometimes." Peter shrugged. "Well, most times."

"Is Rosamund made of the same essence as you?"

"Of course. The universal essence makes up everything."

"Is the universal essence flawed?"

"No." Peter remembered Rosamund's flawless face in the market fair, and how hurt she looked when he told her that he didn't care for her company. "Well, uhhhh, not sure she meant to hurt me. Maybe I just saw it that way."

"Good," Jacob said. "You recognized your ignorance and accepted responsibility for your interpretation of what happened. In truth, nothing happened because you are invulnerable. You can't be hurt by anything outside yourself. What is the second step?"

Peter sighed. "Be open to see the problem differently. Well, if she cannot hurt me, if nothing outside of me can hurt me, then what left?" Before Jacob could say anything, the answer came to him. "Me. I am what left. Am I hurting myself?"

Jacob said, "For the third step, melt the problem's explanations together in the crucible. Then wipe surface clean of slag – the deception in the problem. How did you deceive yourself?"

"I told myself that she … she thought I was a stupid fool."

"Now spoon the lead out of your melt and tell me the purpose behind this deception?"

They turned a corner to climb the hill toward the shop. Peter reflected on his motives while trudging up the hill. After a few moments, he found the answer. "I felt like a stupid fool. I still do. I used her to support that shame."

"Very sharp. Wisdom is like a steel tool – sharp and durable. What's the last step?"

"Act according to my ideal." Peter took a deep breath. "I forgive Rosamund. She did nothing." In that moment, his heart warmed and tension drifted away like smoke. "Ohhhh. I feel lighter, as if something heavy burned away."

Jacob patted Peter's back as they reached the top of the hill. "When you forgive, you burn away the fog around your quarry. What other resentments do you want to burn away? Lothair?"

Peter shook Lothair's baton. "Lothair really did hurt me. I gots proof."

Jacob's laughter produced a series of frosty clouds through which Peter plowed headfirst as he limped into the shop. Jacob closed the doors behind them, pulled the rusty shears from the sack, and gave them to Peter.

"Do I have to sharpen these again?" Peter slouched onto his

mattress. "Wish I could fix them so they stay sharp."

Jacob said, "We can make them sharper and more durable, just as you can be with wisdom. Polish the shears but don't oil them. We're going to case-harden them."

"Case-harden?" Peter shivered in the cold and scrubbed the shears with a wire brush.

From a corner of the shop, Jacob brought a stoneware box to the worktable. He swept away a layer of dust and ash from its lid. "Case-harden is a way to turn the skin of iron into steel."

"Can we turn iron into gold this way?" Peter asked, but he knew the answer.

Jacob coaxed the fire at the base of the furnace. "Only iron can turn itself into gold."

"And we help it on its way," Peter completed the answer. He polished the shears with a whetstone.

Jacob dropped several handfuls of charcoal dust from the bottom of a bin into the stoneware box. After washing his hands, he brought a hemp sack of horse-hoof shavings to the worktable and divided the trimmings into four high piles. "We can fit all four shears in the case, two leaning against opposite sides and two on the bottom. But they mustn't touch each other."

Peter placed one set of shears on a bed of charcoal dust inside the case.

Jacob said, "Cover it with shavings. This is the insult you think Rosamund gave you."

Some of the shavings had become hard as stone from years of storage. Peter covered the shears completely and placed the second set of shears opposite the first.

"That's the pain you think Crayfish caused you," Jacob said. "The third set is anger over the honor you think Gabriel stole from you."

Peter covered the second and third set of shears with shavings. "What ish the fourth?" he asked, already knowing the answer.

"Lothair," Jacob said.

Peter shook his head. "Not ready for that yet."

"Then let's leave it out," Jacob said. "Put the lid on the case and mix some loam to seal it. Otherwise, the air will stink of old grudges burning away."

After Peter sealed the lid, Jacob set the box within the furnace and shut the door.

For the rest of the day and into the night, they took turns tending the furnace fire, keeping it at a constant high temperature. Peter pumped the bellows, chanted softly, and reflected on how he forgave Rosamund and how he could forgive Crayfish and Gabriel. The shop became so warm that he had trouble sleeping when evening drowsiness overtook him.

He awoke the next morning to a mild, springlike breeze drifting from the shop's open garden door and out the open front doors. While he ate his breakfast of stale, brown bread, he listened to the activity in the street as the town's people took advantage of winter's brief reprieve to run errands, conduct business, and visit friends.

At midday, Jacob announced that the case had been heated long enough. They let the fire burn out and opened the furnace door. Within the furnace's white-hot interior, the rectangular container glowed like a crucible, bright orange speckled with small black craters and ridges.

"We'll let it cool," Jacob said. "You'll see the power of steel to make the shears strong and sharp for a very long time. Meanwhile, you can brush and oil the last set of shears."

"I do it later," Peter said.

While the case cooled within the furnace, Peter opened the scroll with Jacob's new Latin translation of Yitzak's book. "You left some Hebrew in the text," Peter said.

Jacob laughed and said, "You'll have to learn the Hebrew alphabet if you want to know the meaning of each letter."

Peter read aloud, "The ten Sefirot and numbers from the No Thing are -"

The town carpenter trotted breathlessly through the shop doors. "Jacob, can you help my wife? She's vomiting blood. It's getting worse and I can't stop it. Please come."

Jacob asked him a few questions: what may have caused the illness, how long she'd been sick and what remedies she had tried. He loaded a sack with several containers: dried knotweed and calendula flowers, St. Johnswort extract, crushed oak bark, and powdered roots of comfrey and celandine. He said to Peter,

"Sharpen and oil the fourth set of shears like you've always done. When the case has cooled, polish the rest of the shears inside." Then he hurried out the door.

Peter picked up the fourth set of shears. He didn't want to brush, polish, and oil them, and then repeat the same messy process a few months later. He recalled the steps for case-hardening. It was simple. He could do it himself. It was time to be rid of his fear of Lothair. Master Jacob would be proud.

The clay box no longer glowed when Peter pulled it from the furnace with Jacob's largest tongs. He didn't realize how much the container weighed until it cleared the furnace opening, slipped from his grasp, and thudded upright onto the floor. The fall broke the loam seal and the lid slid off. Airy rivulets of intense heat danced upward from the open box.

With the tongs, he removed each set of shears, cooled them in the slack tub, and placed them on the worktable. A light gray metal replaced the iron's black grain. Small white blemishes clustered like blisters on sections of the metal. It didn't take him long to polish all three sets until they shone like silver. He marveled at their brightness. Their sharp edges seemed capable of cutting through anything.

"Now I change Lothair," he said aloud.

He gathered several handfuls of charcoal dust into a pot and dumped it into the stoneware box. As he washed his hands in the slack tub, he noticed his shadow flicker on the wall before him. He turned to see flames leaping from inside the container. The box, still very hot, had ignited the charcoal dust.

As quick as he could, he dropped the fourth set of shears into the box and threw the last hoof shavings over it. He fumbled to get a grip on the lid with his tongs.

A throat-strangling stench overwhelmed him. He gagged and dropped the lid. Thin, gray smoke from burning hoof trimmings swirled out of the box and drifted with the breeze out the front door. The noxious smoke squeezed his windpipe and cut his breathing to short, rapid gasps. He coughed, choked, dropped to his knees, and fumbled again with the lid. His eyes watered and his sight blurred.

A second set of tongs grabbed the opposite side of the lid and pulled it away from him. He rubbed his eyes and saw Jacob standing over him, seemingly unaffected by the fumes.

Jacob placed the lid back on the box. "Quick. Seal it. Where's the loam?"

Peter wheezed, "Loam? Not mixed it yet." Gray smoke snaked out from the lid's edges.

"Jacob?" Thomas and Lucus covered their mouths with their cloaks and coughed just outside the shop entrance. "Are you well?" Thomas asked through thick wool.

Jacob smiled and waved to Thomas. "Yes." Still smiling, he said to Peter, "Mix the loam and seal that lid as fast as you can."

The wool merchant from down the hill walked up and gasped between coughs, "God help us. What's that smell?" His hacking wife and children gathered behind him.

Jacob walked to the door. "Just a little accident. Peter is about to fix it."

Peter gagged and scrambled to mix the clay, sand, and water to a consistency thick enough to seal the smoking fissures. The coughing and complaining crowd outside grew larger. Jacob apologized and urged his neighbors to return home.

Peter finally sealed the lid and was ready to flee into the garden when the beggar hobbled up to the garden door. "What stinks?" Crayfish hissed.

Father Kristoph pushed the beggar aside and walked through the garden door. "That smells like burning flesh," the tall priest said and coughed. Robed monks from the fields entered behind him and coughed.

"It's horse's hooves," Jacob said to the gathering monks. "We burn them to case-harden your shears."

Father Kristoph lifted a set of shears and his eyes widened. "It's been changed."

A monk touched the shears. "It's silver." The coughing subsided as every monk tried to touch the shears.

Jacob's voice dropped to a low, serious tone. "It's steel, but only on the surface."

Father Kristoph shook his head. "You turned our shears into silver."

"How?" two young monks asked in unison.

"Wid sorcery," came a loud hiss from the garden door.

A robust linen merchant at the front door exclaimed, "Sorcery?" Behind him, the crowd stopped coughing and grew quiet. By now, the breeze had carried most of the toxic fumes away.

The beggar wormed his way forward and stood next to the monks. "Jews steal and cook babies to make silver."

A shriek pierced the stinking air. "Zelda. Where's my little Zelda. Zelda." The brewer's wife pushed her wide hips through the crowd and into the shop, bringing with her a baby in one arm and a toddler by the hand. She peered into each corner of the shop, tossing her graying hair one way, then another. "What did the Jew do to her? Where is she?"

Crayfish pointed his handless stump at the rectangular box on the floor. "Dere she ish. Burned alive."

Zelda's mother screamed and collapsed to the floor. Her baby and toddler howled. The crowd behind her muttered and gestured.

Hugo shook his fist from the back of the crowd and shouted, "Kill the Jew."

Peter picked up his stick and looked for a way he and Jacob could escape. Throngs of people blocked the doors and windows.

"That case is too small for a child," Thomas shouted above the noise.

The beggar shouted, "He chopped her to pieces."

Zelda's mother screamed again.

"Open the box," Father Kristoph said. "Quick."

A monk picked up a sledgehammer and shattered the stoneware container with one swift blow. A cloud of the throat strangling fumes billowed out.

Zelda's mother vomited. Her baby and toddler gasped for air. All others, except Jacob, backed away, coughing and gagging. Peter held his breath as the toxic, gray smoke slithered on the breeze through the shop and into the street. The town's people hacked and shouted in protest and anger.

Father Kristoph struggled to speak between coughs. "That ... can only be ... burned ... human flesh."

The miller coughed and asked from the street. "What do ... we do?"

"What does custom say?" the shoemaker asked from a window.

"We've never had ... a sorcerer before," the wool merchant coughed his words. "There is no ... custom."

"Put de Jew in a box and burn him," Crayfish shouted.

"Burn his evil tools," Hugo shouted.

Father Kristoph pointed at Jacob's scrolls and books. "Burn his hellish wisdom."

Peter tried to slip between two monks toward the garden door but the beggar's thin claw grasped his tunic and pulled him back.

"Burn de little wolf, too."

A monk took Peter's arm, another his wrist and a third twisted his baton from him.

"They hoof shavings," Peter cried, his heart thumping in his ears. "Really they are. We not making silver. I gots some gold. You can have it if you let me go."

The monks bowed their heads. Peter stopped struggling, aware of a sudden stillness. He looked over his shoulder and saw Bishop Bernard and Countess Lilli in the shop's center. Lothair grimaced just outside the entrance. The coughing crowd in the street had bowed their heads and shuffled back from Lothair.

"Kill the Jew and the serf," Lothair barked.

Despite the hands gripping him, Peter slid behind Father Kristoph's robe and watched.

The bishop crouched as if the odor floated above him. His stiffly smooth chasuble and his tunic's soft folds contrasted with his wrinkled nose, squinting eyes and frowning forehead. "What's that smell?"

"The blacksmith has been burning either animal hooves or horns," the countess said. She stood straight, her face smooth and serene as though immune to the stench. A gold clasp at her thin neck held a blue woolen cloak, which covered her from her shoulders to the ground. She moved to Peter's study table, gliding as though her feet, hidden by the cloak, never touched the ground.

The bishop coughed and said, "How do you know that?"

She examined the scroll with the Latin translation of Yitzak's book. "In the emperor's court, I saw and smelled many things."

Father Kristoph pointed at the worktable and said, "My lord

Bishop Bernard, the Jew has been making silver from our sheep shears."

The bishop studied one of the shears for a moment and then placed his pastoral staff with its ornament of God enthroned before the tall monk's eyes. "This is silver. That," he pointed at the shears, "is steel. As the son of Lord Norbert, you should know that."

Father Kristoph bowed his head low. "But how does he make it look like silver?"

Jacob answered with head bowed, "Seal the tool with hoof shavings and charcoal dust. Keep at constant high heat for the full cycle of day and night. The surface of the tool turns to steel. When polished, it looks like impure silver. Black iron still lies beneath the surface. The process is called case-hardening."

The countess lifted her eyebrows. "That's a technique of the imperial armory." She glided to the worktable, picked up a set of shears and said, "Father Kristoph, wouldn't you rather have tools of silver than iron?" She looked directly at Peter.

The shop disappeared and Peter saw only her eyes. They held him, probed him, exposed him. She looked away, released him, and the shop reappeared. His face flushed and he bowed his head.

Crayfish shook Peter's tunic with his claw. "Dey killed little Zelda to make steel."

"Little Zelda is too small to get through this mob," Bishop Bernard said. "I saw her with other children at the back of the crowd."

Zelda's mother leapt to her feet and shrieked, "Zelda. Come here, Zelda." She ran past Lothair and plowed through the crowd, clutching her baby and dragging her toddler.

The bishop raised his staff and faced the crowd in the street. "Go home and ponder the folly of making hasty judgments." He turned to the priest and monks. "Father Kristoph, it's nearly time for vespers."

The crowds dispersed with a reluctant murmur. The monks released Peter and retreated. Crayfish kicked Peter's backside before hobbling away. Lothair shook his head and marched down the hill.

The bishop pointed at the scroll. "Is this the new wisdom you told me about?"

"Yes, my lord bishop," Jacob answered. "It will be delivered to your scriptorium for copying soon."

When Countess Lilli and Bishop Bernard left the shop, a young, dark headed man pulled a heavy ladened donkey into the shop. His soft, round face seemed unusually tanned for the winter months. He wore an oversized gown and cloak. He bowed from the waist and spoke Latin in a high, child-like voice. "Greetings to God, Master Jacob. I am Dionyses, a journeyman alchemist and metal merchant from Constantinople. I carry sheets of Cypriot copper north and sheets of Cornish tin south. I am sent by Master Theophiles. He told me to look for Lindworm." He pointed at the shop's doorknocker.

Jacob bowed and answered in Latin, "Greetings to God, Dionyses. Theophiles is a friend and mentor. If thy hair were longer, thou would look like another from the shop of Theophiles, the novice Daphne."

The journeyman smiled at Jacob. "I know Daphne well. But for the sake of my safety, I shall not speak of her."

"Stay with us, Dionyses," said Jacob. "Learn from us as we shall learn from thee."

Dionyses said, "Then learn this first from me. I stood at the back of the crowd and heard much of what just happened. In another city here in the barbarian north, an alchemist was accused of sorcery. His neighbors burned down his house with him inside it. Be careful, Master Jacob, and beware."

CHAPTER 38
THE GREEK

A cricket chirped at the shop's entrance while little Dionyses pumped the bellows to the furnace. Despite the heat from the furnace and an unusually warm spring day, he wore both his baggy tunic and gown. Peter wondered why Dionyses never shed his oversized layers.

Dionyses said in Latin, "Your bishop worries because Pope Sylvester died before making King Heinrich the next emperor, no? The new pope will not make him emperor because the new pope does not like barbarians." His high pitched voice dipped and rose in a hypnotic song to the rhythms of the cricket and the bellows. "Why say thou Pope Sylvester was an alchemist?"

Peter answered in Latin, "He and Master Jacob traveled together as journeymen."

"If Sylvester was an alchemist, why did he die?"

Peter yawned and scratched his stubbled chin. "Master Jacob said if it is true that he died, it was because he chose to die."

Yellow smoke began streaming from the vent at the top of the conical furnace and flew out the smoke hole in the ceiling. Peter detected a foul odor. "That smells like rotten eggs."

Dionyses released the bellows. "That is sulfur, the active male. He flees the heat and leaves behind his lover, arsenic. It is good the wind blows away from the town, or your neighbors would riot again. No?"

Peter limped to the open front doors and leaned on his baton. The cricket stopped chirping. He scanned the street to see if others could smell the foul odor.

Children squealed as they chased each other down the hill and out of sight. The wool merchant's wife struggled up the hill with a large pot of water. She waved to Peter before entering her home. A clean breeze cleared his senses. Thank goodness for a west wind.

Dionyses came to the entrance. "Thy countess is very beautiful. She is part Greek. No?"

Peter jumped at the journeyman's soft stroke on his back. With each passing week, the journeyman's habit of caressing him while Jacob was absent made him more uncomfortable. Yitzak had stayed only a few days. Why was Dionyses staying so long?

Dionyses stood on the doors' threshold and asked, "What sort of name is Lilli?"

Peter answered, "It is a short name for Elizabeth."

"Those rings thou made for the bishop were pretty, especially the small one of Saint Elizabeth. That is the name of the lover of Bernard. No?"

Peter shook his head.

The little Greek continued, trilling his Latin r's, "Thy bishop made a rumor that Count Edzard murdered his own father. That way the bishop may rid himself of his rival and have the countess for himself. In my land, our holy men marry or have lovers, male and female. We are not afraid church property will be given to the children of happy, fulfilled priests."

"Bishop Bernard is married to the church," said Peter.

Dionyses stood in front of Peter and asked, "Have thou ever had a lover?"

He probed Peter with large, brown eyes that seemed older than his youthful face. Peter had never seen him shave and assumed Greeks didn't grow beards.

Peter limped back to the furnace. He paused over formulas Dionyses had scratched in the shop's dirt floor and read aloud the pictograms. "Take the sticky, orange gravel you call rah al-ghar." The Arabic word sounded harsh within the Latin speech. "Place in a crucible and then an upside down funnel on the crucible. Apply high heat." He yawned again. He was tired. Dionyses taught him sacred formulas every night until late.

The cricket resumed trilling at the entrance door.

"That burns away the male sulfur and leaves the female arsenic," said Dionyses. He opened the furnace door and, with a set of tongs, removed the glowing crucible containing the orange gravel. A stoneware funnel perched atop the crucible like a bird with its neck bent to one side. Gray powder crusted around the neck's opening. "What shall we do with lady arsenic?"

Peter read the pictograms, "Add it to zinc earth and copper. Apply heat. What is this symbol?"

Dionyses glanced at the symbol on the floor. "Cadmia."

"What is cadmia?" Peter asked.

"Add it to gold to make the dog grow." Dionyses scraped arsenic off the funnel's neck into the crucible.

Peter touched his pouch with his gold pebble. "Cadmia makes gold grow?"

Dionyses dropped into the crucible a cup of zinc earth, which fizzled on the bottom, and then a folded sheet of copper, which stopped the noisy fizzling. "So it appears, but only if thou add no more than one part cadmia to three parts gold. If thou add more, it becomes obvious thou have only diluted the purity of thy gold. Then thou must feed the mongrel dog to the gray wolf, antimony, to restore it to its original nobility." He pointed to a bowl of coarse white powder they had made on the forge the day before in an endless series of heatings, mixings, boilings, distillings, and remixings, in which the proportions of matter, heat, and time were carefully measured.

Dionyses placed the crucible inside the furnace and shut the door. "Look for the proper alignment in the heavens. Heat the gray wolf until its crystals reflect the color of the red lion. Mix the wolf of antimony and the impure dog of gold. With the red lion of fire, gold returns to its noble state again by separating the subtle from the gross, prudently and with judgment."

"That sounds like the Emerald Table of Hermes," said Peter.

Dionyses pumped the bellows. "Yes, the Emerald Table from Alexander the Great."

"Have thou made gold?" asked Peter.

"I have made small amounts of silver from lead, but gold, only once when I extended forgiveness, the philosopher's stone, out from myself and discipline into myself."

"Discipline?" asked Peter.

"Discipline is strength. Strength is made from patience and fed by desire. Strength is attention to details and repetition of formulas until perfect. Strength is disciplined devotion to cycles of calcination, dissolution, distillation, sublimation -"

Peter interrupted, "So many steps, repeated over and over. Why so many cycles, formulas and things?" He pointed at the things Dionyses had brought with him.

Those things lined the shelves in neat order; several basins, stills, funnels, straws, beakers, flasks, cylinders, and vials, many made of clay, or of metal or of a wondrous ice-like material called glass. Peter had seen drawings of these containers in Jacob's books. Many of the vessels contained unfamiliar rocks, powders, and liquids, like bright green pebbles of malachite, yellow orpiment stones, green oil of vitriol, clear syrupy glycerol, red cinnabar powder, fibrous crystal of sal ammoniac, clear burning waters, and acrid waters.

Dionyses said, "Without those things, we could not learn the sacred art of alchemy. Today we use cycles and formulas to crucify lady arsenic, return her to the prima materia. Then we resurrect her, put color back into her body, just as we did the gray wolf yesterday."

"Why crucify everything?" said Peter.

"Because everything is impure, flawed, sinful."

The cricket's chirping annoyed Peter. He limped to the entrance and rapped his baton against the doorjamb. The chirping stopped. "Flaws are deceptions," Peter said. "Yet we crucify others for these sins. Resurrection shows that the biggest flaw of all, death, is also a deception."

Dionyses released the bellows and stepped toward the entrance. His thin eyebrows lifted with bemusement. The shape of his eyes matched those of the countess. "I have never met a Christian who thinks like thee. Look around thee. Everything is flawed, impure, sinful. Thou can see it, hear it, feel it, taste it. It is real. No?" He stepped closer. "Most novices begin at age nine and finish by age twelve or thirteen. It pleases me that thou art older, stronger, handsome, unmarried..." He fondled Peter's hair.

Peter ducked away. "We should finish making cadmia. Instead of so many mixings and heatings, we could chant."

"Chant? Alchemy is no ethereal art. It is of the world. No?" The journeyman scooped from the floor two handfuls of dirty ash. Holding out the dust in his open hands, he walked toward Peter. "This is what we are made of and this is what we must change." He stumbled, pitched forward, and threw the ash onto Peter's tunic.

Peter leaned on his baton and brushed the dirt from his tunic.

Dionyses held Peter's hand away and locked his dark eyes

onto Peter with the same intensity Peter had felt from the countess. "I am sorry, Peter. It was my fault. Let me brush thy tunic clean."

Peter could feel the eyes clutching him.

Dionyses knelt, holding Peter with his eyes, and brushed the dust from the tunic. "Master Jacob said thy next lesson is strength. Close thine eyes, relax, and I will tell thee of strength."

Peter's mind erected walls of distrust to block the probing eyes.

The Greek's tone dropped lower and urged obedience. "Close thine eyes and relax."

His voice dissolved Peter's first wall of resistance.

"Close thine eyes and relax." The Greek's eyelids drooped lower.

Another layer of Peter's resolve fell to the persuasive voice.

"Close thine eyes and relax."

Everything except the Greek's dark eyes melted into a liquid haze.

"Close thine eyes and sleep."

Peter's eyelids grew heavier. He was tired. He wanted to sleep.

"Close thine eyes and listen."

Peter's eyes fluttered shut.

"Listen."

For a while he heard only the rhythmic chirps of the cricket and soft strokes on his tunic.

Dionyses whispered slowly, "Strength is patience that is disciplined by desire to give us balance. To be balanced, things must have equal parts of male and female. Thou need more female. No?"

Peter felt the light touch of a hand on his thigh. The slow brushing of the other hand moved across his hips.

"Empty thy mind and imagine the female, the one thou want, the one in thy dreams."

The whispered words led Peter to Rosamund. He saw her face, her blond hair. She was kneeling before him, brushing him, gazing up at him with blue eyes. The shape of her eyes changed, became oval. Their color shifted to brown like the eyes of the countess and back again to blue. They beckoned him, pulled him, stroked him, excited him. His desire grew.

"Imagine her touch."

One of her hands glided up to his stomach and then down. The fingers of her other hand moved to the rhythm of the cricket's song. Her touch sent delightful waves thrilling over him.

"She needs thy touch."

He needed her touch. His desire for her pulsed like his heart.

The cricket stopped singing.

She stood and pressed her breasts against his chest. "She wants thy lips. Kiss her now."

He kissed her soft, delicious lips.

A terrific blow to the side of his head knocked him to the ground. After a few disoriented moments, he became aware of shuffling nearby.

Lothair's boots slipped on the ash covered floor. He reached toward Peter but slipped backwards. Dionyses held the back of Lothair's chain mail tunic and pulled the struggling warrior away from Peter.

"Stop, Lothair," Jacob called from the front doors.

Peter grabbed his baton and jumped to his feet. He was ready to flee out the back door but hesitated at the spectacle of the little Greek dragging away a warrior twice his size.

Lothair turned around and swung a fist at Dionyses. The journeyman ducked and Lothair toppled over his target. The little Greek stood upright and flipped the tall warrior over his back. Lothair rolled onto his seat and sat, apparently dazed, in a cloud of disturbed ash.

Jacob strode forward and helped Lothair stand.

Lothair shook off Jacob's hands. "Don't touch me, Jew," he howled, his face purple.

Jacob bowed his head and said, "How may we serve you, Lord Lothair?"

Dionyses backed away and bowed his head.

Lothair's chest heaved and his fists trembled a long while before he slammed a leather purse onto the worktable. "Edzard wants the half woman," he pointed at Peter, "to make a gold cup. It's to celebrate his victory over Maynard and the completion of his stone tower. He wants a hunting scene. The little serf is to deliver it himself. Edzard want to see this perverted cripple."

Peter's face burned with a rush of angry heartbeats. "I a cripple because of you. I could be a warrior but you crippled me. You crippled me with this." He shook the baton.

The tall warrior sneered, "You whine like a woman. You could have served Maynard the Fat. You have as little honor as he had."

Peter struggled to speak. "I ... I ..." His teeth clinched. His hands shook. He closed his eyes and concentrated on calming himself. A spring breeze moved through the shop and through him, and its strength filled him. "I have HONOR," he barked at Lothair with the force of a wind.

Lothair fell back a step, as if something pushed him. He steadied himself on the worktable and his mouth fell open.

"Forgive me, Lord Lothair," Peter said. He did not bow his head. Resolute and unblinking, he looked directly at the warrior and saw fright in Lothair's widening eyes. For the first time in almost three years, he did not fear Lothair.

The warrior backed his way to the door and said, "Edzard wants you to make the cup grander than anything you've done for the bishop. When you return it to the castle, come without your sorcerer," he pointed at Jacob, "and without your pervert." He pointed at Dionyses. "You're to come alone. Just you." He stopped in the street and shouted, "But hurry, because the bishop will banish you when he hears about your perversion for loving men." He almost ran down the hill.

Peter asked Jacob, "Loving men? What he mean by that?"

Dionyses turned away and said in Latin, "The warrior saw thee with me."

Peter said in the local language, "No. I was with Rosamund and ..." He looked around the shop. Rosamund and Countess Lilli had not been in the shop. Only Dionyses. Peter's knees buckled and he collapsed onto a stool. "No. Oh God, no." He wiped his mouth. "Yech. He kissed me. And Lothair saw it."

Jacob said, "The doors are open. Anyone walking by would have seen it."

Peter stood and pointed at Dionyses. "He tricked me. He made me do it. He tricked me."

The little Greek's voice pitched higher, his Latin words trembled. "I am sorry. I am so lonely and Peter is so good. I am not strong, not disciplined. I am sorry. I shall leave now."

"Wait," Jacob said in Latin. "Thou must stay at least one more day. Thou must come with us and explain to the bishop who thou really art, for the sake of Peter."

"No," Peter said. "Don' tell the bishop. You gots to send him away. Now."

Dionyses looked at Peter. Tears ran down his beardless cheeks. "Master Jacob is right. I must show everyone who I really am to protect thee, Peter. I was told it was too dangerous for a woman to travel alone in barbarian lands. But I am not afraid anymore. Alchemy made me strong enough to handle a man as big as Lothair. Forgive me for tricking thee."

Peter said to Jacob, "What ish he saying?"

Jacob answered in Latin, "Daphne cut her hair, dressed like a man, and changed her name to Dionyses to protect herself on her journey. Thou did not kiss a man. Thou kissed a woman."

CHAPTER 39
TEMPERING POWER

Lucus beamed from his stool at the worktable. "I just finished my apprenticeship. Now I'm a journeyman."

Peter slipped leather gloves over his hands. "About time. In the past three years you grown to be nearly as tall as me." He opened the furnace door and the heat pushed him back like an invisible hand.

"You've grown, too," Lucus said. "When do you finish your apprenticeship?"

Sweat beaded on Peter's brow from the combined heat of the furnace, the forge, and the summer humidity. He removed the crucible with a set of tongs from the furnace. The crucible glowed bright orange, speckled with a few black pockmarks. The count's gold inside glistened like a lump of soft cheese. He shook his head and said, "Not yet." He returned the crucible to the furnace, replaced the door, swung the bellows away from the forge to the furnace, and pumped air into the charcoal under the furnace.

Jacob pulled an iron from the forge. "It's time you learned tempering power." The fire tinted his white mane red. A coal popped and threw an ember against his arm.

Small, white scars from flying embers and iron flecks dotted Peter's arms. Jacob's skin showed no scars.

Jacob hammered the glowing iron flat. Specks of sparkling rust and flakes of black scale fell away from it. He put the iron back into the forge and asked, "What makes a hammer, a chisel, or a cleaver so strong that it can beat and cut other iron?"

Peter rotated the bellows back to the forge. "Ish tempered," he answered.

Jacob pumped the bellows and watched the iron in the forge. "Yes. Heated and cooled by a dying fire for three days. Heated again, shaped, filed, and then heated once more. Bathed in brine and then in water. Iron is tempered, made strong, with patience. If you hadn't checked the crucible so often, if you hadn't been impatient, the count's gold would have already melted. An alchemist is never in a hurry."

Peter swung the bellows to the furnace again. "Where do you

go now?" he asked Lucus.

"Everywhere. I'll leave with Master Thomas this summer as always. We're going to the Greek lands by way of the river. Missionaries have converted the Magyars and Slavs along the riverbanks, so it should be safer. Then I'll be on my own, travel as a journeyman for seven years and learn the fur trade from other masters." Lucus said to Jacob, "Thank you for the gift."

Jacob replied, "A journeyman furrier needs a good set of scrapers." He severed the rod nearly in two on a chisel, twisted the scraper free, and threw it into the slack tub. "Peter will file and polish them for you."

Peter took the crucible out of the furnace again. The liquid's iridescent yellow swirls appeared to spiral down into infinite depths. "Finally," he shouted. He poured its contents into the waiting loam mold on the floor. Gold filled the mold of the cup and its stem, but not its wide base. He shook the crucible to extract the last drop. "Not again," Peter sighed.

Lucus stood and looked into the mold. "Not enough gold. You need a quarter more."

Jacob removed his apron and gathered blankets, baskets and tools on the worktable. "You'll have to make the cup smaller again."

Peter carefully lifted the mold and poured the gold back into the glowing crucible. "No. Ish already too small. Count Edzard wants a grand cup."

"The count's planning a grand celebration after the summer raids," Lucus said.

Peter nodded. "Going to celebrate at my old village, where he defeated Maynard the Fat. All the warriors will be there."

Jacob paused at the garden door with an armload of baskets and blankets. "Lucus, tell Peter about strength through tempering power." He walked out to the pushcart.

Peter asked, "How you know about that?"

"Master Thomas taught me six powers. It was part of my apprenticeship." Lucus squinted at the ceiling, as though trying to remember. "Strength comes from patience and brings balance. Tanning leather is for me what tempering iron is for you. Both require patience."

Jacob returned for an armload of shovels and axes, and carried them to the pushcart.

Lucus continued, "Master Thomas said that when there is a conflict, study it, open your heart to new ways of thinking about it, form a solution from moral examples, and act on it. All these steps require patience and patience requires that you be strong within. Strength is quiet and doesn't attract attention unless it's lacking."

"Strength ish not quiet," Peter said. "Look at Count Edzard and Lord Lothair. Look at their strength. Ish loud and proud so everyone knows they strong."

Thomas called his former novice from across the street. Lucus ran out saying, "I'll be back for the scrapers tonight. Thank you, Master Jacob."

Jacob returned from loading the pushcart and sat on Lucus' stool. "Lothair, Count Edzard, and all his warriors are examples of fear, not strength."

Peter slouched on a stool next to him and sputtered, "They gots armor, swords."

"They don't need those. Aren't they made of the same indestructible essence as you?"

"Well, yes."

"They're defending the deception they can be hurt. If they'd remember their real strength, they'd need no armor, no swords."

Peter sighed. "You turn my ideas upside down. How can they all be wrong?"

"Some are right," Jacob said.

"Which ones?" Peter asked.

"Who knows?"

"Don' you?"

Jacob smiled and shook his head.

"But you my master," Peter said. "You know everything."

"You are your own master. Take from my way what's true to make your own way."

"But everything you taught me ish true," Peter said.

"Half of it is untrue."

Peter sat upright with a start. "Half?"

"Probably more than half."

"You ... you know which half?"

"No. When you find out, let me know," Jacob said and laughed.

Peter rubbed the creases on his forehead. "How can your lessons be untrue?"

"My way changes with new revelations, just like your own way. Anything that changes can't be true."

"But everything I learned from you, the four qualities of the furnace, the six powers, these all certainly true."

"No thing is certain and only no thing is true. Everything else is uncertain and untrue."

Peter stood. "What? You telling me ... now ... your way ish wrong?"

"Not just now, but from the beginning of your apprenticeship. It is the lesson behind all lessons. Each of us takes a different path on the journey of recovery, back to the nothing from which we came. The number of ways back are infinite and you must find your own way."

Peter began pacing."You didn' tell me this before."

"This is not the first time you heard me say this," Jacob said. "But this is the first time you listened."

Peter stopped and waved his hands above his head. "Why am I your apprentice? If what you teach me ish wrong, then why am I learning from you? What purpose?"

"To be."

Peter waited impatiently for Jacob to finish his answer, until he again asked, "What? To be what?"

"To be, to be, and to be. That's the purpose. It's not to be an alchemist, or a blacksmith, or a furrier, or a warrior. Rather it's to be the essence of what you really are."

"You mean the universal essence? But that something like air. Ish everywhere. I not everywhere. I right here."

"The universal essence isn't like something or everything. It's like nothing. That is what you really are."

Peter frowned. "What am I really?"

"Nothing."

"Impossible." Peter thumped his chest. "I am real. Everything I learned ish real. What about God, or Jesus? What about Moses? What about love or wisdom or ..." His voice trailed off when he saw Jacob nodding. "What about faith?" he whispered.

"Yes," Jacob said. "All things visible and invisible."

"But they real, right?"

Jacob stood and laid a hand on Peter's shoulder. "Their forms are not real. But their content is from the same essence as you. You are greater than you know, greater than everything, because you are nothing."

Peter's shoulders drooped. "But if I ask you ish true, you say nothing ish true."

Jacob nodded.

Peter looked away. The shop seemed too small, too dark. "Everything I did, I did with hope. Did I do it for nothing?"

"This is so hard to understand," the blacksmith said. "Everything we do, we do with nothing, in nothing, and for nothing. This revelation frees us from deceptions. It's wonderful."

Peter collapsed onto his mattress and tilted against the wall. "Wonderful?" he rasped. "How can nothing be wonderful?"

The blacksmith knelt by Peter's mattress and touched his shoulder again. Peter lay down, leaving the blacksmith's hand suspended in air.

The blacksmith stood and walked to the back door. "The days are long. We need to work in the forest. We need charcoal and iron ore. When you finish the scrapers for Lucus and the cup for Edzard, meet me in the forest. Don't be angry about our talk. When we come back from the forest, we'll temper some tools and learn the sixth power of alchemy. Be patient." He stood at the back door in silence for a while, shifting from one foot to the other before leaving.

Peter lay in numb confusion for a long time. Was he a victim of lies? The blacksmith promised to make him into someone special. But now the old man told him he was nothing.

He moaned and whispered, "What have I done all these years?" He pushed his face against the mattress. "Nothing. Why am I doing it?" His fists slammed the mattress. "For nothing. What will I become?" He kicked the wall. "Nothing."

"Peter?" The linen merchant called from the entrance. "Peter? What's wrong?"

Peter sat up. "Nothing. Nothing ish wrong," he said and laughed viciously. "Greetings to God."

The merchant glanced about the shop. "Greetings to God. Where's Jacob? I need a pair of scissors and I'm leaving tomorrow for the low-countries."

Peter climbed up his baton. "Jacob gone away for a few days to cut trees and dig holes." He searched the wall pegs and shelves for scissors. "We don' have any. But come back later. I make you a pair of scissors."

"Thank you, Peter." The merchant smiled and bowed his head before leaving.

Peter fired the forge and placed a rod in its center. As he watched the iron change from black to orange, a glimmer of hope began to glow within him.

"I am not nothing," he said out loud. "I make scissors, and axes, and nails, and pots, and all kinds of things. I am a blacksmith."

He hammered the iron flat with angry grunts. Embers flew in the air when he thrust the iron back into the fire and pumped the bellows.

"I don' need to stay here and learn nothing. I don' need to learn about tempering power. He said ish all untrue anyway. I learned enough. I can leave Jacob and make things in my own blacksmith shop."

He yanked the iron from the fire and cut it over the chisel. With a growl, he twisted the flat piece free, slammed it into the slack tub, and jabbed the rest of the rod into the fire.

"The count may need a blacksmith in the castle. Lothair won' bother me. He afraid of me. I saw it and, if he tries to hurt me again, I use the powers of alchemy to stop him. Those powers not made of nothing. They real. I saw them." He fingered the gold pebble in his pouch. "I never learned how to make gold but I learned how to grow gold."

He released the bellows and searched a shelf for containers and minerals left behind by Daphne. The orange gleam of cadmia caught his eye and he grabbed a nugget half the size of his fist. He pointed it at the unfinished cup and shouted, "Now I can make a grand cup. Now I can grow the count's gold. Won' that impress the count?"

"No," whispered a familiar voice.

Peter jumped with a start. His heart thumped faster.

I shouldn't be talking out loud, he thought.

He scanned the shop but saw no one. He looked out the open doors and windows and found nobody. He set the mold and the cadmia on the worktable and listened. Coals hissed in the forge, birds sang in the garden, and children squealed in the street. But he heard nothing else.

The whisper may have been the counselor. But no, it was probably his own doubt.

He gazed at the cadmia nugget and his doubt fell away. He would combine the cadmia with the count's gold to increase its size and weight. He would make a cup so grand that he would be asked, no, he would be commanded to stay at the castle, away from Jacob and his nothing.

PART III

Putrefaction and Resurrection

CHAPTER 40
ALONE

Despite the cold gloom of the count's stone tower, sweat dripped from Peter's bowed head. He stared at his boots, the timbered floor, and the splintered end of his walking stick. The great hall's only door, a heavy, iron-covered barricade just behind Peter, shut out the summer morning. Drafts of air whined through a few vertical slits the length of a forearm in the stone walls.

The count yapped like a small dog, "Yes. I see it now. My father's last day of life. A hunting scene. Good. We celebrated a successful war with a hunt. There are the warriors on horses. There are the dogs. They're running through a field. There's a wolf. They're chasing a wolf. Or is the wolf chasing them? You there, boy. Look at me."

Peter raised his eyes. A lifeless, tiled fireplace occupied the great hall's center. Beyond the fireplace sat a long table and a lonely high-backed chair. Wooden cups and platters cluttered the table. Stools and benches lined the walls. Against the far wall, steps led through a hole in the floor to the cellar, and a stone staircase rose steeply through the ceiling to the second floor of the tower. A thin, rolled up mattress, probably Gabriel's mattress, leaned on the staircase.

Three ironclad men, Count Edzard, Lord Lothair, and Lord Norbert, stood near the chair. The smallest of the three, the count, held Peter's gold cup close to a narrow beam of sunlight streaking though a wall slit. The cup, nearly twice the length of Edzard's hand, sparkled and reflected points of light that sprinkled the dark walls like a swirl of stars in the midnight sky.

Lothair, the tallest of the three, frowned at Peter. One hand gripped his sword hilt, as though he might need it in a moment's notice.

Lord Norbert, older, slightly stooped but broad shouldered, stroked his graying beard and squinted at the gold cup in the count's hand.

The count tilted his head back, peered down his thin, sharp nose at Peter and pointed at the sculpted scene on the body of the cup. "Are we chasing the wolf or is the wolf chasing us?"

"Ish w-w-whatever my lord count w-w-wishes it to be," Peter said.

Count Edzard turned to the older warrior. "Good answer. This goblet will make Bernard jealous. This boy made silver things for him, but never anything of gold, never this grand."

"If ... if it w-w-would please the count," Peter said, "I can make many things for my lord count ... here ... in the castle. I can be the castle blacksmith."

Lothair shook his head. "We don't want someone who has learned from a master of arts blacker than blacksmithing."

Count Edzard leaned on the back of the chair. "I should have a blacksmith. Are you already a master smith?"

Peter swallowed hard. "Almost."

"Then you're a journeyman."

"W-w-well, almost."

"Have you finished your apprenticeship?"

"Yes, sire."

Lothair waved his hand. "He's lying. He's an addle-headed serf with a crippled leg."

"No, sire," Peter said. "I not addle-headed. I a free man, a blacksmith. I can make many things, w-w-weapons too." He pointed at the crossbow lying on a bench.

The count looked at the crossbow. "Have you ever made a Lombard crossbow?"

"No, sire. But I could. Don' gots to finish my apprenticeship to know all I gots to know."

The count shook his head. "Go finish your training, boy. Come back when you're a master." He handed the cup to Lothair. "Give the boy something for his work. Then make everything ready for this summer's war. I'll leave in two days." He waved to the older warrior. "Norbert, let's go hunting."

Peter bowed his head again as the count and Norbert walked past.

"First you won't let me raid with you," Lothair growled. "Now you won't let me hunt with you."

The count stopped. "Your duties are here."

"My duty is to fight and take what I've won."

"I'll give you a portion of any war booty or ransom. That's

the custom, Conrad's custom."

Lothair's boot tapped the floor. "You only called three warriors to service this time. You can't make much of a war with just three warriors. There won't be much booty to share."

"I'm going to raid Slavic shepherds this summer. I just need two warriors. Norbert will be staying at the castle to supervise the masons and the countess and -"

Lothair snapped, "Is he your marshal, now? What am I supposed to do?"

"You'll stay here and do what Norbert tells you to do."

"God damn it. Why?"

The older warrior snarled, "Because I'm trustworthy." Peter lifted his eyes and saw the graying knight lean forward with his hands on his hips. "I've never slurred my lord's family. Neither am I suspected of murdering his father."

"The bishop's whispers don't accuse me of the murder," Lothair barked. "They accuse him." He pointed at Edzard.

The count stamped his foot. "I know I didn't do it. And if Maynard didn't do it, then another of my warriors did it, someone on the hunt that day. You were on the hunt that day. You disliked my father. You might dislike me, too. Ever since you let Duke Heinrich become king, I've doubted you. Norbert's in command while I'm away. His loyalty is beyond doubt."

Lothair threw his arms into the air. "How long will it be before Norbert's loyalty is doubted? Each year you order more warriors to stay in their valleys, to stay away from you. Now they fulfil their vassalage with sheep, or furs, or grain, or serfs to build your castle. They would rather pay homage with war service. They're becoming poor with little to no war booty."

The count pulled the door open by its iron ring and sunlight flooded the room. "Are they complaining to you? Is that a conspiracy? I must depend on Norbert more than I thought."

Lothair growled, "The only God damned conspirator is Bernard. All his canons are the sons of your vassals and when they inherit their land, they'll give it to him, their bishop. Your father was strong and would have stopped that. That's why he was killed."

"Are you saying Bernard killed my father but spared me because my father was strong and I am weak?"

"Isn't it obvious? He's still weakening you. He's sowing distrust among your vassals."

"I am not weak," Edzard barked. "Bernard is a thieving scoundrel, but I am not weak. Since you believe your lord and protector is weak, I have even more reason to shun you."

Edzard and Norbert slammed the door behind them. The great hall returned to its cold gloom.

Peter jumped when Lothair slammed his fist against the table. "He's a mare's ass," Lothair snarled to himself. "I only want to serve with honor. But he won't let me."

"I don' w-w-want anything for making the goblet," Peter said, bowing his head lower. "Just ask the count to think again about a castle blacksmith." He shuffled backwards to the door.

"Stop," Lothair barked and clunked something on the table. "You're not leaving until I weigh the God damned goblet."

"W-w-weigh?" Peter looked up.

A set of scales stood on the table. Beside it lay several river stones, smooth and round.

Lothair examined the cup. "I hope you've shorted Edzard. For a crime like that, custom lets me cut off your hand. If you bleed to death, we'll be rid of one sorcerer."

Peter gripped his walking stick tighter.

The tall warrior set the cup on one of the scale's dishes and it clanked down against the table. On the other suspended dish, he laid first one stone, then a second, and then a third, all of the same size. He waited. Neither dish moved.

Lothair's eyes grew wide. "What?" He added a fourth stone and the dishes swung up and down until they counterbalanced each other. "There's more gold here, a fourth more than I gave you." He frowned at Peter. "Did you add gold to it?"

Peter bowed his head. His heart beat faster. "No, sire." He wondered what he should do.

The counselor answered silently, *"Do as Jacob taught you."*

Lothair said, "But the goblet has more gold than I gave you. How's that? Did it grow?"

Peter regulated his breathing as Jacob had taught. "Yes, sire."

"How did you do that?"

Peter's heart slowed. "I did it w-w-with ... desire." He opened his heart, knowing his strength lay in the universal essence. The answer to Lothair's question crystallized. "Disciplined desire to make a goblet so grand that I would be told to reside in the castle, that I would be respected, honored, that I would have a chance to become a warrior."

Lothair stepped toward him and his boots came into Peter's view. "Warrior? Humph. Tell me how you grow gold."

Peter stared at the floor timbers. The essence of sturdy wood grain washed through him and strengthened his will, his body. He became as an anvil. "With a nugget of -"

"Sorcery," Lothair barked. He struck his fist hard in the middle of Peter's chest.

Peter felt little more than a brief pressure.

Lothair groaned, rubbed his knuckles for a moment, and then charged, shoving Peter with both hands. Peter stood firm and Lothair pushed himself backwards, stumbling against a bench.

"What the devil?" Lothair yelped. "What the devil has the Jew taught you?"

Peter answered evenly, "To be as strong as the essence in a wooden floor."

Lothair grappled for his sword. "Then I'll chop the wood into splinters."

Peter flowed with the universal essence to the warrior's weapon and wondered if the sheath would like to tighten around the sword.

Lothair pulled at his sword, but the sheath held it tight. He grabbed the hilt with both hands and jerked it again and again. With each effort, he managed to free the sword a little more.

Peter turned to the door. "Lord Lothair, I go now."

"No. The serf will stay until commanded to go."

Peter frowned directly at Lothair. "I not a serf. I a free man. You cannot hold me unless I commit a crime."

"God damn you. You've committed the crime of sorcery."

Peter stepped toward the door, asking it to let him flee. He reached for the door's ring, but before he touched it, the heavy door swung open. A hot gust blew a swirl of courtyard dust inside.

Daylight filled the great hall again. Peter half turned and saw flashes of gold and silver at the back of the room. Countess Lilli stood on the stairway, her abundant jewelry sparkled in the light. She locked her eyes on his eyes and caught him, bound him in a web of her will. His legs wouldn't move and, even when he heard Lothair's sword slip free of its stubborn sheath, he couldn't flee. She held him with her eyes.

The shadow of a cloud darkened the tower.

"You'll always be a God damned serf," Lothair howled. The warrior's raised sword glinted as he stepped between Peter and the countess.

"Don't hurt him," the countess barked and turned her eyes on Lothair.

The invisible bonds around Peter fell away. He sprang out the door and onto the stone platform just outside. He tripped on his walking stick and pitched down the steps to the ground. In near panic, he envisioned the door would shut Lothair in.

Another gust blew past him and a loud thud echoed through the courtyard. The armored door had slammed shut.

He stood and squinted at the stone tower. Did he close the door without touching it? Of course he did. He used the powers of alchemy. He could make things do what he wanted.

He puffed out his chest and imagined another humiliation for Lothair. "My will ish that Lothair be a captive inside." He held up a hand and spread his fingers as he had seen Jacob do.

The cloud passed and the sun warmed his back. The door moaned and popped, as though expanding in the heat of the sun, spreading to fill the doorjamb. Someone inside the tower beat on the door but it wouldn't open.

Lothair's angry baying filtered through the armored door. "Sorcery. Sorcery."

Just as quickly as Peter's powers overflowed, his strength drained away. He wilted like a plucked flower. A mist filled his mind and his thoughts wandered, lost in the gray fog. He wanted to lie down and sleep. But Lothair was beating at the door. Everyone in the courtyard; masons, servants, and foot soldiers, stopped their work and watched him with frowns of fear and accusation. He limped toward the castle gate, leaning heavily on his baton.

He rested a moment at the gate, which the masons were rebuilding in stone. The masons backed away and left him alone with their tools and scaffolding. A couple of foot soldiers climbed the steps to the tower's dais and tried to open the door with no success.

He began the trek down the bluff's winding road. His exhaustion lifted little by little with each step. A morning sky expanded above him and a cool breeze with the piney scent of the forest sharpened his senses. The cathedral spire soared up from the valley, reaching as high as the castle bluff. Distant figures of women washing and drying linens dotted the riverbank beside the free town. A few serfs and a couple of mares loaded with quarry stones snaked up the road toward him.

Halfway down the bluff, his mind grew sharp enough to form a plan. Lothair would publicly accuse him of sorcery. He could seek the bishop's protection by wearing a bell rope around his neck.

No. Despite the bishop's protection, Lothair had killed Paul, the first serf recruited from his village. It would be better to get Jacob's help. He should go to the forest, find Jacob, and tell him what happened.

The air whizzed briefly. Something struck a rock with a loud crack on Peter's left and ricocheted onto the road just ahead of him. There he found the shattered remains of a wooden dart with an iron point.

He looked over his shoulder and saw a foot soldier bending over at the castle gate. The foot soldier stood on a stirrup mounted to the front of the crossbow. He caught the bowstring with a hook on his belt, and, as he straightened, the hook pulled the bowstring up to the back of the weapon. He loaded a dart, shouldered the crossbow, and pointed it at Peter.

Peter stopped breathing.

A tall foot soldier in a yellow hat ran out the gate and stood in front of the crossbowman, blocking his line of fire.

Peter breathed again. "Thank you, Gabriel."

A horse-mounted warrior rode through the gate and past the foot soldiers. He pointed his lance at Peter and spurred his stallion down the winding road.

"Lothair," Peter gasped. He tried to breathe slowly, to feel the powers of alchemy again. "I w-w-will make his horse stop." He held out a trembling hand and spread his fingers. "Stop."

Lothair's horse rounded a hairpin curve and galloped faster than before.

"Oh, God," Peter cried. He turned and ran down the road. He didn't have time to reach Jacob in the forest. Had to make a new plan. Quick.

CHAPTER 41
THE SWORDFIGHT

Peter held his stick higher, away from his churning legs. The steep decline made running difficult. The thunder of Lothair's horse came closer. Peter looked over his shoulder. The warrior pointed his spear ahead. His bowl-shaped helmet flashed in the morning sunlight. His shield bounced on the strap to his shoulder. His horse half galloped, half slid down the steep winding road. Behind Lothair, ran Gabriel, the crossbowman, and two other foot soldiers holding axes.

Time moved too quickly. If Peter couldn't run faster, Lothair would catch him soon.

Half a dozen serfs and two mares loaded with cut stones from the quarry stopped on a bend in the road. They dropped their stones, pointed at Peter and his pursuers, jabbered and milled in confusion, blocking Peter's way. He jumped off the road and skidded down the embankment between the hairpin curves. Lose gravel scraped his calves and followed him in a small landslide to the section of road below. He ran across the road and jumped down the next embankment, and then the next. Each shortcut gained him a few moments. On the road above, Lothair cursed the serfs and mares for delaying his pursuit.

The ground began to level and Peter sprinted across a rocky field of sparsely growing wheat seedlings. He rejoined the road where it straightened and led to the bridge about two hundred paces ahead. He could clearly see the riverbanks dropping abruptly to mud flats and fields of worn rocks. A few women from the town crouched on the rocks. Some washed clothes in the water while others stretched linens to dry in the hot summer sun. A merchant led a horse loaded with bundles from the town to the bridge.

Sweat stung Peter's eyes. If he could make it to the bridge, someone there could help him. He wished he could fly.

The thunder of hoofs came closer. He glanced back again and saw Lothair standing on the stirrups in a full gallop, his spear tip hovering just a few paces behind Peter's back.

Peter ducked left. The spear nicked his right arm, caught his sleeve and lifted him off the ground. He flew forward, his right sleeve leading, propelled by the lance. Time seemed to slow. He soared over the road and toward the river. At the sound of his sleeve ripping, he floated free, weightlessly flying, then descending through the air in a forward arc over the riverbank on the north side of the bridge. He released his stick and held his hands against the approaching ground.

He splattered into a mud flat and sank deep into ooze. After a dazed moment he stood, pulling himself from the muck. His tunic's right sleeve had torn completely away. Blood from a small cut on his upper arm mixed with mud. He wiped mud from his face with the left sleeve.

Lothair had galloped to the other end of the bridge and now trotted back. Gabriel, the crossbowman, and two other foot soldiers had run half the distance from the castle to the bridge with Gabriel far ahead of the rest. The women stopped washing and watched with wide eyes. Peter recognized Hugo, the tool peddler, gaping from the other end of the bridge, holding his packhorse on short reins. Peter's stick protruded from the mud near the bridge.

Peter struggled toward his stick. Mud sucked away his boots and pulled at his bare feet. He grasped the stick just before Lothair stabbed at him with the lance from the bridge above. Peter batted the lance away and ducked under the bridge.

Smooth river stones covered the ground beneath the bridge. A couple of muddy blankets, the beggar's nest, lay between two boulders. Peter caught his breath and wiped his hands on the blankets, glad that Crayfish wasn't home.

Hooves clopped to the near end of the bridge and the horse came into view as Lothair directed it down the riverbank behind Peter. Once on the mud table, the stallion sank up to its knees. It fought to step forward, sank deeper, and neighed.

Lothair cursed, threw down his lance, and jumped off his horse. He too sank up to his knees. He jerked at his sword hilt, held his shield out, and struggled toward the bridge.

Peter turned to flee but his muddy feet slipped on a smooth stone and he fell. He stood again just as Lothair reached the boulder field under the bridge. Lothair's sword finally slipped free of its tight sheath. Peter faced the warrior and swung his stick like a battle baton. The stick slapped Lothair's shield.

The armored warrior jumped back. His sword waved in nervous jolts. Wide-eyed caution replaced his usual frown. His mouth flapped ajar exposing his broken teeth.

Behind Lothair, Gabriel clambered down the riverbank.

Lothair moved slowly forward and swung his sword. Peter knocked it upward.

The warrior slashed back with more confidence, sweeping the sword low. Peter flipped his stick down and caught the sword at his thighs. Its blade cut into his baton. Both men jerked their weapons free.

Lothair swung the sword over his head and down. Peter deflected the downward blow but its force knocked the baton against his head. Stunned, he fell back onto a large boulder and his stick slipped from his hands.

Lothair pointed the sword at Peter's heart. "Where's your sorcery now?" he snarled.

"Remember the countess," Gabriel said, standing just behind Lothair.

The warrior wavered. His eyes darted about. Peter rolled off the smooth stone just as Lothair regained his resolve and thrust the blade. It clanged off the boulder. Lothair lost his balance and staggered forward.

With lightning quickness, Peter grabbed his baton from the ground and swung it at Lothair's sword. The baton hit the sword hilt and the blade flew out of Lothair's hand. The warrior spun from the knock against his hand and fell on his shield against the boulder. The sword twirled through the air and slapped into the mud next to his horse.

Lothair pushed himself off the boulder and scrambled past Gabriel. He plodded back into the mud flat and yelped, "Sorcery." Gabriel strolled after him.

Peter ran the opposite way, out from under the bridge and onto southern bank. The air hissed over his back. A dart from the crossbow shattered a stone to his left and the crossbowman cursed from the bridge above.

At the top of the steep embankment, two panting, sweating foot soldiers waited with their battle-axes.

Peter charged up the embankment.

CHAPTER 42
FLIGHT

As Peter scrambled up the river embankment, Lothair howled "sorcery" again from the opposite side of the bridge. Both foot soldiers backed away a few paces and lifted their battle-axes above their shoulders. When Peter stood at the top of the bank, the larger foot soldier trotted forward and swung his weapon with a loud grunt.

Peter ducked to the ground and the heavy ax swished over his back. The foot soldier lost his balance and fell forward onto Peter's back. Peter sprang up and flipped the foot soldier off his back, as he had seen Daphne flip Lothair. The foot soldier tumbled down the steep embankment.

The second foot soldier charged, slicing the air with his ax. Peter jumped aside and the ax caught his tunic, ripping the seam at his left shoulder. He grabbed the foot soldier's swinging arm and pulled him forward. The second foot soldier toppled over the edge of the embankment and blundered into his comrade.

Peter ran onto the bridge. Just four paces down the bridge, the crossbowman shouldered his reloaded weapon and aimed at Peter. Quick as an arrow, Peter dove forward and swung his stick. The baton whacked the crossbow's stirrup at the front end of the weapon. The crossbowman spun from the impact of the baton. The bowstring fired with a loud slap.

Lothair was reaching for his sword when the crossbow's dart smacked into the mud flat next to his sword. He squawked, fell backwards into the mud, and looked up at bridge.

Gabriel laughed and offered Lothair a hand.

Peter and the crossbowman eyed each other for a long, anxious moment. The crossbowman pulled a long knife from his belt. Peter pulled out his thin, little knife. The crossbowman backed away, his knife and crossbow shook. Peter edged around him and ran across the bridge toward the free town, his knife in one hand, his stick in the other.

The women left their wash and fled the riverbank. Between the town and the bridge, Hugo and his packhorse blocked half the road.

"Stop him," Lothair howled. "He's a sorcerer. Stop him."

Hugo reached for Peter with big, hairy arms. Peter swerved around the tool peddler and sped into the first street of the free town.

"Stop him," Hugo shouted.

Peter slowed at the first crossroads. If he turned right, the road would take him past the monastery, through the wheat fields, and into the southern forest where Jacob was making charcoal. But Jacob was too far away to help and the monastery couldn't protect him from Lothair. Peter would have to hide in the free town. But where?

He sped straight ahead toward the center of the free town.

Several people in the street stopped to watch him run by. Over his shoulder Peter saw Hugo leading three merchants on the chase. Behind them ran the crossbowman and the two ax-wielding foot soldiers. Cries of "Stop" and "Sorcerer" became louder as he wove through the residents, disrupting children's games and women's errands.

Merchants and craftsmen stopped their work to watch the chase. A few joined the pursuit. The crowd following Peter grew larger. His grip on his stick and knife squeezed tighter. Where could he hide?

The street narrowed to the width of a cart. Ahead of him, Father Kristoph and a group of monks turned toward the cries. Father Kristoph pointed at Peter and his pursuers. Peter ducked left, under Father Kristoph's grasping arms, and veered off the street, speeding down a garden path behind the townhouses. He twisted his head from side to side, looking for a place to hide.

At the next street, he cut right. Rounding another corner brought him into the market square by the town stables. He ran through the stables' wide open doors and sprang into the first empty stall. He crouched and gasped for air.

The stable keeper leaned over the stall rail. "Peter? What's wrong?"

Peter crouched lower. "Lothair wants ... to kill me."

"You're not a runaway serf anymore," the stable keeper said. "He can't kill you like he did that poor serf boy three years ago. Didn't he come from your village?"

Peter stood with a start as the answer struck him. He could hide in one of the bishop's chests. The bishop had said that if he had hidden Paul in a chest, Lothair would not have found him. The bishop could hide Peter in a chest, couldn't he?

A child ran up to Peter's stall and shouted, "I found him. I found him."

Peter ran past the stable keeper and the child, back into the market square with his knife and stick ready. A few men on his left ran toward him. He turned right and sprinted toward the cathedral and the bishop's house at the end of the square. The noisy vigilantes followed.

Several residents watched the commotion from their doors and windows. Children left their mothers to run with the pursuing crowd. Peter neared the bishop's house, planning to burst through the door.

Between him and the bishop's door, a flock of sheep bolted in fright. One sheep ran in front of Peter and he veered around it, entangling his legs with his stick. He pitched forward and sprawled on the ground a few paces before the bishop's residence.

Someone jumped on his back. "I gots you," the beggar hissed.

Peter gasped for breath and struggled to his feet. Crayfish slid to the ground, hanging with his single hand onto Peter's tunic like a lead weight.

"Stand clear," someone called.

Several paces away, the crossbowman aimed at Peter. His pursuers ducked away from the line of fire.

"I am ... invulnerable," Peter whispered between labored breaths. "I cannot ... be hurt." He envisioned himself shielded by a halo.

The crossbowman pulled the trigger and the dart snapped into flight.

Peter's breathing quieted. He imagined his halo extending to the crossbowman's missile. Everything seemed to slow. The dart sailed toward him like a feather on a pond pushed by the wind. The crowd watched with unblinking eyes, frozen in time. Not even the sheep stirred. Only the dart moved, sluggish but unswerving, straight for its target.

Peter watched it come nearer. He focused on the missile, wanting to deflect it.

The dart drew closer, showing no signs it would strike anything but Peter.

He concentrated harder.

It continued forward, its path still true and unaffected.

"Oh God, help me," he whispered. Panic shattered his calm. His halo collapsed. He flinched, jerking his hands upward.

With invisible speed, the dart glanced off his baton and then deflected from his knife. It impaled itself into the bishop's door with a loud crack that echoed around the square. Peter wouldn't have known what deflected the bolt had not his knife and stick hummed in his hands.

Crayfish released his grip. "It curved," he shouted. "He made it curve away."

Everyone's mouth fell open and their eyes frowned.

Peter saw everyone's fear. Maybe he could use their fear. He thrust his knife into the air and barked, "Go away."

The beggar scooted backwards squealed, "He gots invisible shield."

The residents shuffled back in unison, as though they were of one mind. Behind Peter, the bishop's door creaked open.

"What's happening here?" the bishop asked.

No one answered. Quiet fright stifled the crowd like a heavy blanket, torn only by the bleating of sheep and the rumble of a galloping horse in a nearby street.

Peter raised both arms and edged toward the bishop's door. "I am an alchemist. I gots many powers."

Lothair galloped into the square and sped toward the crowd. The sheep and the town's people scattered.

Peter turned toward the bishop's house. Bishop Bernard stood in the open doorway. Peter rushed forward and the bishop stepped aside.

Peter whispered, "Forgive me, my lord bish -" Something tightened his tunic's collar and lifted him off the threshold of the bishop's safety. Peter's feet spun in the air until, a moment later, he felt the ground again. But his collar remained tight.

"Forgive me, little brother," Gabriel said. He held the back of Peter's tunic and took away first his walking stick and then his knife, dropping them at the bishop's feet.

Lothair threw his lance and shield to the ground and jumped from his muddy horse. "Hold him still." He jerked his sword with both hands three times before it slid from its muddy sheath. He aimed the sword tip at Peter and ran forward.

Gabriel yanked Peter away from Lothair's charge. The sword and the warrior bounced off the wall of the bishop's house, leaving a smear of river mud behind.

Bishop Bernard jumped back from Lothair and shouted, "Stop. This is my valley. Stop."

Lothair foamed at the mouth like a wild dog. "He's a sorcerer. Kill him." He swung his sword at Peter.

Gabriel stepped in front of Peter. The sword bounced off Gabriel's shoulder as though it had struck an anvil. Many of the iron ringlets in his rusted chainmail tunic shattered and another hole opened.

"No," Peter cried. He struggled to stand in front of Gabriel, to protect him from Lothair. "Leave him alone."

Lothair backed away, his sword quivering.

"Stop it," shouted the bishop. "What's this about?"

"Remember the countess," Gabriel said.

Lothair snarled, "Shut up, fool."

The bishop asked, "What about the countess?"

Gabriel's voice boomed through the square. "She wants Peter whole of life and limb, back to the castle, his master and him."

"Peter and Jacob are free men," the bishop said. "Why are you ordered to take them to the castle?"

Lothair pointed his trembling sword at Peter. "He's the devil's apprentice. I saw his sorcery. So did Countess Lilli."

A discordant chorus rose from the crowd. "We saw it too." "He turned the dart away." "He has an invisible shield." "He's the devil's boy."

The bishop raised his hand to quiet the crowd. "I am the judge for all crimes committed by the residents of my valley. Custom says a free man may hear and refute his accusers before judgment."

Lothair stamped his boot. "He belongs to us. We saw his sorcery first – in the castle."

Bishop Bernard walked up to Lothair and looked him in the eye. "Edzard is hunting in my forest, isn't he?"

"Yes," Lothair growled.

"You send for Edzard and I'll send for Jacob," the bishop said. "I'll go with you and Peter to the castle, since that's where the events began, and we'll conduct the inquisition there."

Lothair's face twitched a few silent moments before he sheathed his sword.

CHAPTER 43
THE TRIAL

Peter paced over the wooden beams of the stone tower's third and top floor until nightfall, when Count Edzard on the floor below ordered him to stop. Peter bit his nails and stood quietly beneath the thatched roof. His tunic and breeches stiffened as caked river mud dried. A framed bed with a mattress and a pillow beckoned his tired legs but Peter preferred to lean against the stone wall and stew in fear, anger, and shame. The count snored below until dawn.

Peter pressed against a wall slit all morning and watched for Jacob to appear on the narrow winding road up the bluff. Several groups of town residents crossed the bridge, ascended to the castle, and later descended, sometimes delayed by serfs and pack animals bringing stones from the quarry. Shortly before noon, Jacob climbed the bluff in the company of Father Kristoph and entered the castle's new stone gate.

Peter tottered to the open trap door, a square hole in the floor and the only exit from the tower's third story. The ladder on which he had climbed to the third floor lay flat on the second floor ten paces straight down. He looked below to an opening in the second floor where a staircase led to the first floor, to the great hall. Muffled discussions drifted up from the great hall two floors beneath. He sat by the trap door and strained his ears but could hear only indistinct words.

After a short while, a big yellow-haired Slav with a dent in his forehead raised the ladder to the trap door and brought him food. Although Peter had not eaten in more than a day, he took only a few bites of a creamy mushroom pastry and a stew of meat in berries and vinegar. His stomach cramped and, as the sun moved into afternoon, the spasms grew worse.

He gave up trying to understand the dampened discussions below and stood again by a wall slit, hoping to see Jacob's white hair among the residents returning to the free town. In the harsh summer sun, he could see clear across the valley to the blacksmith shop, perched on a hill at the far outskirts of the town. Between Jacob's shop and Peter's narrow window crowded over two hundred dwellings, their thatched roofs nearly obscuring the narrow streets that twisted toward the central market square. The massive cathedral and its spire dominated the town. Long and narrow monastery buildings covered a fourth of the town's area.

Dirt fields in midsummer stage of cultivation extended monotonously from the town's outskirts east, north, and south to the forests. The river on the town's western edge marked the end of the bishop's influence and the beginning of the count's.

The ladder thumped against the trap door again. The Slav called, "Come down."

Peter wished he had his baton. At the bottom of the ten-pace ladder, he turned around and saw Jacob, leaning against a post of a great canopied bed in the middle of the second floor. He jumped toward Jacob and cried, "Master, I so sorry."

The big Slav dragged Peter back, leaving a trail of mud chips that flaked off his tunic.

Peter asked, "What should we do?"

Jacob frowned at the stone wall behind Peter. "Just tell the truth."

Peter knew Jacob was right. All the trouble started because he had added cadmia to the count's gold. He would tell the truth, tell how he made the gold of the count's goblet grow. He recalled the formula for cadmia while the Slav nudged him down the stone stairway to the count's great hall, into discussions that echoed off stone walls.

"And what's more," the bishop said, "the great hall is so drafty that a gust of wind could have moved the door. That's why the door seemed to open and shut by itself. Yes, it's a heavy door but its hinges are of such a high quality, made by the blacksmith you hold upstairs, that any breath of air could push the door open or shut."

A few torches lit the great hall. Lothair, Norbert, and two other warriors stood against one wall. In their midst sat the count and countess, he on the chair and she on a stool. Her rich array of gold necklaces, armlets, and bracelets glittered in the firelight.

Fathers Ulrich, Kristoph, and three other canons leaned against the opposite wall, with swords strapped around their clerical robes. Before them strode the bishop, richly dressed and waving his hands as he spoke.

Peter stopped at the base of the stairs, stood next to Gabriel's rolled up mattress, bowed his head, and stared at the hole in a corner of the floor where narrow steps descended into the black cellar. Covered with mud, barefoot, dressed in a torn tunic and ragged breeches, he felt humbler than he had ever felt as a serf.

"And yes," Bishop Bernard resumed, "the door to your tower did stick, but it often sticks in the summer sun, doesn't it? The weight of your tower is pushing against the door jamb."

"What about my sword?" Lothair growled.

The bishop walked to the stairs and stood next to Peter. "Lothair doesn't go raiding with Edzard like he used to. His sword isn't used as much and the sheath probably hasn't been oiled in a while. It's no surprise they stuck together."

Lothair snorted his disagreement.

The count marched up to the bishop and Peter. "How do you explain the boy's invisible shield? Dozens of your people saw it."

"How can anyone see something invisible?" Bishop Bernard asked. "Let's ask the boy."

Father Ulrich walked forward and held the silver reliquary in front of Peter. "Swear an oath before the holy splinters of our Lord's cross to be truthful or suffer eternal damnation."

Peter nodded and mumbled, "I swear."

"Tell us, Peter," Bishop Bernard said, "how the crossbow's arrow curved away."

Peter spoke to the bishop's scarlet stockings and embroidered sandals. "Yes, my lord bishop. It bounced off my stick and knife."

The warriors responded like angry dogs. "Impossible." "Liar." "Improbable."

"Improbable, yes." The bishop raised his voice over the pack. "But impossible, no. We of the true faith, who believe in the Christian God, know that an arrow cannot alter its flight unless it is deflected or God himself intervenes. Father Ulrich, show everyone Peter's walking stick. It has a deep gouge where it deflected the dart. Look at his knife, too. It was dented by another piece of iron. Now tell us, Peter, what made the door of the count's house open and shut."

Peter mumbled, "I asked it to open and shut."

"But the wind moved the door."

"No, my lord bishop. The door granted my wish."

"Then you pushed it with your hands," the bishop said.

"No, my lord bishop. I spoke to the door w-w-with my thoughts."

The count stepped up and waved his gold goblet under Peter's nose. "Did you command Lothair's sword to stick in his sheath?"

"No, sire. I asked his sheath to tighten around his sword."

Lothair growled, "He could ask your collar to tighten around your neck."

No one stirred except Count Edzard, who quietly backed away.

The countess asked, "What did you do to make the door stick?"

Peter held up his hand. "I spread my fingers and the door spread itself until it stuck." He spread his fingers until he heard cries of "No" and "Stop" from the warriors and canons.

Sounds of shuffling and murmurs of "Sorcery" filled the great hall. Father Kristoph said, "The boy's helped by demons. He's turned away from the true faith. He is an apostate."

Peter's heart beat faster. His hands trembled.

"Look at me, Peter," Bishop Bernard said softly. Peter looked into the bishop's face, wet with perspiration and creased with lines of worry. Bishop Bernard wore all his vestments as: the pointed mitre on his head, the embroidered chasuble covering the dalmatic tunic which in turn covered the tunicle, the maniple draped over his left arm, the episcopal ring fitted over a red, gloved finger of his right hand. On his left hand he wore four silver rings, which Peter had cast with images of biblical heroes.

"How do you know you made these things happen?" the bishop asked.

"I let them happen through the powers of alchemy," Peter said.

Bishop Bernard turned to Count Edzard. "Alchemy. The sacred art. Practiced by popes and noblemen of the true faith."

"By kings and emperors, too," the countess said.

The count snapped at his wife, "I'll not serve someone trained by monks, someone who dallies with books, and pictures, and music, who allows the ways of Greeks and other foreigners into our land." The count shook his goblet at Peter. "Tell us, boy, what is this alchemy?"

Peter wondered why no one asked him about the count's gold goblet. "It ish a w-w-way of returning to our golden nature."

"What about the powers of alchemy?" the count barked.

Peter said, "They the powers of faith, love -"

The count barked louder, "They are powers of demons when they enchant my warriors."

"Or frighten half the town to death," Father Ulrich said, shaking a finger at Peter.

"Who taught you these powers?" Lord Norbert asked.

"Master Jacob," whispered Peter.

"The unholy Jew," Father Kristoph said.

Lothair stepped off the wall. "No more talk. Let's settle this the honorable way – the Jew and I in a duel to the death."

"Jacob is no lord," Bishop Bernard said. "You can't fight someone who isn't your equal."

"Let the dirty Jew find a champion," Lothair said.

Count Edzard waved his goblet. "No. I'm leaving tomorrow for war and don't have time for this. Give the Jew a red-hot iron. Do it now. If God protects his hands, I'll spare his life."

The bishop said, "God won't protect him because he's a Jew, regardless of what good or evil he's done. We should ask more questions."

"We already know he's a sorcerer," Father Kristoph said. "His novice is guilty of apostasy. Kill the Jew and his boy and be done with all this tedious talking."

Bishop Bernard left Peter's side and strode into the center of the great hall, his clerical layers of tunics and robes fluttered in his wake. "They are my subjects and the custom of the free town dictates that we must hear their oaths and all their oath helpers, not just their accusers."

Count Edzard snarled, "This sorcery occurred on my land so we should follow my custom. You used that excuse to protect Maynard after he murdered my father on your land."

The countess stood. Her gold necklaces flashed. "A new

penalty must be decided because there is no custom against sorcery neither in the bishop's valley nor in our fief."

The count stood. "Our fief? This is my fief, my castle. I command here, not you."

She lowered her voice and faced her husband. "We will continue the inquisition." The power of her tone tightened Peter's back.

Count Edzard fell back into his chair as if pushed by an invisible hand. "I don't care ... what you want." His words struggled out of his throat. "The Jew and his boy ... die tonight."

The countess said to the Slav, "Take the boy away and bring the Jew."

The Slav pushed Peter up the stairs to the second floor. Jacob stood with bowed head, leaning against the bedpost. In the great hall below, the arguments resumed.

"Master," Peter whispered. "What we gots to do?"

Jacob shook his head without looking up.

The Slav prodded Peter onto the ladder to the trap door above. "Use your powers to help us." Peter said. A spasm cramped his stomach.

Jacob answered with a strained voice, "They're gone."

Peter's feet nearly slipped off the rungs. "What gone? Your powers gone?"

Jacob nodded at the floor.

The Slav punched Peter's legs. "Go on. Keep moving."

Peter struggled with each step. He paused at the top and asked, "Why?"

Jacob shook his head. "Don't know," he choked.

Peter rolled onto the third floor and the Slav removed the ladder. His stomach cramped again as he watched from the trap door. Jacob descended the stone stairway to the great hall.

CHAPTER 44
THE COUNTESS

A soft voice brushed the darkness behind Peter's closed eyes. "Are you in pain?"

Peter wasn't asleep, nor was he awake. He swirled in a nether river between dreams and pain. His body circled in on itself like a whirlpool, arms clutching his waist, stomach alive with biting fish. He opened his eyes.

Countess Lilli bent over him. Several dangling gold necklaces sparkled against her dark blue dress. Straight, black hair hung down past her shoulders. Large, almond-shaped eyes and full, rose-tinted lips dominated her perfectly unblemished face. Above her towered the Slav with the dented forehead.

"Stomach," Peter groaned and looked away.

She growled at the Slav, "Fetch the May butter and warm the stomach ale. Bring the dross, too."

The yellow-haired man disappeared down the ladder.

"My slave will bring what you need." Her voice sweetened again. "Come to bed."

She took his hand and helped him to his feet. He recognized a ring on her finger, the silver image of Elizabeth he had made for the bishop. She led him to the wood-framed bed where the mattress and pillow enveloped him like a cloud. Gray chips of dried mud fell from his skin and tunic onto white linens.

The orange light of a setting sun streaked through the western wall slits and crossed the floor in long bands.

The countess sat beside him and pressed the underside of her wrist against his forehead.

He looked away, uneasy that a noblewoman would touch him as if he were her equal.

"Close your eyes and relax," she whispered. "Close your eyes and relax, relax, relax."

The silky inflection of her tone flowed through him like a gentle brook, washing his cramps away. He closed his eyes and absorbed her softness for a long, luxurious time. She lifted her wrist from his forehead and stroked his cheek. "You have no fever."

Peter drifted, entranced by her voice.

"It's just a stomachache," she cooed. "You're not used to eating fine foods are you? Creams, spices, eggs, meats."

Talk of food sent an acrid belch up Peter's throat and broke the trance. He turned his head and swallowed the bile.

She untied his belt and lifted his tunic. "Let's see what's wrong with your stomach." She pulled his breeches down to his hips.

He tensed to both the nausea and her intimacy.

Her fingers traced the taut ridges of his stomach muscles. "Oooooh," she purred. "Smithing makes a man strong. There's nothing wrong here."

Peter gasped for breath. Her touch aroused him.

She stood and said, "Relax. Regulate your breathing as your master taught you."

He concentrated on breathing slowly and deliberately.

From a tiny vial attached to one of her necklaces, she sprinkled a white powder onto the scab on his right arm. The Slav reappeared with a full platter. She took from it a small container, removed its lid, and dabbed its colorless, gooey contents into Peter's navel. A rancid smell attacked his nostrils. The countess gave him a steaming cup of spice-flavored ale whose aromatic vapors counteracted the goo's odor. She arranged a warm, moist compress on his stomach and his nausea receded. She growled at the Slav again, "Bring a basin of hot water and clean linens."

The big Slav ran back to the trap door.

Peter propped his shoulders up on a pillow and bowed his head. "Thank you, Lady Lilli."

"Don't bow your head, Peter," she said, lowering the pitch of her voice. "From now on, you are ordered to look at my eyes."

Her voice compelled him to raise his eyes to her dark, oval face. Beneath thin arching eyebrows, her large, brown eyes locked onto his. They pulled him until all his attention focused on their deep wells, sucking him in and searching him out at the same time. Everything else, the room, the bed, the cup in his hands, her face, everything sank away and submerged beneath the penetrating gaze of her eyes. Time slowed until it stopped.

"Good," she said finally and turned her eyes to his stomach. "Drink your ale before it gets cold." She pushed the compress, pressing out a few drops of golden liquid that trickled from his stomach to the linens. "Talk to me, Peter. Tell me what you know and ask me what I know."

Free from the spell of her eyes and her voice, Peter groped for words between sips of ale. "My stomach feels better already. W-w-what that?" He pointed to the rancid goo in his navel.

"May butter. I exposed it to the sun for a couple of weeks and then mixed it with the male organs of saffron flowers."

"W-w-what that?" He pointed to the compress around his navel.

"That's the cumin dross from the ale you're drinking. It's arranged on your stomach in the shape of a heart."

"And this?" He pointed to his arm.

"Powdered comfrey root."

"Yes. I know about comfrey," Peter said. "But the other remedies are different from those of other w-w-women, different even from Master Jacob's."

"These are some of the things I learned from imperial alchemists."

Peter fumbled the half-empty cup of ale.

She helped him steady the cup and laughed with a trill that gave him goose bumps. "Yes, Peter," she said finally. "Like you, I am also an apprentice of alchemy."

"W-w-who ish your master?" he asked.

She glided to the wall, her feet hidden by the long dress, and gazed out toward the town. Bands of sunset streaking across the room turned from orange to red. "I am my own master."

Peter nodded. "Master Jacob told me I gots to be my own master."

Countess Lilli moved back to the bed. Her skirt slid along the floor as though she were floating. Her eyes locked on Peter's and her voice inflected down. "How did you grow the gold you were given for Edzard's goblet?"

He was riveted once more. "One part cadmia to three parts gold makes the dog grow."

"Ah, yes." The countess looked away and pouted. "Cadmia. I've heard of that. Arsenic, zinc and copper together can dilute gold to a point before it loses its luster."

Peter sighed. "W-w-why didn' the count ask about his goblet?

Lothair didn' say anything about it, either.'"

"If Edzard had known his gold had grown, he'd have beaten the secret out of you."

"Ish no secret. I would tell him."

"But then he'd kill you to keep the formula secret and he'd start stretching his own gold to increase his wealth, what little wealth he has left. His raids bring less and less booty. The mason's work on the tower was costly and now he's directed them to replace the stockade gate and the walls with stone."

She folded her arms under her breasts. "Only I and Lothair know that you grew the gold, and I've commanded Lothair to tell no one. I command you not to tell Lothair about cadmia."

Her eyes intensified and Peter felt himself sucked beneath them again. "Have you and your master ever made gold?" Her voice seemed distant and near at the same time.

"Yes. One time, Jacob made gold."

"How?"

"Breathing, chanting." Peter spoke as in a dream, with only partial control of his words. "Melt copper and tin in the furnace. Remove slag. Mix them together with zinc earth in equal parts. Add ash. Remove lead. Cool with water. Be thankful in the light."

Her laughter freed him from the trance. "Is that how you made gold?" she asked finally.

Peter nodded.

She leaned over, letting her necklaces swing before his eyes. They twinkled in the dim light. "What are my necklaces made of?"

Peter drained the cup of stomach ale and said, "Gold."

"Brass." She spit the word. "Do you know how brass is made? No, of course not. A goldsmith would know. So would a silversmith and a coppersmith and even a tinsmith. In a more civilized land, a blacksmith might know. But here in the barbarian north, a blacksmith wouldn't know, unless he is a Jew."

She walked back to the narrow window and looked out. "Brass is made of copper, tin, and zinc. When it's polished, like my necklaces, it looks like gold to the ignorant. The Jew tricked you. What you thought was gold, was only brass."

The red streaks of sunset on the floor grew dull. Peter touched the pouch on his belt and felt the gold pebble roll within. Or was it a brass pebble? He stared at the compress on his bare stomach and struggled with Countess Lilli's assertion.

"The night Jacob made gold," Peter sputtered, "a bright light exploded."

The countess stood by a narrow window. "Did it rain that night?"

"Yes. It w-w-was thundering and …" Another twinge of doubt pinched Peter.

"Lightning?" The countess finished his sentence. "The Jew fooled you."

"But another time I saw Jacob change a copper penny to gold in his fist and that happened on a sunny day. A strong light glowed in his fist."

"Was there a light behind the Jew?"

"Yes. A window. But I saw it happen from my mattress."

"The Jew's hand glowed from sunlight coming through the window."

"But later Crayfish gots the coin, and the beggar exchanged it for boots, and food, and much more, and the merchants w-w-wouldn' give Crayfish so much if it w-w-wasn' gold."

"Could you see his hand during the whole transmutation?"

Peter paused to remember. "W-w-well, no. His hand glowed too much and he hid it behind his apron."

"He exchanged the copper penny for a gold coin behind his apron. He lied to you."

Peter pondered this possibility in the deepening gloom. "No," he whispered finally. "Master Jacob ish a good man. He never lied to me or anyone else."

"He's a Jew," she said. "I've never known a Jew that didn't lie. I've never known a Jew that didn't practice magic. He taught you sorcery." She returned to the bed and sat next to him.

Peter stared at her necklaces to avoid her eyes. "He taught me alchemy, not sorcery."

"I saw what you did yesterday, with the door and Lothair's sword. I don't care if you call it alchemy or sorcery. I want to learn how you did those things."

A sudden thump startled Peter. The hulking Slav had placed

a basin on the floor. Steaming water sloshed from it. He dropped folded linens next to the basin.

"Bring a candle," the countess snapped and the Slav vanished. She turned to Peter and her tone softened again. "Wash yourself tonight and tomorrow you will teach me alchemy."

"But I don' ... I don' know that I can," Peter said. "Alchemy ish very hard to understand."

She took the empty cup from him. "I learned my mother's magic and everything the imperial alchemists knew. I can learn what you know in forty days."

Peter bowed his head. "Forty days? Lady Lilli, alchemy takes three years to learn."

"Edzard is going on his war expedition tomorrow. He'll be gone for forty days. You will teach me everything before he returns. Then I'll be able to control him."

"W-w-with your permission, Lady Lilli," Peter whispered. "I gots to go back to the blacksmith shop. Maybe Jacob can -"

She slapped the compress off his stomach and stood. "You can't go back to that dirty, little shop. You and your master have been judged and condemned to exile."

Peter's ears burned. His head bowed lower. "Exile?"

"Exile. Yes. Banishment," she snapped. "You must leave the bishop's valley and the count's fief. You're lucky to escape alive. Some of your judges wanted to bury you in a field and cut you into the earth with an ox-driven plow. Others wanted to tie a boulder around your neck and throw you off the bridge. The bishop and I argued for exile. Had I let you loose tonight, your neighbors would have killed you, despite our judgment. You owe me your life."

Peter picked mud flakes from his tunic. He wished he hadn't argued with Jacob, and diluted the count's gold, and humbled Lothair, and frightened the town. "I w-w-was so foolish."

"Stand up and look at me," she barked.

Peter jumped out of bed and stood rigid. Her black eyes appeared as bottomless holes in the twilight gloom and he fell once again into their wells. His mind thankfully numbed.

"You will stay here, quietly, secretly, for the next forty days. Then it will be safe for you to leave. Only Lothair and I and that stupid slave know you are here." She stared out a wall slit and freed

Peter from her eyes. "Edzard is taking two warriors, three foot soldiers, and that damn, rhyming fool on his annual raid. Since our neighbors are too strong for his puny expedition, Edzard is waging this summer's war on heathen Slavs. He'll travel to the wild lands in the east, kill a few shepherds, rape their wives, steal their sheep. I'll be eating salted mutton all winter. Do you want to be a warrior?" she asked, still looking out the wall slit.

"It w-w-was my dream ... once." He slumped. "So long ago."

She smiled and nodded. "Lothair told me as much. He thinks you're too low bred to be a warrior. But I see great potential in you to be your own master, just as the Jew wants you to be. I'll send you away before Edzard returns, to the fields of the Slavs he killed. I'll send you with a slave to help you build your own house in your own valley, to help you enslave any women or children my husband left behind. I'll make Edzard give you that land as a reward for teaching me the sacred art of alchemy. You will be a lord, a knight, a vassal to me and the count."

"I just a free man and a cripple, too. How could I be a warrior?"

She said, "Edzard's grandfather was only a slave. But you're a free man. Your station is closer to a warrior's than his was when he received his title and land."

Peter clapped his hands. "Yes, of course. He w-w-was a slave. I a free man. I better than he w-w-was. I can be a w-w-warrior." His confidence and his smile faded. "But the first count gots his fief by saving the duke from Magyars in battle. I don' know anything about w-w-war."

"Neither does Edzard. But you and I don't need armor. We don't need a sword. We need only alchemy. With the powers of alchemy, no one will dare war against us. I will make the swords of my enemies stick in their sheaths. I will make the iron in their hauberks rust into dust. I will make their horses kneel before me. I will make Edzard give you a fief."

"In alchemy, w-w-we don' make things happen," Peter said. "W-w-we let things happen. I gots to ask Master Jacob to -"

The countess threw the cup against the wall. It clattered, tumbled to a dark corner of the tower. "The Jew's a fool," she hissed. "He won't help me, can't help me."

Peter said quietly, "Perhaps he lets us use his books."

"I hope I can save his books. Unlike you, the Jew refused my help and left the castle to begin his exile." In the deepening gloom, he could barely see the countess waving him to the window slit.

Peter stepped forward and looked through the wall slit. Against the indigo twilight sky, a fire raged high on a hill across the valley.

She moved across the room toward the trap door and its ladder. "The Jew's enemies took him, beat him, threw him into his blacksmith shop."

Peter could see tiny figures silhouetted against the flames. They seemed to dance around the fire. Peter's stomach began to cramp again.

Her voice rose as she descended the ladder. "They set the shop on fire with him inside."

In a distant part of his mind, Peter heard a knocking as the ladder was removed. He stopped breathing at the realization that the fire burned where the blacksmith shop stood.

Countess Lilli's voice shot through the empty trap door. "The Jew is dead."

CHAPTER 45
MOURNING

Long into the night, Peter stood at a wall slit and watched Jacob's shop burn. At times the blaze flared and exploded when it consumed containers of powders and syrups.

"Should have been patient. Should have been stronger," he whispered again and again. "Should not have argued with Jacob. Should not have used the cadmia. Should not have frightened everyone. How can I repair what I done?" Shame filled his mind like lead ingots in a straw basket. When the straw handle on his mind ripped away from the oppressive weight, he heard an answer.

"Wait."

"Yes. Should have been patient. What can I do now?"

"Wait."

His legs buckled and he slumped to the floor. He leaned against the stone wall and didn't move the rest of the night.

In the dawn's gray light, he stared at wood grain patterns in the floor without seeing them. He heard masons tapping, children playing and dogs barking without listening to them. He sensed the odor of May butter in his navel without smelling it. No thought disturbed his exhausted void until late in the morning, when the ladder thumped against the trap door.

"Are you awake, Peter?" Lady Lilli's voice echoed in the emptiness. Her red skirt shimmered into view, blocking the floor's numbing patterns.

His burning eyes shut against her bright color.

She wiped his navel clean of May butter. "I see you didn't bathe last night. Neither did you sleep in the bed. I brought you a trencher of frumentry. Please take some."

At the thick, wheaten smell of porridge, Peter's stomach rumbled, his only response to her words.

"I had it made just for you. It's plain, made simple for simple tastes. Next week I'll add salt. Then later I'll add milk, then eggs and then saffron. After a while, you'll have nobler tastes. You will be able to eat like a lord."

Peter opened his eyes. She sat on her knees in front of him, holding a hollowed out half round of brown bread filled with cooked grains. The white, shapeless meal steamed under his nose. His stomach gurgled. His mouth watered.

She slipped half a spoonful between Peter's lips. "Edzard left this morning," she said. "I'm sorry about Jacob."

Peter chewed slowly. The warm mush brought him out of empty exhaustion.

"Do you like the frumentry?" she asked.

"I killed him," he mumbled and stared at her brass necklaces.

"You didn't kill the Jew. He killed himself. He could have stayed here like you. He knew the mood of the town. Maybe he thought he could get away." She gave him another bite. "He was old. He would have died soon anyway."

"He w-w-was immortal," Peter said with a full mouth.

The countess stopped, holding the spoon above the bowl. "Immortal?"

Peter swallowed. "He w-w-was older than anyone knew."

She fed him another spoonful. "How old?"

Peter chewed faster. "He w-w-was a slave trader, w-w-when the Slavs lived here, before the Magyars came, before Count Edzard's grandfather w-w-was given this land, before the emperor gave the valley to the church."

"Really? I've heard of other immortals." She fed him again. "How do you kill one?"

"He said alchemists die w-w-when they choose to."

"There, you see. You didn't kill him. He decided to die."

Peter opened his mouth, ready for the next bite.

She held the spoon back. "Jacob told us yesterday that he had lost his powers. Did you lose your powers?"

Peter shrugged and eyed the porridge-filled spoon.

The countess kept the spoon suspended away from his mouth. "Well, did you or didn't you?"

Wisps of white steam wafted from the porridge and the aroma encircled him. He sucked back saliva drowning his waiting tongue. "Don' know."

The spoon did not move forward.

He wondered if the spoon wouldn't rather be in his hand and flicked his fingers open. She jerked back and dropped the spoon.

He caught the spoon and put it in his mouth.

The countess smiled. "How did you do that?"

"Do w-w-what?"

"You took the spoon from me. It jumped out of my hand into yours." She gave him the bread bowl. "Tell me about your powers. Start from the beginning."

Before finishing the porridge, he told her about quiet eating. As bands of morning sunlight shrank on the floor, he picked flakes of river mud from his feet and spoke about reverent cleansing. While the sun climbed to the noon hour and bands of sunlight disappeared, he sighed anxiously and spoke about the calming effects of regulated breathing and chanting. The still air under the thatched roof grew warmer as morning slid into afternoon.

Lady Lilli fanned herself with an empty platter. "Yes, every magician teaches that control of your body and mind is important," she said. "What magic words did you chant?"

Peter wiped sweat from his brow. "Benedicamus Domino."

The countess frowned. "That's what the monks chant. That's not magic."

"Don' matter w-w-what you chant, as long as it calms you. The w-w-words seemed magic to me until I learned Latin. All w-w-words and things are nothing except w-w-what meaning w-w-we give them."

While afternoon sunlight eked through the western window slits in longer bands, Peter spoke at length about the quarry of universal essence in everything, and the deceptions of fear, aggression, and shame that hide the quarry like layers of fog.

"This quarry is my power," the countess said. "I need it to protect myself from danger."

Peter told her that not even the most terrible things were dangerous because she is actually invulnerable.

She dropped the pitch of her voice. "That's what I need, to be invulnerable. How do I make myself invincible? Look at my eyes and tell me."

His muscles stiffened. He lost himself in her dark pupils and the details of the room behind her melted like butter in the summer heat. He recited by rote the difference between form and content, between deception and essence.

Her voice lowered further. "I don't understand. Give an example."

Speaking in a flat monotone, Peter explained how we shape the elements of the universal essence into different forms, just as a blacksmith makes a warrior's chain mail tunic from a shapeless pile of tiny iron rings. The forms mean nothing until we attach our deceptions to them.

She turned away. "So a form is dangerous only because I make it so. Everything has only the meaning I give it."

Peter blinked, free from her trance. "Uh, yes. Like the Latin chant."

The countess stood, gazed out a window slit, and said, "If everything means nothing until we put some meaning on it, then everything is, in its raw state, nothing. And there's nothing more harmless than nothing."

Peter's memory of his argument with Jacob about nothing flickered to life. He rubbed his tense forehead and struggled to understand. A revelation burst through his fog.

"Yes, yes, yes," he said. "Everything ish nothing. We give it meaning, purpose, design. But once we see that it ish really nothing, we free from what we thought it was, free from our deceptions. That ish what Jacob meant."

He jumped to his feet. "It all made of the same thing. But it not a thing. It ish no thing. It ish essence, universal essence. Now I understand. Everything ish the same. All the separate things not really separate. They not real things." He pointed at his chest. "My body ish not real." He pointed at his head. "My mind ish not real." He thrust his hand toward the wall next to him. "The wall ish not real. Ow!" He sucked on his scraped knuckles.

The countess laughed. "The wall is very real," she said, catching her breath, "and very hard. When I know the wall's meaning and learn to control it, then I can pass my hand through it. I'll learn to make it harmless to me but not to others. That will make me invincible."

The ladder squeaked and the Slav brought a meal of lentils in a bowl of hollowed out dark bread for Peter and stewed meat in a bowl of hollowed out white bread for the countess.

She sent the Slav away and they ate in silence in the late

afternoon heat. Peter chewed slowly, delighted with his newfound revelation but wondering about her interpretation.

As they finished eating, the ladder squawked and Lothair's head rose through the trap door. Peter wished he had his stick.

"Well?" she asked Lothair.

Lothair glared at Peter. "All I've got are blistered hands and feet from sifting through ashes. It's still smoldering and it stinks like hell. Some of the God damned monks are praying at the ruins to rid the town of the stench. Bernard is with them, looking like a long-faced mule."

"Gold?" she asked.

Lothair shook his head. "No gold. Just iron. That fat peddler, Hugo, is poking around for iron tools. Edzard stopped to look before heading east to war. His fool, Gabriel, took a ram's horn from the ruins."

"Books?" she asked. "Scrolls?"

"No. Nothing left but that cursed water well."

She waved him away and the ladder squawked again as he descended.

"The bishop copied Jacob's books and scrolls," Peter said.

"I've read them all," Lady Lilli said. "I'm sure the Jew hid a few from Bernard, secret writings Bernard would have destroyed had he known about them."

She put her fingers to her lips for a few thoughtful moments. The ring of Elizabeth on her finger shone in a shaft of sunlight, reflecting tiny details in Elizabeth's silver face and hair. The countess saw him staring at the ring and held her hand out before him. "You made this ring for Bernard, didn't you? The bishop and I are close, like family. When you become my vassal, you will join that family." She stood and glided to the trap door. "Wash yourself tonight and sleep in the bed, not on the floor. We'll continue tomorrow. Without the Jew's hidden books, I'll rely on you more than ever. Do you need anything?"

Peter bowed his head. "If possible, Lady Lilli, I ... uh ... I a cripple and I ... uh ... I need my w-w-walking stick."

The countess climbed onto the ladder. "Why? Isn't it just a form, a deception in an unreal mind?"

Peter's face tingled with a hot flush.

She descended to the bottom and the Slav removed the ladder from the trap door.

Peter washed in the water basin and wondered if Jacob chose to die. His master appeared tired and defeated when Peter last saw him, as though the events had overwhelmed him. Jacob seemed powerless but not resigned. And yet he suffered a horrible death. Peter's grief and shame welled up once more.

He jumped when his baton thumped nearby, thrown from below through the trap door. He caressed the stick, worn smooth at the top where he always held it, splintered at the bottom from his fall off the cliff, chipped and nicked in places where it deflected a bear's claws, Lothair's sword, and a crossbow's arrow. His stick had, like Jacob, been his steady companion for the past three years. He remembered Jacob's patience, friendship and miracles. He opened the pouch tied to his belt and held the shining gold pebble in a band of sunlight.

Should he tell the countess that at least one gold platter lay at the bottom of his master's well? But she had insisted Jacob made brass, not gold. Was this bright pebble in his hand made of brass and not gold? Why did she send Lothair to the charred ruins of Jacob's shop in search of gold? She must have known Jacob made gold.

Peter nodded and whispered, "I gots to teach her alchemy ish not about making gold, but about recovering our golden nobility." Rosamund understood everything he told her about Jacob's lessons in just one morning at the market fair. Surely he could help the countess understand alchemy in forty days. He would honor Jacob's memory by passing on his knowledge. He would make each lesson a memorial to his dead master.

By the light of the setting sun, he dried himself with clean linens, hung his washed clothes on a bedpost, and lay down on the mattress. In an instant he was dreaming that a chapel with golden doors had been built around Jacob's well and that pilgrims came to wash deceptions from their eyes in its healing water.

CHAPTER 46
DYEING

"I wish Grandma Bertha had stayed to see this," Rosamund whispered.

Young rabbits and a wolf puppy ate from the same milk and wheat mush she had placed on the forest floor. A couple of older rabbits watched from under a holly bush, keeping a wary distance from the wolf. But the younger rabbits shared the mush with the thin, adolescent predator. They didn't even flinch when the wolf's crippled front leg twitched with an occasional spasm.

Over the past few weeks she had moved the puppy's food closer to the rabbits' food a little at a time until they were no more than a pace apart. Today she combined their meals into one and they ate together for the first time. This was the reward for her patience. Bertha would enjoy seeing this. The rest of the villagers thought it was crazy.

Rosamund sighed. Her late husband tried to kill one of the rabbits. Life was so much easier without Karl.

Instantly she felt ashamed of the thought, but the shame dwindled as she watched the young animals. If rabbits and wolves can change their minds about each other, so can people.

She picked up both her and Bertha's baskets with hands stained blue-black from picking dyeberries. She skipped barefooted over the soft blanket of pine needles and breathed in the cool, clean aromas of evergreens. Before long, she bounded out of the forest and onto the balks between fields of young wheat, rye, barley, and turnips. She ran past serfs pulling weeds in the furrows. She headed for the smoke that drifted from dye cauldrons on the other side of the stockade wall. That was where Grandma Bertha awaited her. If Bertha's chest had not hurt, she would have stayed in the forest with Rosamund.

When she trotted into the village, she slowed to catch her breath. She walked past a few huts, up the ramp, and into the stockade that surrounded her lord's house.

Halfway down the length of the courtyard, Gisela and two of her helpers stirred two steaming cauldrons on beds of burning deadwood. A fourth woman, Grandma Bertha, sat against the

Lord Arnulf's house in the shade. She wiped her face with her red wool shawl from Count Edzard. Opposite Bertha, clumps of gray wool, already washed clean of animal grease and soaked in potash mordant, dried in the sun on pegs attached to stockade timbers. Alkaline vapors from boiling potash stung Rosamund's eyes and nose.

Gisela leaned on her stick and scowled. "Why didn' you come back with Bertha? Show me those berries."

Rosamund set the baskets at Gisela's feet and knelt next to Bertha. "You better?"

The ancient woman leaned her head against the wall. Her thin, white hair lay matted with sweat to her wrinkled forehead. She rubbed her arm and lisped, "Chest don' hurt anymore. But my arm ish numb. Sorry I didn' finish pickin' dyeberries."

"Wish you had stayed. They ate together from the same frumenty - the wolf and the rabbits - after I called them."

Gisela said, "Only witches talk to wild animals." The other women glared.

Rosamund stood and faced Gisela. "Ish not witchcraft. You gots to see it. The rabbits don' fear the wolf and the wolf -"

Gisela shouted at Bertha, "You gots to stop her nonsense. Why you leave her in the forest?"

Rosamund stepped between Gisela and Bertha. "She didn' feel good. Besides, I can collect enough berries by myself. I not afraid to go alone in the forest."

Gisela shook her head and turned away. "Fear has nothing to do with it. Ish against custom. But a head-strong girl like you don' care about that." She bent her gray head over a pot and rang it with her stick. "This don' bite enough."

Ursula stopped stirring the pot and said, "It makes my eyes burn."

"It gots to make you cry," Gisela said. She motioned to Rosamund. "Go gets more potash."

Rosamund walked with her head high past the women, around the corner, and through the building's back door. Lord Arnulf's lady sat bent over her loom and clapped its boards against strands of spun wool. All the doors and windows were open to a breeze that cooled her house and cleansed it of caustic fumes from the cauldrons outside. Rosamund bowed her head and asked the aged matriarch for another sack of potash.

The lady said, "It's hanging up there with the other dyes. How far along are you?"

"We washing and mordanting the second set of wool," Rosamund said. "The first set ish almost dry. We start dyeing it soon."

In an alcove half full of dye-stained pots, Rosamund climbed on a stool to reach a small, white sack hanging from the ceiling with other sacks of powdered red, blue, yellow, and black dyes. Through the open alcove window, she could hear water sloshing in the cauldrons outside.

"One of those rabbits bit Karl," Ursula said. "She told the rabbit to bite him."

"He was poisoned," Gertrude said. "Gisela bled him but he got weaker and weaker."

Gisela said, "I know more about healing than anyone. But that rabbit bewitched him."

"It was a simple case of bad blood," Grandma Bertha wheezed. "Gisela did all that she knew to do. Sometimes the sick get well, sometimes they don'. You girls should see those baby rabbits. They not bewitched. I take you there myself, without Rosamund."

Rosamund smiled. Grandma Bertha would change their minds.

Ursula said, "His blood was poisoned. She cast a spell on him."

"She consorts with demons," Gisela whispered. "You saw her baby, didn' you?"

"That was a monster's baby," Gertrude said.

Rosamund cringed. Her grip on the sack of potash tightened. She resisted the urge to throw the sack through the window and onto the women.

"Dear God." Grandma Bertha's voice rose in strident tones. "Show a little love for poor Rosamund."

"She cursed for life," Gisela said. "Everybody afraid of her."

"She a sorceress," Ursula said.

"The devil's lover," Gertrude said.

"Hush up, all of you," Grandma Bertha snapped. "You imagine all the wrong things. Open your minds. See her in a differ ..." She paused and screeched like a bird in pain.

"Bertha," Gisela said. "What wrong?"

Sloshing sounds from the cauldrons stopped.

"Bertha?" Gisela's tone rang with alarm.

Rosamund's heart jumped into her throat. She fell off the stool, dropped the sack of potash and ran through the back door. She rounded the corner of the building and saw all three women clustered around Grandma Bertha.

Gisela was kneeling and pressing her ear against the old woman's chest. Grandma Bertha sat as she had before, leaning against the wall, her head back.

"She gone," Gisela said and closed the old woman's half open eyes. Grandma Bertha appeared to be sleeping.

Rosamund knelt, took Bertha's frail hand and squeezed it. "Wake up, Grandma."

"She gone," Gisela said again.

Bertha's hand remained limp in Rosamund's grasp. "Don' go, Grandma."

Gisela stood and walked away. The other women neither moved nor spoke, as though paralyzed.

Rosamund rocked on her knees and waited for Bertha to wake. She wiped the old woman's face with her red, wool shawl. Bertha's hand grew cold. Rosamund looked up into the blue sky with tears welling in her eyes and whispered, "Please, Grandma Bertha, don' leave me here alone."

CHAPTER 47
THE MEMORIALS

Every morning at dawn, Peter awoke to the tapping of stone masons building the castle gate. The Slav raised the ladder from the second to the third floor of the stone tower and brought him fresh water for bathing and the heart of a round of bread, warm and without crust. After a time, Peter's breakfast changed from grainy brown to soft white bread.

One day the Slav presented Peter with a new red tunic of fine linen. Another day he brought a pair of blue breeches. A week later he delivered a pair of leather boots. Every few days the slave left Peter some item of fine clothing: a cloak of finely spun wool, a hand tooled leather belt, a pair of linen gloves, a leather coin purse, and an empty sword sheath. Peter slipped his baton into the sheath and his gold pebble into the purse.

In the late morning hours, he received porridge, at first plain and in later weeks seasoned with salt, and then later with dried cherries, and later with cream and spices added, always served in a bowl of hollowed out bread. Countess Lilli usually ascended when he finished eating. She wore thin dresses of finely woven wool and silk. On hot summer days their garments stuck to their sweating bodies in the furnace-like heat beneath the tower's thatched roof. They fanned themselves with pieces of hardened leather and sipped cool ale from the cellar.

Many pieces of jewelry adorned her elegant neck, arms, and fingers. "The royal craftsmen would be envious of your work," she said and held her silver ring of Elizabeth in a shaft of sunlight. "When King Heinrich sees your work, he'll ask that you make things for him, too."

In the late afternoon, Peter ate unsalted soups and, as the days passed, stews, and then later, meat pastries spiced with a crushed peppercorn. At sunset they burned a candle and talked until the countess finally descended and the ladder was removed.

At night he could hear her in the room beneath talking with Lothair or Norbert or ordering servants. Peter kept still and quiet, as ordered by the countess, to keep his presence secret.

Over the summer, she taught him the manners of the imperial

court: to speak clearly and crisply, to stand straight with shoulders back and head high, to bathe regularly with scented waters, to refrain from wiping his mouth or his nose on his sleeve, to file his nails instead of biting them, to use a knife for cutting food but not for eating, to take small bites, not to speak or drink with his mouth full, not to blow on his food to cool it, not to poke his food with his finger, not to gnaw bones or bite the bread bowls because these were given to the lesser people.

The daily alchemy lessons provided intense discussions. Peter's efforts to make each lesson of alchemy a memorial to Jacob eased his guilt and grief. By teaching alchemy, he learned more about the sacred art in forty days than he had over the past three years.

When the countess didn't understand a concept, her voice commanded his body to face her fully, her eyes directed his mind to recite difficult points fully. The web of her spell wrapped him tighter as her knowledge increased.

In the first days, Peter taught her four qualities required for a furnace of an alchemist. He began with the furnace's reflective walls and how, by cooking our thoughts, by understanding ourselves better through reflection, we can understand others and see that we are all the same.

"When I understand my own motives," Countess Lilli said, "I can better understand the motives of others and I can better counter their plans and schemes."

Peter stressed the importance of the furnace door, how to open the mind to all possibilities, how to open the heart with service to others, and how to listen to spirit.

The countess said, "Serving others is a good way to disarm them, to open their minds to my powers and to the spirits I send their way."

Peter explained that our ideal sets a higher pattern that we, softened by the heat of reflection, could be poured from our crucible into a more beautiful mold.

"My mother is my ideal," Countess Lilli said. "She was a foreigner, a lady-in-waiting, and yet, through her magic, she dominated the imperial court. I, too, will dominate."

The fire of zeal, Peter told her, moves us to action, to change and improve.

The countess said, "I have a burning desire to control my world."

As Countess Lilli's interpretations grew more disturbing to Peter, her control over him grew more complete. He became aware that he was at war with himself. One part of him was a slave to her commands and responded with dutiful recitations. The other part was free and served her with thoughtful answers. Before the slavish part took total control, he resolved to detach himself from the bonds of her spell and to teach her better. Every day he struggled to loosen the control that her eyes and voice exerted over him. With each alchemical power he taught, Peter untied another strand of her web.

He began the second part of the memorial lessons with Jacob's assertion that no teacher can give us powers we don't already have.

"I've seen your powers," she said. "I'll take them and the world will kneel before me."

He explained that the first power, hammering power, is faith plus action. Belief shapes our world.

Countess Lilli toyed with his hair. "I believe you will teach me to be a hammer, the greatest alchemist ever. Belief is powerful. Magic has no power without the belief it can grab and hold." Without warning, she ripped a few strands from his head.

Peter winced and rubbed his scalp.

"You're courageous and obedient, worthy to be my vassal with your own valley," she cooed. "Now that I have part of you, you believe I have all of you." She tucked his plucked hair into her slipper.

A few days later, Peter turned to cleaving power, the recognition of unifying love.

"Yes, love is a tool," Lady Lilli said. "I cleave to others in order to get what I want." She glided to where Peter sat on the floor, his back against the bed and one of his arms stretched over the mattress. She lay down on the bed behind him and rolled over so that the tips of his fingers could feel her breast through her dress, wet with perspiration.

Peter tensed, afraid to move his arm.

She laughed. Her breast lifted and fell against his fingers with each peal of laughter. "With cleaving power," she said finally, "I can manipulate any one."

After a few days of taut discussion, Peter took up the next power. He defined welding power as a way to make visions into things by recognizing that thoughts are as real as things.

"When I concentrate my thoughts, I can weld them to anything," the countess said and pointed at him. "I can make our future real."

Peter saw her halo leap down her arm, shoot out her finger, and strike his chest with glowing, red intensity.

She whispered, "Edzard will fall, Lothair will be banished, and you will be a warrior, a master of alchemy. I will be master of my world. It will be exactly as I envision it."

In time, Peter gave up teaching her the power of vision and moved to the power of the anvil, the willingness to allow the greater will.

"With this power," Countess Lilli said, "everything will bend to my willpower." She snatched Peter's stick out of its sheath and hurled it across the room where its splintered end crashed into a dark corner.

Peter retrieved it and found a tiny gray mouse, nearly invisible against the gray wall, crushed to death by the impossible accuracy of her throw.

She tilted her head back and growled, "If my mousy husband does not bend to my will, I will crush him."

After a few frustrating days, Peter struggled into the next lesson, describing steel power as sharp but humble wisdom.

The countess leaned forward and bit into a fruit pastry Peter held in his hand. Its sticky sweetness oozed onto his knuckles. "After I ensnare the ignorant and gullible, I will suck their wisdom from them." She held his wrist and licked the ooze from his knuckles.

Peter tried discreetly to pull his hand away but her grip tightened. She squeezed his wrist harder. His discomfort turned to pain. He felt her halo devouring his own. He jerked his hand free and sat on the bed, drained and confused.

She took the pastry from his limp hand. "Your wisdom is sharp as steel. It is my greatest weapon and I need it. You're trying to free your mind from my control. Don't do that, Peter."

Peter disobeyed her command. The power of her eyes and her voice over him was slowly waning. The cords of her web were breaking one by one.

One morning the Slav brought him a warrior's undershirt and chain mail tunic.

"These are Edzard's old aketon and hauberk," the countess said. "They're too big for him but they should fit you well. He threw them away because the Jew made him two new ones from Maynard the Fat's old hauberk. Wear these and remember that only I can make you a warrior."

One day in the fifth week of instruction, Lady Lilli did not ascend at her usual time. Peter slipped into his chain mail tunic and looked out a wall slit over the free town, the cathedral, and the ripening fields. For the first time in weeks, cool air filled the tower with a promise of autumn.

He thought of the coming harvests, the market fair, and his new fief. He would build a great house, a church, and a town for merchants. He would ask Rosamund to come to him, if she could forgive him.

He hoped she could. But he shouldn't hope for her forgiveness until he forgave others. Jacob said he couldn't finish his apprenticeship until he wished upon Lothair what he wished for himself. Rosamund seemed capable of forgiveness. So why couldn't he? She understood what he'd said about alchemy that morning in the market fair last year. Countess Lilli, on the other hand, did not understand alchemy.

He shook his head. Why were the lessons going astray? Lilli still thought of alchemy as a way to force things to change outside rather than allowing change inside. Was something missing from the lessons? Perhaps he could teach alchemy differently, in his own way. Jacob told him to find his own way. Peter reflected on a different way to explain the six powers. After some thought, he saw a way to group them into three powers instead of six.

Hammering faith and welding vision could be lumped together to become a power of the mind. That would help her understand ideas and the things that ideas produce. Cleaving love and the anvil of will combined into a power of the heart. That would help her understand the relationships between things. And finally, he came to see steel wisdom and tempered strength as a power of both the mind and the heart. That would help her understand the purpose of ideas and her responsibility for their consequences.

But these groupings seemed shallow. He wanted to teach her something more profound. He regrouped these three new powers into two greater powers. In the first, vision wouldn't work without faith and wasn't pure without love. In the second, strength was misguided without will and useless without wisdom. But still something was missing.

By late afternoon, Peter realized no matter how he arranged the powers of alchemy, none of them were separate from the other. They were all parts of one power, united in one purpose to reveal the content of all forms.

Content. That's what was missing from the lessons. The universal essence.

He had explained the universal essence the first day when he used a hauberk as an example, when he realized what Jacob meant by no thing. Since then he had taught her about forms: faith, love, vision, will, and wisdom – all ethereal forms but forms nevertheless. Next she expected to learn the power of tempering strength from him. How could he reassert the importance of content, the universal essence, to help the countess better understand?

The ladder knocked against the trap door and Lilli climbed to the top. She glowered at him and her scorn pinned him against the wall. He concentrated on his breathing, whispered a chant, relaxed his mind, and his body. He slipped from her eyes to focus on her brass necklaces. She stomped forward until her eyes were a hand's length from his. "Do not try to escape my eyes."

Peter's muscles stiffened again. His body fell against the wall like a rigid timber.

She hissed, "I'm angry enough to kill someone. I could even kill you. Do not tempt me."

CHAPTER 48
THE CONTEST

Countess Lilli backed away and crossed her arms. "Edzard sent a message. He will raid a few days longer. Since he's killing Godless Slavs, he can ignore the church edict and make war for more than forty days. The fool doesn't care that he's holding his few loyal warriors to a longer vassalage duty than required, all for a few more sheep. He probably hasn't taken enough sheep to pay the masons."

She swiped the back of her hand across Peter's chest, and her long fingernails clicked over the ringlets in his chain mail tunic. "My idiot husband sent the message not to me, who rightfully rules in his place when he's gone, but to Norbert, his faithful spy. I sent the messenger back to Edzard and warned him not to ignore me again. I've suffered his insults too long. With the powers I've learned, I will crush him."

She lowered her voice and fixed her eyes on his. "Tell me what's left to learn."

The power of her voice stiffened Peter's already rigid muscles. His words dribbled from his mouth. "All ... powers ... are ... one power." He battled to detach himself from his fear and awe of her, and slowly regained control of his tongue. "It is ... something I have ... just come to realize," he continued. He spoke with the crisp inflection the countess had taught him. "There's only one purpose -"

She swiped her fingernails again against his armor. "You've taught me five ways to achieve my purpose. What is the sixth?"

Peter began a review of the previous lessons, to emphasize the content, the universal essence, but she cut him off. She commanded he teach her only the sixth power.

For the next few days, he tried to teach her that tempering strength in iron requires disciplined patience. With tempering strength an alchemist is working with the universal essence to make an unbalanced world noble again. Whenever she carved selfish forms of strength from his lessons, he patiently led her back to her quarry, to selfless universal essence. Lilli's impatience grew each day. After their discussions, after she stomped back down the ladder, he lay awake at night devising subtler ways of teaching her.

Late one morning, after another sleepless night, Peter watched the countess with detachment as she marched up the ladder and straight into his face.

She growled, "I've heard enough about patience. And don't say another word about universal essence." She lowered her voice and fixed her eyes on his. "Teach me how to strengthen myself and weaken others."

Peter stared back with drowsy, unfocused eyes. He ached for sleep. He longed to be free from her spell. He burned with a desire to help her. He reflected on how she held him in her spell, how he respected her. A revelation came in that instant. She held him because he did more than respect her; he was in awe of her. The only power she had over him was the power he let her have. The strands of her web he had woven himself. In that instant his vision of Lilli changed. Her almond eyes became hawkish. Her black hair didn't reflect light but devoured it. Her soft face hardened like leather.

She barked, "Look at my eyes. Listen to my voice. Tell me how to make myself strong and others weak."

He opened his heart to a patient response and smiled at Lilli. He silently blessed her just as his ideal would. "Our strength doesn't weaken others," he answered softly. "Rather, it makes them stronger." He felt nearly free of her web. One invisible strand still held him.

She frowned and turned away. "These past few weeks, my power over Lothair and others has become stronger. But you are slipping away. You've even stopped that irritating stutter. What are you doing?"

Peter yawned. "I'm learning alchemy, same as you. But you and I see it differently. It frees me. It imprisons you. You're not just hurting yourself, you're dragging the rest of the world down with you."

Lilli cocked her head back. "I don't care if the world is dragged into the cellar. I'll have my powers and I'll rule the world from the cellar."

Peter shook his head. "We need to envision a test for you, for the end of your lessons. It would have to be a test where you direct your powers toward something good, something right."

"I don't need a test. I need the rest of your knowledge. Don't resist me anymore. You owe me your life. I am your countess and you are my vassal and I will get what I want."

"If Jacob were alive, he'd help you understand that it's not about getting, it's about giving, it's about forgiving."

Her eyebrows rose along with her tone. "Forgiving?"

"The test to end my apprenticeship is to forgive and submit to my enemy. You need a test of forgiveness, too."

She squinted at him. "Who is your enemy?"

Peter's face and scalp tingled. "Lord Lothair," he whispered.

"Lothair? Why do you want to submit to Lothair?"

"He crippled me. He hurt me."

"Then you must hurt him back. Forgiveness is a sign of weakness. Show no mercy. The harsher the punishment, the stronger the punisher. What does anyone get from forgiveness?"

"Peace."

"Hah." Lilli paced the floor. "I'll get peace only after everyone has submitted to me, only after I've gotten revenge, true to my namesake."

"Your namesake? But ..." Peter stopped to remember the Bible passages he had read in Jacob's shop. "Elizabeth was a woman of piety. She didn't seek revenge."

"You think Lilli is short for Elizabeth, the mother of the mother of God. I let people believe that. But my mother named me after Lilith, the avenging demoness for women wronged by men. I am the result of a rape so horrible my mother could never have any more children. She raised me to make men suffer. When I become master of Edzard's castle, I'll combine my mother's magic with your sorcery and punish my unsuspecting father." She thrust a trembling finger toward the east. "Any one I can't control, who is strong enough to resist my eyes and my voice, is an enemy." She scowled at Peter.

Peter fidgeted. "I'm nobody's enemy."

"If you have the same secret powers as I and if you're not under my control, then you are my worst enemy." She locked her frowning eyes on his. "Look at me."

He looked back with unfocused eyes and saw a dark fog of

fear swirl about her. A single black wisp snaked away from the fog and wrapped itself tightly around him. He envisioned a blessing, a stream of white love flowing from his heart to her heart. The black wisp and the dark fog retreated. A buried love within her reached out and connected to the white stream. Peter held the connection, felt the connection, became the connection. She swayed, her eyes softened, and a thin layer of light shimmered around her head and shoulders. The air around them glowed and objects in the room blurred. The brass amulet that hung over her heart shone bright like gold. For a suspended moment, they clove together in the universal essence. But her dark fog, sensing it was dissolving into nothing, reacted with terror. Fear fought back. Her frown returned. An invisible black bolt shot out from her and struck their connection and struck it again.

The creaking ladder interrupted their contest and the Slav showed his dented head through the trap door. "Lord Norbert wants to see you."

"Not now, slave," she snapped.

The big man bowed his head. "He gots another message from Count Edzard."

Her dark skin turned darker. "My patience with Edzard has ended. I'll squash him with my new powers." Her glare whipped at Peter. "I saved your life and you owe it to me. Remember that I am your countess and you are my vassal."

She followed the Slav down and a moment later the ladder was removed. Peter heard them walk down the stone stairs to the first floor and exit the building, slamming the heavy, armored door behind them.

Peter rubbed his face and groaned. He had taught Lilli to do harm. Jacob had warned him not to speak about alchemy. How could he undo what he'd done? If Jacob were alive, he'd know what to do.

He peered out a window overlooking the cathedral and free town. If he could escape, he'd find another master of alchemy like Jacob and bring him back here to help.

Peter shook his head. No. Jacob told him to be his own master. If he could escape, he would go on the road, learn as a journeyman from other masters, and eventually become a master on his own.

Then he could return and right the wrong he'd caused. But to be a journeyman, he'd have to finish his apprenticeship, and that meant forgiving Lothair. He would have to submit to the tall warrior and Lothair would probably kill him. He wasn't yet ready to forgive Lothair. Or was he?

He walked to the trap door and studied the long drop to the floor below. No way to escape. He looked at the bed with its mattress, pillow, and sheet. He needed to rest, to catch up on lost sleep. Perhaps he should stay, break the last strand of her spell and teach her the true value of alchemy. It was best he stay. Or was it?

He crossed his arms over his chain mail armor, closed his eyes, took a deep breath and asked what to do.

The quiet answer came instantly. *"Go."*

Peter looked at the bed again and saw a way to escape.

CHAPTER 49
CONSPIRACY

Discord drifted through the tower's narrow windows. Uneven rapping of masons' tools on the castle gate drummed behind strident words from Norbert and Lilli in the courtyard. Peter left the window slit and stuck his head through the trap door in the floor. He heard no sound within the stone tower.

He pulled the bed frame toward the square opening. The bed's legs scraped so noisily against the timbered floor that he dared drag it only one slow finger-length at a time. Sweat tricked with each brief exertion.

He pulled the bed until one of its legs rested against a raised seam in the floor close to the opening. He tied one end of the bed sheet to the leg, tied his fine wool cloak to the opposite end of the sheet and lowered it through the trap door. It dangled too high above the second floor. He pried a loose nail from the bed, tapped it into the split end of his stick, and tied the end of his cloak around it. Now his makeshift rope was long enough.

He roughed the leather soles of his new boots against the stone walls to make them grip better. After a few test tugs on the sheet, he shimmied through the trap door, down the sheet, the cloak, and then his stick. A ringlet in his chain mail caught the nail head in his stick and the cloak began tearing where it was tied to the nail. After freeing the ringlet, he slid to the end of his stick, a long hop above the second floor. He released his stick and the thud of his landing echoed off the stone walls.

Peter crouched for a few moments and listened. Nothing else moved in the building. One pace away, the floor opened for a stone stairway down to the great hall, to the armored door, to freedom. Ten paces behind him sat the count's large canopied bed.

He reached for his stick but it swung beyond his grasp. Before he could jump and tear his stick free, he heard below the main door in the great hall open and shut. He froze, unsure of what to do.

Lady Lilli's voice rose up the stone stairway. "Can your uncle's house hold everyone?"

"Yes," Lothair's familiar growl answered. "Did the message say we meet in three days?"

"Yes. I'm sure it will be a great feast." Lilli's tone dripped with sarcasm. "A third year anniversary. He wants us to bring his chair. We'll gorge ourselves on mutton and listen to him toast himself with his prized gold cup. He'll make us listen again to that fool sing that bloated song about his victory over Maynard. Then he'll take us to the battlefield and gloat some more."

From the sounds of their voices, Peter guessed they stood by the main door.

"Has Norbert left?" the countess asked.

"He's left to get Richard and Anson. I'll get the rest of the warriors. It'll take two days to bring them all to Arnulf's house, along with the bishop and my priestly cousin. I'll leave one foot soldier here."

Peter glanced around the room. Should he hide under the canopied bed or should he climb back up to the top floor?

"I'll meet you there," the countess said. "We should plan a surprise for Edzard."

"I'm afraid, Lady Lilli, that you will be the one surprised."

"What do you mean?"

"Norbert has discovered you're keeping prisoners in the tower. The old fool confronted the Slav about it. When we return from Arnulf's valley, he'll accuse you of adultery and the Slav will be his witness."

Peter heard a crash as if a stool had been kicked over.

"That would give Edzard an excuse to beat me to death." Her words cut with anger. "Everyone would think him justified. Everyone knows we detest each other."

"I know a woman of your standing would never touch anyone lower. I'll swear an oath to that before Edzard."

"Who do you think he'll believe? You, whom he fears, or his trusted spy, Norbert. I know how to stop Edzard dead." Her voice sweetened. "I need help to do it. I'll give you a valley for helping me, noble Lothair."

"Don't toy with me. You also promised a fief of land to the little serf. That's disgusting."

Peter decided to hide under the bed. When Lothair and Lilli discover his makeshift rope, they will rush out of the tower to search for him and then he could escape. He tiptoed toward the bed.

Lilli said, "I don't trust the boy anymore. He has slipped from my control. I will not give him the raw lands of Slavic shepherds killed by Edzard."

"What will you do with the little serf now?"

"I'll use him to make the Jew talk to me."

Peter's heart stopped. His ears burned.

The countess continued, "He loves that boy. If I beat the boy in front of the Jew, tear the boy's limbs off one by one, then the old man will finally tell me his secrets."

Peter gasped. Was Jacob really alive? Who else could she mean? His trembling hands pressed to his mouth to keep from shouting with joy.

His plan changed. He wouldn't escape until he found his master. But how could he find Jacob? Peter looked up at his improvised cord hanging from the trap door above. He could climb back to the top floor, act like he knew nothing, and wait for her to take him to Jacob. Then Jacob would tell him what to do. Jacob would fix this mess.

Peter didn't want to jump for the end of his stick. That might be noisy. A stool would help him reach his makeshift rope. He spied a stool by the count's bed.

Lothair paced below with heavy steps. "Now is the time to let me serve you. These two are sorcerers. They are clever and dangerous. Your inquisitions have yielded none of Bernard's secret plans against us. Let me beat the truth out of them. When Edzard sees that you and I are working to return the free town to him, that we are loyal and honorable, he will discount Norbert's accusation because it is based on a slave."

Peter shook his head as he tiptoed to the stool. Lothair doesn't know what secrets the countess really wants.

Lothair continued pacing. "I want the shepherds' land. It would be my own fief and I'd be away from your dung-headed husband."

"I can give you something better. After Edzard is murdered in your uncle's house, your uncle and his son will be accused of the crime. After they're gone, I'll give you their valley with its fields, serfs, and animals."

Peter picked up the stool and turned back to his swinging stick at the end of his improvised rope.

"What do you mean? My uncle wouldn't do that. He may not be smart but he's an honorable man."

"That's right. He won't murder Edzard. But he'll be blamed for it."

"This must be stopped. Who is the murderer?"

Countess Lilli's voice lowered. "You are."

Her tone pulled at Peter and slowed his steps to a crawl. He felt a strand of her spell whipping around his legs.

Lothair's pacing stopped. "No. I won't." His words strained, like insects struggling in a spider's sticky lace. "Don't use ... your damn voice ... on me. I'm ... honorable."

"Be quiet and look at me." Her tone dropped lower. "Look at my eyes and listen to my voice."

Peter struggled to break free from her spell and hoped Lothair could break free, too. If their positions had been reversed, had he possessed Lothair's training and power, Peter might have pursued his goals as forcefully as Lothair. In a flash, Peter saw himself equal to Lothair, with the same goals, the same deceptions, the same universal essence. Maybe he could, after all, forgive Lothair. Maybe he could submit to him and still be safe. But first, he must find Jacob.

The countess dropped her tone still lower. "You will kill Edzard. He deserves it. He killed his own father."

"No. Maynard ... killed ... the old count."

Lilli spoke again in a normal tone, her voice pitched high and light. "Edzard did it. I was there. I saw it. No one else knows except Bernard."

Peter nearly dropped the stool. Was she the witness?

Lothair's growl reasserted itself. "How can that be? Edzard believes Bernard's lies that Derek's murderer is still alive. He's afraid beyond all reason, thinks he'll be killed next. Why would he be afraid if he's the murderer?"

"When Bernard, curse his soul, violated the sacrament of my holy confession by telling others the truth, Edzard pretended to be afraid in order to take suspicion away from him."

"Edzard doesn't have the courage to kill anyone, unless his victim is asleep like Maynard the Whore."

The countess said, "Count Derek tried to rape me. Edzard saw it and flew into a rage. Edzard stabbed his father in the back, killed him, and blamed it on Maynard."

"Attack from behind. Well, that is something Edzard would do."

Lilli said, "He thinks his father soiled me and he's loathed me ever since."

"He loathed you before his father's murder."

The countess pitched her voice lower. Her words pierced the air in a slow staccato. "He killed his father, he killed Maynard, he wants to kill me, and, when he finds out that I have told you the truth, he will kill you, too. You must kill him."

"I ... honor -"

The countess barked, "Listen to my voice. Look at my eyes."

Peter's muscles tightened again in the power of her speech. He fought to detach himself.

"Before you leave today," she said, her inflection crisp, "I will give you a pouch with a special mushroom I've been saving. On the day of celebration, I'll divert everyone away from the feast table. Maybe I'll show them my new powers. You stay behind and rub Edzard's gold cup with the mushroom. Leave plenty of spores behind because I want him to die that night."

Peter's boots seemed made of lead. Sweat dripped freely from his brow. He hoped they would take him to Jacob before they left for Arnulf's valley.

"Wash your hands after you handle the mushroom," she continued. "I want to keep you. I want to use you. Do you think I committed adultery with that little boy or that old man?"

Lothair answered in a monotone. "No. Secrets. You learned Bernard's secrets."

"What if I learned sorcery? You, the count's strongest warrior, have been under my spell since Count Derek brought me here to marry his son. Now my control is complete."

Peter put the footstool under his hanging stick.

"I have learned to connect with power," she said. "I have learned the power of faith and wisdom and love. I want to show you what I learned about the power of love."

Peter stood on the stool, wiped sweat from his eyes, and grasped the lower end of his stick with both hands. He jerked himself up and heard the nail at the top of his stick tearing the fabric of his cloak. He stopped climbing and swayed on the bottom end of the stick. He heard only soft rustling from the great hall below.

Peter pulled himself halfway up his stick and heard the tearing of his cloak again, louder this time. He paused once more, swinging back and forth. He had only to climb a little higher to grip the fabric above the knot around the nail. His arm muscles shook from the strain. Sweat dripped into his eyes.

His hands, slick with perspiration, slipped on the smooth stick. He scrambled to hold onto the baton. The nail ripped free and the stick slipped out of the knot. He flailed desperately for the torn cloak but managed to grasp only a few ragged threads. He and his stick fell.

His feet hit the stool's edge and flipped it over. His stick clattered down the steps. He tumbled over the open stairway and fell through it head first.

Darkness enveloped everything.

CHAPTER 50
REVELATION

When Peter awoke, the light stunned him. He shut his eyes but an intense throbbing in his head kept him from descending back into darkness. His eyes fluttered open again, looking for a better way to deal with his pain. It took him a while to realize that the light, though strong to one accustomed to the dark of long sleep, was but a tiny reflection of a greater light. The light of day filtered through a fistsized hole high in the wall, so high he'd need to stand on another person's shoulders to reach it.

The ceiling appeared to measure six by six paces. The cool, damp air smelled like a stable at the end of a long winter. Beneath the thick air lay another odor, faint and foul.

He pushed his hands against the cold, wet ground and broke a small stick beside him. He sat up and new pains in his ribs and hips clamored for attention.

"Don't move too quickly," a friendly voice said.

"Jacob," Peter whispered, all pains forgotten. He jumped to his feet and peered into the shadows.

His master stepped forward from the opposite corner. His white hair and beard glowed faintly in the weak light. Spatters of mud dotted his hair, face and tunic. Peter fell into his open arms and they hugged each other for a long time, rocking back and forth like a parent and child.

Peter wiped away his tears. "Lilli said you were dead. I felt terrible. But then I heard you were alive. Thank God." He squeezed Jacob again. "I'm so sorry, master. It's all my fault."

"Don't blame yourself. Nothing happened." Jacob sat and pulled Peter down with him. "Sit down. Be careful. Your head was bleeding and your ribs were bruised when the slave dumped you here. Who beat you?"

"I fell trying to escape, or rather, trying not to escape."

Jacob brushed dried specks of mud from Peter's chain mail tunic. "Nice hauberk," he said. "Blue breeches, leather boots, sword sheath, too. You're dressed like a warrior. You speak like one, too."

"Lilli taught me speech and manners. She gave me these

clothes. Where are we?"

"A storeroom in a corner of the cellar."

Peter strained to see the door, a rough-timbered square in a jagged rock wall. He picked up a slender gray stick protruding from a puddle. "We can dig under a wall with these sticks."

"They're too brittle for digging. Rats have gnawed them. That's a rib bone."

Peter remembered Ledmer, the serf rumored to be buried under the tower. That foul odor he had smelled earlier he now recognized as decayed flesh. He dropped the bone and something scurried away into a wall crack. "Oh, God. What could be worse than this hole?"

"A closed heart," Jacob said and handed him a crust of bread. "You must be hungry. You've been asleep for two days."

Peter gave the crust back to Jacob. "Thank you, master. I'm not at all hungry."

"The slave brings bread every evening. The countess is keeping me alive until she has learned all she can." Jacob bit off a small piece of bread.

"You're eating bread?" Peter's question squawked high with disbelief. "You're not immortal anymore. Did you really lose your powers?"

Jacob swallowed. "We can't lose our power, but we can block it."

"Did the countess block it?"

Jacob's dark eyes glistened in the halflight. "No. We block it ourselves. No one else can block our power."

"How? Why?"

Jacob wiped away a tear. "Remember your first lesson, about the fogs that block our quarry?"

"Yes. The fogs of fear, aggression, and shame. But you don't have any of that, do you? You're above that, aren't you?"

"Every day, for the last two months, those questions have tormented me," Jacob choked and bowed his head. "With all this time to reflect, the answer hasn't come yet."

"You don't hear the counselor anymore?" Peter asked. He squeezed Jacob's hand. "I'm so sorry. Can I help you? I still hear the counselor. I still have my powers, such as they are."

Jacob put his arm around Peter. "Then you are now the leader. Our roles are reversed."

Peter asked, "Have you been in the cellar all this time?"

"Yes, ever since the trial," Jacob said. "We were both condemned to exile, but Countess Lilli kept us imprisoned. If Bernard or Edzard knew what she's done, they wouldn't allow it. She comes down here early every morning with many questions and leaves around mid-morning with no answers. She's getting angrier as each week goes by. How has she treated you?"

As the faint light inside faded with the setting sun outside, Peter related how she lied about Jacob's death, how she promised him a fief of land, how she cajoled him, teased him, threatened him, how he taught her alchemy, and how she combined his lessons with her mother's magic to strengthen her spells. "All she has to do is look at you and speak. Her eyes and her words catch you, hold you. She can make you do what she wants. I gave her the power of alchemy. I shouldn't have done that."

"You couldn't give her something she doesn't already have," Jacob said. "The power of alchemy is in every one. We can use it to prophesize or to belch. The choice is ours."

As night fell, the last hint of light within the storeroom dissolved into total blackness.

"Count Edzard is in danger," Peter said. "Lilli is going to poison him at Arnulf's house and blame it on Lord Arnulf and Father Ulrich. It's terrible. We've got to stop her."

Jacob sighed. "Don't judge what's terrible and what's not. If we don't judge, we don't have to forgive. Lift yourself above it all. Disentangle yourself."

"And let the count die? And let innocent people take the blame. No. We've got to talk to her, show her how wrong she is."

"We can't make others right. We can only make ourselves right."

"I'm not trying to make others right." Peter's voice rose. "I'm trying to make the world a little better."

"What's good, what's bad, and what's a little better depend on how we see the world. When we change ourselves, the world changes. What's most important is what we think."

Peter stood up in the dark. "Yes, that's true. What we think is important but useless if we don't act on what we think. All your lessons taught me how to act in the world, with the world, as the world."

Jacob said, "Detachment was one of those lessons."

Peter waved his arms in anger. "Yes. Yes. Detachment from selfishness. But too much detachment makes us aloof and that cuts us off from kindness, from compassion, from connecting with the universal essence. If I withheld knowledge that Maynard was innocent for the sake of detachment, I'd be ashamed. Maybe that's why your power is blocked. Maybe a fog of shame surrounds your quarry."

Peter could almost feel Jacob frowning in the darkness. He regretted his outburst. "I'm sorry, master," he whispered.

For several moments, only the scratching of unseen rats disturbed the silence between them. After a long while, Peter heard his master standing.

Jacob asked, "How do you know the count will be murdered?"

"I heard Lilli planning it. She'll do it at the count's feast, a celebration of Maynard's defeat. She's going to divert everyone's attention away from the feast table while Lothair poisons his cup."

"Lothair wouldn't do that," Jacob said. "He's too honorable."

"Lothair doesn't want to do it but she's got him under her spell. She controls him with her voice and eyes. She's going to blame it on Lord Arnulf and Father Ulrich because the feast will be prepared at their house."

"When is the feast?" Jacob asked.

Peter paused to reckon time. "How long did you say I've been here in the cellar?"

"Almost two days."

Peter shook his head. "It's too late. The feast is tomorrow. If we could escape, we'd need a full day to journey to my village. It's already night. We can't do anything anyway."

"Why is she doing this?" Jacob asked.

"She hates the count. He insulted her too many times. And he killed his own father, too."

"You shouldn't believe Bernard's rumors."

"It's true. I heard her say it. She's the witness the bishop told us about. She said old Count Derek tried to rape her and Count Edzard saw it and killed him and blamed it on Maynard. You saw it. Isn't that what happened?"

"No."

"No?" Peter gasped. "Well then, what happened?" He waited a very long time before Jacob answered.

"It's true that Derek attacked her," Jacob spoke slowly, as though he were thinking of something else. "But Edzard never saw it, and doesn't know what his father did. Old Count Derek and Bishop Bernard brought Lilli here from the imperial court to marry her to Edzard and thus reduce the tension between Bernard, who serves the emperor, and Derek, who served the duke. But they both had hidden motives for choosing Lilli. Derek wanted to revive the lust of his youth when he raped his way through dark-skinned peoples of southern lands. He stalked her until he found an opportunity to attack her. He believed he was filled with new virility because he drank so much vervain tea."

Peter said, "You gave him that tea."

Jacob said, "Yes. He requested many potions after bringing Lilli to the castle. He said he needed the herb that's plentiful in southern lands to ward off the spells of witches and to attract the favors of women. It was obvious why he wanted it. While the warriors and their wives hunted wolves in the forest that day, Derek hunted Lilli. But he lost sight of his prey when Maynard interrupted his pursuit."

"Lothair sent Maynard to find him," Peter said.

"Yes. When Maynard found him, Derek vented his frustrated lust on the young man, just as he had when Maynard was an unwanted child left unprotected in the hands of a predator. But the child was now a man and he fought off Derek's attack and fled."

Peter said, "That's how Maynard lost his ring."

"Yes. Lilli heard the fracas and came upon the scene as Maynard was fleeing. She taunted and enticed Derek. It was clear she intended to control him for her own purposes. She seemed completely surprised when she lost control of him and he attacked her. But he had spent his strength in his struggle with Maynard and she managed to stab him in the back with a knife she used for collecting herbs. The wound cut all feeling to his legs. While he lay helpless on the ground, she took his sword and plunged it through the knife wound."

Peter whispered, "You watched it and did nothing because you were ... detached."

"Yes. Picking mushrooms, berries, and herbs in the undergrowth, hidden and unconcerned about the tragedy that befell Lilli, Maynard, and Derek." Jacob laughed, shocking Peter even more. "Thank you, Peter."

"What for?" Peter asked.

"Now it's clear why the counselor picked you for my apprentice. For years the shame of ignoring, of withholding my knowledge of the old count's death, weighed heavy on me. It hid under a mask of detachment, a detachment that became indifference. And now, here in the castle, faced with the countess and the truth she represents, this mask blocked my power and held me in a prison of my own making. Thank you, Peter, for saving me from myself."

The scraping of wood against stone interrupted Jacob. A thin shaft of firelight shot into their midst. The rough door creaked open just enough to allow a large, rough hand through.

"Take your bread," the hulking Slav grumbled. He held a crust of bread in the extended hand and a torch in the other.

Jacob said, "Enough with indifference. It's time for action." Instead of taking the bread, he pushed the door open.

CHAPTER 51
FREEDOM

The big Slav dropped the bread crust and threw his shoulder against the door.

Jacob pushed the door open with one hand, seemingly without effort, and stepped over its threshold.

The Slav dropped the torch and pushed the door with both hands.

"Get out," Jacob said to Peter. "Quick. Ride to the count." He opened the door wider.

"Stop," the Slav shouted and slid backward. He pressed his dented head against the door and grunted.

Peter ran out and jumped over the Slav's torch on the floor. The flickering light of the torch revealed ale kegs lining the walls of the cellar, cured meats and sausages hanging from the ceiling, and the waisthigh stone wall of a cistern brimming with rainwater. He stumbled through thrashing shadows until he found the steps leading up to the great hall above. He called, "Over here. This is the way out."

The Slav leapt away from the door and tried to push Jacob back into the storeroom. The blacksmith remained unmovable. The Slav jumped behind the blacksmith and tried to drag Jacob backwards. But the alchemist stayed in place, rooted to the earthen floor like an old oak.

Peter ran back to help his master.

Jacob waved him away. "Go to the stables. Get a horse. Ride to the count's feast."

"I don't know how to ride horses," Peter said.

Jacob said, "It's the only way you can get to your village before it's too late. Just remember your lessons."

The Slav jerked, pulled, pushed, and cursed Jacob with all his strength, all in vain. He roared in frustration.

Peter walked backwards. Faith, he told himself, have faith. "Are you coming?" he shouted.

"Yes. Later. Go quickly," Jacob said. "Save the count. And Lothair, too."

"I can do it," Peter whispered and ran up the steps to the first floor. A torch set in the wall lit the great hall. His stick lay where he had lost it, next to Gabriel's mattress at the bottom of the stone stairway that led up to the second floor. Peter grabbed his stick, yanked the nail from its split end, and bounded over benches to the armored door.

From the cellar he heard the Slav bellowing, "Help. Stop the boy. Help."

Peter pushed the door open and ran down the steps. The Slav's cries pierced the humid night and echoed off the courtyard walls. He looked at the starless sky and wondered if a thunderstorm would cover their escape. For a moment he paused and connected with the heavy air, cleaving to their common, loving essence.

A peal of thunder overpowered the Slav's calls. A gust of wind roared through the courtyard. Thunder and wind continued to smother the Slav's every cry. Lightning illuminated Peter's way to the stables.

Inside the stables, a riotous spectacle confronted him. The horses kicked their stalls and snorted in fear of the noisy storm. A foot soldier and the conscripted serfs stumbled in the dark from stall to stall, hushing the animals, and tying the gates tighter. Only one horse remained calm and Peter ran to his stall. In a flash of lightning, he saw a white star on its forehead and recognized the animal as the one that had twice bitten him. He backed away and gripped his baton tighter.

He took a deep breath and envisioned himself safely mounting the horse. He silently asked the horse's permission. The stallion bowed its head. Peter untied the gate and walked out into the courtyard, into the windstorm. The horse followed, without a bridle or saddle, and Peter climbed onto its bare back.

The foot soldier stepped from the stables, pointed at Peter, and shouted, "We're under attack."

The air tingled with energy. Peter reached out to feel the air, to feel its will.

The foot soldier ran forward and pointed his cross bow at Peter. "Stop. You are my prisoner. What lord are you, sire? Where are you from?"

"I was a prisoner," Peter said and pointed his stick at the top of the stone tower.

A finger of lightning jagged across the sky and struck a corner of the tower. Thunder blasted the air and shook the earth. A shower of shattered stones from the tower's top floor rained onto the courtyard and chased the foot soldier back into the stables. Peter's horse stood still, unaffected and untouched.

Jacob staggered out of the tower's entrance, dragging the big Slav with him. Jacob waved and shouted, "I'll catch up to you. Go now. Go quickly."

Peter's horse lurched forward, nearly throwing Peter by its suddenness. It galloped through the courtyard and out the gate.

The lightning and thunder quit altogether. The river faintly shimmered in the valley below. Peter couldn't see the steep road in the darkness. He made no attempt to guide the steed. Instead he trusted the horse's wisdom. The stallion trotted down the twisting road, turning at each unseen hairpin curve, sometimes skidding to a near stop, sometimes leaping over an invisible obstacle, but never seeming to stray from the path. Peter bounced on its back, his legs hugging its flanks, one hand clutching its mane and the other his stick. He no longer thought of the white-starred horse as the dumb, unpredictable brute he had once feared, but rather as a skillful, intelligent animal he now trusted.

When they reached the base of the hill, the horse broke into a gallop. They flew past the stone quarry toward the glimmering river. Just before the bridge, a shadow appeared before them. The horse shuddered and stumbled. Someone or something screamed and knocked against Peter's crippled leg.

The stallion slowed to a trot and clopped across the bridge. Peter looked over his shoulder. Someone lay on the road at the far end of the bridge. The horse may have trampled that person. Time was short and Peter had to move on to warn the count. But he couldn't leave that person helpless in the road.

"Wish I had more time," he whispered.

He pulled at the horse's neck and shouted commands he had heard the warriors use with their steeds. Pressing with one leg against a flank and then another, he turned the horse around and directed it back across the bridge.

Each moment seemed to linger longer. Sounds of the river babbling beneath the bridge slowed to a low gurgle. The clouds above parted and stalled in place, allowing a full moon to shine on the valley. In the moonlight he saw, lying prone on the road, the beggar.

Crayfish raised his head and cried, "Oh, God. My leg ish gone. Oh, God."

Peter dropped his baton, slid off the horse, and bent down to examine the contorted limb, broken at the shin below the breeches and twisted to a right angle, the same leg that had already been broken twice. The beggar's bare feet twitched, his boots lay where they were thrown on opposite sides of the road. Blood trickling from torn skin at the break appeared black in the moonlight.

"I'm sorry," Peter said.

"Dree times," Crayfish groaned. "Broke dree times. Custom says ish gone. Oh, God." He raised himself on an elbow and struck Peter's head with a balled fist.

Peter fell back and balled his own fist. "No," he whispered. "Must have patience. Must be strong."

He knelt again beside Crayfish and whispered a chant. Despite another blow from the beggar's fist, he felt himself cleaving to the universal essence. For an instant he became the beggar, feeling the beggar's fear, frustration, humiliation, and hidden beneath all that, the beggar's perfect quarry of universal essence. He put one hand on the beggar's knee above the break and one hand around his ankle.

"Stop," Crayfish shouted. "What you doing?"

"I'm forgiving you," Peter said. With one quick jerk, he snapped the leg straight.

Crayfish grunted once, fell back, and lay still.

Peter glanced around for something to make splints. He saw nothing but his baton. He stood, held his walking stick up to eye level with both hands, and said farewell to his crutch for three years. He lifted his crippled leg, balanced himself on the other foot and brought the stick down hard against his raised knee. The thick baton broke cleanly in two and a loud crack echoed off the stone quarry. He set each half on either side of the beggar's broken leg and tied them in place with shreds from the beggar's torn breeches.

A short time later, he delivered Crayfish to sleepy monks in the monastery. He gave the monks his gold pebble from the leather purse and asked them to care for the beggar. "You must promise not to punish him if he curses," Peter said.

"Yes, sire," they answered with bowed their heads and carried Crayfish to their infirmary. Jacob caught up with Peter at the monastery, riding bareback on another of the count's horses.

"Master, I used my powers," Peter shouted. "I used them to escape. We're free."

"We won't be free," Jacob said, "until you submit to Lothair and I submit to Lilli."

"I'm ready," Peter shouted.

"Me, too," Jacob said.

Peter pushed the heels of his boots into the stallion's flanks and it jumped forward. Jacob followed Peter across the market square, through empty streets, past gaping residents awakened by galloping hooves and standing in their doors. Peter's horse outran Jacob's and, at the edge of the free town, Peter paused where the blacksmith shop once stood to let Jacob catch up.

On a patch of blackened ground, the ruins of the forge, the furnace, and the low walls of the well shone faintly like ghosts. The moon's reflection in the well appeared like a large silver platter. At the bottom of that well lay at least one gold platter. But Peter no longer needed gold.

When Jacob's horse came alongside, Peter directed his horse down the narrow road out of the free town, past fields ready to harvest, and into the black forest. The thick leafy canopy shut out all moonlight and cast a shadowless darkness over everything. Peter and Jacob crouched behind the necks of their sweating steeds, unable to see the way before them, never striking tree branches that reached into the trail to snare unwary travelers, never stumbling over logs, rocks or water filled holes that littered the way, never straying into putrid bogs that waited to swallow the careless, never encountering predatory animals that hunted along the path at night. They rode forward, blind, trusting, brimming with purpose, flowing in universal essence, racing toward the dawn.

CHAPTER 52
DISCOVERY

At dawn, Rosamund and a few other serfs picked mushrooms and berries at the forest boundary for Edzard's feast. Rosamund knew where the best mushrooms grew deep in the forest, but the others refused to cross the forest boundary and cursed her when she continued forward alone. After a time, she harvested a basket full of choice mushrooms.

When she walked out of the forest and saw the sun had already risen past mid-morning, she knew she had tarried too long. Most of the count's feast had probably already been prepared. The women would scold her for being late. Gisela would beat her with her stick again. She ran toward the timbered stockade across freshly mowed fields and around haystacks.

She ran until a prized stone mushroom bounced out of her basket. She stopped a moment to retrieve it and to catch her breath.

In the fields before the stockade, smoke from several cooking fires flew on a gusty breeze. The serfs would eat turnips and brown bread outside the stockade while the nobles would eat meat and pastries inside Lord Arnulf's house. Behind the fires, a flock of sheep, driven to her hamlet by Count Edzard, grazed on a slope of the shallow ditch surrounding the stockade. Huts of her hamlet clustered around the earthen ramp that crossed the grassy ditch and connected the stockade with the village.

At the top of the ramp sat four naked children, slaves tied to each other and to the stockade gate. Count Edzard had taken them and the sheep from Slavic shepherds in the eastern valleys. Rosamund thought of her lost child and wished she could return these children to their mothers.

Warriors, ladies, and churchmen began filing out the stockade gate and down the ramp. The countess, dressed in black linen overlaid with sparkling jewelry, led the way. Noble women in their red, blue, and yellow dresses followed and laughed, along with their children and armored husbands. The count's hunting dogs trotted obediently with the throng. The Bishop shone bright in his white raiment. Father Ulrich and other canons followed, wearing swords and chain mail tunics over their dark robes. Lord Arnulf and his lady hobbled beside their priestly son.

Gabriel lumbered head and shoulders above the crowd. His ridiculous yellow hat and the ram's horn tied around his neck were clearly visible from a distance. Since his arrival with the count, Gabriel told Rosamund about Peter's trial, his exile and the riot incited by jealous merchants who burned the blacksmith shop. Gabriel gave her hope, saying Peter would someday return, wiser and welcomed.

It seemed someone was missing from the noblemen. She put down her basket and counted on her fingers. She tallied six canons including Father Ulrich and Bishop Bernard, and then, following Count Edzard, eleven warriors including Lord Arnulf and four foot soldiers including Gabriel. Yes, one warrior was missing; Count Edzard's tallest, strongest warrior.

The countess called the serfs to abandon their cooking, and they left the fires unattended to follow her and the nobles. Her words wafted on the breeze and Rosamund felt those words tugging her toward the crowd. She picked up her basket and started running again.

She recognized the unmistakable limp of Gisela among the serfs. The old woman looked across the fields and shook her stick in Rosamund's direction. Other women turned and glared.

Rosamund no longer felt compelled to join Gisela and the crowd. She stopped running and slowed to a walk.

The countess stopped in a freshly mowed wheat field beside the village and near the ramp. Priests, warriors, and their families stood in a semicircle around her, the count, and the bishop. Serfs crowded behind the noble families. At the top of the ramp, the stockade gate swung shut.

After another hateful glare from Gisela, Rosamund decided to bypass the crowd, steering away from the hostile women who stood between her and the stockade ramp. She angled toward the back of the stockade, aiming for a hole in the wall, to bring the berries and mushrooms directly to the fireplace inside Lord Arnulf's house. Rosamund walked past the neglected cooking fires with their spits of roasting mutton and pots of boiling turnips, and she continued forty to fifty paces before turning down into the grassy ditch. After wading through the sheep, she climbed up the green incline to the stockade wall, to a gaping hole of wood rot common to timbers anchored for many years in moist earth.

As she was about to duck through the hole, she heard the countess. Rosamund hesitated and looked back at the crowd.

The countess called loudly, "Even the horses know our mastery." She pointed at the nobles' horses, tethered to a rail and kneeling with their front legs. The crowd stirred and the horses neighed.

The sight of the animals' strange behavior disturbed Rosamund, but her first duty was to deliver the contents of her basket. She turned to enter the stockade.

"Stop." The countess' voice boomed with such authority that Rosamund's feet stuck to the earth as though they were caught in deep mud. The countess pointed at Count Edzard. He and everyone else stood still, as if they were also stuck in mud. She fixed her eyes on her husband and motioned him closer. He started toward her, as though jerked on a rope.

Rosamund forced her concentration back to the task of bringing her basket to the feast table. She pushed her legs forward and ducked through the hole in the stockade wall. Once inside the stockade, she moved again with ease to Lord Arnulf's house.

A hot breeze blew past her, circled back and gusted at her again. It blew dust in her eyes as though angry. For a fleeting moment, the breeze seemed directed from afar, searching for anyone moving freely outside the authority of its mistress, the countess.

"That ish a crazy idea," Rosamund whispered to herself. She rubbed dust from her eyes, swept strands of blond hair from her face, and pushed the front door of her lord's house.

The door remained shut, barred from the inside.

Behind her, the hot gust spun itself into a dirt devil. Rosamund ran down the length of the house, past shuttered windows to the open back door. The dirt devil seemed to follow her. She sped inside and nearly bumped into Lothair.

He stood clad in gray metal and nearly invisible in the darkness. He faced away from her and seemed unaware of her presence.

She glanced around for a suitable place to leave the basket.

Two long, rough tables stretched down each side of the building's sixty-pace length. Between the tables, the fire in the central fireplace threw light on evenly spaced timbers that supported the roof. The aroma of simmering raspberries and blackberries drifted from small pots next to the fire. Shallow alcoves, some of them curtained, lined the walls. Next to her near the back of the house, a third, shorter table connected the two longer tables into a "u" shape. Wooden stools, cups, and platters indicated where the nobles prepared to eat. At the center of the shorter table and close to the back door, Lothair stood beside the only highbacked chair in the house. His arm moved in a circular motion.

She peeked around his side to see what he was doing. He held the count's bright, yellow cup in one gloved hand and with the other gloved hand pressed the cup's inside with a large, dried mushroom, a stone mushroom. No. Wait. What was it? It had collar around its stem. It was a death cap mushroom. Was he poisoning the count's cup?

Lothair placed the cup before the chair, put the mushroom into a pouch hanging from his sword belt, turned, and looked at Rosamund with glazed, expressionless eyes.

"Forgive me, Lord Lothair," she mumbled.

He didn't answer.

Rosamund dropped the basket on the head table. She had to find Lord Arnulf. The count must be warned. She backed toward the open rear door.

The dirt devil whirled into the house through the back door and slammed the door shut before dissolving into stillness.

Lothair blinked and frowned. "Why aren't you with the others?"

Her voice quivered. "I ... I gots to go now."

Lothair reached for her. "What the devil did you see?"

Rosamund dodged his hand. "Nothing," she cried. She jumped to the back door, pulled its ring handle, but it refused to open. Something told her to move away and, as she did, Lothair's sword struck the door where she had stood.

She tried to scream but dust blew up from the floor and choked her. She ran for the front door, coughing and gagging. In the wavering light from the fireplace, she knocked over stools and scattered spoons from the tables while weaving between support timbers. She fell against the front door and struggled with the heavy beam that barred the main door. She threw the beam aside with shaking arms and grasped the door ring. Lothair slammed his weight against the door, cutting off her escape.

She ducked again and Lothair's sword sliced above her head. It crashed into the wall and showered her with chips of dried mud.

She scrambled over a table and ran the length of the building. At the back of the house, she ducked into a curtained alcove filled with dyeing pots.

A couple of cauldrons and stirring sticks clanged against each other as she clamored over them in the dark. She climbed onto a cauldron and fumbled for the alcove's shuttered window. The shutter stuck fast. Its handle wouldn't turn. She yanked the handle with both hands, as the alcove curtain behind her ripped open. The handle broke off in her hands and she tumbled backwards in startled terror, falling into a waist-high kettle. Swirling dust choked off her screams.

Lothair lifted his sword, nearly touching the sacks of dye that hung above the alcove entrance. The fireplace flickered behind him. He hesitated. "It's better I spill your blood by the count's cup. Then I can say I killed a damn conspirator, and saved his dung-filled life from your poisonous mushroom." He lowered his sword and reached for her.

She picked up a long stirring stick and knocked his hand away.

"You'll need more than a stick," Lothair growled. He became still and cocked his head, as if listening.

Above the noise of her pounding heart and gasping lungs, Rosamund heard the low rumble of distant, galloping horses.

CHAPTER 53
SUBMISSION

Peter galloped out of the forest and cut through a freshly mowed field ahead of Jacob. He directed his steed around a few haystacks and headed straight for the crowd gathered in a field near the base of the stockade ramp. As he rode closer, Peter could see everyone watching the approaching horsemen with wide eyes, everyone except his grinning brother in his yellow hat and the frowning countess in a black dress. At the top of the ramp four naked children gestured at the riders and huddled in terror. Peter leaned forward and asked his horse to slow to a trot.

Countess Lilli raised her hand. Her rings and bracelets flashed in the sunlight. Over the rumble of hooves, she shouted, "Stop."

The horses stumbled and fell, throwing Peter and Jacob into a haystack about thirty paces before the crowd. The stallions rolled over and jumped up, panting, sweating, their legs shaking from the long journey. The horses cantered to the shade of the nearest tree.

Jacob helped Peter out of the haystack. The sweet scent of fresh hay mixed with aromas of boiled turnips and roasted lamb. Although Peter had not eaten in over two days, he wasn't hungry. He spit straw from his mouth and brushed it from his chain mail tunic and blue breeches.

A few warriors and priests edged closer and asked each other, "Who is it?"

"Looks like a young lord and his slave," Norbert said.

"I don't recognize him," Father Ulrich said. "Must be a foreigner."

"That's no lord, you fools," the countess growled. "It's the sorcerer's boy and he brought the sorcerer with him."

The priests and warriors unsheathed their swords. One of the hunting dogs crept forward and growled.

"What are you doing here?" the count yipped like a frightened dog. "You've been exiled for sorcery. Both of you. Go away."

"Lothair isn't here," Jacob said to Peter. "He must be in Arnulf's house. Go to him."

"Why don't we go to Arnulf's house together?" Peter asked, preferring to face the count, the bishop, and all their vassals with

Jacob by his side than to face Lothair alone.

"It's time you end your apprenticeship and submit to Lothair. It's time for me to submit to Lilli and tell Bernard and Edzard what she's done and what she's planning." Jacob bowed his head and stepped forward.

The priests and warriors shuffled backward.

"Go away. I command you to go away." Count Edzard's yip changed to a whimper and he crouched behind Gabriel. "Go away. Go away."

Peter's elder brother smiled and waved Jacob's shofar, the ram's horn, in the air above his yellow hat.

Peter avoided the eyes of the countess and studied the crowd a moment longer. "Rosamund isn't here either," he whispered.

A muffled scream from the stockade startled everyone.

Peter's heart stopped. "Rosamund," he called and sprinted toward the stockade.

Countess Lilli barked like an angry hunting dog, "Stop. Stop. Stop."

Peter's boots grew heavy as though they were again made of lead. He struggled toward the ramp and fought to break that last stubborn strand of her web. He had faith that he could detach himself from her spell.

Lilli cried, "I said s-s-stop." Her voice lost its fierceness.

When Peter heard the countess stutter the same way he had once stuttered, it struck him that she was not superior but equal to him, just as flawed and as perfect as he was. With that bit of wisdom, he cut the last strand of her web as cleanly as if he wielded steel-covered shears. His legs regained their lightness and he flew up the ramp.

At the top of the ramp, the naked children stumbled over each other to get out of his way. A length of rope tethered them to each other and to the gate.

He pushed the gate open, but something grabbed one of his boots and held him back.

"Kill him," the countess screamed. "Kill the Jew, too."

Peter turned around. A dog pulled at his boot. Another dog barked fiercely in front of Jacob. Two more dogs charged up the ramp. One dog clamped its teeth into Peter's forearm below the chain mail sleeve. The other dog circled and howled. Peter spun on one foot and swung the stubborn dogs biting his boot and arm in the air. Their teeth pierced deeper in the violent struggle. He lost his balance and fell. The third dog snapped at his neck and caught its teeth in the chain mail ringlets of his collar. Peter thrashed on the ground in a cloud of dust and panic.

Another scream from Rosamund inside Arnulf's house cut through his panic. He couldn't help Rosamund as long as he struggled to defend himself. Only with defenselessness could he help himself and her. He lay limp on the ramp and surrendered to the dogs. With a stream of love from him to them, he made a connection with his captors, cleaving the love from his quarry to their quarries. He silently asked if they would let him go.

The dogs released his arm and his boot. He pried his chain mail loose from the obliging canine at his neck while the other two dogs sat placidly panting. He saw Jacob stroking the head of a dog sitting at his side while Lilli gestured frantically at the docile dog.

Peter sprang up and said, "Thank you," before speeding through the stockade gate. He hit the house's front door running and it burst open.

At the back of the darkened house, Lothair lifted his sword with one hand. The polished blade flashed in the light pouring through the open door. The other hand held Rosamund's head and her thin, exposed neck against a table. Unaffected by her flailing fists and feet, he turned and squinted into the light.

"Lothair. Stop," Peter commanded with forceful authority like the countess. "Let her go."

Lothair released her and she slipped under the table. He raised his hand to shield his eyes. "What lord commands me?"

"Peter, apprentice to Jacob, the master blacksmith from the free town of Bishop Bernard," Peter said. He envisioned that Rosamund would embrace him and that Lothair would lower his sword. He wiped the vision clean of his fear of Lothair and replaced it with a desire to help the tall warrior.

Rosamund ran to Peter, tears streaming down her face, and they embraced. She shook and sobbed on his shoulder. He pushed his cheek into her silky blond hair and whispered, "Thank God."

Lothair frowned and pointed his sword at Peter. "How did

you get out of the cellar? Where's your God damned walking stick, your baton?"

Peter smiled. "Don't need it anymore. You can put your sword down. I won't harm you. I am going to surrender to you."

Lothair grunted, "Don't trick me with your sorcery."

"I'm not a sorcerer. But I know how to break Lilli's spell and I can help you get free. You'll have your honor back."

After a long moment, Lothair lowered his sword. "Yes. My honor is ... tainted. She's got me twisted ... in a witch's web."

The door behind Peter slammed shut, plunging the room into darkness again. Peter turned and saw the glint of Lilli's eyes and jewelry by the door. Her dark dress, hair, and skin blended into fitful shadows cast by the central fireplace.

"The boy brought the Jew," she hissed. "He's telling Edzard and Bernard about our plan. But he's a Jew and no one will believe him. Besides, Bernard belongs to me and Edzard will too, if he survives." She locked her eyes on Lothair. "What are you doing?"

Lothair hunched over and turned his head, but his eyes remained fixed on her. "The boy ... help." His words strained for control.

"Fight it," Peter said. "Don't let her rule -"

"Do not listen to the boy." Her tone dropped and her words squeezed out between clinched teeth. "He is my enemy. You are my vassal and you are honor bound to serve me."

Lothair jerked upright, as rigid as a support timber.

Lilli pointed at Rosamund. "What is she doing here? Why was she screaming?"

Lothair answered in a stone, cold monotone. "The girl came in the back door. She saw me with the death cap. I will kill her at Edzard's chair - put the mushroom in her hand - claim that I caught her poisoning the count's cup."

"That might work. It'll give me time to decide how to handle the Jew." She pitched her voice lower. "Kill the girl now."

Lothair strode forward stiffly and raised his sword. His entranced eyes seemed to look through Rosamund.

Without a thought, Peter stepped in front of Rosamund and barked, "Stop, Lothair."

The warrior faltered, slowing to half steps as he moved around the fireplace.

"Peter." Lady Lilli's voice oozed like a sweet pastry. "Listen to me. I'm your master now. Tell everyone the Jew is a lying sorcerer."

Peter raised his hand and spread his fingers. "Lothair, stop."

Lilli's voice dropped lower, her tone demanded obedience. "Look at me, Peter. Tell me how you escaped the castle. Give me those powers of escape. Look at me."

Peter kept his back to the countess and walked toward the faltering warrior. "Lothair," he imitated Lilli's commanding tone. "You are to act according to my will."

With the broad side of his sword, Lothair slapped Peter out of the way.

Rosamund fled, slipping around Peter and behind Lothair. The tall warrior stumbled after her.

The countess cooed, "Peter, go help Lothair. Don't you want to submit to him?"

"Stop, Lothair" Peter lowered his voice. "You do not have to do what the countess says. Do what I say."

Lothair moved in starts and stops, as if obeying conflicting masters. He swung his blade slowly at Rosamund and split a wooden platter on a table.

"Stop, Lothair." Peter's voice trembled. "She doesn't have a spell on you. She controls you because you believe she can. You think she's superior to you. She's not." He grabbed the back of Lothair's chainmail tunic and pulled. The tall warrior dragged him forward.

Rosamund threw a stool and Lothair batted it away.

"Stop, please," Peter cried. "You can be your own master." He jerked the back of Lothair's tunic.

Rosamund picked up an iron pot from a dark alcove and held it before her like a shield. Lothair knocked it from her hands with a sweep of his sword. She fell into the alcove and crawled into a large overturned cauldron stained with dye.

Lilli's voice reached out with silky subtleness. "Surrender to my will, Peter."

Peter gave up his attempts to control Lothair, gave up his willfulness. Lothair swung his sword backward. Peter released

Lothair's tunic and grabbed Lothair's sword hilt. Peter gripped the hilt with both hands and waited, unsure where the flow of universal will would carry him.

After an unnaturally long moment, Lothair grunted as if lifting an anvil, and slowly swept both his weapon and Peter forward. Peter lost his grip and tumbled into the alcove where Rosamund cowered. He banged against some cauldrons, sprang up and placed himself between Rosamund and Lothair.

The tall warrior paused and blinked his eyes. He appeared startled, as though he suddenly remembered that Peter was also in the building.

"Think of the wisdom of what you're doing," Peter pleaded. "See it differently. The countess promised you a valley, that valley won't set you free. I know you're honorable. You're frustrated and hurt. You want the same things I want. You can rule your world without being ruled."

Lothair's sword trembled in the firelight. His eyes darted and face twisted as though he struggled to understand.

The countess moved closer. "Lothair, you have no wealth, no land, no honor without me. You will do as I say." She flashed angry eyes at Peter. "Are you strong enough to die with your sorry serf girl?"

"I have the strength. But spare her," Peter said and looked over his shoulder at Rosamund.

Rosamund looked up from the overturned cauldron through her tears and smiled at Peter. She seemed at peace with death.

His fear detached and fell away. He smiled back at Rosamund with relief.

From behind the tall warrior came Lilli's venomous hissing, "Kill the boy."

Lothair's blank expression returned. He jerked his sword above his head. The sword's point caught one of several sacks hanging from the alcove's ceiling.

Peter dropped to his knees. "I forgive you, Lothair," he said, "for the love of God."

Outside the building, a long, single wail from the shofar, the ram's horn, sang for atonement.

CHAPTER 54
LIGHT AND DARK

Peter closed his eyes and bowed his head.

Lothair grunted and the air moved.

Peter awaited the blow of Lothair's sword and accepted death. Tension drained away. The desire to control life crumbled and fell off like rusted armor. He floated free, lighter and airier. His world and his plans plummeted away as dense and leaden weights, worthless to the flight of spirit. Serene knowledge of his real worth flowed through him and washed out all fear, aggression, and shame.

His mortal shell dissolved. Light exploded. The light stretched beyond all understanding - limitless, timeless, and formless. Joy carried him through the light, and he flew in every direction at once, without effort, buoyed by radiance. He soared into the realm of totality where he felt no separation, no differentiation from anything, anytime, anywhere.

He alighted in a place that was everywhere and nowhere. He rested for a time with no beginning and no end. He experienced all things as one thing. Compassion for everything, everyone, everywhere, and every time without exception cascaded from him. He embraced it all and it all dissolved in his embrace, dissolved into nothing, into No Thing. He embraced the No Thing and It embraced him.

Gratitude overflowed and he whispered, "Thank you."

He listened to his whisper and became aware that his tongue could still speak, his ears could still hear. He touched his lips and felt hot breath from his mouth. His body still lived.

He blinked his eyes open and returned to the piddling reality, or unreality, of the world. He still knelt in an alcove of Arnulf's house, just as he had before the explosion of light. He checked himself for blood and found instead that much of his gray iron tunic and blue breeches had turned golden yellow. All the windows and doors stood open, and the light of day filled the building, blanching shadows and blending forms. Hard edges that separated one thing from another blurred in his teary sight.

Small movements disturbed the stillness. A few of serfs peeked through alcove windows. Rosamund rubbed her face with both hands in a gold tinted cauldron behind him.

Lothair sat on the ground just outside the alcove. The light of day reflected a yellow luster off the warrior's chain mail. He wiped an eye and asked, "What happened?"

"Alchemy," Peter answered. Peace and plenty filled him. "Lead returned to gold."

Lothair examined his metallic tunic. "Gold?" After squinting at his armor a few moments, he jumped to his feet and shouted. "My hauberk turned to gold." He lifted his sword and it reflected a yellow sheen. "My sword, too." He kissed the sword hilt. "By the holy bones of Saint George, is this alchemy?" The warrior's face and beard had turned yellow also.

Lady Lilli hurried to Lothair's side. A sprinkling of gold dust sparkled on her black dress. "Quick. Everyone's coming through the stockade g - g - gate." Her words rushed with panic. "Kill the b - b - boy and the g - g - girl."

"Don't use your voice on me." Lothair turned his head away. "Don't use your eyes either. I've been under your God damned spell too long."

With sudden force, the countess slammed an elbow into Lothair's stomach. The warrior stumbled backwards to Peter's alcove.

Rosamund grabbed Peter's shoulders and pulled him back, away from Lothair's stagger.

"You will do as I say," Lilli screeched and snatched the golden sword from the stunned warrior. "I control you."

Lothair's yellow lips gasped for breath. "I'll do as ... I please. I am ... my own master. I need no fief of land from you. I have enough gold now to buy a kingdom. I'm free."

Countess Lilli waved the sword with both hands. "You will do as I say or I'll kill you."

"You can't hurt me." Lothair reached for the sword in Lilli's hands.

The countess jabbed the sword tip into one of Lothair's unprotected forearms. Lothair jerked his hands back and rubbed his wound. Blood from a small cut below the hem of his metallic sleeve smeared across his yellow arm and turned it orange.

She pushed the sword tip against Lothair's armored chest. "I am stronger than you know. I can kill you like I killed Derek."

Lothair's yellow jaw dropped open. "You killed Count Derek?"

"He broke from my control and attacked me," the countess hissed. "I killed him with his own sword. If you don't follow my voice, I'll kill you with your own sword. Listen to me. Listen and look at my eyes."

With a blurring sweep of his arm, Lothair ripped the sword from her hands. He raised the sword and its tip caught the bottom of another sack hanging from the alcove's ceiling.

"I'm a sorceress," Lilli shouted and beat him with her fists. "I'll damn you with a curse."

A black cloud engulfed Lothair. At the same time, all the windows and doors slammed shut. The building returned to darkness, a darkness far blacker than before. Peter shut his eyes and covered his mouth as the black fog filled the air along with the sounds of coughing, stools breaking and tables crashing.

After a few moments, the heavy dust settled to the floor. Peter crawled out from the alcove and stood up. A weak tongue of fire from the fireplace struggled to light the house.

Lothair sat on top of the collapsed head table with his back to Peter. He appeared blacker than any thing in the darkness. On the ground nearby lay Edzard's gold cup, tarnished with spots of black. "I feel so heavy," he groaned.

"I cursed you," the countess snapped. She sat on a stool a few paces away, barely visible in her black dress. The specks of gold dust on her dress had vanished. Her jewelry no longer flashed in the firelight but appeared dark as lead. Her eyes blazed from her soot-smeared face.

Lothair grunted to his feet. He lifted the front of his chainmail tunic and bowed his head for a closer look at the metal ringlets. "What's this? Where's my gold?" He picked up his black blade and grunted louder. "My sword is heavy as lead."

Lilli's voice dripped with sweetness, "I turned your gold into lead. Come back to me and you'll have your gold again."

"No. You God damned witch. Give it back to me now." Lothair swung his lead sword down at her.

Countess Lilli jumped away and the sword broke the stool. "Lothair, stop," Peter called.

The warrior struggled to lift his sword. The blade bent up where it had struck the stool. "Turn it back to gold," he bellowed.

Countess Lilli ducked behind a thick support beam and cried, "I d - d - don't know how."

Lothair swung his bent sword and the countess ducked behind a thick support beam. The weapon struck the beam and its blade broke off just above the hilt.

Peter rushed forward to stop Lothair but a light blinded him before he could take two steps. He shaded his eyes with his hands.

"Don't touch her, Lothair." Jacob's voice boomed from the blinding light that streamed into the house through the open front door.

Lothair stood still. He seemed darker than lead in the bright light. His broken sword lay on the ground next to a support timber. Lady Lilli crouched behind the timber, her scowl streaked with black smears.

Jacob walked through the light and stood near the fireplace, followed by Bishop Bernard, Lord Arnulf, Father Ulrich, and the other priests and warriors, their swords unsheathed and ready. They all looked grim except the bishop, whose face contorted with anguish. The count entered last and hunched behind his warriors close to the open door. The foot soldiers waited just outside the entrance. The warriors' wives and children crowded behind the foot soldiers. The serfs opened alcove window shutters one by one and peered inside.

"Forgive me, Count Edzard," Lothair said, bowing his head. He dropped his sword hilt to the ground. His face appeared as black as his armor. "Your wife wanted me to poison your cup with this mushroom." He pulled the death cap from a pouch and dropped it to the floor. "I resisted her but she put me under a spell. She's a sorceress."

"Bastard," the countess spat. "He's lying."

"Peter knows who's lying better than any one," Jacob said.

Everyone focused on Peter. He stepped forward to stand next to Lothair. "Countess Lilli is no sorceress," Peter said, "but she did plan to poison Count Edzard and blame it on Lord Arnulf and Father Ulrich. The countess controlled Lord Lothair the Angry, but only because he believes she is stronger. He is at heart an honorable man who would rather do good than evil."

The countess pointed at Peter. "He conspired to kill you, Edzard. The Jew was part of it, too. I stopped them. And what's more, Lothair, not Maynard, murdered your father."

Jacob said, "Count Derek the Ram, your father-in-law, was killed by you."

"Hah. Ridiculous. I'm a woman. He was four times my size, six times stronger."

The bishop shook his head and whispered, "Oh, dear child. Jacob saw you do it. He was a witness."

"I was the witness." Lady Lilli's tone softened. "I told you that in confession. I know at that time, I told you Edzard killed him. But that's because he hates me, he's mean to me. Lothair did it. He did it with Edzard. They did it together."

Bishop Bernard's voice trembled. "Jacob saw the murder."

"He's a Jew," Lilli hissed. "You can't believe a Jew."

"I didn't believe him until ..." Bishop Bernard choked and bowed his head. Tears filled his eyes.

Lord Arnulf asked Countess Lilli, "Can we believe what you say?"

"Of course," she snapped.

Father Ulrich said, "Everyone heard you say that you killed the old count."

"What?" Her eyes flashed wider, her black lips parted.

Norbert said, "After we opened the doors and windows of Arnulf's house, we heard you admit it to Lothair. When you said you are a sorceress and cursed Lothair, we shut the windows and doors to protect ourselves from your curse."

Rosamund stepped up next to Peter and said, "I heard her."

A serf at a window whispered, "Me, too."

"I did, too," said another. A murmur of agreement spread through the crowd.

"Derek attacked me," Lilli shouted above the murmur. "The warriors were hunting wolves in Bernard's forest. I was hunting herbs. Derek left the hunt and tracked me." She fixed her eyes on the bishop. "He tried to rape me. I had to defend myself."

From the open door Count Edzard barked, "Kill the witch."

The bishop waved a hand. "No. Wait. Remember there's no custom for sorcery."

Norbert said, "But there is for murder."

"No," the bishop said. "It was not murder. It was self defense. We need an inquisi -"

The count cut him off. "A woman isn't judged like a man. I can kill her if I want to. It's my right. Let's kill the demon's mistress."

The bishop moved in front of the countess. "I will defend her."

Edzard wagged an accusing finger at the bishop. "You will defend her? You have aligned yourself with Satan. Don't you call that apostasy? Everyone here is a witness to your conversion to sorcery. As someone guilty of apostasy, you forfeit your possessions and your life. You have given me back the free town."

The bishop shook his staff at Count Edzard. "I am no apostate. I am looking for the truth."

Edzard shook his sword. "Sorcery is your truth when you defend a sorceress. Your powerful friends can't help you now." He pointed at Father Ulrich. "Kill the bishop and the countess."

The little priest stepped next to Bishop Bernard. "Your reasoning is deceptive. I will not answer a murder with more murders." The other four canons stepped forward and stood beside Father Ulrich and Bishop Bernard.

The count waived his sword. "Your noble canons have turned their swords against their fathers and against me, their rightful lord. I declare them all outlaws."

All five priests lined up with the bishop to face eleven warriors. Father Ulrich stood opposite his father, Lord Arnulf. Each lifted a sword ready to battle.

CHAPTER 55
THE LAST BATTLE

The crowd outside Lord Arnulf's house hushed. Inside the house, the canons and the warriors said nothing. They held their swords ready to parry a blow, but neither moved to strike first.

Peter heard only his heart beating in his ears. He pulled Rosamund close to him and edged closer to Jacob. Perhaps his master could protect them from swinging swords.

After a few moments, Count Edzard howled from behind his warriors, "What are you waiting for? Kill them."

No warrior moved forward. They looked at their sons with pained concern. The priests watched their fathers with frightened resolve.

Peter heard the bishop whisper to Lilli, "Run out the back. I'll hold Edzard here."

The countess pushed the bishop away and barked, "Stop." The warriors and canons flinched, then lowered their swords. She raised her hands, spread her fingers and lowered her voice. "Listen to me. Look at my eyes, all of you. Do as I say."

All the warriors and priests turned toward her. She locked her eyes briefly on each one but skipped over Peter, Jacob and Rosamund. She whispered in low voice, "Listen to me. You will listen and do as I say." The air thickened but it didn't hold Peter. The others, however, seemed stuck in place.

Lilli's tone pitched lower than Peter had ever heard. Her voice gravelled as if possessed by some otherworldly evil. "I cannot let the spineless Edzard win like this. No one is to hurt Bernard because I want that pleasure for myself. All of you will let me escape and none of you will pursue me. I will return later for my revenge."

The countess glided soundlessly backwards, keeping her eyes on her bound captives. Her black dress slid along the floor, over the fallen ruins of the head table, to the back door. When she opened the door, a couple of serfs fell forward from where they were listening. They squawked and fled, falling over each other in their haste. The disturbance broke her hold on the noblemen and they lifted their swords again.

Behind her, a gust of wind blew a dirt devil up from the

stockade's dusty ground. She stepped into the whirlwind and together they spun out of sight.

"Stop her," the count squeaked. "Go after her."

No one moved.

Count Edzard slapped the broadside of his sword against the back of nearest warrior, Lord Norbert. "Are you a mouse or a warrior?"

Norbert stepped away and growled. "She's your wife. Get her yourself."

Gabriel ambled past the foot soldiers at the front door and entered Arnulf's house. He waved Jacob's shofar and sauntered up to Edzard.

The count grabbed Gabriel's rusted chainmail tunic with such force that a few more holes ripped in the brittle armor. "Go get Lilli. Bring her back."

Gabriel smiled. "Countess gone. Through stockade hole, through harvested fields, through forest bogs, through -"

"Shut up." Count Edzard slammed his fist into Gabriel's chest. "Get the dogs. Hunt her down."

The elder brother didn't move and continued smiling. "She took the dogs to forest bogs. But she'll be back, back on track."

Edzard barked at his warriors, "Bernard is still here. It's your duty to aid me in war. Kill him. Kill all the priests."

Jacob nodded to Peter and whispered, "Tell them about the Peace of God."

Peter caught his meaning immediately. "Wait," he called. He raised his hands and stepped into the space between the opposing swords. "Haven't the warriors sworn an oath to follow the church's Peace of God?"

Lord Arnulf lowered his sword. "We swore an oath to God to spare clerics in time of war."

Edzard growled, "Forty days of war are finished. We can attack the priests."

Peter said, "You, my lord count, extended the days of war."

Arnulf said, "We cannot attack them." He returned his blunt sword to its worn sheath. The other warriors nodded and all but Edzard slid their weapons back into their sheaths.

Edzard pointed his sword at Peter, "Don't listen to the God

damn boy. He's nothing. We can kill Bernard. We can burn his town. We can burn his cathedral."

Peter pointed at the bishop. "If you burn the cathedral, you burn the reliquary of the Holy Splinters."

The bishop boomed with authority, "I am the protector of the Holy Splinters from the cross of our Lord. Anyone who threatens to burn their sanctuary is an ally of the devil."

The warriors turned away from the canons and faced Edzard with accusing eyes.

"We … we outnumber them. Kill them. Kill somebody. If you c - c - cowards won't kill them, then …" Edzard pointed his shaking sword, "… then kill Lothair."

The tall warrior bowed his head again. Peter looked up at Lothair's blackened face. A golden yellow color showed itself in places beneath Lothair's bearded chin.

Norbert said, "A person who plans murder but does not carry it out must be exiled."

"No. No. No." The count stamped the earthen floor.

Norbert said. "That is the custom from Konrad, your grandfather's fair and just marshal."

The count howled, "My grandfather be damned. Konrad be damned. Custom be damned." He pointed his sword at Norbert. "You're my last faithful vassal. Go kill Lothair."

"Your father would have followed custom," Norbert said.

"My father was a fool. He gave up fighting Bernard. He married me to that witch. If Lilli hadn't killed him, I would have killed him myself." The count jabbed his sword tip into Norbert's ribs. "I am your lord. I command you to kill Lothair."

Norbert unsheathed his sword again and walked toward Lothair. The gray warrior stopped a pace before the tall warrior and said, "Lothair, you have plotted against your lord and you will be punished. You have dueled with a sorceress and your sword lies broken on the ground. You will need a good sword wherever you go in exile." Norbert thrust his sword, hilt first, at Lothair. "Within my sword's hilt is a holy relic of Saint Peter. Take my sword and may it protect you."

Everyone but the count emitted an audible sigh.

"There's nowhere I can go," Lothair mumbled.

Peter tapped him on the shoulder and said, "Go east, to the lands Edzard took from the Slavs. Rule them wisely."

Rosamund whispered, "Take the slave children with you. Return them to their mothers. They be grateful and forever loyal to you."

Father Ulrich patted his cousin on the back and said, "Edzard won't bother you. He can't govern his own fief, let alone a faraway valley. You can be your own lord."

Lothair took the gray warrior's sword and sheathed it. "I will work to regain my honor." Lothair held his head high and marched toward the entrance. The warriors and priests stepped aside to let him pass. The count gasped and shuffled backward until he bumped into the frame of the main door. He thrust his shaking sword at Lothair. With a casual sweep of his armored arm, Lothair brushed the sword aside and strode out the main door.

After a moment of frightened indecision, Count Edzard scampered along the wall, past curtained alcoves and overturned stools, to the broken head table at the back of Arnulf's house. He picked his gold cup off the floor, tucked it under his sword belt and howled, "Damn you all." With the clumsiness of near panic, he stumbled out the back door.

Jacob said to Gabriel, "Remind Edzard to be careful with his gold cup because it's poisoned."

Gabriel laughed and skipped out the back door.

Peter hugged Rosamund and they held each other for a long time. He wiped her tears and felt her fear dissolve as she melted in his arms. He too melted in her arms. In that embrace he sensed again the lingering compassion of universal essence and a residue of radiance from the realm of totality.

While he held her, Jacob cleaned and dressed the dog bite on Peter's arm. "Don't stop hugging her," he said. "That hug has greater healing power than any herb."

Bishop Bernard sat on a stool and stared out the back door. His eyes teared and his lips quivered as though grieving.

The warriors and canons milled around the room discussing the morning's events. The warrior's wives and children entered and began repairing broken stools and tables. Arnulf's wife pulled gloves over her hands and picked up the death cap mushroom.

"Burn your gloves after you bury that mushroom," Lord Arnulf said to his lady.

"What was that black powder on Lothair's face and hauberk?" Lord Norbert asked.

Arnulf examined a torn sack hanging limp and empty from the ceiling of the alcove where Peter had submitted to Lothair. "Must have been black dye. Seems he ripped it open while struggling with Lilli and spilled it all over himself. Powdered dyeberries and crushed bark of blackthorn and black alder."

"What did he mean when he said his hauberk had turned to gold?" Norbert asked.

Arnulf pointed to a second torn and empty bag. "That would be this other dye. Ground flowers of chamomile, goldenrod, and marigold. He thought his hauberk had turned to gold. But it was just powdered yellow dye." Arnulf bent over stiffly to pick up Lothair's broken sword blade. "Mother of God. This is heavy."

Father Ulrich touched the black blade and scratched it with his fingernail. "It's soft. This isn't iron." He turned to the bishop. "What's it made of?"

Peter, Rosamund and Jacob stepped up for a better look.

The bishop wiped his eyes and felt the blade. "Is it lead? Why would Lothair carry a sword of lead?"

Arnulf picked up the sword hilt. Beneath the black powder, it shone bright yellow. "There's no yellow dye on his sword hilt. What metal is this?" He put the broken sword hilt on the bishop's lap.

"It's made of ..." Bishop Bernard hesitated, raised his eyebrows and whispered, "gold?"

CHAPTER 56
THE JOURNEY BEGINS

The serfs sang and danced around smoldering cooking pits in the fields outside the stockade. The warriors shouted and cheered in games within the stockade wall. The festivities grew louder as the afternoon shadows grew longer.

Peter and Rosamund rested in a haystack from their feasting, drinking, dancing, and singing. Peter wore a clean black tunic borrowed from Lord Arnulf. Rosamund checked the bandage on his dog-bitten arm. Her every touch seemed to speed the healing of his wound. She said, "Ish a good feast, even without Count Edzard, our guest of honor."

Gisela hobbled on her stick toward them, followed by her helpers. They carried Peter's chain mail tunic, linen undershirt, and blue breeches. A few paces before the haystack, they stopped and bowed their heads.

"Lord Peter," Gisela rasped. "We cleaned your hauberk, aketon, and trousers of powdered dyes. We thank you for saving Lord Arnulf and Father Ulrich from Countess Lilli's plans. The whole village ish thankful."

Peter stood and said, "Rosamund had already spoiled Lilli's plan before I arrived. You should thank her."

"Yes," Gisela said. "Rosamund ish a ... brave girl."

The women left and Peter walked behind the haystack to change into his lordly clothes. When he returned, Jacob and Gabriel stood next to Rosamund.

Jacob said, "Norbert is sorry you won't come to his castle and learn the art of war. Bernard is disappointed you won't come to his palace to be one of his canons." He slid Lothair's broken sword hilt into Peter's sword sheath. "They want you to keep this as a reward for your bravery. There's enough gold in that hilt to engage many blacksmiths to make many swords."

Peter's face buzzed with a blush. "I always wanted a sword."

Jacob chuckled and said, "At least you have half a sword."

"I don't care about swords. I don't care about gold. I just want to be an alchemist. Isn't it strange? I always wanted to prove myself in war. But today, in my first real battle, I stopped war from happening."

Jacob nodded. "That's the best way to prove yourself. Nobody knew Lothair had so much gold. Bernard asked if alchemy had anything to do with this gold."

Peter asked, "What did you tell him?"

"Nothing."

"Does the bishop understand the difference between nothing and No Thing?"

Jacob smiled. "No. But he will someday."

"What will we do next, master? Rebuild the shop? I'll use this gold to pay the bishop his tribute for the loss of your shop."

Jacob shook his head. "The bishop has waved the tribute. He also plans to declare we were wrongly accused. But many in the free town will always believe we are sorcerers and we won't be welcomed. We can't go back. Not yet. Besides, you will learn your next lessons on the road. You are a journeyman now. We can begin our journey together, but you must eventually go off alone and learn from other masters."

Rosamund kissed Peter's cheek. "I gots to go with you this time," she said.

Peter remembered Daphne and asked Jacob, "A woman can be an alchemist, can't she?"

"Of course," Jacob said. "You read the writings of Mary the Jewess and Kleopatra the Copt, didn't you? Some alchemists think those women are the greatest of all masters."

Peter kissed her cheek. "We'll ask Lord Arnulf to free you from bond. Today, he'll grant us any wish. We'll get your cloak and boots and then we can go." He kissed her lips, lingering to absorb the soft pleasure.

Gabriel waved his yellow hat to the west, past the celebrating serfs and their village. "On the road with monks and lepers, minstrels and pilgrims, masons and peddlers, masters and students. The journeys of journeymen are to master the masters."

"It's best you stay here," Jacob said to Gabriel. "You are Edzard's only friend now and Peter will need you when he returns."

"How do you know I'll return?" Peter asked.

"You must atone with Countess Lilli."

"What do you mean?" Peter asked, but he knew what Jacob meant.

"You were told not to speak of alchemy until you knew what it is. But you not only spoke of it, you tried to teach it."

Peter rubbed his forehead and nodded. A fog of shame settled around his inner quarry. "Yes. I taught her badly. All she learned from me was how to hurt herself." He turned to the eastern forest. "I must find her and help her."

Rosamund took his hand. "Wait, Peter."

Jacob placed a hand on Peter's shoulder. "You can't do it now. When you return to complete your master work, you might be able to help her."

"She'll suffer until then. I can at least put her on the right path."

Jacob shook his head. "All paths eventually lead to the source. Her chosen way is the right way for her at this time. At another time, she may find a better way."

"I've got to do something. I'll forgive her, or submit to her like I did with Lothair."

"Lilli is a far greater challenge than Lothair ever was. The two of us together can't help her today. You must be patient. To truly help her, you must be better prepared." Jacob turned Peter away from the eastern forest. "Let's begin your preparation. Let's start the journey."

Jacob led the way to the hamlet and the stockade. Rosamund smiled and swung Peter's hand with each step. Gabriel blew short, spirited notes on the ram's horn with every other step. The villagers stopped singing and dancing to watch the approaching procession. They bowed their heads as the four honored companions passed.

"Always uphold the gold," Gabriel said and blew a blast on the shofar so loud that even the noisy warriors within the stockade grew quiet.

Peter looked back at the eastern forest. Someday he would have to return.

CPSIA information can be obtained
at www.ICGtesting.com
Printed in the USA
FSOW01n0252271216
28831FS